CAMP FIELD CAPABLE
America's Fabulous Fifties, Book 3
By Cindy M. Amos

Dedicated to

The steadfast men and women
of Coleman Company in Wichita, KS
who work on the assembly floor daily
to build the highest quality products and gear
that entice America to go camping.
Ad Astra per Aspera
"To the Stars through Difficulties"

ACKNOWLEDGMENTS

The author would like to acknowledge the following
for their support and encouragement of this book:
Coleman Company Museum & Outlet
iStock for vintage black & white photograph
Pamela Bower for final proofreading
Cynthia Hickey of Winged Publications
& The Inspiration of the Holy Spirit

CINDY M. AMOS

Who can abide on the sacred landscape of God, to dwell on his holy hill?
The upright man who controls his tongue and honors an oath at any cost.
This is an unshakable man who shall not be moved.
Psalm 15: 1-5 (Abridged)

Chapter 1

Encouraged by the mildness of early April, Mason Porter strolled the grounds behind the main warehouse with heightened interest. Today, the new marketing campaign would launch a line of camping equipment that had the potential to keep Coleman Company solvent through the next decade. His recent hire marked the threshold of a new era, where advances in materials would open new horizons for the questing camper. The pending demonstration capped a productive week in his plastics lab, where he molded the future.

Since the weekend approached, he gave some thought to exploring his new territory. With greening grass poised to overtake the winter-brown landscape, the bustling metropolis of Wichita represented an adventure ready to happen. A train whistle punctuated the vivacious downtown area, replete with industrial warehouses and brick-fronted stores where merchandisers promoted their wares with great success. The city had outgrown its turn-of-the-century Cowtown heritage with an understated sophistication he found typical of the thriving Midwest.

An electronic crackle filled the air while several marketing staffers milled about on the elevated platform. Lined with an array of the company's products, he caught sight of the green metal cooler where a fishing pole rested in leisure. If he had his way, those heavy ice-toting contraptions would be history within the decade. Plastics rode a wave of incoming popularity in the industry. He would insure that their incorporation into the product line would be duly stamped with the Coleman trademark of quality.

"Testing one, two, three," a man spoke into the microphone. He straightened and smiled, shooting his thumb into the air to reflect his success. After taking a cue from his associate, he returned to the stand. "Ladies and Gentlemen, we plan to start in a short minute, so if you could take your places around the platform, we'll let the cameras roll to capture the launch of our spring advertising campaign. Be good sports and react with enthusiasm, would you? I'm sure Glori will appreciate it. Thank you." He bowed and departed for the back of the stage.

Mason reviewed the platform and decided to head for the far left corner. That would give him a head start to his car, a slate blue Plymouth Belvedere. That car helped him enjoy the twisted commute along the Little Arkansas River to his rental house up in Valley Center. Only the tiny shack's price was convenient, yet the area off of Meridian Avenue proved much quieter than here in town. As the crowd of gathering employees amassed, he chose a spot up front and kept his eye on the green cooler, archaic dinosaur though it was.

A peppy young woman walked the front of the stage in a complete sweep and paused once to add a picnic hamper to the collection of camping gear on display. In center stage, a pea-green tent sprang up, held in place by a metal pole. The front fly rippled in the breeze while the rear pole became similarly rigged, giving the tent's roofline two peaks.

When the woman returned, she carried four soda bottles pinched between her fingers. She studied the array and made a beeline for the green cooler. In fluid motion, she bent to place the bottles on the cooler's lid. A Hollywood wink accompanied the task, the flirty gesture directed right toward Mason.

Aware the cameras were rolling to track her every move, he pretended to catch the wink in his clutching hand, and then tapped his chest. Only two weeks with the company, he'd play it straight into their planning book, as this campaign would make or break this summer's sales. Since engineers came at a healthy price tag, he would help earn his keep with a bit of melodrama, if it helped keep the company profitable.

A tall man walked with stiff steps toward the microphone. He tapped it until an audible thump echoed from the speakers. After fingering his abbreviated black mustache, the man held up a script and then regarded his audience with a curt smile. "Ladies and gentlemen, thank you for being here for our illustrious announcement this afternoon. I'm Edgar Sterns, director of Marketing and Sales, welcoming you to the kickoff of our new promotional campaign, 'America Goes Camping.' Let me assure you, with the economy on the upswing and summer on the horizon, there's never been a better time to hit the road for recreation. But you don't have to take my word for it. Here's the incredible Glori Dawes, straight from our Human Resources Department, to tell you more about the campaign."

The roofline on the tent flopped. Soon, a leisure version of the winking woman appeared, her wavy hair wrapped in a bandana. As she strolled to the front, she pretended to warm her hands over several crisscrossed limbs in a makeshift campfire. She acted somewhat startled to notice the crowd. "Oh, hello there. It's been a long workweek, hasn't it, my fine friends?"

Several chiding answers made their way back toward the stage, chased by a couple of "amens." Mason hid a sliver of a smile by propping his chin in his palm. Not sure what he'd expected, an exchange of direct dialogue had not even made the list.

"I'm excited for springtime, luring us back outdoors." She hoisted a lantern and pretended to check on the mantles inside the globe. "That means Memorial Day weekend is almost here—and summer won't be far behind. The distant wayside opens to scenic parklands, where winds whisper through vast canyons and comb through giant sequoias, calling us outside to view America's most amazing landscapes."

She changed directions and began walking toward his corner of the platform. Spirited, she seemed enigmatic up there, a fire sparking her blue eyes to convey an excitement impossible to contain. When she squared her shoulders to the audience, her fists found her hips. "I'm here to extend an invitation to my fellow countrymen. Come on, America—let's go camping. It's going to be so much fun, just pack up your gear, ice down your cooler, and head out on the highway for the backwoods. This is our country, the land of the free...and the home of the magnificent. Let's get out there and see it. Well? What do you say?"

Good-natured cheers echoed back in response. Mason examined the crowd on either side to find everyone wholeheartedly vested in the kickoff. When he refocused on the stage, the speaker had wandered over to his corner of the platform to take possession of the fishing pole. After noticing him, a smile pushed two dimples into her pretty cheeks. *Goodness, so this is Glori Dawes.* Up close, she became the indelible, incredible company spokesperson.

The tall man returned to the microphone. "I hope you like our camping theme for this promotional blitz. Our hope is to show Americans what gain there is to be leisure, to venture forth into the unexplored parklands with capable equipment that lends surety to their camping experience. The only factor we cannot control is the weather, so we'll be sure to have them check the forecast before pulling out of the driveway."

Glori rose from where she'd been seated on the cooler. "One small thing before we launch out, Edgar. You promised me a traveling companion, remember? So, where is he—my camping husband extraordinaire? You can't expect me to pitch this tent by myself, after all." She skirted the campfire and tightened a loose line at the tent's entrance.

The tall man turned to the audience. "That's right, gentlemen. Next week, Marketing will take applications and hold tryouts to fill the role of leading male camping enthusiast to furnish Glori a partner for the duration of the campaign. There will be some travel involved, at company expense, so we can film on location at some of America's popular national parks."

Glori leaned into the microphone. "I haven't picked my favorite locations yet. Mount Rushmore beckons, but there's Yellowstone with Old Faithful, Yosemite, Grand Canyon…too many to pick from, yet I must." She laid a finger beside her temple to appear thoughtful.

"While Glori is busy working through her location dilemma, I can at least get her hitched…for stage purposes, I assure you." He smiled enough his mustache tipped crooked. "My assistants are handing out the application forms as I speak. Simply drop those off in front of the marketing office in the mailbox labeled 'America Goes Camping.' Mr. Coleman is convinced the perfect candidate waits right here within our workforce, so let's not disappoint him, shall we?"

Glori walked to the far end of the platform, pointing out the men distributing the papers. In continuous motion, she covered the length of the stage and swept a hand through the air as if to sprinkle some magic dust over ordinary men to make them more compatible.

In fine-tuned assessment, Mason studied the stage props, eyed the stiff host, and tried to block out the hubbub of the crowd. That left him with the spokesperson in center focus, a vivacious woman with slender ankles and twinkling blue eyes. By direct comparison, she made the plastics in his lab uncomely. For a split second, he entertained the possibility of applying.

Knowing a straight-laced engineer would not make malleable material from which to craft a stage mate, reality grated across his fanciful daydream. He had no chance at all. The realization came with an ingratiating sound, like someone had pulled a nail out with a crowbar.

A glance back at the stage revealed instant trouble. The fishing pole tumbled from its propped position. The spokeswoman's once sparkly eyes now widened. Her whole frame trembled. The apex of the tent disappeared from view as structural failure overtook the platform. A heave from the back forward made the stage's surface lurch. A woman in the audience shrieked. Reverberation wracked the sound system, and the microphone pitched into the crowd.

With time of the essence, Mason moved toward the corner post. "Glori, over here. Make a jump for it." To accentuate the command, he extended his arms in a catch position.

Amid the din of confusion, she locked gazes and started to move toward him. The sound of snapping lumber from midstage became deafening. A dreadful shift seemed to tug her feet right out from under her, compromising her leap.

To counter the disaster-in-the-making, Mason ran several steps toward her and tried to cup his arms under her hurtling frame. Wooden slats from the underpinnings shifted toward them at the same moment she came into reach. In a whirling motion, he locked his arms around her and tore her away from the shattering platform. Intent to gain some distance, he sidestepped through the panicked crowd and headed straight for the Belvedere.

Glori moaned and laid her head back against his chest. Slivers of blue came and went beneath her eyelids. Her legs dangled limp from his left arm.

His heart pounding, he managed to get the passenger door open and sweep her inside. He knelt and sat on the edge of the floorboard. Patting her hand, he tried to bring her back to consciousness. "Glori, are you all right? Please, say something if you can."

Her head rolled to one side. "My tent is going to be a royal mess after that debacle."

He laughed and squeezed her hand. "No matter. They'll get your gear shipshape in no time. All you need is a camping companion, and you're off to Sequoia National Park, or wherever your heart desires."

"My ankle is throbbing. Do you think you could run me home? I need to elevate it pronto. I suppose it could use a soak, too."

Heady warmth overtook him for a brief second. Though not her stage mate, at least he could claim the take-home consolation from the kickoff event. Not bad as compensation went, it lengthened the time he got to examine her beautiful face. "My dear Glori, your chariot awaits." He tucked a fold of her skirt into the car and slammed the door shut. While no one seemed the wiser, he slid into the driver's seat and absconded with his prize, a surprise ending to the workweek as a man could conjure up.

~

Glori squeezed her eyes closed and reopened them. The handsome stranger with kind brown eyes that had once beckoned to her now failed to disappear. The familiar rear gable of her landlady's home stood sentinel above the car, so she'd experienced a minor sense of direction along the way. What a shame the white-hot pain from her right ankle muted the entire scene.

"You simply must allow me to help you—just this once," he said from a squat position outside her door. "Let's evaluate the current damage without causing more." The way he turned his head made it something of a tease. He held out his arms, intent on carrying her inside.

She rose off the leather upholstery and balanced on her left leg. "I can hardly let some stranger take me in his arms just like that. What would people think?"

His arched brow lowered as a smile hooked into his cheek. "No stranger here, only the new materials engineer. Mason Porter, humbly at your transport service, Miss Dawes. That right ankle is already swollen, which leaves me not to care about what others might think."

She wanted to shake her head, but nodded instead. If only she could think through the agony, a remedy might show itself in the plain light of day. A pulse of pain throbbed from the tender joint.

He stepped closer. "Please, do as I say. Put your arms around my neck and hang on. Is there a key to proffer at the door, or do we go right in?"

As she began to reply, he swept her off the ground. To offset her imbalance, her arms flew around his neck while her cheek came to rest against his collarbone. The faint smell of Aqua Velva softened the unexpected contact. "No key, as my landlady Mrs. Brougham expects me around this time daily." After two jostling steps, she thought to ease his haste. "Slowly, please, Mr. Porter. We will get there in due time."

He made a throaty affirmation and became more deliberate in his movement. "If I'm to respond to your every whim, then you must call me Mason. That makes us mutual friends, not hero and rescued damsel."

"I admire those terms, Mason. Plus, I'm grateful the company had the foresight to hire such a sturdy engineer. Who knew I would need the support?" When he glanced down at her, she managed a slight smile.

"That platform was an atrocity of design, even for a one-time event. I may have heard the nail pull out that sent you plunging into the crowd. Just for curiosity's sake, I might go back and examine it further."

"I've heard engineers tend to be systematic, though you are the first one I've ever met in the flesh." Her thumbs betrayed her, stroking across his hairline as if to prove his realness.

He counted under his breath as they ascended the rear steps. Turning sideways, he crouched. "You get the knob, Glori. My hands are full of camping wanderlust right now."

She sighed and reached for the door. "My apartment is to the left down the hall a bit. Mrs. Brougham is an old family friend. My rent helps her keep up the place, and she gives me privacy in return. I love these old grand dame mansions, though the raised ceilings make it hard to heat in wintertime."

He stepped through the threshold and shoved the door closed with his shoulder. "Tell me when to halt, then. I'll see if I can deliver you without striking your foot against another setback."

"I wish you were more funny than correct. I hesitate to think what walking through the plant might be like on Monday." She unclasped one hand to indicate the right entry point. "Let me get it. Sometimes, the door sticks."

"Maybe the old foundation is settling." He squared in front of the doorframe and halted.

She squirmed to get enough moxie on her push, and the door complied without much resistance. In a few measured steps, the distance to the divan vanished. When he knelt to deposit her on its cushion, their separation threatened. Rushed to express her gratitude, she stroked a finger along his chin and eased onto the familiar silk brocade. Her ankle protested the touchdown in wincing pain. The swollen area held a purplish cast that spoke of tissue damage.

Mason reached for her hand and bowed. "Dear Heavenly Father, lend us your strength when we are weakest, and heal Glori's ankle injury in your everlasting mercy. Though frail as dust, we are still your loving children. In the honorable name of Jesus we pray, amen."

She reclined her head against the padded upholstery, which set a solitary tear loose from the corner of one eye. What a debacle the hastily-planned kickoff turned out. In no shape to do anything about such a catastrophe, her weekend took a vacant turn toward lame.

He patted her shoulder. "I'm going to make you an ice pack. Requesting permission to assault your refrigerator and rob its freezer compartment." He gave her a sideways look to make her think twice about crossing his plan.

Glori blocked her eyes with the back of her hand. "Permission granted—but don't make the compress too heavy. You can use the tea towel on the oven door."

In half a minute, she heard him ratchet the release arm of the metal ice cube tray, followed by the cracking of ice. The faucet never ran, so she'd have to refill the tray later. Maybe she could put weight on the ankle by late Saturday. She exhaled audibly and almost missed the sound of his footfall returning.

"Here you are—one not-so-heavy ice pack ready to take down the swelling." He hoisted the tea towel for her inspection, its ends knotted for containment.

"Really, I am causing you too much bother. Please, ease that into place and leave me here in solitude, feigning a rapid recovery. I'm sure you need to be on your way. It's Friday night, after all."

He took meticulous care to surround the swollen anklebone, coaxing a few bumps smooth under the towel. "You're right, it's Friday. That's hamburger night for me, so I'm making a run to the Old Mill Tasty Shop for a double order." When she started to protest, he placed a finger across her lips. "My treat, so will that be a hamburger or cheeseburger for the star of 'America Goes Camping?' French fries or onion rings? RC Cola or A&W root beer?"

"Make that the fallen star, but you do leverage your offer with better than average bait. I'll have a cheeseburger with fries and a root beer, please. Leave the door unlocked and just let yourself back in. I doubt I'll be getting up any time soon." She caught his salute and gave a finger wave while the first pulse of cold stung her tender ankle. Seconds after the door clicked closed, the telephone began to ring. One glance at the conversation bench revealed the call would remain out of reach. Down and out, she might as well act the forlorn part, so she did.

Chapter 2

Mason shouldered through the door with dinner-for-two filling his hands. "Knock, knock. Is anyone in here still conscious?"

Glori pulled up and braced on two toss pillows. "Yes, I am awake, and the throbbing has subsided for the most part. Please come in."

"I raced back as fast as I could. Too bad I didn't have one of my prototype plastic coolers with me to provide some insulation." He set the carry-out carton on the coffee table and bent to check her ankle. "Let me put this ice pack in the sink for now, or a puddle will ruin your divan."

"Please do. My ankle is plenty numb. Ooh, something in that bag smells delicious."

He picked up the tea towel and immediately had to trap a drip in his cupped hand. "Do you need anything else from the kitchen?"

"An anti-inflammatory tablet might help. The aspirin are on the shelf over the sink."

"No, I've brought you something much better. I'll wash my hands and be right back." He hastened with his melting load and managed to ditch it in the deep enamel sink before it could spread its seepage. Spotting the bar of Ivory soap on the rim, he lathered up and knocked the faucet on with his knuckles. Once satisfied with his rinse, he dried his hands and returned to the front room.

"This root beer is bringing me back to my good senses." She took a long sip through the straw and closed her eyes, humming.

He wished he had remembered to offer medication before dashing out. Still, the present moment proved better than later. He reached into his pocket and handled the folded paper sleeve with care. "Here, this will take care of the ankle pain, and any other aches associated with it." He opened his mouth to prompt her to do likewise.

"Wait. What is that?"

"It's a B.C. Powder. The medicine comes in powder form, to make it fast-acting."

A flicker of recognition lit her eyes. "Take a B.C. Powder and come back strong?"

He tucked a smirk to one side of his mouth. "Someone's been watching too much television. Lean back now, and take your medicine like a cooperative little camper."

She opened her mouth and tilted her head back to comply. Her eyes tracked his every move until the fine dust found its target. She winced and reached for the root beer again.

"Oh, I should have warned you. It's notoriously bitter, but it works like a charm. Let me unpack our dinner. Do you want to watch the nightly news?"

"Heavens, no. The audio would be my worst enemy right now. Pull up the green chair and sit across from me. That way I can steal one of those delectable onion rings while you're not looking."

He pulled out two burgers and set the one marked with a "C" on the waxy wrapper in front of her. When he turned to locate the seat, he found a slim club chair with straight wooden legs capped by metal rings. "Are you fond of the Danish modern style?"

"Not really." She grabbed for a french fry, located a catsup packet, and raised her gaze to look at him. "My mother received the chair as a gift, and promptly passed it along to me. She likes her pieces more padded, as you might imagine."

"There's something to be said for functionality," he replied, dragging the chair along the hardwood floor. "Of course, that's an engineer's perspective."

"Though you have me quite intrigued with this engineering thing, I think we should pause our conversation to give thanks for the food. I would like to offer grace, unless you object." She blinked as if to ask a question.

"No, not at all. Please do, as I'm blessed to be here and not eating alone." His neck steamed at the admission. Perhaps he had said too much. In retreat, he bowed to pray.

"Thank you, God, for the abundance of this table, and for the act of chivalry delivered in my dire need of it. Give us grateful hearts, that we might return the praise to you. In Christ we pray, amen."

"Spoken with grace, which makes the next portion of our conversation a touch flat by comparison—but I truly must press for more information." He fished an onion ring out of the oil-soaked paper basket and waved it like a conductor's baton. "Are you originally from Wichita?" He smiled before he bit into the fried treat. The onion pulled out of its coating, a tasty reward.

She unwrapped her burger and peeked beneath the top bun. "Yes, my grandfather moved to town from rural Kansas. My father went to Topeka for college, returned to work for Mr. Coleman, and married my mother, whom he'd met at a church social. I lived in Emporia to obtain a journalism degree, but came right back when Coleman Company offered me a position in Human Resources. I handle employee benefits and get to write for the company newsletter."

"I read through last month's copy of Coleman News. I deemed it a real crackerjack. Now, as fate would have it, I'm eating with one of its writers. Fancy that." He stopped to take a giant bite from his hamburger, lest he set free any more superlatives he might regret later.

Her eyelids flitted closed when she tasted the cheeseburger for the first time. A spray of faint freckles decorated the bridge of her nose, complimenting the red tones in her stylish blonde hair. Her long reddish lashes seemed to fan the air as they swept open. "This is truly saving me at the moment. I don't even remember stopping for lunch today."

He held up a finger in protest as he cleared his throat. "Pay yourself first, my dear Miss Dawes. That mantra is both sound business sense and good personal advice."

"I'm afraid I don't have a good business mindset—not like Mr. Coleman, anyway. When he shifted the company's production away from oil heaters and gas floor furnaces as the market shifted, he buoyed the company's health with our new emphasis on camping gear. I welcome that direction, because I think it holds much more promise."

He nodded and took another bite of his burger, comforted that his dinner mate had tuned into some of the critical acclaim the administration received in the industry. A dense pocket of mustard made him reach for his soda. The fizzy sweetness offset the tangy detour. "I admire his mantra, 'Don't let life put you back on your heels. Lean into it.' It speaks of flexibility, much like my plastics research. Here, won't you try the onion rings?" He held out the basket and allowed her to partake.

Glori made a selection and held the ring up to her encircled lips. "How's this for a perfect fit?" She laughed and downed the morsel.

Fond of how her eyes sparkled when she jested, he admitted that his weekend had gotten off to a phenomenal start. His first week's triumph had been locating The Old Mill Tasty Shop for a first-rate hamburger. Now, his second week's triumph might be adding a scintillating individual with whom to share it. He dared to hope for as much.

She took a sip of root beer and set down the cup. "Drat the contest for my camping partner next week. I don't have a spare moment to review those silly applications. There might be some real work waiting in my department mailbox deserving more immediate attention."

Prodded by a touch of commiseration, he smiled and reached for the largest onion ring. "Now Glori, American citizens must get permission to go camping. There go our summer profits if they don't." He gave her a delving look and chomped the onion ring in half.

"Perhaps I could be so bold as to suggest that you apply—and put me out of my selection misery, Mason." An earnest reflection shone beyond the tease, enlivening her eyes.

Caught between duty and a dare, he squinted at her. "Would you truly make my plastics research play second fiddle for my time?"

A wry smile curled her lips, but commotion at the door stopped her from replying.

A short woman stalked into the room, her brow furrowed. "So you are here, Glori Dawes. What kind of nincompoop won't answer her phone?" Her red-painted lips stuck out in protest.

A man shoved in behind her and slammed the door.

At the loud report, Glori pressed both index fingers to her

temples. Like a strutting ballerina, she lifted her swollen ankle from the cushion. "A crippled nincompoop, I suppose. Now, you've found me, Midge. Try not to bring my headache back with your aggravated arrival. By the way, this is my rescuer, Mason Porter. He's a new engineer working with plastics."

When the fellow turned in his direction, Mason recognized him as the feckless narrator for the camping skit, the man from Marketing with the abbreviated mustache. Unappreciative of the interruption, he bit his tongue to crimp a sardonic reply. Maybe these two intruders would go away like pesky flies, and their cozy dinner-for-two could continue into the blissful night.

The woman paced to the living room window and lowered the Venetian blinds with a metallic rattle. Before returning, she pressed the television's power button to awaken the giant inside the cabinet. When the newscaster blared out breaking news from the Brussels World's Fair, she adjusted the volume knob to tolerable.

Not missing his chance, the man skirted the coffee table and knelt by the divan. "How dreadful to end the filming like that, Glori. We searched frantically, but couldn't find you anywhere."

"No, Edgar. You were too late. Mr. Porter had already swept me away to his well-cushioned car, where I immediately asked to be brought home. The pain in my ankle nearly blinded me, it was so intolerable. I'm medicated now, and he's brought me dinner. I guess you might say that the evening is looking up."

The woman stepped closer and gave him a hasty inspection. "I'm Midge Kerr, Mr. Porter, Glori's assistant. Thank you for saving her from a more abrupt collision with the pavement in the back lot. We'd never get the summer campaign off the ground if matters had turned out worse."

"Just doing my gentlemanly duty, Miss Kerr, I assure you." He bundled the empty wrapper and found the audacity to offer Glori the last onion ring. When she accepted it with a private smile, he regained some confidence. He stood and faced the stiff man whose expression proved more unyielding. "I don't believe we've met." He offered his hand with the greeting.

The man's gaze shifted away to regard Glori, and then returned to him, as cold as ice. "I am Edgar Sterns, director of Marketing, also widely known in Wichita as Glori's fiancé."

The bottom dropped out of Mason's stomach as the dinner ambience crashed. A loud commercial advertisement came on TV, tossing an imbecilic jingle around the room as the tension mounted. Finally, the narrator extended his hand for a limp shake. "I suppose you can be going now, Mr. Porter. We promise to take good care of Glori from here on out."

"I trust you will." In a parting gesture, he crushed the fop's knuckles with a working man's grip and nodded at Miss Kerr. "She's already taken a B.C. Powder for the ache, so no more medicine until bedtime."

The assistant finally found a servile smile. "Thank you, Mr. Porter. I'll prep a soak in the tub next. A touch of Epsom salts is always good for what ails you."

Intending to make a more personal farewell to his hostess, he stepped around the man's skinny blockade to approach the divan. "I suggest you not overdo it this weekend, Glori. You may feel like a new woman in a couple of days." He winked with the delivery, snapped his fingers, and pointed at her injury. "Feel free to come see us in Manufacturing—when you can spare the steps."

"I certainly will, Mason. And you consider my suggestion, if you will." Her eyes held a secret message, one not desecrated by mere words. "Bless you for your catch today."

Retracting from her presence with forced willpower, he exited through the door, content to have it resist closing, an apt departure for a recalcitrant hero.

~

At Midge's insistence, Glori stood to her feet. The rush of blood made her ankle throb in a matter of seconds. Running water echoed from the tub through the nearby doorway, making her appreciate the apartment's brevity. "This may be the most ungainly hobble west of the Mississippi River tonight," she teased while angling for the hallway.

Midge turned off the television and began to follow her. "I don't know what happened out there. One minute, we have the camera crew in session, and the next, the whole sha-bang collapses to the ground. I sent Andy into the rubble to retrieve the props, so we can still use them in the park shots. Goodness, what a near catastrophe."

She gestured for her to come closer and placed an arm around her shoulders. "I take it no one else was hurt in the mêlée."

Midge blew out a long breath. "No, it didn't even cross our minds that you might be injured. I am sorry to have stormed in here shooting off my mouth like a reactive Ricky Ricardo on a Lucy-induced tirade." She rolled her eyes and placed an arm around her waist for support.

Glori took a gimpy step and touched the heel of her injured foot. The resulting pain caused her to yelp. "Spanish cursing might have made a different impression on our new company engineer. You may have to make amends at some future opportunity, Miss Kerr."

"Duly noted," she replied in quick relent. "Let's get you into the tub and end all the excitement. To tell you the truth, that hamburger smelled like the perfect dinner tonight."

"I would be game for that," Edgar said, coming in from the kitchen. He drew a cigarette from the box in his shirt pocket and fingered its length. "Remember to call your mother, Glori, before she hears a more tragic report from someone else."

"And you remember my no smoking inside rule, Mr. Sterns," she replied with disdain in her tone. He'd been around enough to wear on her nerves. Thank goodness she had already eaten dinner—with a true gentleman, no less. Suddenly, the idea of being alone suited her mood. "Just get me inside the bathroom, Midge. I can handle it from there."

"Okey-dokey. Tell me, where is your other shoe?"

Stunned, Glori paused and grabbed for the bathroom door frame. "I cannot even remember having it on."

"I previewed the film footage," Edgar replied. "You are wearing two sneakers in the skit. It looks like your new friend may have a foot fetish—or at least bear a fondness for women's shoes." He grinned like a turncoat and headed for the apartment's main door.

Glori touched her toes to the floor, needing all the balance she could muster. "Edgar, just one more thing before you leave."

"What's that, my darling?" He raised a dark brow as if to taunt her.

Midge insisted on possessing her remaining shoe, which she jacked off without untying. With a cordial tap on the back, her assistant shifted out of the bathroom to depart.

"Never foist our engagement status as social leverage again, or it will vanish into thin air, much to your discomfort." She sliced him with a defiant look before stepping onto the tile floor.

"And your discomfort, as well," he replied.

Midge ended the stalemate in her typical style, shoving him out with her mocking laugh.

Alone at last, Glori pressed her forehead against the mirror, dealing with a discomfort deeper than her anklebone. Her thoughts flitted to the handsome engineer who smelled of Aqua Velva and wore bands of steel for arms. Perhaps a materials expert could detect the difference between fake veneer and real wood. The eyes never lied, and she was confident she'd read genuine interest in his.

Chapter 3

Mason positioned the test slab across the open mouth of a metal ice chest to better elevate it. The putty-gray plastic had satisfactorily hardened to a stiff plank, but he had to know if it was uniform in composition. This polypropylene had just come onto the manufacturing market last year. Uses ran the gamut from drinking straws to pressure pipe systems, but he determined to coax a state-of-the-art insulated ice chest from it. One thing remained evident—the weighty galvanized version of Coleman's trademark cooler needed to fall by the wayside.

A lanky man dressed in khaki work clothes strolled into his area of the fabrication shop. "Wednesdays are tough, because a man can hardly tell if the workweek is coming or going." He shook his head as if to authenticate the claim.

"That's the pure truth." He stepped toward the man, allowing the break. "Mason Porter, the new materials engineer."

The man nodded with a tight smile. "Don Merritt in lantern assembly. What manner of plain beast do you have there? I've never seen the likes of that substance before."

"It's a plastic polymer called polypropylene. Don't let the way it looks fool you, because I can make it any color of the rainbow. What I'm testing for at this juncture is lightweight strength, uniformity, and durability. One day soon, I'll create a mold that can cast the modern replacement for this old tub." He gave the galvanized metal ice chest a patronizing pat.

Don chuckled and scratched his head. "I think we'll keep the metal in our lanterns, for the time being anyway. I understand that product flammability is a key consideration for materials selection.

Ice chests make the perfect guinea pig for a new concoction like plastic. No one's going to set a cooler on fire."

"Excellent point, Mr. Merritt. Feel free to stop by my corner of the shop from time to time. I need someone staring over my shoulder to see if I have made any notable progress."

"Oh, I could have Mack Insley, the floor supervisor, poke his nose into your research." He glanced across the shop floor, as if a threat was imminent. "You'd have to answer a bunch of questions, though, as he knows nothing about plastics. It might not be worth your time."

Mason offered his hand for a brokered truce. "We'll call it good for now. I'm running some quality tests next. Let me know if you ever need any inspections."

"We've got a million-dollar seller coming down the assembly line with an impeccable track record, Mr. Porter. If we converse a decade from now, I hope you can say the same about your plastic cooler." He extended his hand and shook to seal the challenge.

Soon lost in thought, Mason positioned the ultrasonic apparatus and began to conceptualize the inspection's stages. He wiped his palm over the transducer and decided to refer back to the reference manual for the proper sequencing. Locating the tube of lubricating gel, he positioned his record book to readily receive the data and took the manual in hand.

Technical jargon demanded his utmost concentration. He checked the calibration on the gage so it matched the diagram. With the transducer as the listening device, the receiver had to properly "hear" the defects, or his testing would be for naught. For some reason, the shop grew uncomfortable with its stagnant air and weak lighting. The limitations might have been imagined, though he wasn't given to finding fault.

Convinced he had readied the machine with adequate skill, he turned on the power. A captivating process, his graduate studies had insured full exposure to ultrasonic inspection. He reached for the lubricating gel and ran a test line down the center of the sample plank like putting catsup on a hot dog. With a steady hand, he ran the transducer through the gel, pausing at the marks he had drawn down the length of the sample.

He eyed the gage simultaneously as the transducer rode its linear circuit, concentrating on any deviation he might detect. Two pitting blemishes caught his attention as he passed, but his interest focused on structural anomalies more than cosmetic defects. The continuity of the material proved impressive. *My word, this plastic is phenomenal stuff.*

Movement off the end of the table distracted him from the end of his run. Glancing up, he thought to tell Mr. Insley to mind his own business for the duration. Instead, Glori Dawes stood in front of him, her gaze shifting from his sample to his face. "Well, will wonders never cease? My favorite HR representative has wandered into my quadrant for some inexplicable reason."

"Greetings, Mr. Porter." One eyebrow arched as she made her assessment. "May I touch this gray plank of sample material? I've never seen anything quite like it."

"Extruded polypropylene, please meet Miss Glori Dawes, a human cast in her own pleasing form. That's an engineer's way of saying how good it is to see you again."

"I'm here for your introductory tour, Mason, but I see how inconvenient it is for you."

"Not at all. I was just finishing up a test run. Let me turn off the ultrasound gage."

She reached for him in reactive response. "No, please. Show me what you're doing here. I'm intrigued with this apparatus. Plus, I should know something about this newfangled plastic, in case I have to write a column about it. I don't like to be caught off-guard."

Momentarily unsure of her sincerity, Mason wiped his thumb against the transducer to remove the excess gel. "All right then, we'll start with a pair of these." He grabbed a spare set of safety goggles and handed them to her. Something of a test, most fashion-conscious women would not tolerate wearing the unattractive headgear.

Glori surrendered her personnel file and fitted the goggles in place. When she glanced up at him, the frames magnified the attractiveness of her blue eyes. "Is this what you had in mind?"

Perhaps the most honest answer would be that he'd had it the least in mind, but with a five-foot-six beauty hovering over one's work, such a telling confession could wait. "You're wearing those properly, yes. Now, let me show you how to listen for defects."

"Listen? Do you mean I trust my ears? Oh, golly. I'm untrained as they come."

He stepped closer with the tease, but couldn't subdue his pleasure as a grin leaked out. "Not your ears, my dear Miss Dawes, the ultrasonic gage has a receiver that does the listening. Place your hand in mine, and we'll run the test line down the sample. I'll clue you ahead of time that some minor pitting has blemished the surface in a couple of spots, so watch for those on your read-out there."

She slid her slender fingers around the transducer while moving closer. "My word. Isn't this something?"

"Yes, it is," he assured her, careful to leave his gaze welded to the plastic. Again, he guided the transducer along the gel line to let the instrument interpret the test area.

"There," she said, "I see pit number one."

"Good work, Glori. Have patience now, for what else you might find." He took his time finishing out the run, content to have her shoulder blade pressed against his chest, even for the briefest duration. Inches from the terminating point, the gage indicated the second pit.

"Again, pit number two. This is fascinating. I may lose my heart for doing HR work at this rate." She turned and gave him a spark-lit look over her shoulder.

Mason stood straight and confiscated the transducer from her. "Polypropylene is becoming a useful polymer due to its adaptability. Still, it might not be the right polymer for our purpose. The Brits have developed a high-density polyethylene that's being used in packaging. I plan to explore that option next."

Glori pulled off the goggles and stepped away from the instrument. "What characteristics are you aiming for by using plastics? I mean, where's the gain?"

"Here's one." He lifted the plank off the galvanized chest and hoisted it up and down. "You try this." He handed it over.

She took possession wide-eyed. "Oh, my. It's much lighter than I supposed."

"Lightweight is one favorable property. Add moldable, affordable, strong, and avoids degradation to the requisite formula, and I think we have a winner—plastics. Which type will best serve our purpose is the more refined question."

She rested the plank back on its stand and retook possession of her file folder. "Let me get back to my task at hand. Be honest now, Mason. Have you any time for my introductory tour? If not, I will consider myself enlightened to your plastics work and beat a hasty retreat back to my corner of HR." She bit her bottom lip, though her eye contact remained steady.

"You don't seriously expect me to take a pass on that offer, do you, Miss Dawes?" He couldn't keep his brow from furrowing as he delved for her mutual receptivity.

Her lips pursed as she tapped her chin with the file. "Mercy me, no. Break my heart another day, Mr. Porter, but do humor me for the tour this morning."

He glanced at his watch, keen to add a conditional. "I'm yours for the duration—but only if it ends with lunch in the cafeteria. Dare you etch that sort of defect into your reputation?"

"Flaw duly noted, as we shall have that lunch together, so help me God."

He held one palm up as if taking a pledge, but the hand that would have foresworn on the Holy Bible wrapped around her forearm instead. With divine aid, he remembered to flip off the power switch on the ultrasound gage to end the test. The results would be telling, most definitely. He embraced the interruption as heaven-sent, because it certainly felt that way.

~

Glori jabbed the succotash with her fork, wondering why she'd selected the hot lunch today. "Tell me, had you an ounce of national pride when Explorer One left the cradle of its launch pad at Cape Canaveral back in January?"

"Yes, a considerable amount," Mason replied. He picked up his last potato chip and waved it at her. "Eisenhower plans to solidify our commitment to space exploration this summer, so we can surpass those rascally Russians. Rumor is that he'll make the new aeronautical agency civilian-oriented, not military."

"That speaks of a peaceful mission into the outer unknown, so at least we're not leaving it to the warmongers. How refreshing." She pushed her plate away, quite done.

"Last month, the Vanguard One satellite launched and has successfully transmitted information back to earth as a result of its solar technology. It would appear that satellites are the wave of the future. Say, is that succotash any good?"

"Please, help yourself. I'll allow you to run that taste test and report back your own results." She scanned her fork over the plate in the same fashion he had leveled the transducer.

Mason laughed and reached for her plate. "Did your mother never tell you there are people starving in China?"

"Help me absolve my conscience, then, by cleaning my plate for me. Mercy, there were twenty-five applications for my camping partner in the Marketing mailbox this morning. I'll confess that over half of them are men twice my age. Great balls of fire. That should fuel a campground scandal, shouldn't it?"

He chewed the soppy vegetable mix, shaking his head. Though he seemed a man of measured response, he could not hide his mirth at her predicament. After taking a lengthy drink of water, he leaned toward her. "What is it that you're looking for, Miss Outdoorsy? Tell me your idea of the perfect camping partner. I understand the part about not being too decrepit, but what else would you desire?"

She leaned back in her chair and closed her eyes, lest she be altogether too transparent. "He has to know his way around the campsite—and how to operate our equipment."

"I see. Is there anything more?"

"For the camera's sake, he should be a bit taller than me, but not by much, so it looks like we're well-matched. I don't want his feet to be poking out beyond the tent flaps when we bid the camera goodnight."

"Perhaps you should have the goodnight scene cut after the toasted marshmallows are shared at the campfire." He snickered and returned her plate. "As delightful as this lunch has been, I'm afraid I must report back to the shop. Thank you so much for the inspiring tour. We must have walked the length of a football field four times over."

She pushed back in her chair and reached for the empty plate. "Look at that. I didn't complain about my ankle once—or ask you to carry me any part of the way."

"No doubt that Epsom salts soak did the trick," he replied with a wink.

Embarrassed by the heated flush working up her neck at the personal attention, Glori headed for the dish disposal station. With no idea how to prolong the lunch date, she grasped at an elusive straw. "I hope you have something fun in mind for your Good Friday off."

"Not really. I live in Valley Center in a small rental, but there's not too much to explore up there." He dumped his apple core into the garbage and moved toward the door.

"I'm escorting my darling niece to the Riverside Zoo on Saturday for the annual egg hunt. Admission is half off for the Easter holiday, so it's a fine time to visit. The zookeepers plan to bring the alligators up from their wintertime basement lair, which is always a rousing spring ritual. I hope there's time left for amusements at Park Villa Arcade, to let her play the games."

"You've piqued my curiosity with the alligators. Is this attraction in downtown Wichita?"

"Yes, right on the river off McLean—the west bank. I highly recommend it, especially if the weather is good."

"Well, I may see you down there, Miss Dawes. I'll be the slightly taller man being amused by cold-blooded reptiles held outside of their natal geographic region." He leveled his hand from the crown of his head and swept it over her hair part.

Aware of his reason to size up their heights, Glori puckered her lips and feigned disdain. Nothing could have been further from the truth. She'd all but asked him to apply as her camping mate again. Maybe the alligators held more endearment from the crowd than a camping HR representative who had a sudden fondness for engineers. "Off to your plastics then, Mason."

"Always a pleasure, Glori." With his eyes full of merriment, he tipped an imaginary hat and walked away.

Midge stepped up and blew out a belabored breath. "Good golly, Miss Molly. I thought that bore would never leave. We have to redeem your afternoon schedule, or you'll not possess a spare minute to review those applications."

Glori watched as Mason stopped to shake a floor foreman's hand while departing the cafeteria. The aforementioned task was not to her liking, not in the least. "I should be so lucky," she replied, her tone as deadpan as she could manage. Midge's nudge didn't help her plight, though it did set her in forward motion.

Chapter 4

The Arkansas River seemed to draw a cool breeze through the low-lying park. Mason questioned the propriety of chasing a doting aunt to the Easter egg hunt, when that time should have been devoted to her darling niece. Still, from the invitation in her tone, he guessed Glori would welcome the intrusion. Lacking anything of promise to occupy his time off, he'd driven in with embattled hopes of finding her in the crowd. The arched billboard for Park Villa Arcade flanked the far river bank. He steered the Plymouth toward the small zoo.

One matter that had given him cause to toss about after retiring last night was this issue of her being engaged to the smidgen-mustached Edgar Sterns. From every sign conveyed by Glori's overt friendliness, she didn't consider herself betrothed. Or perhaps he'd been reading too much into that feminine reaction. Still, leisure time together—especially with an innocent third party— would provide a rather good testing ground. The more time he spent with Glori, the more he learned. Attraction could be an unfed lion, always roaring for more.

After parking, he strolled toward a crescent of loosely-collected families along a grassy field. Animal cages lined the far side of the meadow. A high-pitched cry echoed beyond a line of catalpa trees, so he tried to imagine what type of cage occupant might have made the noise. Off the right side of the crowd, a blur of color turned into a fanciful game resembling "London Bridges Falling Down."

"I'm a lonely little petunia in an onion patch," the woman sang with gaiety.

"Won't you come and play with me?" the little girl added with a pleading tone. Her thin arms reached up as if to pluck a cloud from the sky.

Recognizing Glori, Mason stopped to observe the exchange for a few seconds longer. Tender in every aspect, her attention radiated around the child. She'd never looked more beautiful, relieved of corporate duty and carefree in the moment. Agonized that her playful expressiveness might change upon his sudden appearance, he knocked his baseball cap back and tried on an oversized smile. "Say, was that the Easter Bunny I saw hopping through the lion's cage just now?"

Glori straightened from hovering over the child. "Hello Mason. I certainly hope you're mistaken about spotting the Easter Bunny. We've been searching for that rabbit high and low. Please, come meet my sweet niece Linda." She positioned the girl to face him and locked her arms like a daisy chain around her neck.

"Hi, Mr. Mason. Are you a friend of my aunt's from Coleman?" The child wrinkled her nose with the interrogation.

He stooped and placed his hands on his knees. "That's right. We met at Coleman Company a few weeks ago. Your Aunt Glori gave me an introductory tour of the entire plant. It's a fascinating place, as you might imagine."

"They won't let me go inside, not until I'm ten," she replied. A quick glance at her aunt won her a nod of approval.

"Historically, W.C. was pretty strict about allowing children in the workplace," Glori said. "With safety ever an issue, I can't really blame him."

He shrugged. "That's the senior Mr. Coleman?"

"Yes, he was the founder of the company. We lost him just last year. His son runs the operation now."

A shrill whistle sounded between the crowd and the animal cages. Several men in similar uniforms stood at the top of a small knoll. The middle man raised a megaphone to his mouth. "Is anyone ready to hunt Easter eggs?"

The children gave a collective squeal. Prancing in place, Linda reached for the basket cradled on her aunt's arm. Several precocious participants walked out onto the field, causing another blast from the whistle.

"Hold on, you older children. Parents, we'll start with the five and under group. Please have them join us at the starting line to your left. When we blow the whistle again, it will be children only, so please have them ready at the starting line."

"I have to be with the older children," Linda said, her mouth twisted in protest.

"But look how much more room you're allowed to hunt eggs in," Glori replied, her hand sweeping the expansive field. "Plus, you're almost fast enough to catch me now. More space will be to your advantage."

Mason squatted for an additional strategy session. "Remember to keep a sharp eye for color and curved shapes nestled in the grass. This is almost like looking for butterflies—only on the ground, not in a bush."

Her eyes widened for a few seconds as she processed his instructions. "Okay, I'll hunt butterflies on the down-low." She turned to her aunt and nodded. After the whistle blew for the younger children, her basket began to swing with an antsy rhythm.

Mason rose to find Glori inching closer, her lime-green polka dots hard to miss. Soon, she hovered off his shoulder. He rewarded her with a cryptic tease, one eyebrow arched for added intrigue.

"Waiting one's turn can be an authentic life lesson," she said under her breath.

Pushing against the vagary of the comment, he bristled to think he might have to wait through her engagement to demonstrate further interest. His resolve waffled. "Me or her?" he asked, his tone a touch testy.

Though humor shone in her eyes, her lips tucked into a lopsided circle and resembled a crooked heart. "Use it if you need to, my fine friend. I was speaking to the temperament of a child. Patience is more than a virtue. On occasion, it's a necessity."

In half a minute, they would be standing alone on the sidelines, with darling Linda hunting eggs. He would be clear to state whatever he dared, though such directness might spoil the remainder of the outing. As he took a breath of fresh air, a sense of calm washed over him. Perhaps he could wait his turn at that. He would be charming company in the interim.

Engineers always pursued the steady state, lopping off both unpredictable tails of the Bell curve in favor of the predictable rise and fall of consistency that lay between. Statistical analysis made for an odd referee for courtship—if that was where this new friendship might be headed.

At a loss of focus, he remained unaware of the second hunt commencing until a blur of lime green passed him by, headed for the starting line. He reached for her out of involuntary need, his hand landing on the pink scarf tied around her waist. A playful tug rendered it his by full possession.

Glori reached back and swatted at him, her fingertips sweeping his non-penitent hand. "Use it if you need to, my fine friend," she teased over her shoulder. The accompanying wink stated a different case, one that held more weight than pink chiffon.

He stuffed the scarf inside the buttoned placard of his knit shirt, hoping the zookeeper's efforts at hiding dyed eggs could be undone in a matter of minutes. "Like butterflies on the down-low," he called to Linda, equally anxious to get the show on the road. When the girls broke into a run for the starting line, their lithe tandem movement doubled his anticipation.

~

"I hardly think they should pull at them like that," Glori said, fighting a constricting of her chest. Confrontation always had the same suffocating effect, which made her the supreme peacemaker. Too bad the alligators had so few allies in the crowd. Another leering jeer went up from some rowdy youths gawking at the man-versus-beast scenario.

"Why don't the gators want to go into the pen?" Linda asked. "They'll like it once they get in there."

Mason lowered to her. "I think it's the trip to get there that bothers them. God didn't give those creatures long legs for walking any great distance. They probably like to swim more than they prefer to walk."

"Plus, they love basking in the sun, so being outside will be much nicer through the summer." Glori gave him a quick glance, her face flush with heat.

"See, now they've added the proper motivation," Mason replied.

When he pointed up the ramp, Glori hesitated, but turned to look. A squatty zookeeper dangled the raw leg quarter of a plucked chicken in front of the reptilian foursome. Suddenly, a belly-sliding race ensued. In no time, the gate behind the loathsome animals closed and ended the transfer's tugging conflict. More chicken pieces appeared from a bucket while one unlucky employee addressed the delicate task of removing the tape from the animals' snouts. Once that individual cleared the perimeter fence to safety, the crowd began to applaud. Indifferent, the alligators tore at the raw meat until the last scrap was devoured, a savage process.

"Pretty impressive show," Mason said, leaning toward her.

"I like the bobcat better," Linda replied. She gestured with a piece of taffy garnered from the egg hunt. "Too bad he sleeps inside his tree trunk den all day."

"I'm getting thirsty," Glori interjected. "Is anyone else ready for Park Villa Arcade?"

"I am," Linda squealed. She pocketed the taffy and locked hands with them both to pull toward a new destination.

Glori obliged and fell into step with Mason. "So, how's your skeet ball prowess, Mr. Porter?" She flexed both brows to stimulate his response.

"Madame, you've never seen such hand-eye coordination, I assure you."

Linda stopped pulling and relaxed her lead. "You won't win that one, Mr. Mason. Aunt Glori never loses at skeet ball."

"Best two out of three," he countered without hesitation.

Glori shook her head while giving him a sideways glance that lingered. "Okay, it's your money." A smile flickered into place, though she'd done her best to keep it subdued. Getting to know Mason proved to be a challenge, one she found repeated delight in addressing. "Tell me something about yourself."

Linda stiffened her arms and used their momentum to start a hopping game. After the second try, she got fairly good at it. The third hop seemed almost collegiate in proportion.

"I have an older sister. She lives in Scottsdale, Arizona, where it's dreadfully dry. They don't even have a decent lawn for my two nephews to play outside." He produced her scarf and held it out in surrender.

"Aha, boys in your family—I could have guessed." She snatched the sheer pink band and tried to reattach it to her waistline, but found the handicap of using one hand too constraining. With Linda holding tight to fuel her hopping gait, she could only manage to hook the scarf around her neck.

"Please, allow me," Mason insisted. He walked backwards while guiding the scarf around her waist. "Now, put a finger on the tie and help me with the bow."

Working left-handed, Glori attempted to provide the needed assistance. Her focus fell on Mason, who seemed intent on accomplishing his task. In her up-close inspection, she discovered a small mole off his right earlobe that took on impish personification. For the life of her, she couldn't determine why she enjoyed the study of it so intently, or the masculine jaw it graced.

He righted his posture after a final tug and hoisted Linda for her next jump. "Did you see anything that met your approval, Miss Dawes?"

Stirred by his effect on her, she quickly fished for a deflection. Her pulse raced while Linda landed the perfect leap. "Beat me at skeet ball, and I'll confess. Humility has a cleansing effect on me, but if I win, the truth remains locked within these lips."

He nodded as he examined the entrance arch above the arcade. "Lemonade comes first then. I don't want any excuses when I beat you fair and square."

Linda tugged at his arm and delivered a stern look. "Like I told you, Mr. Mason—my aunt never loses at skeet ball."

"You mean not until today, Linda Lou," he replied, tweaking the girl's nose.

She laughed in a giddy ripple. "Until today," the child repeated with a snicker.

A light sweat began to trickle down Glori's back. Though the loose linen blouse allowed her skin to breathe, she suddenly felt stifled. Music wafted from the arcade area, and the smell of popcorn filled the air. When Mason held up three fingers to the lemonade vendor, she fought the urge to tear away and rack up the first round of skeet ball—just for practice. A thought that she might lose caused her shoulders to shudder, despite the increasing heat of the day. By golly, she'd really gotten herself into a pickle this time.

"Here's your lemonade, my fine friend," Mason said, jutting the cup toward her.

"Press it right between my shoulder blades," she quipped,

absconding with the liquid relief before he could make good on her request. The first syrupy mouthful brought back a bit of confidence with it. She chewed the ice, hoping for a steady hand and sharp-eyed deliverance.

~

Mason stood beside the Belvedere, airing out the interior. When he opened up the rear passenger door, his surprise lay within plain sight. "Would anyone here know how to use one of these gizmos?" He gestured to the oversized ring standing on the floorboard.

Linda sucked in a breath, her palms clamped on her blushed cheeks.

"A hula hoop?" Glori sounded incredulous, her expression frozen.

He wondered if he'd made a mistake. "They had them everywhere at the grocery store yesterday evening. Since I knew Linda would be with you today, I wanted to bring her a little something. It's made out of Marlex plastic. You'd be hard pressed to span this circumference with wood."

"May I?" Linda asked, reaching for the hoop.

"By all means, yes," Mason replied. "I hope you like yellow."

Glori encouraged the child with a pat on her shoulder. "It's her favorite color." In no time, the vacuous ring encircled the girl. Gyrations soon began, yet the hoop didn't remain suspended. "Try going faster, dear. Really give it a whirl."

Mason noted the ring stayed gravitational for twice as long the second time. "There, I think you're onto the proper way. Keep trying. It's all in the hips."

Glori stooped and picked the hula hoop out of the grass. "Let me get it going for you, Linda. Arms up. Now, spread your legs out some. Here we go." She slung the hoop around the child's ribs and, by some miracle of gravity, it kept rotating.

Mason clapped. "Ah, we should have counted. Otherwise, how will we know when she's set a new record?"

"Count next time, dearie, while I talk to our friend, Mr. Porter in private." Glori nodded toward the driver's side of the car and led the way around the car's chrome grill.

Picking a smudged insect off his metallic paint job, Mason followed her several strides back. Maybe she would give him a hushed lecture about spoiling Linda with an impromptu gift. He stood guilty as charged, if purchasing a plastic hoop equated to spoiling.

Glori hovered near the side view mirror, fingering its rim. When she looked up at him, a fleeting smile crossed her complex expression. "I'm penitent to some degree, though it's been a lovely day. I fell from grace at the skeet ball arcade, such a tragic loss." Her deepened smile caused dimples in her cheeks.

He stepped closer under the heightened allure. "Was there not some confession attached to your penalty for losing? Oh, yes. In humility, you were going to reveal a truth about what you approved of in your case study earlier." He raised a balled fist to his lips and cleared his throat, intending to soften his tone. "I'd be eager to hear that revelation."

She sighed, locking her gaze on his. "That tiny mole off your right earlobe had me transfixed for the most inexplicable reason. Perhaps you were standing too close to give me a fair chance."

He tweaked his lips to one side. "That pesky thing? I try to shave it off each morning to no avail. Funny that it caught your eye. Engineers typically come without many accoutrements, Miss Dawes."

"You're a fine-looking man, Mason Porter. There, I've said it—my penalty for losing at skeet ball. Consider it a rare occasion, as I'll bring my best game next time, and you'll have to do the confessing."

"I worried that you might read me the riot act over buying the hula hoop for Linda. How wrong can a man be?" He reached up and wrapped his fingers around hers atop the mirror, stroking her hand with his thumb.

"That was so thoughtful. Why would I condemn such a generous act?" Her voice broke at the rendering, causing her to turn away.

Sensing a cloud eclipsing the honest moment, he stepped closer, leaving only the mirror separating them. "Is there something more, Glori. Please tell me, so we'll not leave the day in ruins. We've simply had a wonderful time."

"Twenty-eight," Linda shouted from the far side of the car.

Glori swept her hair back from her face and turned toward him. "Please don't leave me on that 'America Goes Camping' campaign with some ungracious lout for a partner." Her eyes rimmed with tears as she straightened her shoulders. "It could be so much fun with someone more remarkable to explore a national park together. The deadline for applicants is Monday at noon. I ask you to reconsider, Mason. Please, do it for me."

He watched a scarlet tide wash up her neck as her revelation turned to all-out begging. A season of disrupted work would be the last thing he'd sign up for, yet a spontaneous decline was far from his lips. Even maligned with tears and flushed with the poverty of imploring, her beauty overtook his common sense at such close range. "I...couldn't do it for you," he admitted in a husky voice. When her chin tipped low, he lifted it with a finger. "I could only do it for us."

Their finger-touching collapsed into a sweeping hug that lasted only long enough to wet his neck with her tears. She found her radiant smile and set the day back on track again with it. "Silly me, letting a sorry game of skeet ball lessen me to this." She pulled away and went up on her tiptoes to spot the girl over the car.

"Best out of three games, you mean," he said with a wink. "Something tells me you'll have your revenge, so I'd better keep up my competitive edge. Can I drive you over to your car?"

"No, thank you. We need a few more minutes together. I told my sister I'd have her back by five o'clock. We may have spoiled her dinner with too much popcorn."

"Oh, thank goodness you didn't say spoiled by the hula hoop. I wouldn't be able to sleep tonight under the weight of that guilt." He pulled the driver-side door open and let the Plymouth cool off inside.

"Thoughtfulness is weightless, my fine friend." She touched the tip of his nose and ran away, like a fairy godmother administering a pixie wish prior to departure.

He watched her go, cherishing the tiny wave she sent him after picking up the hula hoop for transport. The child clung to the far side of the ring, which caught a section of scenic riverbank right in its frame as they walked away.

The camping campaign flitted to mind, lacking any problematic patina in the least. Time spent together could come in many forms, as the collapsing stage had already taught him. He had until Monday at noon to decide his fate, or step aside for some other clod to escort Glori. That raked over the coals of a distant campfire, one he had no awareness of having lit. He dragged a knuckle across a wet spot on his neck as he dropped into the Belvedere to head home.

Chapter 5

A massive headache cramped Monday morning, so all the tranquility of Easter Sunday's sunrise service trickled through a crack on Glori's desk between in-baskets. Two elderly managers had opted to take retirement at the end of April, and she couldn't seem to find the correct forms to complete their cessation package. The hunt shifted her attention away from the noontime deadline for a camping husband. Right now, that selection process would color her afternoon dark unless something miraculous happened.

Midge stopped at the corner of her desk. "I have this week's schedule done. Are you ready for your copy?" She pulled the yellow page out of her carbon copy stack and let it flutter into her top bin. "For a woman who's about to gain a cozy camping partner, you don't look too charged up about it. Why the long face?"

"That's my focused expression, my friend. I have half a day to get a full day's work done. Then, 'America Goes Camping' gets my gut-wrenching attention, until I make a selection and seal my fate—at least in the eyes of my countrymen."

Midge contorted her face. "It's not like you're going to martyr yourself, Glori. If it would help, I'll pick a husband for you. Surely one of those sixty-six candidates has some on-camera charisma to offer." She fanned her neck with the schedule while craning over the desk.

Glori brushed her away like a bothersome fly. "Thanks, but no thanks. I've seen Edgar's script, and there's lots of hand-holding and embracing at sunset, that kind of thing. I've got to really sell the happiness of leisure while radiating contentment in my husband's arms. If the tiniest part of that chemistry could be genuine, it would make my job so much easier."

A mischievous grin cracked apart two red-painted lips. "Most of those fellas are not up to snuff. At least half of them are too old. That should help you narrow it down. Grandma used to say 'your spunk will take you where you need to go,' so that's what I'll wish for your afternoon."

"Thanks, Midge. Remember to post Andy's copy of the schedule over by the mailboxes. He'll be through the HR office around eleven."

"Roger that. Oh, here are the leftover blank applicant forms Edgar gave me. He doesn't think anyone else will drop in today." She nudged the stack onto her desk and twirled away so fast her hemline took on the shape of an evening primrose.

Glori shut her eyes to regain focus. The winnowing process for the campaign tightened like a noose around her neck. Perhaps it was affecting her circulation, because her thoughts began to muddle. When she opened her eyes, the stack of blank forms taunted her. Fed up with the distraction, she took the handful of papers, opened her bottom drawer, and shoved them inside. A nervous tic sent a tremble across her top lip.

Unsatisfied with the interim outcome, she grabbed a single copy and placed it front and center on her desk. Not above facilitating her own ideal resolution, she printed a man's name in the applicant space, added the corresponding department of employment, and circled the signature line for completion. As she shoved the drawer closed with her foot, she folded the application twice and stuffed it down her neckline for safekeeping. Now, near-to-her-heart held a double meaning—at least until the clock's hands split the noon hour.

~

"The hierarchy of substances is abolished: a single one replaces them all—the whole world can be plasticized." Mason rehearsed a dramatic introduction to his role in materials engineering for a professional meeting with the Wichita Council of Engineering Societies tonight. Still searching for an affiliation beyond the bounds of work, this problem-solving group might just be the ticket. No doubt he'd find some likeminded souls at that portentous gathering.

He took a round-about route returning from the men's room, where he'd erased the morning's latest debacle with the polypropylene polymer. When he'd plied the sample with a reasonable amount of pressure, it had bowed unmercifully. That gained him a lap full of ultrasonic gel which soaked his slacks. Now, he looked like a kiddy pool accident victim, all washed up with no supporting data to bear out his time investment.

Distracted by his own quandary, Mason scarcely noticed the heightened pace in the lantern assembly area until the siren consigned to the emergency eye wash area sounded with bell-like clarity. Two men dashed toward the rear of the vacuous workspace, where a plume of smoke rose above the assembly platform. Mack Insley, the floor supervisor, shouldered by with hastened steps.

Weighing the offer of assistance against mere curiosity, Mason shadowed the authority figure to the scene of the commotion. Despite attempts to initiate first aid, the victim still thrashed on the floor, his dark face clamped protectively by two quivering palms.

Don Merritt strode in Mason's direction. "And that's how a venerable track record goes up in a puff of smoke." Dread laced his words of ridicule.

"What in the world happened in here?"

"An explosion at the test station. The guy's a veteran, too. He knows our lantern inside and out. They run an ignition test on one out of a hundred. After he fueled it up, the whole thing exploded in his face."

"Lord, please have mercy," he replied in empathy.

Don shifted closer and dropped his gaze. "The Lord may have had nothing to do with it."

Before he could ask what that insinuated, two brusque firemen dashed in to take over the medical care. Two more uniformed men made a beeline over to the accident scene, where one began to take pictures with a boxy camera.

Don raised his hand to his mouth and began to speak behind the subtle cover. "We've had some issues with a temperamental gasket sealing off the fuel line. That rubber comes all the way from South Africa. We hold the patent for the lantern design, the mantle construction, and the mix of fuel. Nonetheless, we're undone by the smallest part in the whole works—a vapor-leaking gasket that could choke your pinkie finger."

Mason shook his head. "We need an inspection procedure for that rubber gasket, sooner than later. Something may be amiss in their vulcanizing process."

"I'd like to see us make our own seals," Don replied.

"I'd be glad to throw this out at my engineering meeting tonight for general discussion. I'll let you know what their consensus is tomorrow at morning break. Can you wander over to my station? That might offer us more seclusion to keep the discussion confidential."

"Count on it. I like a man who is solution-oriented." He offered his hand to seal the deal.

Mason pumped the fabricator's hand, wishing he could promise more than inquiry. As they parted, the firemen carried out the victim, a thick-trunked man who repeated the name of Jesus over and over like a rivulet of unraveling faith. The hurt evident in his supplications knifed through Mason's midsection. Not fond of the work world when it tilted out of productive balance, he wandered back to his research lab area more than a degree or two off-kilter.

~

The phone rang out with an insistent tone, startling Glori at her desk. Immersed in documenting the retirement package for her departing managers, she'd lost all track of time. She reached for the receiver and gasped when she read eleven forty-five on the clock.

"You don't have to get breathy just because it's me on the line, darling" Edgar teased.

"No—I caught sight of the time slipping by."

"Right you are. I called to ask you to come down to Marketing. We might take a picture of you pulling out a handful of applications from the mailbox at the apex of the deadline. You could foster a surprised look on your face to ham up the moment."

"I'm sure I can come up with something akin to shock. How long is it going to take me to wade through all that bachelor brouhaha to find a winner?"

A smug rumble emanated from his throat. "I can help you cull through the ne-'er-do-wells with a preferred recommendation to keep things running smoothly."

"Oh, do you have an ace-in-the-hole selection for me?" An ounce of caution caused her last word to warble. Edgar always had his own personal agenda to promote, so his perspective might be skewed from the outset.

"Lloyd Cox anteed up when I approached him about the possibility of joining our marketing campaign. He and I are set to become business partners on a side venture, so having him around during the shoot might come in handy."

"Lloyd Cox should have stayed with his family's produce business. He has a half dozen incompetency complaints against him, all filed by fellow workers. Remember, Edgar, I work in HR. All roads lead back to our department, good or bad. Besides, I think Lloyd is shorter than I am. What would that say to America? That Glori Dawes likes her men stocky, so they don't have to duck tree limbs out on the trail? Ha! I think not."

"You never know when to simply close your mouth and cooperate, do you, Glori?"

"Let me prove you wrong on that. I'll be down in five minutes. Goodbye." She slammed down the receiver and stared at the clock, daring it to advance. The minute hand ratcheted forward, ready to rub up against the ten. Exhaling, she whispered a prayer, tapped her chest, and rose from the desk.

Lacking any resemblance to a trip down the matrimonial aisle, she regained her poise and headed for her assistant. "Excuse me, Midge. Would you be interested in viewing the culmination of the campaign's applicant process? Edgar wants me to come down and exude curiosity at all the applications in his mock mailbox, so they can get a few snapshots."

"Sure, I'd like to take a gander at that scene. Let me follow along behind you to stay off-camera, though. I only agreed to be your wardrobe lady so I could hit the trail to the national parks next month with the rest of the crew."

"You always lend me balance, Midge. Be it pep band, cheer squad, or good ole Triple Star Ranch summer camp, the original mud sisters have to stick together." She crooked and held her pinkie out to extend the familiar gesture of sisterhood.

Midge gladly slipped her finger into the symbolic clasp. "I'm surprised Edgar is allowing you to pick. I figured he would press a thumb on that scale to favor one candidate over the rest." She puffed her perm into place as they walked, attempting to neaten her appearance.

"He happened to mention Lloyd Cox to me, since they have some business interest together, but I let it go in one ear and out the other." She let a smile flicker across her face as they turned down the hall toward Marketing.

"What about you, Glori? Do you have a hunch for the selection?"

She shook her head. "Not from the applicant pool anyway." She checked her watch. With seven minutes until the top of the hour, she had little time to pull off that miracle. Somehow, the tiny mole near Mason's sideburn flashed to mind like a period punctuating the end of a sentence. She should let attraction's epitaph sound its own lingering death knoll and release that notion.

"Oh, there's Edgar. He's already dismantled the mailbox. Someone's sure ready to get the camping show on the road." Midge waggled her plucked brow. "Is it past the noon hour already?"

"No. Six minutes and counting, though. Help me stall him, will you?"

"Why? Are you hatching some last-minute scheme?"

"Not unless you count divine intervention as a scheme. I'm rather fond of calling it a miracle. Go for it, Midge," she said under her breath.

"Hold up, Edgar," Midge called. "Let's get a picture of all of us with that mailbox. I think the Marketing Department deserves to be recorded in the annals of this grand adventure."

He stroked his mustache, looking contemplative. "You always one-up me, Midge. And to think I was only planning to capture Glori in the moment. We're all in this together, after all."

To continue the stall tactic, her assistant reached for the knot on his tie and straightened it. "There, you always look sharp in blue, Edgar. Now, stand between us and turn the mailbox sideways, so the door end points to Glori."

She tried not to roll her eyes as she tucked in beside Edgar to set the pose. Dying to look at her watch, she avoided the obvious connotation. Buying time became agony as the photographer shifted positions and took several exposures. "This mailbox feels heavy."

"It should," Edgar replied. "I filled it with all the completed applications, with the hopes it would look farcical when you grabbed them out." He froze for the pose and then dropped his affable expression. "Okay, now let's get Glori by herself, opening the lid to extract the potential winner." He yanked the mailbox clear until it almost banged against the office door.

"Wait a minute," Glori replied. "It's not even noon yet. You're jumping the gun."

Edgar towered over her. "I grow tired of waiting. It's a fox chase anyway—a modern-day snipe hunt. This is a pretend husband you're selecting, which isn't legal and binding beyond the campaign. I hope you can keep that in mind, in light of your true engagement."

She glowered at him for even bringing it up, until a commotion down the hall distracted her. A man barreled down the straight stretch, his arms resembling windmills as he bore down on the Marketing office in a run. A remarkable vision, she made out Mason Porter's flushed face.

Edgar stiffened. "I'm afraid you're too late to apply, my good fellow."

Mason skidded to a halt, his heels scuffing the waxed floor. "Too late?"

Pulsed with a surge of amazement, Glori stepped toward him. "Not late at all. The noon siren hasn't sounded yet." She snatched the folded application from her neckline, and pulled a pen from her pocket. "Please sign here, Mr. Porter. That's all you need do to apply."

Mason took control of the pen and scrawled his John Hancock within the circled space. The moment his hand touched the mailbox door, a distant siren began to blare.

Without a second to spare, Glori snapped her fingers at the photographer to cue him into readiness. Next, she grabbed the latch and reopened the mailbox, removed the folded application from the front, and pinched Mason's shirt collar to draw him closer with the other hand. In one fell swoop, she pressed his application to her chest and welded a kiss onto his forehead with so much melodramatic fervor, the smack echoed down the hallway to chase away the trailing siren. She heard the camera's shutter click in rapid fire, capturing her decision-making moment.

"Criminy, Glori," Edgar said, his tone full of rebuff. "Get on with the selection process."

"It's over already." She pressed a few wrinkles out of Mason's collar, allowing her fingertips to touch his neck on the sly. "I have my camping husband right here."

Edgar harrumphed and escorted the mailbox inside his office, turning his back to the entire scene. The door had barely clicked closed when Midge started snickering.

Glori examined Mason from the soles of his shoes to the top of his head. When her gaze met his, she let it linger. "What should I say to my new camping husband? I hope that you're capable." She arched her brow ever so slightly to allow the statement to hang between them.

"Well, my dearest Glori Dawes, you're about to find out." He bowed and offered his elbow. "Would you be available for lunch?"

"Yes, by every chance, I would be." She took his arm, confident she touched a miracle in doing so. After a step or two, she turned and smiled in relief over her shoulder. Though meant for her mud sister, the camera clicked to immortalize the gesture. *So let the campaign begin.*

Mason pulled her closer. "Did you think I wasn't coming?"

"Not for a moment. I wasn't about to launch without you." She couldn't stop the girlish giggle that came next. Why should she? Miracles didn't happen every day, at least not in Kansas.

Chapter 6

Starved for something to eat and some professional camaraderie, Mason followed the hand-printed signs around the hallway at Douglas Place to locate his engineering society meeting. Unfamiliar with this stretch along the Arkansas River, it held a beauty while exuding commerce. Maybe their meeting room would overlook the river for a scenic view. He spied the final sign that bore a black arrow and approached, trying to keep his expectations realistic.

He walked into the elongate room to find approximately forty white-shirted engineers milling about the congested area. Steam arose from a buffet table along the closest wall. On impulse, he strode across the room to seek out the view from the third-floor window. A segment of the river's blue waters reflected the lowering sun, melding with the murmur around the room.

A man stepped up and singled him out. "Hello, and welcome to the Council meeting tonight. I'm Weston Durand, Quality Control at Cessna Aircraft." He offered his hand with the greeting, along with a fleeting smile.

He shook hands. "Mason Porter, a first-time attendee. I'm a materials engineer for Coleman Company. It looks like a sizable group you've got here."

He tipped his head toward a nearby stage. "We try to keep the programming current, to stimulate the membership. Sorry if it seems we've tipped the balance with all the aviation-related engineering. There'll be plenty of common ground for broader application, don't you worry."

"I'm working in plastics. We'll be modifying our antiquated

metal coolers with lightweight plastic versions before the next decade begins, if my research stays on track."

The man raised one brow into his receding hairline, his eyes gleaming. "Plastics? How fascinating. You'll have to meet Duncan Reed. He just shared a related journal article with me the other day at lunch. Long-chain synthetic polymers are molded for lightweight strength and durability. Am I right?"

"Yes, exactly. I'm working with a polymer called polypropylene right now, but it lacks all the qualities I'm searching for, so the hunt continues."

Weston folded his arms and tapped his chin. "Are you able to test for quality control?"

"Yes, I test everything," he replied with a laugh. "I use ultrasonic inspection mainly."

A microphone hummed with feedback from the platform. Weston pointed to a tall man situating his papers at the podium. "That's Duncan Reed. He's speaking tonight. Talk about leading the pack in brilliance. We've worked together for five years, and he still puts me on my heels. Because of him, Cessna holds a remarkable safety record others in the industry are trying to emulate. My continuous improvement paradigm infuses everything he does."

"Wow, I hoped to fall into such a superlative lot, and now it seems I'm right where I need to be." He took a deep breath. Associating with a deep thinking group could not have happened at a better time, given his chaotic work day. "We had a rare failure on the lantern line today that bears further inspection."

The man gave him a knowing look. "Don't let it pass without a closer look. The tyranny of the urgent cannot fluster a savvy engineer."

He chuckled. "That should be my adopted mantra. Otherwise, I'd be happy to sit in my corner of the shop and conduct my research and development without interruption."

"R and D without interruption?" the tall man echoed, humor playing on his features. "That would be a luxury, now wouldn't it? Council President Duncan Reed, at your humble service."

He offered his hand for a shake. "Mason Porter, sir. I understand you're speaking tonight. I look forward to that program."

Weston leaned between them. "He's a plastics engineer with Coleman. We should have him sit with us to find out more about his courtship with polypropylene."

A plump man dressed in a white apron began to beat a spoon against a silver dome. "Dinner is served," he announced. "Start the line to the right where the plates are stacked."

Reed gestured to the far table next to the window. "Please do join us, Mr. Porter. Tell me, where did you get training in plastics? I find the material's diverse applications fascinating."

"My PhD is from Purdue University." He tilted his head as if nothing more needed to be explained. Maybe there weren't too many Boilermakers around these parts.

Durand laughed right out loud as Reed began to walk toward the food queue. "Purdue, Iowa State, and George Washington University are all well represented then. We've got a veritable brain storm erupting at our table. Got any fresh fires that need putting out?"

"Try that explosion on our million-dollar lantern line this morning," he quipped, following along. "Really, this meeting couldn't come at a better time for me." As he shook his head, he decided to hold back the inane part about volunteering to be someone's camping husband in an interruptive sidecar of springtime fun.

"Ignition system problems are always provocative," Duncan added as he took a plate in hand. "There's nothing like troubleshooting a product designed to burn up everything but itself."

Weston snaked behind him and grabbed a napkin and fork. "At least you can keep your feet on the ground. Try keeping a problematic product airworthy. It's a lofty ambition."

"Stop skewering your paycheck, Durand," Reed teased. "Hey, this lasagna looks good. Lorna Rae won't cook it anymore. She claims it's too involved."

"She was a great cook two kids ago," Weston replied. "They have a girl and two boys."

"Any children in your family?" Mason posed, having noticed his wedding band.

Weston shook his head. "We're still trying. If God's willing, this would be a good year."

Mason gave an understanding nod, ready to soak up everything he could from this group.

Reed turned back as a plank of lasagna hit his plate. "We both met our wives at work. Do you have an equally conducive environment at Coleman?"

Before he could help it, Glori's fiery eyes came to mind. Maybe he could drop a hint in her direction. "Perhaps. Today at lunch, I became engaged to the enigmatic spokeswoman in our spring advertising campaign called 'America Goes Camping.' I'll tell you more at the table. It's quite the blue-eyed distraction for an unsuspecting materials engineer, I assure you."

Reed arched back in laughter. "Golly, I do remember those days of early courtship. I became so discombobulated, I almost couldn't function at work." He grabbed a yeast roll bigger than his fist and headed for the table.

"How about you, Mr. Durand?" he probed. "Did you have smooth sailing through courting your wife?"

The man's face blanched. "No, the company's first jet crashed just beyond my fingertips. Myla ended up in the hospital in the process, so our courtship suffered through a light-touch phase before I could clinch the deal. Looking back, it only lends us a funny story to recall now."

Mason managed to get a reinforcing hand under his paper plate when the server endowed him with a healthy portion of lasagna. The melted cheese on top made him want to dig into it right there while standing in line. A gray-haired woman pushed a roll onto his plate to crown the full meal. He pilfered a decorative lettuce leaf from a platter of butter pads and turned for the table. Wedged between Iowa State and George Washington University alumni, he would be in the perfect position to gain ground tonight, an outcome surpassing his every expectation.

~

A highlight of the year, the scholarship candidates sat scattered among the Soroptimist Club members at their spring meeting, a culmination of quite the winnowing process. Committed, Glori donated her time to foster their mission of education opportunities for women in need of intervention. Where money lacked, the Soroptimist scholarship could bridge the gap and open doors for winners to pursue higher education and better their lives. As treasurer, she made sure they emptied the coffers for the scholarship endowment each year.

A doe-eyed high school senior sat two seats down. She glanced in the young woman's direction, but she seemed reluctant to break the silence. At least her dinner plate sat empty, an efficient job.

"Please don't be nervous, young lady. You've already proven your character by being a finalist. We hope you enjoy sharing dinner and our program with us tonight." She leaned closer across the empty chair. "This has been our primary point of business for three months now, so if it looks like we're cherishing the evening—we are." She chased the claim with a tiny wink.

"I read the program highlights," the student replied. "The other candidates are highly accomplished. I don't know how to compete, quite honestly." A nervous finger traced down her off-center braid. "My only real shortcoming is that I was born the fifth daughter of a middle class wage earner." She shrugged and stared at her plate.

Touched by the admission, she patted the girl's hand. "I'm Glori Dawes—an only child—but don't hold it against me. I worked my way through journalism school to aid my father's backing. It's always fitting to do what you can to bolster your own situation. First and foremost, though, you have to keep your eyes on the goal. For any college student, that should be to graduate with a diploma." When their gazes finally locked, Glori could sense she had taken her encouragement to heart.

"I'm Leslie Taylor, Miss Dawes. Thank you for helping settle my nerves. My sisters compete with me all the time, so you'd think I'd be used to it by now."

Glori smiled in a wince. "The stakes are higher here. Many recipients will have their dreams delivered to them tonight. Still, as I said before, all are winners to some extent. Oh, here's our acting president, Darlene Wilson. I bet she's ready to begin the program. Excuse me while I cue the servers to clear the tables." She scooted back with a nod and wiped her lips before surrendering her napkin.

As Glori passed the chapter secretary, she patted her on the shoulder. So much successful planning had been put into this award banquet, and all she had to do was write the check to pay for it. Knowing their account had accumulated plenty of depth to underwrite the scholarships, she began to let the thrill of sharing the wealth buoy her spirits. She gestured to the leading dining room attendant, and the table service commenced in earnest.

"This is the fifth year we've teamed with the East Side Country Club for our awards banquet," Darlene said. "Let's pause to give their staff a round of applause for the delectable Salisbury steak dinner tonight." She clapped away from the microphone as her gaze scanned the room. "I cannot say enough about how beautiful the audience looks to me, as women of every age meld into a sisterhood of life experience. Thank you, candidates, for joining our membership tonight for this auspicious occasion."

Glori held in her pleated skirt and tiptoed behind the seating to regain her place at the table. When a middle-aged server took her plate to stack it, Glori touched her elbow in gratitude. In a split-second decision, she took the chair immediately beside the nervous high school senior and settled in for the presentation.

At some point during the president's summation of the Soroptimist's mission, Glori's focus began to wane. Sated by the full meal and content in the warm room, a lackadaisical wander took her on a side path that led right to Mason Porter. Chivalrous, he not only saved her from a painful decision earlier today, but he held her captive with his insights and exuberant attention all through lunch. Had she not been at Coleman for three solid years prior with no glimmer of such a companionable match-up? Except for the dullard Edgar Sterns, hardly anyone noticed her.

She closed her eyes and recalled Mason's expression while doting on little Linda after the egg hunt. How might he regard her, should they be away from work in private company? A tiny hope birthed in her chest, one that could foster the chance of something more, should two hearts concur, and a loving God allow it. Despite the campaign's mandatory script, they could still infuse the adventure with genuine togetherness. Yes, that would be her goal—to know the man-behind-the-character better as they posed against a backdrop that spoke of American pride.

She inhaled deeply as the program reached the first award announcement for a partial scholarship. Only half-listening, she returned to her dream world and the vista of four carved granite faces flashed to mind. Majestic, the edifice of Mount Rushmore would certainly speak to the marketing audience. When Mason's profile perched against the scene, she could almost see the tiny mole along his sideburn. She pressed her lips together to collect herself.

"And the recipient of our first award is Bonita Grinnell," Darlene announced.

Glori applauded as the heavy-set student made her way to the platform for pictures. Hugs and tears were exchanged at the podium while the photographer got in position.

A gasped breath sounded beside her. "I'm not sure I'm going to make it through the entire program," Leslie confessed. She patted her cheeks as if to bring up some color.

Glori leaned closer. "Here's how I approach such trepidation. I want to claim all the blessings God has in store for me, plus I want to stand aside and allow others to receive their due blessing as well. Remember, he's a generous God and cares for each of us dearly."

Her expression warmed. "That's a great perspective, Miss Dawes."

"The rest is as simple as taking your next breath." She nodded at the platform and cradled her hands in her lap. Try as she might to digress to Mount Rushmore again, the fanciful aside refused to return. Eight more scholarship recipients came forward when called, each one more precious than the last.

"Now, ladies, we'll conclude our evening with the grand scholarship," Darlene said. "As a reminder, this award equates to a full four-year scholarship at the Municipal University of Wichita, including allowance for living on campus, plus meals and textbooks." Darlene stopped and clutched her notes to her chest. Her bottom lip held the slightest tremor. "It is my highest pleasure to announce the name for the Soroptimist grand scholarship— Leslie Marie Taylor."

The young woman bent double, her forehead resting on the table. A sob escaped confinement and set the stage for authentic appreciation. With white-knuckled resolve, she pushed back from the table and stood to her feet. Though tears tracked down her cheeks, she made her way around the dining room's perimeter and ended at the podium for the bestowment.

Elevated by the moment, Glori pressed her clasped hands to her sternum. "Thank you for hearing the fifth daughter, dear heavenly Father," she whispered. "And what of the only child, Lord? Shall you hear the quiet clamor of her heart, too?" She blinked to bat away the tears, but her caked mascara only seemed to make them launch. When Leslie held up the certificate with a bashful smile, she remembered to applaud, the proper response for the door of opportunity opening—whether orchestrated with a human touch or not.

~

Edgar tried to quell his irritation at being so close to the kitchen door. At least at this hour, the greasy spoon's business had slowed to a trickle. He regarded Lloyd Cox across the table. "This planning session is well overdue. We have only three months until my assets become liquid, so that I can purchase the building and get the needed renovations underway. We don't want the lounge to miss the holiday party business when it picks up in December."

"Looks like we have to reformulate our plan for consulting one another more regularly, since your pie-in-the-sky plan to get me hitched to Glori Dawes didn't pan out. I'll consider that my bad luck, because I wouldn't have minded cuddling her close, scripted or otherwise." He lit a cigarette and took a long draw, steeling his gaze.

Edgar cleared his throat. "Well, she navigated around me so fast I couldn't guide her selection. The plastics engineer will be easy enough to manipulate. I'll write a tight script, control the scenes, and then demand Glori's free time as her fiancé. Look at it this way—you won't be burdened by the camping trip, so you can stay in town and get the interview process underway."

"Those girls will be more to my liking, full of curves and not afraid to use 'em. It's best for me to handle the hiring anyway, if I'm to be in charge of payroll."

"That's our agreement, the building is mine and the staff is yours. Now, we need that third partner to take care of the liquor supply. Then, we'll have a true party destination."

"Only it looks like a regular bar."

"That's correct, Lloyd. It's a bar, with ancillary services. Right in the heart of Delano, where no one would suspect it."

"Not even your dear mother," Lloyd replied with a leer.

"Especially not my mother. You should be aware that Glori doesn't know either. She thinks I'm underwriting a business venture more in line with a restaurant."

"Not the liquor or the ladies?"

Edgar smiled and pressed a crease into the paper placemat on the table in front of him. "In three months time, it won't matter what she thinks regarding the nature of my business. Until then, she's as handy as any promissory note can be. We'll all play-act our way to the finish line like upstanding citizens. The gentlemen's club will happen, and it will be the smartest secondary income a man has ever earned, mark my word."

"Get us a link-up for the liquor supply then. I draw the line at booze. Guess that makes me a people person." He grinned and showed off his uneven teeth.

Before Edgar could respond, the server appeared with the platter containing their order. Two plates swamped with beef gravy slid onto the table. The blue plate special looked anything but. It made him doubly glad not to be going into the restaurant business. Hopefully, it wouldn't keep him up tonight with heartburn. No, he had the unresolved liquor issue to accomplish that. *One devious step at a time, old chum.* By the end of summer, he'd have much more interesting asides than marketing coolers and camping gear. He'd write the script for an obvious outcome, one that had him sitting in the catbird seat.

Chapter 7

At Don Merritt's invitation, Mason had been inspecting the cluttered lantern assembly line with intense scrutiny for the better part of an hour. The assembly process proved to be well honed, typical of repetitive fabrication. He would likely need to delve deeper into inspecting individual parts, a time-consuming trail that split into many divergent directions. That consideration made him exhale with frustration.

Mack Insley, the hands-off floor supervisor, walked toward him. After giving cursory attention to a dust-covered column dividing two labor groups, he ambled closer. "You've migrated out of your little neck of the woods, haven't you, Mr. Porter?"

"Indeed I have, Mr. Insley. After a worrisome conversation with Don Merritt, I thought to conduct a superficial inspection over the lantern assembly line to offer him some suggestions. I'm afraid nothing glaring has surfaced from my efforts, well-intended though they were." Heat began to build from the midmorning sun filtering through a row of high-set windows. Mason rolled up his sleeves to offset the sweat beading his brow.

The lanky man stared down the length of the assembly table, seeming lost in thought. A dozen workers continued to tap intricate parts into place. Metal works were ultimately topped with a glass globe to protect the incandescent mantles that provided the company's infamous light. Insley finally cleared his throat. "My admin contact tells me Mr. Coleman plans to tour the assembly floor prior to lunch. I think it best if he finds you back in your lab with a plastic something-or-other in your hands." He cut his eyes at him in a dismissive gesture.

Cooperation seeming the better part of valor, Mason backed away. "I suppose you have a solid point there, Mr. Insley. Still, if there's any opportunity to apply my inspection techniques, please have Don Merritt call me."

"We'll keep that offer in mind, Mr. Porter. Enjoy the rest of your day." He walked away, patting the glass globe placement worker on the shoulder as he passed.

Mason headed toward his lab, running aspects of the lantern assemble sequence through his mind one last time. A tiny error hid among the stronger work, big enough to cause a bang, yet tiny enough to go unnoticed to the naked eye. *Could it be human error?* Fortunately, plastics were much more definitive, where he could mold and make a solid friend in the process.

~

"Lenard Sanders lost his left eye in that lantern explosion," Glori said, hopeful for some commiseration. "To add further anguish to his wounded state, his sick leave benefits will be used up by next Friday."

Midge shoved the manila folder into the file drawer. "Call me crazy, but I don't think a one-eyed man makes the best inspector for our lantern line."

"No, I hope to find a more passive role for Mr. Sanders, but short of putting him in the cafeteria, no epiphany has dawned on me yet. His sick leave shortage has to be my first concern. Too bad he can't have my sick days. I haven't used one since I started work here. That's three years of untapped accrual."

Midge turned to face her with a knotted brow. "Do you think one person's benefit could be swapped out for another? Do they allow it?"

The idea took flight like an eagle over fish-laden waters, circling for further consideration. Glori sketched a stick figure on her notepad and labeled it "Sanders." Next, she drew arrows from several directions, all headed toward the character. "What if we pooled our sick leave benefits? I could ask for donations in the increment of one day. If only ten generous people agreed to donate, Lenard could stay home recovering for two more weeks."

"I totaled those sick day benefits for you at the end of last year. I bet we have over one hundred fifty employees who have accrued leave in excess of a month. What would one day matter—if they chose to give it away?"

Too filled with kinetic energy to remain seated, Glori stood and grabbed her sketch pad. "Can you get your hands on that summary, Midge? I'm going straight to Mr. Coleman with this benefit-donating idea. It's going to make the newsletter tomorrow in a headliner request for support. All I need is senior-level approval to get it in ink. Then we can use your summary to verify donations from the participants."

Midge snapped her fingers. "Pose it like this to Mr. Coleman. Instead of subtracting a day off the employee's record, we'll simply withhold the accrual day that's coming the end of June."

"You're right—that rounds out the second quarter benefits. Midge, thanks a heap. I couldn't ask for a better assistant. Hold down the fort while I'm gone." She pushed open the door with her best friend's chuckle chasing her into the hall. With an exhale, she straightened and tried to walk taller, her usual tactic when encountering a giant in the industry.

~

"So you see, sir, with the aid of injection molding, we can make the plastic cooler any size or shape we want." Mason gestured from corner to corner on the sample bottom segment he'd molded earlier. "I understand you're used to marketing the coolers by the volume held inside, so we can continue to adhere to that standard."

The company president leaned forward, his gaze locked on the prototype product. "Good, this materials change is going to represent a drastic leap as it is. No need to forego the sizing standard that has worked so well for our metal coolers in the past."

"No, sir. I agree. We stay with the standard volumes…and replace the metal with plastics for a lightweight ice chest that the public will receive with enthusiasm. I feel certain I can have that model perfected and ready for mass production by early next year. We'll take the new decade by storm." Having turned into something of a cheerleader for his own employment, Mason stroked the rounded corners of the plastic mold in front of them.

The man shifted on his seat. "One more request of you then, Mr. Porter. Since you seem so capable, I'm certain it will not faze you in the least. My late father was devoted to the steel-belted cooler in our product line. He considered it our tough-and-ready-for-anything option."

Mason took the mention as a punch in the kidney. Hired to renovate the old line of coolers, now he fought an implausible sentimental attachment. He scarcely knew what to say.

"Hear me out, if you will. I like this plastic molding technique. We can knock it out of the park with this addition. But some of our customers want the tried and true, so here's what I'm thinking. We can still give them the steel-belted cooler, but I want it reworked top to bottom. Speaking of bottoms, there's no reason it couldn't have a plastic bottom like this. The steel belts wrap the sides in durable metal to withstand manhandling during use, but we should improve it where we can with plastic. Can you marry the two components? I guess that's what I'm asking you as the expert materials engineer." He opened his palms as if to set the challenge.

Piqued, Mason had to lend a cursory thought or two to the concept of a hybrid cooler. No doubt, his passion would be the all-out replacement to plastic, but he could lend his expertise to the upgrade of the steel-belted model as well. While he paused, a colorful figure stepped between him and the company's commander-in-chief.

"Excuse me, Mr. Coleman." Glori gave a tiny glance over her shoulder at him before redirecting her attention. "Pardon my interruption, but I'm working against a deadline for this month's newsletter and needed your approval on a certain matter before its inclusion."

"Go ahead, my dear Miss Dawes. I take it you've met our plastics engineer, Mr. Porter."

Mason noticed the red blush filtering up her graceful neck and cut the awkward pause short. "Yes, sir. I met Miss Dawes at the campaign kickoff several weeks ago, to my sincere delight."

Glori pinched her lips and gave him an approving nod. "In fact, Mr. Porter caught me when I fell off the platform, saving me from a tragic destiny on the pavement." She stepped sideways until they were shoulder to shoulder. "You might deem it an act of reciprocation, but I've since selected Mr. Porter as my campaign husband to lure America into a camping frenzy this summer. Tell me, Mr. Coleman, do we look well-suited for the duty, in your inestimable opinion?" She tilted her chin down and looked at Mason with a hint of flirtation.

Mason stared at his shoes, not prepared for the role-play effort. Still, he needed to send Glori a message of interest. He feigned a cough, covered it, and then dropped the hand to his side. In subversive countermove, he stroked his pinkie against hers.

"You're a splendid couple in every regard," Mr. Coleman replied. "I'm pleased with the match-up, as it will suffice to introduce my expert plastics engineer to our admiring public."

"Well, I don't know about that, sir. Let me clean up this last mold and give Glori a chance to salvage her deadline." He removed the sample from its stand and shifted to an adjoining table in the lab. While he eavesdropped, he could sand off the overrun seams to make the casting appear flawless. For the first time, he sensed the tightrope between campaign husband and materials engineer. The dual roles would require balance, but he was up for the challenge.

"Regarding Lenard Sanders and the rapid consumption of his sick leave, sir," Glori began. "It occurred to me that he might need an extension for a few weeks, since he lost his left eye in the lantern explosion. Anyway, I immediately thought to offer him some of my unused leave, when my assistant Midge mentioned that over one hundred fifty company employees possess in excess of over one month's time. I'm asking you to consider allowing the employees to pool their benefits for the purpose of contributing them to a fellow employee in good standing—yet in dire need of the gift."

The company president sat contemplating, his elbows on his knees and his folded hands tapping at his chin. He resembled Rodin's "The Thinker" statue, but in a more modern light.

Mason maintained the steady shushing of the sandpaper's rub against the plastic surface, eradicating the test sample's seam. His opinion of Glori grew by bounds, as her heart for the well-being of fellow laborers was to be esteemed. By contrast, he was an overeducated pauper.

"It would have to be voluntary," Mr. Coleman said, "and I'd need each sick day donation in writing. Let's run it through your HR office, Miss Dawes. Go ahead with your newsletter solicitation for tomorrow. I'm actually curious to evaluate the response. Count on me stopping in by Friday, to see if this takes hold or not. I hope for Lenard's sake, it soars."

Once the impulsive idea struck, Mason had to follow through. He forsook his sanding sweep and directed his gaze at Glori. "Miss Dawes, let me be the first to volunteer a sick day for Mr. Sanders. I'll sign the paperwork once you get it in place."

Glori turned her head quizzically. "Mr. Porter, you're our newest salaried employee. By the end of June, you'll have but one sick day accrued. Truly, I was expecting the old-timers to carry this charitable effort forward."

Mr. Coleman held up a finger between them. "No conditionals, Miss Dawes. Open the opportunity up for those who feel inclined to contribute. Then it will be a blessing when an individual steps up to donate. Thank you, Mr. Porter, for what could be construed as the widow's mite, by way of example."

Caught short in the spotlight, Mason's shirt collar seemed to shrink. "Is there any way to remain anonymous with this benefit contribution?"

Glori shrugged her shoulders and pointed her pen tip at her president.

"No, I prefer not to sequester such a selfless act in anonymity," Mr. Coleman said. "In fact, for the following month's newsletter, I want an alphabetical list of all contributors posted. I sense the need to set a limit, so only one sick day may be donated per employee. We'll see what that gives us to work with, as far as Lenard's well-being goes."

"Rest assured I plan to find a light duty job for Mr. Sanders upon his return," Glori said. "Right now, I don't have the faintest idea what it might be."

Mr. Coleman rose to his feet. "Walk with me, Miss Dawes, while I visit lantern assembly. Perhaps something might come to us, if we put our two heads together." He set out for the door, a purpose-driven man.

Glori took a step toward the rear table. "No need for concern, Mason. I'll hide your name in the middle of the alphabet on the donors' list, placed there with admiration for the first gift."

"You're the angel of mercy, Glori. Good luck with your endeavor for Mr. Sanders. I'll watch for your newsletter in the cafeteria rack tomorrow."

She began to walk away, and then hesitated. "Better yet, look for me by the employee bulletin board signing up volunteer sick day donors. Perhaps we could have a real, live lunch date afterwards."

"A man like me should be so fortunate," he readily replied. "I'll see you then, I guarantee it." His role-playing might need coaching, but his real-life character was on point like a bird dog in the tall grass, ever ready for an opportunity such as a lunch break shared with a beautiful woman. Also, it would offer him a chance to sign up as a contributor. New to the working man's world, he'd never held a company benefit before. A sick day donated up front would not be missed in light of his promising long tenure, knock on wood.

~

The noisy hubbub of the cafeteria co-mingled with the aroma of spaghetti sauce on Tuesday's hot plate special. Glori neatened the stack of blank donor sheets and tried to quell a tremble in her knees. They had posted the newsletter half an hour ago. From where she stood, it looked like a third of the copies had already been taken.

Midge approached her with the chalkboard balanced in her hands. "Here you go, Glori. My stomach is growling. Let me grab a sandwich and report back to my assignment later. It doesn't look like you're being swamped at the get-go, anyway."

"Thanks for your inspiring support, Miss Kerr. Go procure your ham sandwich. I'm more anxious than hungry at this point." She nodded for her assistant's dismissal and quickly scanned the block print headlining the chalkboard. *Sick Days for Lenard Sanders* summarized the entire ploy. She braced it against the cafeteria's rear wall and stood off to the side. At second glance, she noticed the slender piece of chalk and decided to safeguard it. Satiny in her grip, she inched her thumbs up to the midway mark and snapped the chalk in half. One piece decorated the chalkboard's tray and the other disappeared into the pocket of her jumper.

"Good day, Miss Dawes," an aging woman said. "Thank you for this month's newsletter. We enjoyed reading it over lunch." She nodded her salt-and-pepper coif at the huddle of women standing behind her.

"Thank you. It would seem the mantle seamstress crew is content to keep good company today." When the woman's eyes began to soften, Glori knew her familiarity with staff had scored some momentary favor. Though her wardrobe had not changed since the forties, the devoted employee deserved her respect.

"Well, we don't want to keep you waiting. We're here regarding Lenard Sanders and his need for extended sick leave. We discussed it at our table and want to be among those who offer up a personal sick day on his behalf. Are we in the right place to do so?"

Glori's eyes began to mist as she reached for the stack of blank consent forms. "Yes, bless you, ladies. I need you each to print 'one sick day' and sign on the bottom line. As stated in the article, your accrual will be diverted to Mr. Sanders at the end of June, closing out the second quarter." She distributed the forms and offered the volunteers a handful of ink pens.

The woman nodded over her shoulder. "What might you intend for the chalkboard, Miss Dawes?" She glanced at the paper and looked up again.

"I thought it would be fitting to list our donors here by name," she replied. "As you can see, I've not had the opportunity to incorporate my idea yet."

The veteran seamstress crooked her finger at a younger woman in back. "Sadie, I'll have you do the honors. Put a heading first that reads Mantle Department, so the rest will recognize that we took the lead."

A flicker of a smile warmed Sadie's expression. She turned, found the chalk, and began printing the listing. By the time she finished, eight names had been recorded.

Glori collected the forms one by one, not trusting her voice to adequately carry in the noisy dining hall. Too emotional over the support, she now had over a week to extend Lenard Sanders' recovery. She read the older woman's name, Ramona Hathaway, intent on memorizing it for future reference. "Bless each of you," she whispered as the last form came her way.

The old woman straightened her shoulders. "Coleman is a fine place to work. I'm a Wichitan born and raised, but I don't know the first thing about building airplanes. Thank the Good Lord there's another respectable employment option."

Someone standing behind her murmured her consensus, and another voice followed it. Soon, two men were standing behind the group. Sadie secured the chalk and gave her a farewell nod. By the time the mantle ladies had left the cafeteria, half a dozen men replaced them in line.

Rushed by the urgency to be methodical, Glori reached for a salt shaker and weighed down the stack of completed forms. Those signatures stood solid as donated time in the collective pool for Mr. Sanders. Though the chalkboard could be erased by an errant elbow swipe, those forms represented permanent records, and she would guard them as such.

Repetition became the name of the game, as a steady stream of employees fell in line to make their donation. Glori started a second column on the chalkboard, leaving room for a third listing should this pace keep up. When the number of volunteers exceeded two dozen, she grew hopeful to reach a month of added recovery for the wounded man.

The cafeteria had begun to thin out. Glori glanced around the room, but couldn't spot Midge anywhere. A handful of men from the portable cooking stove assembly line came forward to sign away the sick day. She nodded her appreciation. Her stomach growled, and she wondered if a sliver of spaghetti would be left for her.

Someone touched the small of her back. Mason appeared off her shoulder with a pepper shaker in one hand, his smile crooked into place in attractive admiration. "Look who's the most popular girl in town...the incredible Glori Dawes."

"Incredibly hungry, that is. Tell me you have my lunch procured already. I think they're shutting down the serving line."

"Two spaghetti plates are reserved on the southwest corner table, awaiting your attention, my dear." He took the stubby chalk from her fingertips and guided her away from the group.

Midge bumped into her trying to slip into place. "All right, boys. Keep 'em coming. It's only a solitary sick day we're asking for. You all look healthy as horses, so let's hope and pray you'll never miss it. Who's next to sign up?"

Glori allowed Mason to lead her away from the carnival hawking presentation of her assistant. She dusted her fingertips across the bright fabric of her plaid jumper, only to have Mason offer her a wet napkin instead. She took it and studied him for several seconds. "That sign-up sure went from trickle to avalanche in a hurry."

"Well, you gave folks a chance to do a good deed…and they took it." He guided her into the chair and sat close by. Two steamy plates of Italian food represented favor of another kind. "I'll bless the food—and the outcome." He reached for her hand and held it feather-light. "Dear heavenly Father, we thank you for pouring out your abundance before us in both the food and the goodwill. We pray for Mr. Sanders, asking you to heal him as only you are able, amen."

Glori planted her napkin across her face, in part to shove back the tears that wanted to fall, but also to block out her endearing lunch partner. His prayer had touched a soft spot in her heart—or had it been the sincere tone of his hushed voice? Awareness of her companion magnified as she took her first bite of spaghetti and tried to regain her balance, if only she could.

Chapter 8

Since melodrama seemed to rule the workday, Edgar decided to play it to the hilt. He plopped Glori's copy of the campaign script onto the corner of her desk so hard, several other papers flew off. "Here it is—your requisite dialogue for the campaign. Of course, I only have the first location scripted. I'll need our second stop specified by next week."

Glori secured a teetering file folder before accepting the script. "Okay, okay. I'll give my national parks map further study this weekend. I can have that selection to you by Monday."

Hopeful for more than her divided attention, he braced his hands on the edge of her desk and leaned toward her. "Do be mindful of the distance between the two parks, my dear fiancée. This script starts against the backdrop of Mount Rushmore. Please don't ask for the Everglades next. Let's be reasonable with one another, shall we?"

Glori glanced up at him. "We agreed that I could select the locations, but I promise to take the car caravan into consideration. How many vehicles do you anticipate?"

"With the camera crew coming in from California, I think we can get by with one car. We'll pull a trailer, if necessary, to fit the camping gear."

"We're personifying 'America Goes Camping,' so let's not appear stingy with the gear allocation. If we have it in our happy campsite, then the average consumer will want it in theirs."

He twitched his mustache to one side. "That's the spirit, Glori girl. I'll confess that I'm looking forward to our time by the campfire, when the camera isn't rolling, that is. It might seem like old times at summer camp."

"I hope to devote my time to the project cast and crew," she replied all too quickly.

"Hey, what's Mr. Handsome doing in our humble office?" Midge asked, flapping the papers in her hand as she passed.

"Hello Midgey," Edgar replied. "You're delightful all dressed in pink this morning."

"I don't know if it's the rayon fabric or the three-quarter length sleeves, but I'm roasting in here today." She blew a breath down her buttoned-up cleavage in an attempt to cool off.

Edgar waggled his brow. "Well, if you decide to peel off a few layers, please step down the hall to my office. It may spur my creativity for scene two of Glori's gear-selling campaign, if a mock campsite can even be considered alluring."

"You just might be surprised," Glori replied. The toying glimmer in her eyes seemed unfamiliar, like she'd been hiding it.

Out of time, he stood straight and glanced from one woman to the other. "Please remember that Friday is canasta night at my folks' house. Glori, you're obligated for dinner as my fiancée. Midge, you're invited by proxy to play in for her, to help me win a game or two. I'm afraid I have business to attend to beforehand, so you'll have to drive yourselves over."

"Three more months and counting," Glori replied, scarcely looking up. "Do you have one of these scripts for Mason?"

"Yes, but I'm having Andy deliver it, because I have more important things to do." He smirked and headed for the door. The precocious engineer would remain the least of his worries.

With a campaign to orchestrate in less than two weeks, he'd better get the packing of Coleman gear underway. Only the most tantalizing products would do, which is why he'd picked Glori Dawes to showcase their line in the first place. Her charm could market a bedpan and make it sell, though he'd readily steal the credit for setting her up for ultimate success. Too bad she underappreciated his influence, though he had plans to change that.

~

The rough-hewn planks of the shipping crate made for a focal point of attention inside the lab's doorway. Mason had waited a month to receive this special shipment from England, and he could hardly contain his excitement when the loading dock crew had delivered it to his lab. Stamped with black ink, the splintery planks read "HDPE" for high-density polyethylene. At long last, he had a material with the tensile strength required to cast the outside of the all-plastic cooler. Two crimped iron bands later, only six nails stood between him and his dream product.

A knock sounded from the doorway. "Uh, Mr. Porter, sir?"

Mason turned on the balls of his feet to address the disruption. He saw a youth standing at the entrance, a ball cap hiding his eyes. "Yes, I'm Mason Porter. Can I help you?"

The visitor shrugged one shoulder until it almost touched his ear. "I don't know about that. Today, Andy is helping Mr. Sterns in Marketing."

"Oh, does Mr. Sterns have a message for me?" Mason relaxed his grip on the crowbar and left it on the table. When he approached the messenger, he noticed his wide-set eyes for the first time. "Good job finding the right lab. You've had to walk quite a ways with your delivery. Thank you for dropping it by."

Meek mannered, the youth surrendered the routing envelope to him. "Mr. Sterns said not to come back until after lunchtime."

"Oh, is that right?" Mason glanced at his wristwatch. The cafeteria wouldn't open for another twenty minutes for its first seating. Sterns didn't want to be bothered with an early-returning messenger, it seemed.

"Andy could help with your big box."

Mason blinked, trying to get a better read on the character offering his services. "Well, I could use some help. That's for sure. Would you mind wearing safety goggles, Andy? That way, if this wood crate shatters, we've got your eyes protected."

At the offer, his face enlivened. "Sure. Andy learned to be safe at work. He can wear goggles and then help break open the box."

Placated that the risk factor was next to nothing, Mason produced his spare goggles and adjusted the band looser. "Here you go, Andy. Let's put your hat on the table and get these in place." Relieved that his helper readily complied, Mason gave him a few seconds to get the eyewear situated. "Okay now, Andy. Do you know what this is?" He hoisted the gunmetal gray tool and gave him a good look at it.

"Andy doesn't know."

"This is called a crowbar. You can use it like the back of a claw hammer, only it's longer, which gives you more leverage." When his explanation produced a clouded look, he tried to simplify matters. "You hold one end, and you crank up on the nailed plank with the opposite end. Let me show you first, and then you can try. That's called the 'you watch and I do' approach."

"Andy watches first," he replied.

Pleased, Mason pushed the crowbar's slot into place on the corner plank. "A worker in England, far across the ocean, hammered this nail into place. And now that this crate has been delivered to the right location, we can take that nail out to open the box. See how I level the bar in place, and then I push down on the far end?" He began to leverage some power on the crowbar to pry out the corner nail. Even with the simple tool, it took some effort. With a grunt, the end plank splintered and finally released the set nail with a screech.

"Andy thinks that sounded like the deck falling," he quipped with a smile.

In a rush of remembrance, Mason recognized the lad as the campsite helper on the day of the campaign kickoff. "Say, that's right. You were there helping Glori Dawes set up her campsite, weren't you?"

He shifted his weight from one foot to the other. "Andy likes to camp."

Mason held out the crowbar for his possession. "That's great—and probably why Mr. Coleman wants you to work for his company."

He nodded and took the tool. "Mr. Coleman treats Andy nice, so he gets to go to Mount Rushmore to help Miss Glori. You have words to practice speaking…in that package."

Mason eyed the envelope, an intruder on his pragmatic day. "Now, we change our approach, Andy." He looked at him with a serious expression. "Next, it's the 'you do and I watch' approach. This tells me if you learned from watching me."

He grinned for a fleeting second. "Andy likes to learn something new every day."

"That's great. Today, you will learn how to open a shipping crate. Try to hook the crowbar under the back corner there, so we can free up one whole side."

"One whole side," he repeated, "gone open with the right manpower."

Mason chuckled and placed a hand on his shoulder to guide him. When the crowbar resisted going into proper position, he slid his fingers down the iron bar and made the proper adjustment. "Okay, now you have to pry and give it some real Andy-power."

After his knuckles whitened, the youth began to grunt in brief huffs. The three-inch nail began to back out of the plank. "One more time." With that warning, he pushed the bar into compliance and the arched nail slid out, releasing the slat.

"That was amazing Andy-power," Mason said as he motioned for the crowbar.

"Andy has power. Andy doesn't use power to hurt people, though." He wiped his hands as if to be shed of the association.

Mason took an extra second to survey the conundrum of a boy-man in front of him. "You see where power is handy, right Andy? At work when a man uses the right tool, it lends him even more power, which means he has to be careful."

"Andy has careful training, too."

He nodded and proceeded to loosen the closest side. "I'll do my corner, and then let you do your corner, so we can finish. Would you like to see what I've ordered inside the crate?"

He nodded and tapped a stubby fingertip on the goggles. "Mr. Sanders didn't have much careful."

A chill ran down Mason's back, as he'd underestimated the youth's ability to reason. "That's right, son. Mr. Sanders needed goggles, but didn't wear any at the time of his accident. When we make mistakes, we have to learn to do things better the next time."

"Andy can crack a crate open next time—that he can do." This time when he slipped the crowbar into place, the nail yielded to one continuous pry.

Hesitating before lifting the planking away, Mason examined the youth's face. "I want to show you something pretty fancy. This crate is full of sheets of plastic. I need your help to stack them all over there, behind the lab table. Can you do that with me?"

"Andy lifts three ice blocks at a time. He can lift your pretty fancy plastic." He squared to him and made his biceps bulge as if to prove it.

This time Mason had to chortle. What might have been an

awkward chore now came delivered with efficacy in the arms of a gentle giant. "You know what? I'm going to call you Handy Andy."

He tucked his lips into his cheek for a lopsided grin. "Handy Andy is getting hungry."

Mason chuckled as he positioned his helper on the far side of the crate. After lifting off the packing material, the first smooth sheet of high-density polyethylene came into sight. He stroked across it with an admiring touch, getting a rush from its potential. "HDPE at last."

Andy made a loud catcall whistle. "Pretty plastic all right."

Amused by his unpredictable companion, he let go a hardy laugh. Soon, they were both laughing like loading dock imps. The first sheet lifted out with ease, linking them with a stiff bridge of limitless potential. Mason guided it into place, and from there, built a stack of state of the art material for coolers-in-the-making.

~

The back entrance to the old mansion greeted her with familiar weathered siding. In a manic press for time, Glori had forty-five minutes to change clothes and retouch her makeup to appear presentable at dinner tonight. For once, she was relieved that Edgar wouldn't be slinking into her private apartment, smelling like a smokestack and offering his cloying attention. She would dote on her parents, and then speak on occasion to his pompous parents, passing yet another contrived night of playing the darling fiancée.

Midge always threw a fine diversion into the mix, so they appeared more of a threesome instead of a happy couple. A solid part of her original oath, they'd upheld the engagement ploy for over six months now. It grated her nerves more than ever. At least the camping campaign would offer a purposeful diversion. She slid from the driver's seat and walked to the rear portico.

After unlatching the door, she remembered to check her mailbox. There, clasped to the curved hook beneath the box was a white envelope, clipped in place with a clothespin. The amateur rigging of it made her smile. She pulled it clear, but left the clip in place. Intrigued, she hummed as she let herself into the apartment.

Allowing the shoulder bag to slide off her arm, she dropped onto the divan and tore open the envelope's flap. The faint scent of a man's aftershave heightened her attention. She flipped open the plain note card and let its message play across her line of sight.

My dear Miss Dawes, Although the campaign script arrived at the lab for my immediate study, I cannot give this role any justice without the support of my counterpart character. Would you care to join me for lunch Saturday, so that afterwards, we might practice these lines together? I'll pick you up at twelve o'clock sharp. Please bring your script and your incredible smile. With stage right affections, your rookie acting partner—Mason Porter

A phone number scrawled across the bottom of the note sorely tempted her, though her mother had taught her a proper woman never calls a man. She unbuttoned her shirtwaist dress as she headed for her closet. The formality of the Sterns' Eastborough mansion would require something nicer, maybe crepe. Edgar most certainly did not deserve the upgrade. If she hurried through the transformation, she would have more time to make that call.

Her pulse increased and soon her muddled thoughts made her all fumble-fingers. She could barely operate the back zipper, and had to leave the final three inches for Midge to finish. Threatened at the thought her driver might drop by early, she skipped the makeup refreshing and headed straight for the phone. For once, the old-fashioned conversation bench bequeathed to her by her grandmother didn't seem too remote to use. She snatched up the note card and settled into place, dialing the rotary plate one number at a time, an eternity of sequencing.

After two rings, a man's voice spoke. "Hello?"

"Yes, hello. I'm calling for a rookie actor who needs some prompting help. Might I have the right number?" She held an innocent lilt in her voice to keep the inquiry innocent.

Mason replied with a ready laugh. "Yes, thank goodness you've called. I took my engineer's mantle off at the front door, but the plaid-shirted actor is timid and shy. He might develop a stutter or perhaps something worse, if not given the proper rehearsal."

She crossed her ankles and fidgeted with her lace hem. "Oh, I see. That sounds dreadful for a man who has to charm an entire nation into going camping. Perhaps I should intervene, if it will salvage the quality of the whole campaign."

He made a throaty noise as if contemplating her remark. "*You are the whole campaign*, Glori Dawes. Paint me as part of the backdrop, a lesser face carved onto Rushmore's granite to give your glowing countenance proper contrast."

She thought to draw him out some. "What a shame I can't have that red plastic cooler on the bench of my picnic table, showing America how creatively brilliant my plastics engineering friend is. In a year's time, it could be quite the rage."

"Hmm, have you chosen red for a reason, Miss Dawes?"

"Silly man. Red is the standard company color. All our title labeling is done in red, Mr. Coleman's favorite color, so of course, our coolers will be red. I recall an expert telling me he could make the plastic cooler any color at all. Can you manage that, Mr. Porter?"

"You shall have your red coolers, an avalanche of red, if you prefer it that way. Now tell me, when can I pick you up tomorrow for our lunch date?"

"Well, is it a date—or a rehearsal? That might make a difference in my answer." She coiled the receiver line onto her finger and then released it. Her breathing grew shallow as the pause lengthened.

"Glori," he breathed into the phone. "Please don't leave me to make a fool of myself. I truly need the rehearsal…but I utterly desire the date. I'm a man backed into a corner—"

"No—or if you are—I've placed you there myself, dear friend. In as much, I'll concede to call it both a date and a rehearsal. But here's the deal, we simply must have fun with the script. We'll add actions to the lines and use props to simulate the camping gear. Once we get the rhythm of it, we can ad lib expressions and really send America a believable message."

"I'm as genuine as they come."

"Better than genuine, Mason. Thank you for asking me out. I accept with great pleasure."

"Yoo-hoo," Midge called through a crack in the door.

Glori cupped the receiver with her hand. "Gotta go. Midge is here. See you tomorrow close to noon. Goodbye for now." She pressed a finger on the cradle to end the call as a tube of red lipstick headed in her direction.

"Are you ready, mud sister?"

Glori moaned. "Can't you just play in for me at dinner, too?"

"That should raise Mrs. Sterns' horn-rimmed glasses, my

friend. Let's go have a nice dinner, and then I'll take the canasta table by storm afterwards."

"Midge, honestly, what would I do without you?"

"Honey, life is not for the fainthearted. Between the two of us, we have it covered."

"I wish to high heaven I could shorten this infernal engagement."

Midge froze in midstep. "You're not serious, are you?" Her eyes widened.

"I don't mean to your detriment, dearie. I mean it for my freedom." When Mason popped to mind, she rose from her seat and tried to forget their conversation. He needed a date, and she needed a break-up—from her engagement. The pressure began to pinch worse than her high heel shoes, but she'd have to wear them both tonight anyway.

~

His unceremonious return from a hamburger run made it seem like a sad Friday evening. Mason traced the Little Arkansas River as he drove alongside its length to regain access to his rental home in Valley Center. The lonesomeness of the journey accentuated the acute contrast to his plans for Saturday with Glori. She made him miss what he didn't know existed. What a conundrum of crisscrossed involvement that generated.

After a left turn, he slowed for a dirt road that would deliver him to his neighborhood. Rows of knee-high corn stalks marked the perimeter of an ambitious vegetable garden. He'd seen an elderly couple tending it on several occasions, sometimes well past sundown. A wheelbarrow sat beside the roadside ditch with a figure hunched over it.

Surprised by the sight, he slowed to make out the situation. Two worn buckled shoes hung out of the wheelbarrow's bed, while the old man fanned the contents with his straw hat. Fearing a medical crisis, Mason pulled the Belvedere onto the grassy shoulder. "Hello, neighbor. Is there anything I can do for you?"

The old man straightened to regard him. "Might be handy to get a lift for the missus. She's plum tuckered out tonight. I thought I would have to roll her back home."

Mason threw open the car door, determined to help. "No need for that, sir. That's why God made gas-powered vehicles, so man wouldn't have to walk everywhere anymore." His chide soon produced the intended effect.

The man chuckled and wiped his brow. "Much obliged, young man. This here's Polly, and I'm Herman Nelson. We live two houses down on the left."

"Well, how about that? You're my next-door neighbors. My name is Mason Porter. I'm glad to finally meet you." He shook the man's bony hand and glanced at the woman crumpled into the wheelbarrow.

She gave him a tiny finger wave of recognition. "I'm all in, Mr. Porter. Help get me to your car, and I'll be tickled for a ride to our back door."

"Yes, ma'am. You've got it." He bent and placed a supportive arm around her shoulders while her husband gave her hand a yank. When he lifted her out of the wheelbarrow, she seemed to weigh nothing at all. "How about you ride up front with me? Mr. Herman can ride in back."

"Don't forget the lettuce, Mahster," she replied, her eyes cutting to her husband.

The old man tucked a crinkled wad of plucked leaves into the crook of his arm and tagged along behind them. He grunted when he stepped out of the roadside ditch to reach the car. "We sure 'nuff appreciate this ride."

"My pleasure. Friday night is ruined if a man doesn't have some kind of company."

"I expect you're right about that. Do you work in town? I don't ever see you at home."

Mason drew in a tight breath as he eased the woman into her seat. Once he closed the door, he helped the man inside. "I do. I leave out for Coleman Company daily during the week."

The man pressed his lips together until his chin almost touched the tip of his nose. "Good people, those Coleman men. Sorry to hear the senior Coleman passed away last year. Level head on that set of shoulders."

Mason crossed around to the driver's seat, thinking about the lingering influence of the company's founder. "Yes, I'm grateful to work in such a stimulating environment."

"Do you cook?" Polly asked.

He shook his head and threw the car into gear. "Enough to get by, but nothing to brag about, really."

"Then you wait an extra second when you drop me off. I'm going to bring you some leftovers to keep in your ice box, in case you don't have anything to eat for supper."

"Well, I'm coming back from eating a hamburger out, but I could have it for dinner tomorrow night."

Herman patted the back of the seat. "Never turn down an offer for food, young man. That's a survival strategy for a skinny bachelor."

In silent rebuttal, Mason tried to flex his muscles, though he knew deep down the man was right. "You two might want to give some thought to cutting your gardening time a little shorter as the sun heats up. By the end of May, summer weather will be back full force."

"It used to be easier to adjust to the heat," Herman said. "I can't just let that ten acres sit idle, though. No, as long as I can walk, I'm gonna tend that garden."

He glanced at Polly and caught the apprehensive look in her eyes. She seemed to have less inclination to meet her demise between the planted rows. "Maybe you should sell the ten acres. This close to the river, it should bring a handsome price."

"Are you lookin' to buy?" Herman asked.

The idea didn't seem too unattractive at the moment. "Possibly. If you get in the humor to sell, knock on my door and let me know. In the meantime, I'll save up my pennies."

"You've got yourself a deal, Mr. Porter. Take the first drive there, and circle around back. That will leave fewer steps for Polly to make. Always think of the woman first, and your life will be a lot easier in the long run."

"I sure need to be thinking along the long run," he replied. When Miss Polly giggled, he gave her a guilt-ridden smile. Slowly but surely, he was learning how to live.

Chapter 9

No, Mason, really. I think you should have the fishing pole in your hands when you say that." Glori followed the suggestion by handing the yardstick across the concrete patio table in her landlady's burgeoning flower garden. "Okay, let's try it again."

"There's nothing but wide open spaces out here, where a man can hear himself think." He stood and pointed the yardstick skyward. "Here's what I'm thinking at the moment—that trout would be great for supper tonight. I'll be back in a couple of hours." He whisked off the bench's end, pretended to grab the cooler prop, and left her sitting alone.

"I'll start the campfire for you, darling," she called with a wave of her hand. Almost an aside, she decided to test his boundaries. "What? No kiss on the cheek for a beloved wife?"

Mason looped around a redbud tree and returned with a questioning expression. He took the script in hand and gave it a cursory glance. "No, Glori. I don't see any exchange of affection written into this scene."

"That's right—and you won't, because dull Edgar has written the script. You and I may have to be spontaneous, as the scene plays out. You know, we do what's right in the moment."

He retook his seat and wiped a hand across his face. "All right. I know we need to make the actions seem real. I'll try to remain more attuned." His brow furrowed, and his expression grew complex. "I'm working through a difficulty. Give me a moment."

Self-conscious for having brought up the intimate subject,

regret started to swamp Glori's intention to draw him out. "Wait...if it's me that keeps you from reacting with affection, I could try to be more pleasant." Even as she offered it, the solution seemed lame.

He stared at the concrete table, his fingertips skimming across the script. He started to speak, but then stopped. In a deafening slap, he laid the yardstick down between them.

She exhaled, wondering how to prompt a resolution. The advertising script had been written with amateurish dialogue that lacked any emotional depth. Still, with a sincere tandem effort, they could lift it out of mediocrity. Perhaps she should suggest strengthening several lines with their own version to see if it would play out in a superior fashion.

Mason shook his head. "Glori, I cannot have you thinking that your charming demeanor could be any part of what's wrong with this scenario." When he looked at her again, his eyes held a hint of warmth. "In truth, I find you immensely attractive." He wove his fingers together as if mustering his courage. "Therein lies the problem between us, if I can be honest. I could be more expressive toward you were it not for one tiny entangling detail—your ever-present engagement to Edgar Sterns."

So worried that the fault might be some lacking attribute on her part, Glori almost laughed when he targeted the insignificant betrothal. She clapped a hand over her mouth and looked away. Nearby, a crepe myrtle coming into bud made for a soothing diversion. She needed to be forthcoming, as she would not have her integrity besmirched by some plotting marketing director. "Please, listen as a friend would, and recognize the thread of truth in what I'm about to tell you." She fingered the markings on the yardstick and tried to measure out her words.

"I seek nothing but the truth," Mason replied, one brow arching to punctuate his statement. "I'm already in one level deep in this play-acting, so everything else has to be real."

Glori steeled her features. "The engagement is a charade, in no sense legal or binding. Grandfather Sterns left an endowment for Edgar, which he's eligible for at age thirty, or before so, if he holds a promise of marriage for a period of ten months. This is the seventh month of our cordial agreement, a deal struck so Edgar can undertake a business opportunity he claims cannot wait two more years."

Mason leaned back and crossed his arms. "So Sterns meets you in the hallway one day and asks you to pretend to be his fiancée like it was a casual business transaction? I find that hard to believe, quite honestly."

She pushed against her throbbing temples. Another layer of deceit would have to be revealed. Yet she could only go so far. The rest had to be protected. Air seemed to evacuate her lungs, and she struggled to breathe. "While two old friends spoke in confidence, somehow Edgar eavesdropped and overheard several critical details. When he proposed his betrothal scheme only days later, he repeated enough relevant information to hold it over their heads and force his agenda. To keep things from becoming uncomfortable for all involved, I took what seemed the easy way out and agreed to be his devoted fiancée for the ten-month duration."

"The more you reveal, the more uneasy I become." He worked his cracked lips together and tried to swallow. "You've allowed yourself to become trapped, largely for Sterns' benefit."

She leaned toward him and reached out for his hand. "I thought little of the sacrifice when I made the vow, as I had no one special lending me any masculine attention. No one until now, that is. Hence the rub, I suppose. Mason, you have to know there's nothing between Edgar and I. Certain rules have been established to keep him at arm's length. Any show of affection is play-acting of the senseless sort, trivial and of no meaning to me—or to my heart."

He rose and began to pace about the slate surface of the patio. "What of your heart, Glori Dawes? What kind of woman pledges marriage to one man and yet desires to keep company with another?" He raised his palms to accentuate the incongruity.

Caught between two pretend worlds, it now left her in an excruciating reality. Glori stood to confront Mason. He at least deserved an answer. If this was a dismissal of their friendship, she would brave it like a lioness. "My heart remains pure and chaste, Mr. Porter. I have chosen to protect a close friend and assist a work associate with his forthcoming inheritance. In less than three months, I will break the engagement with my chin up and my dignity intact. My single regret may be that I didn't have the foresight to believe someone like you might show up with genuine interest. Compared side by side, the absurdity of my former romantic agreement is loathsome to me, but I cannot break the vow at this point in time."

"Cannot—or will not? You wear a diamond on your ring finger, yet ask me to show you affection. Well, this conflict has begun to keep me awake at night as I toss and turn about what to do. None of this is of my making, and the more I learn, the less I can stomach it. I'm not sure I can be your camping husband, Glori, as much as I want to spend time with you."

Stunned by the unexpected sting of pending separation, she grappled for a foothold. "But I selected you out of sixty applicants. And you signed the form, agreeing to the terms of travel and such. Please, stay with the campaign, Mason. I won't demand anything from you except what the occasion might naturally entail." She tilted her head to soften her plea, though it caused the first tear to escape. "I can't imagine being with anyone else, cross my heart. I'm asking you to stay with it, and lend me some forbearance." Her knees trembled, so she sat back down.

He grabbed the top of his head and smoothed his brown hair back, his eyes fixed on the slate. "Your oath is an abomination to me…and possibly to God as well. Scripture says to let your 'yay be yay and your nay be nay,' avoiding vows altogether. God gives us boundaries like that out of love to protect us. Now, look at the entangled web you're caught in." He shook his head, snatched his script off the table, and headed for his car.

As tears swarmed her squeezed-shut eyelids, she reflected back on a vulnerable young woman whose belly protruded from an unwelcomed seed. Friendship counted for something—if not in this world, then maybe in the next. Her cheek met concrete as the crying fit won out.

~

By Wednesday afternoon, Mason reaped the reward of his solitary focus on work. The prototype of his first design for the all plastic cooler emerged from the injection mold process looking like a work of fine art. If he had turned sculptor, then rectangular high-density polyethylene boxes were poised to be the next nouveau trend to close out the decade. The cooler's curved corners and inset handle grips provided plenty of fresh design to admire.

"Now, for the ultimate marriage of layers," he muttered. In steps, he retrieved the flexible interior liner he had cast on Monday out of polypropylene. He eased the white liner into place and tamped down its corners to achieve an exacting fit. After eyeing the match-up, he fingered the seam closed around the rim, trying to envision the heated bond to be conducted on the assembly line. To simplify matters, he could design a right-angled flange along the rim which could be glued flush to the outer shell. He liked that revision immensely. Mastic would be less hazardous during assembly, since heat could readily deform the plastic and mar the cooler.

He wrote some notes in a lab book, taking pains to measure the lip of the lining to better create the surface adjoining the two layers. Once he exhausted the details of such a merger, he pushed ahead to his next challenge—a lid that topped the whole works. A flat uninterrupted surface, it could double as a campsite seat or a cleaning station for a fishing outing. With that slippery task in mind, he thought to lend the top surface more texture to better enhance grip.

Lost in a frenzy of intensive note-making, he failed to hear the lab door until it clicked closed behind the intruding party. Venturing a glance, he saw Glori standing in the entrance area, her gaze fixed on his latest creation. Magnetically drawn, he dropped his notebook on the table and stepped toward her. The small napkin-draped plate in her hand stirred a deeper sensation. "Welcome to my lab, Miss Dawes, as always."

Her eyelashes fluttered in a shy response. "Forgive my boldness, but I hosted a retirement party for two longtime employees this afternoon in the product showcase wing. Since your enigmatic company was missed, I thought to deliver this token of the hole it left in my day." Any trace of reticence melted at her confession. "Have I worked through the lunch hour already?" He stepped closer and took the offering from her with a wink.

"It's two-fifteen, Mason. I suppose that's how time slips away from the creative geniuses among us." She maneuvered past him and stood close enough to the cooler to caress the outer shell. "You cast the new cooler in Coleman red. It looks magnificent, like you hand-carved it out of a block of ice." Her airy tone elevated the praise.

Unready for a critique, her delivery struck him in a vulnerable spot. "I had a dear friend suggest the red coloration. The liner will remain white, and I'm still conceptualizing the lid." He paused for a bite of the cake and let the sweet butter cream frosting recalibrate his mood.

She turned to him, her eyes rimmed with emotion. "This is perhaps the most incredible thing I've witnessed all week. It's a snapshot forward in time, when the future arrives and sweeps you away with it. Do you ever get a sense of that, Mason?"

"I'm being swept away, all right," he replied, motioning with the fork. "I thought it had more to do with this scrumptious cake and the scintillating company who delivered it."

"Truth be told, are you glad to see me?" Her bottom lip trembled a bit as she folded her hands together, waiting for his reply.

"I'm ecstatic for all of it—the break, the cake, and the companionship. There, I'm both honest and hungry for more at the same time." He took a whopping bite of cake to prove it.

A furtive blush worked up her neck. "The campaign departure date had been set for May eleventh. With no complications in film production, our first TV advertisement will hit the air on June sixth, a Friday night. Ladies Home Journal is holding open a half-page ad for the June issue, the earliest we could make it in print. Mount Rushmore will have two new stars to profile. I trust you'll be ready for our marketing debut."

He eased onto a stool at the end of the table. "If I can leave the lab in solid shape, with the new casting fully tested for durability, then I can embrace the great outdoors with open arms." He rested the plate on the table and gestured as far as his arms would stretch.

The smile it birthed seemed full of admiration. Glori's eyes twinkled as she stepped closer. "Would you like to use a pseudonym for the campaign? I don't have to call you Mason, if you want to protect your privacy."

He let another bite of cake melt in his mouth while squinting in contemplation. The name he really wanted popped to mind. *Abolish the engagement hindrance and full steam ahead.* "Mason is fine, and I hope you'll remain Glori, as I'm growing fond of saying it. I wouldn't mind a 'darling' being thrown at me from time to time, either."

Her lips parted with a growing smile. "Of course, I'll remain Glori then. It's a privilege to call you my camping husband, Mason. I thought I might have forfeited that privilege earlier and am relieved that we'll still share this opportunity to promote the company. It's no small endeavor to get America excited to go camping, but our future depends on it. Since I'm partial, I'd like to request that your cute red cooler come along for the trip. Would that be possible?"

The crux of the matter played out akin to their friendship. He'd pose it as such and let her decide. "You tell me if it's fair to show the purchasing public a product that's tantalizing—yet unavailable on the market. What would that say? Here it is—but you cannot have it?"

She stepped closer and ran her fingertip over his shirt collar. "You cannot have it yet—but it's coming available soon—and you won't be able to do without it." Her knuckle skimmed his chin before she moved away toward the door. "Thank you for the rectangle of red. I'll hold that as a personal favor a friend dedicated to me."

"A secret favor," he replied, "for an inspiration that cannot be found on mere paper."

"Have a productive week, Mason. Edgar intends to call a crew meeting early next week for cast and behind-the-scenes supporters. I hope to see you then." She pulled the door open and disappeared like a cloud of purple cotton, a color that made her sky-blue eyes even more unforgettable.

He continued eating until the slab of cake was gone. Thoughts of the shapely delivery person remained, wrapped with keen interest like Saran film around an untouchable piece of temperamental equipment, a polyvinyl chloride wrap begging for his immediate attention. The campaign would be a tactile barrage of personable exchange, offering none of the analytical safety his developmental lab provided. He'd have to be careful of that interface, mindful that mastic was better suited for plastic. Yes, he'd avoid the heat of an emotional fire, as much as humanly possible. Under pressure to perform, he hoped to remember how to camp.

~

Edgar shuffled through the snapshots, eager to meet his new

employees. "Only three? We need double that many girls, even to start."

Lloyd Cox shifted in the booth. "There, the redhead. She's something else. Her resume listed kissing as a hobby. That's how I knew I was on the right trail with her. She mentioned having some acquaintances of a similar friendly persuasion, so I'll pursue that lead next."

"Good. I may have found a new location for us by the downtown YMCA. It was a breakfast joint that went under. From all appearances, it won't require the renovation that the grocery store in Delano would have." He shrugged and took a second look at the photos.

"A gentleman's club means the joint will have to switch shifts from morning to nights. I hope there aren't too many bars on that block."

"Nothing upscale, like we'll be doing. With traffic coming and going at the YMCA, it may be easier to blend in without attracting unwanted attention."

Lloyd shook his head. "I don't know how you think like that, circling like a pack of wolves isolating a weakened kill. I'm a simple man who acts and reacts."

Edgar swirled the brandy sniffer in his hand. Overhead lighting shot sparkles over the back of his hand. For an instant, their progress seemed magical, as if meant to fall into place. "I'll address the liquor partner issue before I leave town for the camping campaign next month."

"Looks like you get all the adventure." Lloyd hoisted his glass and tipped it toward him. "Hope your campsite holds some hidden perks."

"There will be plenty of suggestive looks around the campfire, believe you me." Edgar lifted his glass and clicked it against his partner's, intending to christen a voyage of exploration that went beyond the bounds of duty. He always preferred a layer of subterfuge beneath his primary purpose, as it fed his diabolical thirst for something more.

"You'll like the redhead there," Lloyd said, tapping the photo.

"Perhaps I'll like them all," Edgar replied. The brandy burned all the way down his throat, as exacting executive privilege held its own set of perks. He was in charge—of the gentleman's club and the camping campaign, the possibilities playing to his strengths. "You won't mind serving as bartender now and then?"

"Suits me fine. A man's gotta stand somewhere. Go ahead and put me behind the bar."

Edgar smirked at the relative ease of staffing the club. Now, he just had to secure four walls around his planned mischief. What a liquor-soaked house of ill repute it would be.

Chapter 10

The week began burdened, as if a trolley car had unloaded in Human Resources. Glori worked hard to rid the end-of-the-month tasks from her pressing to-do list. May first fell midweek, and with Midge's help, she had made it without an hour to spare.

May Day should be filled with satiny ribbons and bonny lasses dancing around the Maypole, but she was a businesswoman with a multitude of tasks to conduct. An ounce of redemption, she'd found a nosegay of lavender blooms clipped to her mailbox on her way out this morning. Such a little act of consideration knocked the rough edge off her day. She bent and sniffed the tucked-in treasure to regain her tranquility.

"I just finished recording those employee work hours for April," Midge said, "if you want to check my ledger. I'm heading down the hall to the ladies room. After that, I might hit the break room for a snack. Want anything to boost your spunk?"

"I guess not. My aqua pedal-pushers are already fitting tight. I plan to wear them at Mount Rushmore the first day we film."

Midge snapped her fingers. "That reminds me we need to go over your wardrobe one evening this week. I'll be right back."

Before settling in at her desk, she scanned the room and found a cluttered mess. Having the historical records dumped by the barrister shelving didn't help matters, but Herb Ebert, the company historian, had to retire due to deteriorating health, so the Proof Books that catalogued the company's history sat idle. A month of rainy days would not allow her to tackle that project.

She pulled up at the desk to placate her throbbing temples. An herbal remedy, she inhaled through the lavender bunch while the matching purple ribbon tickled her nose. A job posting to shore up the lantern assembly line waited for her attention next, or she'd miss the Wichita newspaper's deadline. Compelled to move forward, she began typing the qualifications.

"Excuse me, ma'am. Am I in the right place?"

Glori looked up to see a meek figure standing just inside the door. Her face seemed instantly familiar. "I know you from somewhere, young lady. Was it the Soroptimist dinner?"

The youth's jaw dropped. "Yes, Miss Dawes. I won the scholarship to attend college that night. I'm Leslie Taylor, reporting in for Sergeant's Temp Services as the admin assistant requested for Human Resources."

Glori pressed a hand to her temple to quell the last nagging pulse of pain. "Well, will wonders never cease? I guess Mr. Coleman thought we needed a backup since Midge Kerr and I will be on location shooting the spring sales campaign. Is this your summer job with the temp agency?"

The young woman approached her desk. "Yes, it is. I come with little experience, but I'm strong on attention to details and have thorough follow-up. I can answer the phone and take messages, as I did that at my last position." She placed a one-page resume on the corner of her desk and waited for further instruction.

Glori blew her bangs from her eyes and gave the document a cursory glance. Once she recognized the temp service emblem on the letterhead, all seemed in order. "Okay, great. Here's what we'll do. Midge and I are here until May eleventh, so we have almost two weeks to train you. On top of the employee matters that surface, we'll set up an ongoing project for you. Tell me, do you like history?"

Leslie's expression brightened. "I'm quite fond of it, actually. Give me a museum to roam any day. There's so much to learn by looking back."

"Perfect. You'll need a table, so I'll send Andy to get one for you. Our company historian retired last week. All his documents have been turned over to us. Just as I suspected though, as his health began to fail, so did his ability to keep up. The company's Proof Books are behind at least half a year. There's a stack of advertisements and newspaper clippings that have to be chronicled in order and added to the Proof Books. How's that for a time-filling project?"

"What a beaut," Leslie exclaimed.

"Upsy-daisy," Midge called through a crack in the door. In her hands, she balanced two Nu-Grape sodas and a pack of snack crackers. She dipped a shoulder and pushed the door further open. "Well, that turned out to be a run down the gauntlet of ill-preparedness. At least I had enough change." She swooped in giving her best impression of Lucille Ball.

"Midge Kerr, I'd like to introduce our new temporary admin assistant, Leslie Taylor. Mr. Coleman has hired Leslie to hold down the fort when we hit the campaign trail."

"Oh, thank goodness for reinforcements," Midge replied. "We'll try not to overwhelm you, young lady." She sat a soda on the desk.

"She's willing to take on the Proof Books project between tasks," Glori added. "What a blessing to have an extra pair of hands around here—and a willing spirit."

Midge blinked as if to reset her mental state. "Well, I could get Leslie started by teaching her how to verify the employee work hours for April."

"Perfect, Midge. I really need to get this classified advertisement into the paper, or I forego the deadline for Sunday's listing. Before lunch break, I'll get Andy to set up that table, so Leslie can have a work station."

"Sounds like one big girl party—only we're not painting our nails and chatting about men." Midge winked and retook her seat.

"Welcome to the girl party, Miss Taylor," Glori repeated in a teasing tone. "We are glad for the pleasant company, rest assured." Thankful that an easy payout to the temp service would be all that was required for the new assistant, she returned her attention to the Royal typewriter to resume where she'd left off.

Soon, Midge's peppy banter led the new employee through the gamut of counting hours. The morning regained a productive cadence between the clicks of the typewriter and the tapped keys of the adding machine. May first ticked away in another working day. With Human Resources as the heart of the thriving company, Glori sensed everything would turn out fine.

She even had memorized her scripted lines, which was likely more than her counterpart could claim. A smile surfaced despite the all-business demeanor of the office. After the last word was typed in place, she tore the paper from the roller and placed it atop an outgoing mail envelope. For added inspiration, she sniffed the lavender nosegay one more time. She'd help Mason deliver his lines to perfection once the camera was rolling. Yes, with the gentleness of a deer fawn, she would coax him along. *What pleasurable work that will be.*

~

Upon completion of his second review of the modified liner design, Mason selected the polypropylene material to feed into the modified injection mold. Before he could examine the set-up further, the lab phone rang. An objectionable moan marked the trip over to his desk. "Engineering, Porter here."

"Hello, Mason, it's Weston Durand from Cessna. Do you have a minute this morning?"

"Yes, you've caught me in the nick of time. How are things in the airplane industry?"

"At work, things are moving along nicely. I'm really calling about the Council of Engineering Societies meeting next Monday night. Our guest speaker has fallen through, so Duncan Reed suggested that I give you a call. Before you give me a blatant 'no' for asking so late, let me add that we try to get out of the conference room twice during the year. Would it be possible for our members to meet you at Coleman and tour the various product assembly rooms? Duncan has really wanted to cast a critical eye on the safety management there ever since you reported that explosion at the lantern testing area. In that spirit, we could offer some valuable off-the-cuff collaboration."

Buoyed by the potential for professional support, Mason assessed the possibility. "It sounds like an on-the-spot inspection. Am I willing to sign up for that level of scrutiny?" He laughed while he checked his desk blotter for any conflicts. Only his note for the engineering society meeting marked the day.

"I can tell Duncan to go light on you guys, but the man typically has only one gear, and that's forward drive at full speed ahead."

"Let me give you a conditional yes. Maybe I should clear it

with admin first, though I know the second shift laborers will still be working. I might also seek out an assistant tour guide with more depth of knowledge. I'd be happy to give a plastics demonstration in my lab, if that type of activity would interest the membership."

"Now you've got me hooked. That's exactly what Duncan had hoped for, some added technology thrown in for good measure. We'd start at six o'clock. From there, you can make the tour last as long as you want. Count on twenty-five of us at the most. Here's my phone number, if you'd be kind enough to call back and confirm."

Mason scrounged for a pen to record the rapid-fire sequence. For some inexplicable reason, the sound of Weston's voice lent some validation to his research work. He could hardly wait to demonstrate the plastics' injection mold technique. "I've got it. This sounds great. Really, you've shot a boost of adrenalin in my direction. Coleman welcomes the Wichita Council of Engineering Societies with open arms. Tell Duncan Reed his critical eye is most appreciated here. We only stand to benefit from such intense scrutiny."

Weston chuckled in response. "Caution, my friend. There's always a trickle-down effect from his findings. I've never met anyone else that can hold a candle to that guy's intuitiveness."

"Perception is embraced, though I might drag a broom across the lab floor beforehand, so he doesn't think I'm a total schlep at rudimentary housekeeping." He paused to let a laugh rumble up the phone line. "Hey, thanks for the diversion this morning, Weston. I'll take a break and go seek out that admin clearance now. Let me confirm after that, so you can get the word out to the members in time. Goodbye."

He returned the receiver with an exaggerated exhalation. He had one friend in admin, and she made for a pretty top-notch tour guide, too. He exited the lab, remembering to flick off the lights on his way out. Solitary of purpose, he approached his destination and spotted Andy stepping out of the Human Resources office. "Hey, Handy Andy. How's your day going?"

"Hey, Mr. Porter. Andy helps the new girl. She looks nice."

Mason gave the young man an affable slap on the shoulder. "I'm here to do some girl-watching, too. Did you see Miss Dawes in there?"

"Oh, yeah. Miss Dawes needed Andy's help, so she called. Now, they have a table."

"Good show. I know she appreciates the strong help."

Andy glanced up and flexed his muscles, a big grin on his face. "Close to lunchtime."

"Too close. You'd better get going. I predict they'll run out of barbeque pork sandwiches today. The hot lunch is chicken pot pie." He grimaced in disapproval.

Without another word, Andy shot down the hall toward the dining area.

Mason pushed open the HR office door and peered through the crack. Glori had just taken to her feet, a paper in her hand. He extended the opening, anticipating her exit.

She retrieved an envelope out of a stack and crammed the two together in haste. In an instant, she acknowledged his presence with an unbridled look of pleasure, though she didn't stop striding. "Come along with me," she insisted. "I'm racing a deadline to get this classified ad into the newspaper." She led down the hall until it opened into a clerical pool. "Sally, this has to go out to the Eagle ASAP."

"Maybe I should send it by messenger with Andy. It's only a couple of blocks."

"Andy went to lunch," Mason replied. "I can run it down for you." He took the ad and folded it into the envelope. When he looked up, Glori seemed flabbergasted. "No, really. I can carve it off my lunch break. It's the first of May. I've hardly been outside all week. How do you expect me to stay in shape?" He winked and started toward the closest door. Before he could shove it open, he sensed someone at his side.

"Hope you don't mind some company," Glori quipped through tight lips.

He held the door open and trailed her into the pleasant spring day. "I hoped for an audience with you, and now I have one—if I can keep pace."

"Before I hear you out, I get to pose my own question." Her fingers found the crook of his elbow and latched on, connecting them. "Would you know anything about how a darling lavender nosegay made its way to my front stoop this morning?" She surveyed the intersection and began to make the crossing without breaking her gait.

"I know nothing—and everything—about that nosegay. It spoke of spring, so I could only think of one destination."

The corners of her mouth twitched. The rest of her body remained all business. Chrome-trimmed cars began to form a line waiting for the traffic light.

Mason spied the newspaper office on the corner up ahead. "How easy would it be to allow a professional engineering group to tour the Coleman facility next Monday evening at six? I've been asked to fill in for a guest speaker who fell through. Two of the officers are especially interested in seeing my plastics lab."

"Oh, I bet they are." She paused at the heavy glass doors.

He pulled at the brass handrail and opened the door. Thinking to add to his set-up, he opened his mouth, but stopped in deference to the hubbub inside the lobby.

Glori approached the front counter. "This classified has to make the Sunday paper. Please put it on the Coleman account." When the clerk held out her hand, Glori snapped her fingers.

Reactive, Mason slid the envelope into her possession without hesitation.

"Thank you for putting a rush on it for me. We appreciate the newspaper's support."

"We're here to serve the community," the clerk replied with a vapid smile.

With no time to study the surroundings further, he got the door for her. Humorous, her steamroller imitation could have flattened a less attuned escort. Back in the light of day, a length of sidewalk promised time for further discussion. "About that engineering society tour—"

Glori pivoted in front of him so fast, they collided. Her delicate fingers found his forearm to steady the merger. "Old Mill Tasty Shop is only a block out of our way. Please say we can go." Her blue eyes searched his face with keen interest.

Relief mingled with attraction as he studied her up close. "We most certainly can. I've never been a big fan of chicken pot pie anyway."

"So that's it—a culinary escape to an open flame grill?"

"And extraordinary company," he added. "Plus, you can split my onion rings with me, which is my ploy to get you to say you'll help me get the tour approved."

She began walking again, her elbow tugging at his. "Come right this way, Mr. Plastics. Your request is being processed even as we speak." This time her smile held more of a tease. "Expediting such a request might cost you a chocolate milkshake."

"Hmm. Only if we can split that, too." He tightened his hold and mimicked her stride. "These officers, Duncan Reed and Weston Durand, are men to be admired. Some of their problem-solving stories are epic in nature. I've fallen in with a cerebral lot with the engineering society, and thank God above for it."

"Keep thanking God, then, as I want you to bless the food I'm about to consume. What a break to get out of the office. When they off-loaded the unfiled historical records and lagging Proof Books on us after the company historian retired, it just about sunk my ship. Saints be praised, we had a temp ordered, and she's already tackling the job. As a bonus, I knew the young lady. She won a full-ride scholarship from my Soroptimist Club a few weeks back."

"So that's the nice new girl Andy mentioned to me in the hall." He waggled his brow for effect. "I have to give Handy Andy more credit every time we meet. That guy is unassuming at first glance, but he truly has something to offer."

Glori negotiated around a newsstand in front of the drugstore. "If you two clicked so well, maybe you should consider Andy for a camping partner. Edgar groused to Midge that he had to share a tent with a mere messenger boy."

Mason spotted his favorite burger joint up ahead and gained a step to get the door. "Sounds like I need to do Andy a favor and rescue him from a pompous tent-mate." He held the door open, hearing a stifled chuckle as Glori walked by.

"Midge and I get the family-sized tent, the one that will be featured in the photo shoot. Want the corner table?"

"That's perfect." He led her down a meandering path of misaligned chairs to the ideal lunch spot. "I don't really know how we arrived in this predicament, but I plan to enjoy every moment of escapism that comes with it." After helping her into a chair, he caught the attention of a server and held up two fingers. "We'll take the cheeseburger basket with two root beers…and add a side of onion rings. Fast service is appreciated."

"Two Number Fives with beers and rings, coming right up,"

the woman replied.

Mason settled into his chair, his eyes drinking in his lovely companion. "I never knew a classified ad could make my day."

Glori ducked her chin. Reaching for a napkin, she slid one into his proximity. "How about the ad I wrote that lured *you* to Coleman?"

"Work of art," he exclaimed, accepting the napkin. "A real Michelangelo." Her blush was his reward for summoning the paints, and it was the most comely shade of pink he'd ever seen.

"It was the first time I'd ever typed the word 'plastics' in my career."

"Look at me, expanding your horizons." He found her hand under the table and spoke the grace over the food. Soon, their efficient waitress appeared with heaping baskets of nutrition. Contentment blurred with lunch as onion rings mimicked lip circles and laughter ruled the table. He soaked it in like a tonic, thinking he'd have to get out of the lab much more often.

Chapter 11

Edgar assumed the head chair at the conference room table, intent on taking and keeping the lead. Marketing would call the shots, which he would make perfectly clear to all involved. They had less than three minutes to report in, or he'd have to ratchet up the expectation heat.

Midge walked in and took the chair to his left with a fleeting smile. "I can hardly afford to take time out of this crazy workday. May has been a beast so far."

"Your tempo is about to shift, Midgey, so take heart." He touched his mustache to appear more affable. Checking his notes, he missed the next two characters entering.

"Here's your leading lady and your gear set-up expert." Glori took a seat beside Midge while Andy maneuvered around Edgar to sit on his right side.

"That leaves the head of this quintessential American family missing and presumed dead," Edgar joked with a smirk.

"Not at all," Mason said as he walked through the door. "I still have a minute to spare. Your watch is running fast, as usual, Edgar."

Fighting back a loathsome response, Edgar took his notes in hand. "Cheer, cheer, the gang's all here. Let's get started with our campaign itinerary. Thanks to Glori's keen selection prowess, we have three locations to shoot footage in as classic American landscapes."

"Location Number One is Mount Rushmore, South Dakota," Glori said with a high pitch.

Edgar pushed on. "This national memorial was originally billed as 'the world's biggest roadside attraction.' That's an eleven hour drive from Wichita, so we'll embark at seven o'clock on May eleventh in hopes of shooting some still photography at the nine o'clock floodlight presentation. On the twelfth, we'll be met by the Rinehart Filming crew at the park to shoot video of our camping family with the presidential backdrop."

"I've read the morning light is best for capturing the edifice," Mason added.

Glori turned to him. "We'll eat breakfast that morning in the Carver's Café, which gives us a place to wait for our link-up with the film crew, in the event they get delayed. The view from inside the cafeteria is said to be phenomenal."

Edgar snapped the papers in his hand. "Plus, not having to cook at the campsite will get us to the park gate early, to better avoid long lines. I cannot emphasize enough how critical time management will be this entire trip. We have to stay well synchronized and make ourselves available at any given moment if the backdrop dictates. Contracting the film crew is costly, as you might imagine."

"We could stage making coffee at the campsite," Mason suggested. "I'm an early riser."

"Andy wakes up early, too." The youth made a fist and cuffed Mason's shoulder with it in a friendly gesture.

Relieved to see the two buddy up, Edgar took a sidetrack from his notes. "We'll have three tents, with the women's tent in the focal point for staging the shoots. I'll have a modest two-man tent on the perimeter. Mason, have you made any accommodation plans?"

"Yes, I have a five-man tent, so Andy is camping with me."

Edgar nodded and added the note, somewhat grateful for the privacy. "Let me also mention how important concise packing will be. Midge, all the wardrobe cases will have to share the trunk with the camping gear, as we'll only have the company sedan and the filming van, once we make the rendezvous."

"I can accommodate the hanging wardrobe items on the rod across my back seat," Mason offered. "Plus, my trunk can hold personal duffel bags."

A prickle crept across Edgar's forearms. "What? You're planning to drive, too?"

"Of course. My Plymouth Belvedere is roadworthy. If I'm going to see iconic America, I plan to view it out of my own windshield."

"Well, that certainly alleviates the crowdedness of having five adults traveling for eleven hours in one car," Glori said. "I'll be happy to ride along with you, Mason. The backseat always makes me queasy, anyway."

"Welcome aboard, then," Mason replied.

A bit steamed at the turn of events, Edgar felt the urge to move on. "We'll embark for Stop Number Two when the film crew gives the go-ahead. Fortunately, that won't be a far drive."

"Location Number Two is Devils Tower National Monument, Wyoming," Glori said.

"Jeepers creepers," Midge exclaimed. "I've always wanted to put my peepers on that monstrosity—and now, here's my chance."

Glori chuckled. "Well, quite frankly, it was both in the vicinity and in the right direction. Plus, there's a prairie dog colony on the park grounds that I intend to examine up close."

Edgar couldn't mask his choking response.

Mason held up a finger. "That setting might pluck a few American heartstrings."

"Prairie dogs are extremely social animals," Glori added. "They even communicate."

"Well, here's a communication—the main shoot has to take precedence at every location. Once we enter the park's main gate, we'll allow the film crew to lead. That way, they decide what has scenic potential—and what doesn't."

When Glori's bottom lip poked out, Mason cleared his throat. "Perhaps we need a caveat, say if we have a majority vote to stop at a secondary location of interest, within reason. Not to forfeit the day's schedule, but we may pull into some once-in-a-lifetime setting that could be snuffed out in deference to our ultimate destination. I wouldn't want that to happen."

"Say—I like that," Midge replied, "having a vote, I mean. We're all adults on the same mission for the campaign. That doesn't mean we can't enjoy ourselves along the way."

"All in favor of having a vote for secondary stops, raise your hand," Mason proposed.

Edgar clenched his teeth. Of course their vote came in

unanimous, despite his intention to rule like an autocrat. That could easily turn dictatorial, should the conditions warrant it. For now, he'd concede to move ahead. "Fine, so noted. Time for the third wave of the campaign."

"Location Number Three is Yellowstone National Park," Glori announced. "We'll have grizzly bears, bison, and bighorn sheep to see across two million acres."

"Oh, me oh, my," Midge replied.

"Mud pots, geysers, and cutthroat trout," Mason added with a smile.

Edgar stood. "We'll hold shoots along Yellowstone River and Lake, Grant Village, and lastly, at Old Faithful. Mr. Coleman specifically asked that we make that geyser the grand finale of the film sequence, so the script will definitely reflect his request."

"I don't believe I've seen that particular script," Mason said, his brow arched.

"You will in due time," Edgar promised. "Everything will be family-oriented, coaxing America out to view its national treasures. Since we won't have children in our starring family, we'll be sure to include a few in certain scenes, with parental permission. What am I forgetting?"

"Expense per diem," Glori replied. "Since we're camping, I don't see us topping out."

"I'll cover the group meal expenses," Edgar added. "You're responsible for any souvenirs and frivolous expenses along the way."

"Frivolous?" Midge questioned.

"Ice cream and such," Glori replied with a toying smile. "We can always lock our wallets away in the car's glove box when we're out on a shoot."

"Right—don't ask for trouble, and you won't find any," Edgar said. "We cannot afford to slow down for trouble resolution, and we cannot afford inclement weather once we start out."

"You'd better be a praying man, then," Mason said. "Some things are beyond our human control."

"Well, I'm in charge of everything else," he insisted. "Should any issue arise—excluding blisters on your heels and possibly poison ivy—come to me for direction. Are there any further questions?" Silence followed, a positive sign that he'd been thorough enough. Maybe he could go write that second script this afternoon.

"Andy's glad to go along," the youth said, his fists pumping the air.

"Me too, partner," Mason replied.

Glori fell into Midge's exaggerated hug across the table. "I can hardly wait to start. America Goes Camping—here we come!"

Mason slipped from his seat and leaned toward him. "I'll record mileage to turn in as a professional expense. Other than that and the campground fees, I'll absorb my other expenses."

Determined to maintain control, he locked gazes with the leading man. "I'll see whether we have funds left for your mileage tab once we return and total the damage to my budget."

"And I'll assume responsibility for what the camera records," Mason countered. With a nod, he left the conference room like a man on deadline.

"Edgar, I hope you didn't alienate my camping husband already," Glori said as she rose from the table. "What did you tell him?"

"Basically, that I'm in control," he replied with a patronizing grin. "Same newsflash goes out to all—Edgar Sterns is the boss."

"Yeah, of a traveling circus," Midge added, turning for the door.

"You can catch more flies with honey," Glori quipped.

"Let's hear it for cooperation then," he pressed. A tamp of his paperwork sounded like a firecracker exploding. "It's my way— and the highway." He gave her a domineering look to squelch any further comeback, which seemed to do the trick. The threesome left with arms interlaced.

"Grizzly bears, indeed," he muttered. He would have to lock the coolers in the trunk, a small act of theft prevention, all things considered. There were more frightful things out in the night, the kind that mosquito netting and tent flaps failed to thwart. He spent the distance back to his office mulling over the prospects. Such side projects amused him. Life was to be lived in layers, and he grew fond of the deeper ones, the kind that went unseen.

~

Mason doubled back up the admin hall, aware that he'd forgotten to pose his idea to Glori for wardrobe coordination. He pushed the door to HR open and found her at the four-drawer filing cabinet. "Sorry for the interruption, but I forgot to mention a possible solution for insuring our clothes match for each individual shoot."

"Oh? Midge and I just made plans to get together on Wednesday after work at my place. Would that suit you?"

He glanced between the two women, feeling a bit like a cart pulled behind a matched team. "Sure, include me. I thought to load my rack across the backseat and place my best sports shirts on it. That would give Midge's discerning eye the opportunity to match our clothes."

"I can put tape labels on the shirt collars," Midge replied, "so you could keep them in order. I really like that idea."

"It works for me," Glori added. "I hope you have something that goes with polka dots."

Midge caught her fooling expression and broke out in a snorted chuckle.

A young woman stepped closer with clippings in her hand. "Excuse me, Miss Dawes. I think I can file these both topically and chronologically, because I found a heading labeled 'Lanterns' under a series of product listings."

At hearing the subject matter, Mason turned to give the worker some attention. He spotted a large newspaper clipping with a camping lantern featured in a photograph. "May I?"

"Please, pardon me," Glori said. "Mason Porter, this is our new temp, Leslie Taylor. In addition to being our anchor in HR while Midge and I travel, Leslie is this year's full scholarship winner for my Soroptimist club."

"Congratulations, Miss Taylor. I'm sure college will start soon enough. Until then, I suggest you enjoy this summer—especially working for Coleman. You never know where your work experience could lead you."

"Thank you, Mr. Porter. I'm thrilled to be here, I assure you. This cataloging work is fun, too."

He fixed his gaze on Glori. "May I review those lantern clippings? I've been trying to help Don Merritt inspect that assembly line. Maybe I don't know what I'm searching for."

Glori waivered while a look of puzzlement crossed her features. "I don't know what those articles could tell you."

"Neither do I, but I'm willing to invest the time to find out." He held up an open palm to receive the clippings. "Mr. Sanders might appreciate someone willing to dig deeper."

Glori exhaled. "Okay, you may borrow this stack. I'll have Leslie hold any more out for you if she comes across them. Now, I really must shoo you out of this office. Midge and I will be working nonstop until five o'clock as it is."

Mason took possession of the articles with a nod to dismiss the helper. Not quite finished, he shuffled closer to Glori. "You aren't forgetting the engineering society's group tour this evening at six, are you, Miss Dawes?"

She found the file she'd been searching for and pushed the file drawer shut with a gliding pop. "Not in the least, Mr. Porter. However, it may be embarrassing on your part to be found locked up in a records vault because you failed to heed my kind warning."

A guilty smile marred his professional deportment. "I'll see you at the front entrance just before six o'clock then. Fancy that— I'll have all of my favorite people together on tour."

"Scram, Sam," Midge called from her desk, her flame-red fingertips brushing him away.

Though Glori had turned her back to him, he could still hear her melodic laugh. Buoyed by the promise of more time together after hours, he made his exit with a little extra reading material in hand. He thought to pick up a soda in the snack room, a rush of liquid sugar to keep his molecules flowing. That group touring tonight might have some sharp questions, so he had to stay focused. What he didn't know, Glori would—which made them the perfect team.

~

At ten minutes past five o'clock, Glori pushed a paper back into her in basket, determined to leave it until tomorrow. That decision left her in a hybrid frame of mind between Scarlet O'Hara's need to defer and Pollyanna's rose-colored glasses. "Dear me. I'm all over the place."

"Not me," Midge replied. "I'm outta that door. See you tomorrow, kiddo."

"I have to stay for that engineer group tour at six. I need a miracle boost and maybe a change of heart, too."

Midge stepped back toward her desk and began rummaging in

the top drawer. "What's wrong with your heart? Oh, I get it. You don't want to spend more time with Mason Porter. Don't look now, but in ten days, you two are going to be inseparable."

Glori took her head in her hands and leaned over her desk blotter. "This time, you've got it all wrong, mud sister. Maybe backwards even."

Midge stepped closer, rolling her eyes. "How could I have it backwards? Wait. You *want* to spend more time with Mason Porter?" She tossed a Baby Ruth candy bar onto her desk. "Here's the miracle boost part. For the rest, I'm not suggesting what to do."

"Isn't this when you tell me to follow my heart, Midge?"

"No, this is when I remind you to take a three-month delay to following your heart. Don't screw this up, Glori, or your picture will be in the paper for a different reason, not because America is falling in love with your camping lead." She made a tiny growl in her throat as if to ward off the potential situation, and then twirled her full skirt toward the exit.

Alone, Glori scanned the messy office, her gaze blurred by weariness. Low on options, she grabbed the candy bar and unwrapped it. The first bite began to change her spent attitude, its chewy caramel dissolving in her mouth like a magic potion. Her thoughts shifted to Mason.

She didn't need to hoist a clean-burning Coleman lantern to see where their relationship might be heading. To fall in love would only benefit the lacking campaign script. For every other scene in her life, it would pose a detriment at the present time—but like the candy bar, she craved more. Her next bite proved better than the first, and in no time, the entire candy bar had vanished riding a delectable whim.

Chapter 12

Excited to have these two aspects of his Wichita life intersect, Mason stood at the plant's front entrance peering out the plate-glass door for his guests. Only a few cars passed by, indicating a slow-down of Monday's rush hour traffic. That should work in the group's favor as members sought out parking in the lot across St. Francis Street.

A glance at his watch told him he had five minutes to spare. The sound of heel clicks echoed down the hall behind him. He turned to find Glori approaching, a shapely silhouette. "Hey, how's my favorite tour guide doing this evening?"

"I think the pace got to me today. My energy level is sustaining on low, and only because Midge tossed me a candy bar on her way out."

Stricken by his own negligence, he touched her elbow. "We'll grab something to eat right afterwards, if that would help. We should be done by eight."

She reached up to fix her hair, breaking his connection. "By eight-thirty, I may be face down on my pillow, losing consciousness with this killer day."

He chuckled at her admission. "Thank you for taking on this extra duty. I'll follow your lead until we get to my lab. If there's a way to route us to my corner last, that works best for what I have planned."

She blew out a breath and squared her shoulders to his. "Fine, I'll make that scenario work for my purposes, too." She blinked, and her expression hinted of vulnerability. "Mason, should I sound like I'm wearing down, please interject into the tour's narrative to provide me some relief. I'm not sure how long that candy bar will keep me aloft."

"Yes, of course. You have my word. I'll even watch for it, so thank you for calling the possibility to my attention." A man approached along the sidewalk. "Oh, here they are now." He pushed open the door and ratcheted up his congeniality as host. "Welcome to Coleman Company. Good to see you, gentlemen."

Duncan Reed filed in with his lanky stride, nodded at Glori, and stood behind him. Weston Durand came in next, escorting two attractive women. Six more engineer-members pulled up the rear.

Mason gestured with his arms at shoulder height. "Already, I must amend my greeting. Welcome ladies and gentlemen. I hope you didn't have much trouble following my directions."

"No, none at all," Duncan replied. "Please, introduce your associate, Mason, and then I'll introduce our troops."

"Yes, it's my pleasure to introduce the director of Human Resources, Glori Dawes, who also writes the company newsletter among other miscellaneous tasks. In fact, Glori is set to star in the company's spring advertising campaign."

She punched a fist into the air. "America goes camping!"

"I'm game for that escape," the light-haired woman said.

"I'm the society's president, Duncan Reed, and this is my wife, Lorna Rae." He extended his hand to Glori.

"Nice to meet you both," Glori replied. "I'll expect you to be among the first to hit the road this summer to take the family camping." She sealed the sentiment in a wink to Lorna Rae.

"That would be a dream, Glori—to leave my laundry basket behind," she teased.

Mason chose the man standing to his left to introduce next, a familiar face. "This is our treasurer, Weston Durand, who leverages us to pay our dues on time."

The man laughed at his commentary. "Glori, please meet my wife, Myla. We both work at Cessna—at least they haven't thrown us out yet."

Glori found her smile. "Hello, Myla. So nice to meet you."

Duncan stepped forward and introduced the other six members accompanying the group. All had aviation affiliations attached to their names. "There. I think we're set. Please indoctrinate us on everything from the company's history to its latest success."

Glori moved beside him. "I'll cover the history on our way to the product showcase room, where we've established something of an archival display that dates back to nineteen-o-two." She paused to send a flicker of a smile to him. "Our plastics engineer holds our latest success secret, so we'll end our tour at Mason's experimental development lab. I think he has something special lined up for us there."

In the spotlight, he soaked up her attention and played the imp. "What can I say? Injection molds could switch the humblest of engineers into show-off mode." The confession readily earned him a laugh. "Please feel free to ask questions as we go. I'm sure Glori won't mind." He touched her elbow to turn over the group to her control.

Her gaze traveled from Duncan Reed's sturdy height down to Weston Durand's earnest expression and finally alighted on his face. "By all means, ask away. We don't usually have a tour group of this distinguished caliber. Should I fail to have the technical details at my disposal, I can research them and let Mason bring the answer to your next meeting."

Duncan readily snickered and bowed his head. "Miss Dawes, I believe you just lent my snooping tendencies some legitimacy. Bear with our technical bent as we go, I implore you."

Lorna Rae bumped her shoulder and leaned closer, speaking against the back of her hand. "I've found ignoring the technical bent also works effectively."

"Given the right moment," Myla added.

"Off we go then, to the product showcase room," Mason said, "where they don't typically allow engineers to roam."

Weston slapped his shoulder as the group began to follow Glori up the hallway. "She's marvelous. Do all the women working here look like that?"

Mason shook his head, trying not to beam his pleasure. "Not hardly. That's the company's incomparable Glori Dawes, which is why she's in the lead role of the spring campaign—to win the hearts of America."

Weston started to say something, but squelched it when Myla gave him a squint-eyed look. He waggled his brow instead, and then stepped up to walk beside his wife.

Glori turned to face the group at the doorway. "It all started when founder W.C. Coleman spied a bright-glowing lantern in a shop window in Kingfisher, Oklahoma. Through tweaks and improvements, he moved that gasoline pressure arc lamp business to Wichita, Kansas in nineteen-o-two, and set up shop. During World War I, Coleman Company made over one million lamps for farmers to ensure food production for military consumption. You'll find that theme repeats itself over the first half of the century—Coleman produces and the U.S. military uses—and sometimes it happened in reverse. By nineteen fourteen, he'd sold fifty million lanterns."

Duncan raised a finger to interject. "I read that infantrymen in World War II forged their daily existence with some kind of soldier's cook stove. That fact made an impression on me."

"Yes, it's been reported that the two most important pieces of noncombat equipment for the Second World War were the Coleman pocket stove and the Jeep." At that declaration, Glori threw open the double doors and gave access to a room filled with an array of lamps, lanterns, cook stoves and a thousand other products, including small kitchen appliances and huge oil furnaces.

Once Duncan had proceeded toward a shelf of artillery shells, Mason approached the tour guide. "You're lending me new appreciation for my employer."

"I hope you can hear the admiration in my delivery."

"See? You should drop any ideas you have for that Jeep," Myla said, punching Weston's side with her elbow. "Pick something off these racks, for pity's sake."

Mason tamped down a smile at the not-so intimate exchange.

Glori redirected the conversation. "Purchases are indeed possible. We can loop back to this room after the tour for me to ring those up. Coleman welcomes your business and guarantees any product for life."

"I'd like to return," Duncan said, nodding to his wife who had a lamp in her hands.

Mason gave Glori a quick wink, mindful of her exhaustion. "Take two or three more minutes in here. We probably should press on after that."

Glori shifted closer. "I want to wow them with the mantle assembly room next. It makes an indelible impression, and it's the largest such operation in the entire world."

With her influence reverberating to his core, he leaned toward her to respond in a whisper. "Everything you say moves me. How on earth can that happen?"

Her eyelids fluttered closed. When they opened, a smoky look came his way. "Every signal doesn't require a bright-glowing lantern, Mr. Porter. Would it please you to shop the showcase store?"

"Not at all," he replied in a low tone. "I've found my selection right here." Try as he might to put his engineering hat back on, the mix of technical and personal intrigue had him off-kilter. When Duncan Reed gestured for him, he stepped away to regain his composure. At this juncture, camp stoves made better sense, anyway.

~

The companionable interaction between members of the tour group managed to fuel Glori's enthusiasm for the task at hand. Mason had virtually taken over in the lantern assembly room as the topic of the maiming explosion took center stage. Grateful to stand mum on the sidelines, she admired the intuitive exchange while the problem-solving foray ran its course. Many of the solutions involved processes she'd never heard of, hence the technical swamp that mucked up the tour's progress. Fortunately, only Mason's lab remained.

Lorna Rae stepped into her proximity. "Not to cut out on the demonstration, but Myla and I need to set up the dessert spread for the men. That's part of the reason we tagged along—but not entirely. This place is amazing."

"Could you suggest where we might set out Lorna Rae's cake?" Myla asked.

She looked close by, but nothing availed itself as clean enough. That left only one spot kept hygienic for that specific purpose. Plus, it was half the distance of the employee snack room. "Let's crash the cafeteria's dining area. Surely we can find a corner table that fits the bill."

"Are we close to the end of the tour?" Lorna Rae asked.

"Yes, there's only Mason's lab left to go. I think he wants to hold a demonstration of his plastics technique."

Myla waited for the men's noisy exchange before continuing.

"Here's the thing—they'll go on like that all night, so we've learned to offer food as the final stop. We could sneak back out to the car and get the treats while this winds down. Would you mind missing the plastics demonstration, Glori, so you can show us where to go?"

Fully anticipating Mason's expertise-in-action, she had to balance that against the woman's reasonable request. "Fine, we women will cut out and do our own thing. You had me over one of those Mary-versus-Martha barrels a second there, Myla, but this is definitely the right way to keep the evening moving. Let me excuse us and hand the tour baton to Mason." She stepped away to rejoin the men.

"The slightest imperfection in one part could put the entire product at risk," Weston said as he fingered the top ring of the lantern's housing.

Mason stood transfixed on the assembly line, his dark eyes unblinking.

Glori straightened her posture. "Gentlemen, we have half an hour remaining, which lends you enough time for Mr. Porter's plastics demonstration. I understand that refreshments will be served immediately afterward, so the ladies will now depart to set this up. I'll leave you in Mr. Porter's capable hands." She turned to him. "Please join us in the dining area, where the cake will be waiting for a different kind of inspection."

His sullen expression vanished. "Who could say no to that?"

Duncan laughed. "That's my downfall precisely."

"Your salvation, you mean," Lorna Rae replied.

Myla hooked an elbow through Lorna Rae's arm and soon connected Glori to the departing parade. Barely out of the assembly room, she turned to her with animated blue eyes. "The men always give us that 'how could you leave now?' look, but you won't see one of them refuse a piece of cake later. Talk about predictable."

Lorna Rae hummed in agreement. "Their genius mentality is difficult to shut off, so it often overcrowds other aspects of life. They walk a fine rope, one that lassoes the world's technical problems for closer evaluation, yet also threatens to choke off the essence of life happening right at their fingertips."

"Fatherhood has been good for Duncan," Myla said. "Lorna

Rae definitely gets credit for making him a more well-rounded individual."

Lorna Rae reached for the door. "I'm certain Weston will be the same, Myla."

"If God will entrust us with children, that is." Myla's dark bob swung across her cheek as if to hide her expression.

Glori pressed the door open, not sure what to make of the candid conversation. All three of them seemed to be in different stages of life, full of both conundrums and momentary victories. "I'll watch you to the parking lot and back. Sometimes, the hobos show up downtown, looking for a borrowed park bench to spend the night."

"Back in a flash then," Lorna Rae replied. She grabbed Myla's arm and jaywalked in a diagonal to the parking lot.

Tired, Glori tuned out as thoughts of children and family swarmed her consciousness. A streetlight blinked on above the Coleman front awning, casting long shadows onto the sidewalk. She had a good life here, but that didn't mean she couldn't ask God for more. "Lord, bless these women with happy homes. Teach me to be mindful of what honors you the most, amen."

Lorna Rae stepped over the curb, balancing a broad box in her hands. Soon, Myla appeared right behind her lugging a brown paper bag in her arms.

Glori opened the door and stood aside. "Ooh, time for the party to begin."

"Cake always means a party," Lorna Rae replied. "This is my original recipe, one I don't make often anymore. It's Duncan's favorite."

"That's how she hooked him," Myla added.

Glori led the way toward the dining area. "You ladies are highly informative. This behind-the-scenes chatter may be useful to me in the future."

"Are you two dating?" Lorna Rae asked in a low voice. "I mean, the way he looks at you, it's destined to happen."

Glori gestured to the right, unsure how to respond. Perhaps their play roles would suffice. "Our time of togetherness is certainly near on the horizon. I selected Mason to be my campaign camping husband from a company-wide contest. We leave in ten days to start filming."

Myla brushed shoulders with her. "You definitely have some chemistry brewing on the back burner. Better not let that attraction heat to a fast boil, especially if the camera is rolling."

Another pot came to a boil—the upwelling need to tell the full truth. She pointed with her left hand. "Right through this doorway. Well, here's a hindrance that bridles the whole potential relationship." She flexed her ring finger to make the diamond ring on it dance.

Lorna Rae twitched her lips. "Phony—or matrimony?"

"This will be perfect for the cake, over here," Myla said.

Glori wiped her hand down her skirt. Not that her bad luck charm would rub off, but now she felt exposed. "Not matrimony, that's for sure. I took a tangled oath to protect a girlfriend. Plus, I'm helping a young businessman look more presentable, so he can obtain his inheritance early. That makes me taken at the moment— my ring finger mainly, but not my heart."

Myla took a glass jug of tea out of the paper sack. "Pardon me for saying it, but that's a doozy of a hindrance. Goodness, there must be a better way to transport this iced tea."

Glori smiled at her predicament. "Let's pose that conundrum to these clever men."

Lorna Rae fanned out the stack of napkins. "I had a wedding ring on my finger the day I met Duncan Reed. God was merciful to me, though, and I never had to wear it again—or the pretense it represented."

Myla pushed her wavy hair back. "It's better to live with genuine emotion. If something authentic grows between the two of you, then one day, you'll have to rectify the situation."

Glori's throat thickened. "I don't mean this to sound like a cop-out, but I have less than three months to go. Once my oath draws to its completion, then all parties can satisfactorily go their merry ways."

Lorna Rae stood erect by the cake, looking contemplative. "If only Mason can abide by such a compromise, that is—for three more months. Duncan reads this world in black and white, where the truth has no shady in-between. It took him every ounce of self-control to stay on his side of the divide separating us—until one day, he risked the crossing."

Glori stared at her, apprehension constricting her chest. "What happened then?"

Lorna Rae looked at Myla, and then at her. "We were married within three months. That's how love is."

"Yes, there's a ripeness to it," Myla added.

"A time for every purpose under heaven," she acknowledged in a whispery voice. Why the fragment of Scripture came to mind, she couldn't comprehend, but it shook her to the core.

"Here we are," Duncan called as he walked in beside Mason. "It's time to have some of my wife's indescribably great cake."

Glori regarded Mason, whose hands were behind his back. "How did your plastics demonstration go?"

"Ta-da," he replied, pulling a white plastic lid from out of hiding.

Weston produced the prototype cooler's red base in the role of able assistant and placed it on the floor.

With animated gestures, Mason settled the lid into position and placed two open palms on each end. Applying slight pressure, he combined the two components for a perfect match-up. "Here it is, ladies and gentlemen, the future of the Coleman cooler."

"As I live and breathe, I've got to have one of those," Myla exclaimed.

"I've made my request for one also," Duncan said with a grin.

While Mason pretended to slice and chop something on the cooler's lid, Glori couldn't stop her eyes from misting at the monumental scene. The look of satisfaction on Mason's face became a part of the memory—a genius and his invention at play on the template of her heart.

"Here, sweetie." Lorna Rae extended a plate with a giant slice of cake centered on it. "Go give Mason his reward, and don't let him miss that look of appreciation in your eyes."

"Right, this one's for him."

Two forks appeared in front of her. "I made it extra large, so you two can split it." Lorna Rae gave her a furtive grin and returned to the serving table.

Her instincts numb, Glori stepped to the cooler where Mason knelt, inspecting the top seam from each angle. She squatted beside it to gain his attention. When their eyes finally met, she didn't rush the exchange. "You truly made this tour unforgettable."

He hung on her inspection, and finally gave the cake a glance.

"Who knew it would be cause for celebration?"

"God only knows," she whispered in return. "And maybe a certain someone else who's paying extra special attention."

One brow hitched in response. "Have some cake with me?"

"Now who's starving?" She stuck a fork into the corner and hoisted chocolate cake to his lips. When his mouth opened, it gave her great pleasure to feed a plastics expert his treat. Her first bite of cake was sensuous in its own right, and it was soon followed by a second.

Mason winked and dug his fork in for more. The ample serving soon disintegrated to mere crumbs.

Two cups of tea made their way into their private dining spot. "Why can't my tea jug come in something like that instead of glass?" Myla posed.

Glori looked at Mason and could almost see the cogs of contemplation turning. "Our insulated picnic jug?"

"In plastic," he replied, his face animated. "Lightweight yet strong…that splendid idea deserves to happen."

"The jug could even be made to match the cooler—like a set," she posed.

Mason's eyes flared wide. "It's going to take the camping world by storm." When Lorna Rae offered him a second slice of cake, he accepted with enthusiasm.

Glori eased onto the cooler to sit. The new product was durable, lightweight, and sure to make a splash on the market. Now, she had to convince its developer to bring it along on the campaign trail. The cake's sugary influence soon took over, and she floated on a cloud of make-believe. Mason's glances sent the trip into a higher stratosphere, where she happily existed until someone mentioned the lateness of the hour.

"Hey, Miss Tour Guide," Mason teased. "Can you two be separated?"

She stroked the cooler's red side panel. "No, I don't believe so." No higher praise came to mind, and when she saw the appreciation reflect in his eyes, any need to elaborate vanished.

Chapter 13

Mason stormed into the HR office, determined to get the bottom-line truth. He found Glori hunched over a montage of newspaper clippings on a cramped table in the corner. "Aha. There you are. I ran into Andy in the dining area, and he mentioned the script for Location Number Two is out for our use. Like a hound dog, I'm sniffing out my copy."

"Thank goodness you're proactive, as I may not have gotten to your lab with it today." Glori put her hands on her hips and gave him an evaluative scan. "You've been molding something again today. I can see it in your eyes—that preoccupied look."

"Guilty as charged, though it's no disservice for a man to be engrossed in his work. For your information, I've been casting quite the potbellied insulated jug out of high-density polyethylene. Only the beverage inside will weigh anything, as I've made it as light as a feather."

"Bravo, our plastics engineering expert. Too bad history cannot be molded the same orderly manner." When she brushed her hand to indicate the mess scattered across the table, a small clipping took wing and headed for the floor.

Quick to react, Mason cupped it in his hand. "A recent lantern article? Are there many more of these?" He pulled it closer to read the type. No sooner had he read of the newsworthy mishap, when Glori slipped it from his grip.

"There's a spattering of this type. I don't know where Herb got all these. I think he had connections at the central library. Others were sent in by customers." She raised one eyebrow as if giving the collection further thought. "The Proof Books were intended to chronicle the company's products and their impact on the nation. Maybe Herb was micromanaging the task after he began to slow down with old age. At any rate, Leslie is having a tussle trying to get these entries in order. She's resorted to putting similar-themed entries on a page together."

Mason steeled his gaze while reaching for the stack related to the infamous Coleman lantern. "Just as an unexamined life is not worth living, failure to heed the criticism of a consumer denigrates the product's integrity. Because I'm inspecting the lantern assembly for flaws, given Mr. Sanders accident, I'll review this latest round at my desk in search of a possible common denominator."

Glori threw up her hands. "Fine, Mr. Porter. Go dot your I's and cross your T's. I doubt Leslie will miss those for a week or so. Try to have them back before our departure on the eleventh. As for your script, it's here on my desk." She crossed over to retrieve it, her tailored navy dress highlighting her every movement.

Please to be receiving everything he wanted, his attitude grew smug. "Do you trust me to deliver my portion of this dialogue, or do you want to reserve some time to go over it with me?" When she offered it, he grasped it with alacrity, hopeful to inherit some feminine proximity.

She released it as if she were shunning a claim. "No, you go over it first by yourself. If you have any problems, give me a call. We're on overload in here, trying to cram a month of tasks into two weeks."

He paid her with a slow nod, jutting the script's folder under his elbow. "If I have a rough spot, I may drop by your apartment to talk it out some evening."

"Try to call beforehand, just in case."

He tilted his head, unable to fathom what might need predicating with a phone call. "Are not drop-by visits an open sign of true friendship?"

"Or fodder for vicious gossip—to hear my mother tell it." She held up her left hand and wiggled it enough the diamond ring flashed a warning. "Given the circumstances, meeting in public places would be preferred."

His good humor exited before he could. Clamped in place as an outsider looking in, he pivoted on his heel and took leave before any other barbs of invalid suspicion landed in his direction. Marching in retreat down the hall, he considered his options.

Perhaps the best strategy would be to embody the quintessential American husband, abide roughly by the script, and not miss an opportunity to extend a personal touch to the scene. His efforts would be targeted for the camera's benefit, but he was a man—not a performing robot. When it came to Glori Dawes, play-acting affection landed outside of consideration. He had accumulated a vault-full of authentic attraction, and the campaign hadn't even launched yet.

~

The warehouse loading bay lent the right amount of anonymity to get his midday task done. Edgar looked around, a stranger to these parts where men actually used their brawn to conduct a day's work. He smoothed his mustache and searched casually for his contact, unsure if this affiliation would pan out for his side business. Should all three partners work in the same facility, it might appear collusive—or prove convenient. Careful, his skepticism tainted his typical opportunistic bent.

A tall figure maneuvered around a forklift and made its way toward the oversized door leading to the loading platform. After checking the activity there, he turned and came up the aisle. Once he got within speaking distance, he stopped. "Mr. Sterns? You wanted to see me?"

"Yes. I have a business proposition to make. I'm looking for a third partner for a side venture, one who has experience with stocking liquor for a nightspot in downtown Wichita. Someone told me you have family in the wholesale distribution business locally. Is that right?"

He folded his arms. "Yes, my brother runs a food services business. They branched out to include liquor sales three or four years ago. I'm not sure I want to take on a side business. Are you going to make it worth my while?"

"I think the profit-sharing split will be to your liking," Edgar replied, sensing the need to step up his effort. "First, I'm covering all upfront expenses for the club's location. The second partner is in charge of managing personnel. It's handling the liquor I find daunting, which is why I'm availing the opportunity for a third partner to share in the profits."

"You mentioned a club—not a bar?"

"We're billing it as a gentleman's club, to reach a more selective clientele."

"That sounds sophisticated. Are you going with an aviation theme? That might draw in more men."

He warmed at the suggestion. "How clever of you to suggest it. That might be just the ticket to drive our renovation. We hope to be a haven of sorts, so why not be a hangar, too?"

The man gave a low chuckle. "Let me talk to my brother. If he can assure me of available inventory, then I'm your third partner. I'm approaching this opportunity like a hobby—because I already have a job."

"Good. I'll wait to hear back from you. My office in Marketing is private, so feel free to call me there. Can I ask for your commitment prior to the eleventh? The spring campaign starts then, and I'll be out for almost two weeks."

"That seems reasonable. You should hear back from me by the end of the week. Hmm, I'm intrigued at the prospect of a side venture, now that it presents itself."

"The idea's contagious, I assure you. Hold down the fort out there in camping gear land." Edgar turned away, sure he had the right man. Another key piece of strategy fell right into place.

~

Trying to feel like less of a turncoat, Glori paced the front room of her apartment awaiting Mason's arrival. At Midge's insistence, the time had come to coordinate wardrobes for the filming episodes. A steady hum from her bedroom spoke of her assistant's continued dedication to the task. For her, it only bred heartburn.

Regretful that she'd flashed the engagement ring to ward off Mason's interest, she now wished for some way to iron out the relationship wrinkle it caused. Short of shucking the talisman off her finger and slipping it into the end table's drawer, the solution escaped her. Still, he'd sounded like a true sport on the phone earlier and spoke of the distance from Valley Center as if it were nothing. She blew out a breath, trying to collect her rambling thoughts.

Midge marched out with a square-collared linen blouse in her hands. "I think we should stay clear of white. It might cause glare under the midday sun. Let's be bold with our colors, so you'll be the focus of attention."

"Right you are. Pink and lime green come to mind. Imagine me standing in front of Mount Rushmore's gray granite." She regarded her helper with sincerity.

"Golly me. I had in mind green trees for the background, but you're totally right for the first stop. Let me reconfigure my layouts on your bed." She disappeared back into the bedroom with a low whistle.

"Mason will be here any minute. I'll try to stall him until you're ready."

Midge clasped the door jam and turned to her. "Practice your script for the Devils Tower scene together. Timing may be more important on that one."

Heat began to creep up her neck. As written, the camping scene included preparing a meal over the Coleman portable cook stove together with Devils Tower looming in the background. The scene held every opportunity to turn awkward, should Mason not be simpatico with the endeavor. The door chime sounded, cutting her worrisome progression short.

She wiped her sweaty palms on her pedal-pushers before pulling open the door. Instead of a familiar face, she saw a neatly tied bundle of asparagus masking the caller. Earthy and non-imposing, the childish prank lowered her apprehension.

Mason peeked out from behind the offering. "Straight from my neighbor's garden to your table, my fair lady."

She smiled and motioned him in, taking the bundle as he passed. "Midge is in my bedroom laying out the possibilities with my casual clothes. I think she needs a few more minutes. Want to practice the second location script at my dinette table?"

"You are reading me like a cheap dime novel, I'm afraid." He motioned for her to lead the way. "At first glance, the dialogue seems stilted, though I like the cooking scene."

"You do? I'm surprised...in a pleasant way." She tucked the asparagus in the fridge and nestled into her usual seat. After gesturing to Mason, she retrieved her script from the far chair.

"I thought we could cook breakfast. Male viewers would like seeing bacon sizzling under the cook stove's influence." He sat across from her slowly, watching as if to gauge her response.

"Yes, we could have the coffeepot going, too. That always speaks of hominess. I think we're onto something. Yesterday, Edgar delegated the food procurement to me. I plan to start with one cooler full of perishables, and supplement with canned goods. We can always restock as needed. We'll take advantage of the occasional roadside café, as well."

"I hate those Vienna sausage things," Midge called from down the hall.

A lopsided smile crimped Mason's lips. "How about tossing in a couple of cans? Andy and I might eat those while fishing at the campground pond."

She pulled a notepad from between the salt and pepper shakers. Noting the request, she jotted down a few more breakfast items. "Does anything else come to mind?"

"If the company is paying, how about steaks one night?" He ran a hand across the table's wood finish, looking impish. "I mean, we want America to covet all aspects of our camping experience, right?"

"Dear, me. Look who's becoming quite the behind-the-scenes schemer." She listed steaks and added new potatoes. "Aluminum foil has a multitude of uses. I'd better bring some along. There, I've started a list, anyway. Let's move on to the script practice."

"I wondered if we could we try something a little different?"

"In what realm?"

"Real conversation between a man and his wife, not this stilted 'does the tower seem somewhat foreboding?' kind of tripe. I say we make it our own version, while still keeping with our purpose of highlighting the gear."

"If it will help you speak with more fluidity, then I'm all for it. By Location Number Two, we'll be better versed in our mutual reactions anyway. Before Edgar can adversely react to the switch-out, we'll have the entire scene filmed." Something about that tickled her funny bone, so she stifled a giggle.

"Give me one more minute, and then I'll be ready," Midge called.

"I've never seen you look more radiant than you do this morning." Mason over-expressed the line, giving hint to the initiation of his acting.

Ready to meet his match, she reached for his hand. "I can't get enough of this fresh air. We should get out more often. This magnificent view is reviving me."

"I think the coffee is almost ready. What do you think of a brisk hike this morning after breakfast? From the trail map, we could make it around the tower's perimeter and back before midafternoon." His buttery delivery ended with a thumb rub across her knuckles.

"Let's pack some light snacks to bring along. I don't want to be in any hurry to leave that unforgettable landmark."

"This day is ours to spend any way we want. It's is our chance to leave civilization behind. I'll strap the insulated picnic jug to my pack…you bring the camera."

Glori had to break off visual contact. The pretend trek had sent her soaring straight into dreamland. Unable to imagine what it might be like to speak those endearments with iconic scenery in the background, her throat went dry. As if to fan the flames, Mason turned toward the door, highlighting the intriguing mole along his sideburn.

"Would now be a convenient time to coordinate wardrobe pieces?" Midge posed from the doorway, looking from her to their guest.

"Perfect for me," Mason replied. "Let me go get those sport shirts from the Belvedere." He shoved back from the table, giving Glori's hand a pat. "Don't pull up the tent stakes yet, Miss Dawes. We've only just begun to consort."

Midge snickered as he departed. "Just heap those shirts on the sofa, Mason. We'll cull through them and find the right matches." The apartment door soon snapped closed.

Glori propped her elbows on the table and dropped her head into her hands. "Mercy, me oh my. This is going to be one devilishly interesting camping trip."

Midge reached around her for some red grapes in the fruit bowl. "I'm excited as all get-out to see America's wonders. Of course, I'm not the one sitting in front of the video camera."

"If you're trying to make me feel better, it's not working, mud sister."

Midge popped a grape into her mouth, and then caught her around the neck with her elbow. After clearing her throat, she began to hum a few notes of a familiar tune. "Oh, the Triple Star

Ranch is the truest and the best. It keeps on going, and it never takes a rest. It has one yell, and they yell it altogether. It goes like this—Triple Star forever. Hum-dum-dee-dum-dum—summer camp.”

Glori leaned into her full-figured friend, grateful for a trustworthy haven. “That’s probably the last time I ever camped. I’m not exactly the poster model for outdoor living.”

“No, but you will be. ‘Determination’ is your middle name, my friend.”

She shook her head, wondering when life had become so complicated. Six years ago, they had been mere teenagers. Adulthood wore a burdensome frock, and she was more than ready to shuck it for some leisure camping clothes.

Mason poked his head through the doorway. “I dropped my shirts on the divan. Did someone start singing campfire songs without me?” He looked between them with a suspicious stare and finally robbed some grapes from Midge.

Glori stood and struck him playfully in the chest with her script. “That’s one thing I refuse to do on-screen for America— sing at the campsite.”

“Warning duly noted,” he replied. “Come on, Midge. Wave your wand of match-ability and turn us into the Bobbsey twins.”

She walked under his arm, squinting with her critic’s role. “That’s not the rugged manly image we’re going for, Mason. You are not re-enacting a primary school reader, after all. With Elvis demoted from the King of Rock and Roll to a lowly buck private in the U.S. Army now, women are searching for a new heartthrob on whom to fixate their attention. Given a fresh haircut right before we leave, your mug just might fit the bill.” She gave him a whopper of a wink and made her way over to examine the shirts.

“I’d rather be the Plastics Pauper than King Creole,” he teased.

Glori considered his heartthrob potential with an admiring scan. “It’s difficult for the camera to paint an adoring picture of the mind, my brilliant friend. You’ll have to demonstrate your masculine charisma in some other fashion.”

“Which apparently starts with coordinating clothing.” He feigned a headache, gripping his temples. “What manner of fakery have I gotten myself into?”

She spotted the smile driving dimples into his clean-shaven

cheeks and had to resist touching the merchandise. She patted his bicep instead. "Things would go easier if you'd just bring me that red plastic cooler and let me use it at my campsite."

He blocked her at the doorway by lowering his arm. "Don't you wish you could? You're only attracted to my creative mind, if I'm reading you right, Miss Dawes."

She gave him a coy look before ducking under the block. "Love me tender—like Elvis says. Only you get a campfire thrown in to loft sparks into the night sky. How fortunate."

He moved closer to whisper in her ear. "You better put some marshmallows on that grocery list. That sweet exchange might make for a tender picture at the campfire."

Outmaneuvered, Glori couldn't stop the thrill of expectation as they hovered near the doorway. Goodness, that man could set a mood with his mere words. She blinked and tried to refocus. Maybe she should make the grocery note before she forgot his request.

"Here," Midge said, hoisting two shirts in the air. "This is Day One of filming—lime green polka dots paired with solid olive. For the night photo shoot prior to that, I think we'll go with something to match the flags along the Avenue of the Presidents, with Glori in red and Mason in royal blue. In the spotlight's glare, that should strum a few patriotic heartstrings."

"We'll need that kind of vivid contrast against the granite," Glori insisted.

"Goodness me," Mason quipped with a shake of his head. "Even the color wheel is dead-set against me. I cannot forgive those Hollywood film moguls, with their Technicolor plotting for out-loud color—all to make more movie revenue. It's a capitalistic scam, I tell you."

Midge placed the paired attire together and gave him a stern corrective look. "We're not going back to black-and-white, thank you, Mr. McGillicuddy. However, for the sake of completing this wardrobe exercise, I'm quite willing to reconsider the silent movies."

"Let's give Midge a head-start here while we go see what's blooming in my landlady's garden." Glori hooked his arm and pulled him toward the door.

Mason resisted. "Wait. Grab more of those grapes, will you?

That reminds me, we should have plenty of fresh produce to serve at the campsite.”

Glori separated and stepped back into the kitchen with forbearance. “Pick up grapes to go—check. Add fruits and vegetables to the grocery list—check. Was there anything else?”

“You got the bacon down, right?” He winked and trotted toward the front door.

“Look. He knows when he’s worn out his welcome,” Midge said with a smirk.

“We need to brush up on our outdoorsy glow anyway,” Glori replied. She crooked her pinkie at her friend, but Midge was too immersed in fashion to return the gesture. As she stepped outside, she contemplated the transition from one kind of friend to another, as childhood pinkie grips gave way to other fleeting touches. Her “love me tender” comment flashed to mind, making her wish for a retraction in the worst way.

When Mason smiled at her from the garden’s entrance, she took a moment to reexamine that retraction. On second thought, pinkie handshakes weren’t all that sustaining, and—like the fruit— might bear an expiration date. She joined him under the arbor, full of expectation.

Chapter 14

Ill-equipped to handle this sort of endeavor on his own, Mason hefted the duffel bag and took the front steps to the YMCA. His arms sore from mowing the yard for the first time yesterday, he knew his physical state needed improvement. Fortunately, the May issue of the Coleman newsletter had proffered a coupon for a month's discount membership. He had just over a week to gain some muscle tone, which would likely come in handy for the campout.

He entered the marble-trimmed foyer and headed for the sign-in desk. After two signatures, he had a member's card in hand and free reign over the facility. The weightlifting area attracted him the most. He made quick work of changing into gym shorts and a T-shirt, rolled his work clothes into a wad, and stuffed them into the gym bag. Now, he was ready to work up a sustained sweat.

A solitary lifter had just relinquished the bar to head off to the water cooler. Mason changed the free weights on each end and practiced a bicep curl or two in evaluation of the load. Adequate to start, he faced the mirrored wall and began a set of fifteen repetitions, alternating in squats on occasion. His left arm protested, but he held his ground and finished the set. He left the bar on a mat and stepped over to examine the durability of the weight bench next.

"Hey, are you done here or just getting started?" a man asked.

Mason turned to find the weightlifter had returned with a conical paper cup in his hand. Built square like a linebacker though a couple of inches shorter than his height, the guy looked like a regular lifter. His tank-style undershirt threatened to rip at every seam. "Just getting started, but don't let me hold you up."

"Say, I was looking for someone to spot me on the bench, if you've got an extra minute. I'm Billy Dean Connelly of the Wichita Police Department." He offered his hand.

He grasped it with intentional firmness. "Mason Porter, a new engineer at Coleman Company. It's my first visit to this YMCA, so I'm just getting my bearings."

He tucked a knowing smile into one cheek. "Skip the gizmos along the front wall. They're all promo gimmicks geared at shaking out your fat, so the muscle tone can magically seep in. Don't believe it. Free weights are the best tone-up tool, if you ask me."

"Guess you have to stay in shape for the job, right?" Mason motioned to the bench, so the officer could take possession.

He lowered into position on the black vinyl seat. "It pays dividends to stay fit in my line of work. You never know what kind of devious goings-on you might walk up to unexpectedly. At the point of confrontation, one party will exert superior strength, and I aim for it to be me."

"Well said. Are you ready for the bar?"

"Stack it up by forty, will you?" He exhaled and stared at the ceiling.

Mason clamped another twenty-pound disk on each end. In a careful lift, he maneuvered the whole rig over the policeman and shifted it into his grip. "I'll spot you and count the reps." After reaching twenty-five, the man's arms began to shake beneath the load, so he moved closer.

Three slow-motion lifts ended the series. "Take it," Billy Dean grunted.

Mason lifted the warm bar from the man's heaving chest and found the floor with it as soon as possible. He spied a pair of dumbbells and proceeded to do a set of triceps curls, dipping them over his shoulder. His tone-up would not build the massive wall of muscles his partner boasted, but an engineer didn't need that kind of bulk-up, a convincing out for his late efforts.

"Got a date for a movie coming up with my best girl," Billy Dean said. "Leslie Caron stars in 'Gigi.' Boy, I could look at her all day. Too bad that pompous Maurice Chevalier shares the starring role."

"He's an old goat, isn't he? Surely they can't be cast as the romantic pair." He reached a full count and set down the weights.

"Naw, the old Frenchman is supposed to meddle in his young nephew's business, the poor sap. Hollywood always has to mangle up the romantic pair, so they don't get to straight-out fall in love. Guess that would be too bland. Still, I'm looking forward to MGM's Metrocolor spectacular."

With his hands on his hips, Mason drew a breath and reflected on his not-so-straight path to romance. It didn't lack for color. Glori's sky-blue eyes outshone Leslie Caron's penciled-in manicured looks any day. "Guess you and your gal should show California how the Midwest goes about it in the romance department."

He clapped his hands. "We could at that—only nobody's asking a regular Joe like me. Let's go one more round with that eighty-pound bar, my friend."

"You've got it, Billy Boy." He grunted with the lift and took care to set the bar perpendicular to the bench's length, relenting only when a more capable set of hands took hold. He watched for signs of overexertion, which arrived just short of two dozen lifts. "Good work." He secured his grip and lifted the bar away. When he turned back around after setting down the leaden weights, the policeman had sat up on the bench.

"Truth be told, 'The Bridge on the River Kwai' was much more to my liking, but it was Libby's turn to pick. So it goes, in the back-and-forth rounds of courtship."

Mason fired off a line of the war film's familiar whistled tune that allowed the men to construct the bridge in synchrony. That earned him a sheepish grin from the lawman.

"You're all right, Mason Porter. I come in about this time every Tuesday and Thursday. If our workout times collide again, I'll let you go first on the eighty-pound bar."

Mason laughed. "Okay, but start at forty pounds for me, and let me creep up from there. I'm an engineer, so the heaviest thing I have to lift is our old clunky cooler. If my lab work goes as planned, that thing will be replaced by something much more lightweight."

"Which means I can lug it further into the backwoods. I'm going to love that, for sure."

Appreciating the new insight, he pointed a finger at Billy Dean's muscle-braided chest. "Lighter translates to packed-in further. I'll have to add that to our promo material. For now, though, I need to figure out a workout for my legs."

"Try the ankle weights in the corner. The stairs up to the running oval are especially good for a workout." He winked and pulled a towel across his shoulder. "I'm headed for the shower. Don't stop until those calf muscles squawk, Mason."

He shot him a thumbs-up and began to fish out the weight straps from the corner. Thanks to the mower's workout the day before, his calves immediately protested. The ankle weights proved to be an imprisonment of a heavy sort, but up the stairs he headed, the catchy bridge-building song looping through his mind. The path of self-improvement typically held a sting, but at least he'd met a friend along the way. At the top of the stairs, the unattended track invited him along, so he added two laps to his premier workout. Soon winded, the whistling ceased, but he stuck with the endeavor until soreness forced him to surrender. Hunger soon took up its routine acquaintance, driving his next decision while in town.

~

Edgar felt the need to be a bit tightlipped, given the rental management agent had accompanied them downtown. He'd cued Lloyd twice already to cease his banter, but outright discretion failed the man. The front door lock fell open after the agent gave it a solid tug.

"Right this way, gentlemen. The building's available for your possession the first of June. I hope you'll find it adequate for your needs." He gestured with a stubby arm and then fiddled with his tucked shirttail. "Let me get the lights on." He wandered back into a narrow hall, and the front room soon illuminated.

Edgar spotted the brass trim around the bar and thought it spoke of a masculine clientele. The amber-colored pendant lights also had a heavy look to them, not effeminate in the least. The wall behind the bar held three plate mirrors in succession, which gave the room the appearance of being larger. That might play to his advantage as well.

"Eight tables with five captain's chairs each," Lloyd said. "Add that to a dozen bar stools for your occupancy total."

"I think the occupancy totals around fifty-five," the agent replied. "Let me show you the back rooms behind the kitchen area. They allow for inventory storage and cleaning equipment."

Edgar withheld comment until this part of the building passed his inspection. They had more goings-on in mind than the bar up front, so the facility had to accommodate the full range of activities. He turned the corner at the end of the hall to discover two square rooms of equal size. A twin bed would hardly fit either space. *Blast the luck.*

"Not that you'd want to haul bottles of liquor down from upstairs, but there is an empty loft apartment up there that the building owner asked me to mention. The stairway is exterior but sturdy, right outside the door opening to the rear alley. Anyone interested in that portion of the building?"

"Possibly, but not if you're going to gouge me with a stiff rent increase," Edgar said, his tone icy.

"I think you could have it for fifteen dollars more a month. And if you want to attempt the rent-to-own option, having both floors would be required."

Lloyd's round face scrunched into a question mark. "Do we need both floors?"

Edgar leered at the man's incomplete grasp of the business concept. "Trust me, Mr. Cox. You'll be relieved to have the extra space at our availability, I assure you."

"Right this way, then," the agent said. "One dusty overhead apartment, coming right up."

Following on the man's heels, Edgar tested each step for stability since the apartment had gone unused for so long. Even the landing at the back door seemed solid. The door creaked open to a straight hall that split the floor space in half. Two spacious bedrooms filled the rear of the apartment, giving way to a central outdated kitchen that overlooked a boxy living room. At quick inspection, the apartment had loads of potential.

The agent wedged his bulk into the kitchen's galley space and flipped on the faucet. A gasp of air resulted which gave way to a spit of murky water. He shut it off and looked at them. "We best check the plumbing between the floors before we run much more water. No telling what shape those pipes are in."

"Would that be a matter for the owner to address?" Edgar

asked. "Any renter would expect running water and electricity, at a minimum."

The man ran a hand over his balding head. "Be glad to get back to you on that answer. Can I at least report that you'll take the upstairs along with the street-level bar under the terms of a one-year lease?"

Edgar fingered his mustache, enthused for the plan. "I'll accept the terms of that agreement, if you'll put it in writing. Be sure to include the rent-to-own clause, to be decided at a later date."

"I'll have the terms in writing by the end of the week," the agent replied. "Can I ask you to stop by our downtown office to sign the necessary forms?" He gestured toward the back door.

While Lloyd began the descent, Edgar rolled the timing around in his mind. The stairs soon clicked under his feet like seconds off the clock, giving the impression time was moving ahead too fast. At the bottom, he stopped the agent in the alley. "I'm headed out of town for an extended period on the eleventh. Do you think I could gain occupancy by the first of next week—to begin the refurbishment work prior to my departure? We hoped to be in business by June first."

The agent shook his head. "I know my client wouldn't mind. He's ready to get the income flow reconnected. My hat's off to you young men. You've got gumption to get things rolling, where others would just see an old brick building that's outlived its usefulness."

Edgar chuckled at the man's compliment. "We'll get her feeling like a spring chicken again, don't you worry. Let me plan to stop by your office on Friday. You have my name and contact information for the contract, right?"

"Yes, sir, Mr. Sterns. I'll see you Friday then. Go ahead to the front door and let me turn off this light from the hall."

Edgar strolled across the wood-planked floor as though crossing a Wild West frontier. An opportunity of the satin-sheet type awaited their immediate future. He'd have to put the crimp on Lloyd to get the rest of the staff lined up by the end of the month. Tired of breathing stale air, he stepped onto the sidewalk out front to wait on the rental agent.

Lloyd lit a cigarette and exhaled smoke into the evening air. "Well, that sure worked out, though I'm uneasy about the outdoor access to the second floor. That will be hard to keep secure. Hope you've got your money all ready to go."

"Don't worry about my part. You just make sure you've got the girls lined up." To make his point, he emphasized it louder than necessary.

Before Lloyd could reply, a man rushed by from the adjoining building. When they locked gazes, Edgar recognized the cocky plastics engineer who insisted on making eyes at Glori. Burned by being nailed in place at his future establishment, he had no choice but to acknowledge the man. "Good evening, Mr. Porter. I trust you enjoyed your…pursuits." He gestured at his gym shorts and added a maniacal grin.

Mason glanced between him and his associate. "Yes, Mr. Sterns. I had a nice workout, but I'm more than ready to flee the premises for the quiet privacy of Valley Center." He nodded and stepped to a blue car parked along the street curb.

The sound of the lock being manipulated closed jarred Edgar back to the task at hand. From this night forward, there would be a fine line of cultural compatibility between the two neighboring buildings. Unknowledgeable about physical fitness as a moneymaker, he knew his bar business would be profitable. The comparison ended with similar addresses, although the two clienteles might have the opportunity to intermix. The alluring thought made him smile. Up the street, a pair of taillights illuminated, and the Plymouth pulled away from downtown Wichita with a defiant rumble.

~

An annual affair, Glori tripped up the side steps to her parents' house to get the upkeep task underway. She threw open the glass-paneled door to the study and crossed the empty book-lined room toward the light. "Yoo-hoo, Mother dearest," she called in a loud voice.

"In the kitchen, Glori-girl," her mother replied.

She banked left and headed for the back of the house, only to discover her mother bent over the sink, peering down the drain.

"I've lost my wedding band down the garbage disposal again. Come fish it out for me. Your hands are thinner than mine." She puffed her hair from her eyes in exasperation.

Glori sat her purse on the counter and slid the watch off her wrist. Without a second thought, she slipped her left hand down the disposal, feeling around the sharp blades until she touched a trinket riding atop the remnant vegetable peelings. In a pulse of rebellion, she thought to turn on the whirring gadget to see which ring would be salvaged. No, she needed more than an accident to rid her of that menace. "Here it is, shiny as new." She popped the band onto the countertop and wiped her hand on a tea towel.

"Now, I'm ready for your beautification services. Where would you like me?"

"Hmm. Let's stay on the linoleum in case of a spill. I have three colors for you to choose from this spring— light, medium, and dark."

Her mother returned the band to her finger and pulled out a chrome dinette chair. "I bought two new skirts this week to go with the slimmer me."

"I commend your weight loss, Mother. That shows a lot of willpower." She fished into her purse and produced the three bottles. "Here we are with 'Pink Blush,' 'Coral Cravings,' or 'Mulberry Shadows.' Which polish do you like?"

She kicked off her Keds and rubbed across the top of her foot. "I realize it's early in the season, but I'm partial to the darker one."

"Then 'Mulberry Shadows' it is." She put the vial on the table between them and pulled out a chair to sit down. "Your Betty Beauty Parlor pampering service is now in session."

"This timing couldn't be better for me, as the church choir is having its spring get-together on Saturday. I have a new pair of heeled sandals to lend me a little more lift on those risers, so I needed my toenails done in the worst way."

"Feet always get neglected, at least mine do." She took her mother's foot in her lap. "We leave town for the campaign filming a week from Sunday. Edgar estimates we'll be gone ten to twelve days, depending on how efficient the film crew can work." She began to shake the bottle until the tiny bead inside freely rattled.

"How many Coleman folks will be in the clips?"

"Well, five of us are going, but only two of us will star in the features as a camping couple. Midge will be my sidekick. She's in charge of wardrobe—and she's taking that assignment seriously. We're going to share the family tent that will be featured with all the Coleman camping gear."

"Goodness, I hope you young people enjoy that. I wouldn't want to sleep on the ground for that long." She adjusted her glasses to the end of her nose to keep the beautification in focus.

Glori took a long swipe on the right big toe. The polish covered the nail, thick and pliant. "Ooh, I sure like this color in the direct light. Maybe I'll do mine in the same color, though I had the pink in mind at first glance."

"Edgar will be dashing as your camping husband, dear. Be sure to give him lots of feminine attention."

The touchy topic had surfaced sooner than later, but she wouldn't misinform her mother. "No, Mom. Edgar has his hands full directing the script and keeping the crew on task at three national parks. We had to line up another Coleman worker to play the part of my husband. Remember? I told you they held a contest. I selected a new employee, a plastics engineer, as my campaign husband. His name is Mason Porter. He holds a PhD from Purdue University."

Her mother hummed and leaned back in the chair. "Is this Mr. Porter attractive? I'm sure they wouldn't let just anyone take the lead role like that."

"He is, though he's quite reserved about it. Midge thinks we have good chemistry together. I've reminded Mason that the camera cannot see his scholastic merit, so he needs to portray his charm in a more outward-going manner. With a bit of coaxing on my part, I think we can make the exchange seem natural enough for promotional purposes. The company's summer sales are hanging on the effectiveness of this campaign, so we simply have to be convincing." She swiped color onto the second toe and had to re-dip the wand.

Her mother made a throaty sound. "You're liable to put Edgar in a compromised position, don't you think?"

Feigning concentration, she bent closer to her task. How could she argue the abject meaninglessness of a play-within-a-play? Besides, Edgar had leverage, not vulnerability. Of that, she was quite certain. "Edgar is a grown man who can handle the pretense of a staged relationship. Plus, he wrote the original script. How much more in control can a fiancé be?"

"Well, I suppose." She shifted in her seat. "Your father seemed less adept at handling it, as you've put it. When he saw Judge

Jacob Whitcomb whispering in my ear at the club's Christmas party, he made an absolute stink of a scene. That cuffing played out well for me afterward, mind you, but imagine what the other bystanders thought of us at the time."

"Maybe they thought Daddy loves you to an extreme," she replied. In a dab, the pinkie toe received its color crown. "There, I'm done with this foot. Switch for the other one." She arched her back and gave the mulberry color a swift evaluation. It had a boldness about it, despite not being bright red, Maybe she'd let Midge wear the brassy colors, and she'd play toward another color spectrum, one with less pizzazz, but possibly more intrigue.

Her mother filled her lap with her left foot. "Promise me this— that you'll let Edgar know exactly how you feel, should a rub arise. As his fiancée, you owe him that much."

In three consecutive swipes, she had the left big toe covered. With the polish so thick, she doubted the need to coat it again. Maybe she could start painting her own nails, before she ran out of energy for the beauty shop task. She re-dipped the wand and started down the angled smaller toes.

"Glori, please say you'll promise me. As your mother, I might know a bit more about the behavior of men than you give me credit for."

"Fine. I hereby pledge that I'll tell Edgar exactly how I feel about him, should a riff occur. Otherwise, we'll leave the play-pretend on the stage for when the cameras are rolling." She dotted the last two toes and began to blow the polish dry. "Really, Mother. You tend to worry too much."

"Sometimes, I worry just right," she quipped with a tug on her earlobe.

The three-quarter carat diamonds had escaped Glori's notice before. An ample backlash for jealous behavior, Glori doubted she'd receive any similar payback.

"Who's in charge of the food?"

"I am. Do you have any suggestions?" She slipped off her sandal and began to shake the bottle of 'Mulberry Shadows.'

"Pack more food than you think you need. And pack some car snacks separate, like in your purse."

"I'm taking a trail pack instead of a purse. Mine looks like a binoculars case. Do you approve?" She glanced over in time to see ten wiggly purple-tipped toes, happy as can be.

"Certainly, as long as it contains a tube of pale lipstick, a first aid kit, and the snacks. They truly will help the miles speed by."

"That's good to keep in mind for the first day of travel. It's eleven hours up to Mount Rushmore. We hope to take snapshots at the floodlight program that first night." She brought the color wand down and leveled the coverage across her toes, uncertain of the dark selection.

"Midge can keep you looking fresh. Remember to smile before the scene ends. People expect happily-ever-after, even for commercials. That's why a smile ends every toothpaste ad."

"Mother, you realize that clean teeth represent their product's ambition."

"Well, in your case, hold up a piece of camping gear. Still, you need a smile on your sweet face. Promise your mother that, too."

Glori switched feet, tiring of the coaching session that tended to dominate their relationship. "I promise to smile whenever it's fitting, Mother. When you see the commercials, you'll know I'm doing that for you. Okay?"

"That's my Glori-girl," she replied, looking content.

Glori finished painting her toenails, which left her with ten purple piggies and two heavy promises that she hoped she could keep. The smiling task seemed easy enough, but telling Edgar how she felt might generate a bit more honest exposure than she'd planned. Maybe mother didn't know best in this scenario, where half-truths jangled against pretense in the worst way. At least the food tip was a good take-away. She would stock up on the heavy side and fault inexperience if she still didn't have it covered. With a flourish of her hand, she capped the bottle and brought the Betty Beauty Parlor session to a close for the evening.

Chapter 15

Mason tried to keep his eyes on the highway ahead, but with two shapely legs clad in aqua blue jutting from the passenger seat, it wasn't easy. He checked the fuel gauge again, and it still read over three-quarters of a tank. So far, they had made excellent time.

Glori pulled out the road atlas and soon held the state of South Dakota front and center. "It looks as though Horse Thief Lake Campground is along Highway 244 on our direct approach to Mount Rushmore. I reserved three campsites right along the lake. We girls claim the most scenic one."

He smiled and signaled to pass an old truck. Fortunately, the opposing traffic was light. "You always get top billing as the star of the show," he teased. A glance in the rearview mirror revealed Edgar had taken the passing lane as well. The hanging wardrobe pieces blocked the rest of his back deck, so he'd have to depend on the side view mirrors more. "Read me that travel guide entry again."

"I'd be happy to oblige your request." She swapped out the two books and found her marked spot. "America's colossal tribute to its presidential history presents itself on the upper granite face of Mount Rushmore National Memorial, some five thousand seven hundred and twenty-five feet high."

He whistled and winked when she looked up. "Now, that's a grand tribute."

"'Begun in nineteen twenty-seven under the direction of Gutzon Borglum, the edifice was completed in nineteen forty-one under the guidance of his son, Lincoln. The heads of four great presidents are featured in the carving—George Washington, Thomas Jefferson, Abraham Lincoln, and Theodore Roosevelt.'" Glori paused and rested the guide book against her chest.

"This seems the perfect location to launch an American camping campaign."

She smiled and stared out the windshield. "This is a great country with many lovely landscapes. I hoped to find one that summed up patriotism and the land, which is why I picked Mount Rushmore."

"I'll predict we'll shoot our best footage there," he quipped. "Call it beginner's luck."

"No luck…I've been praying like crazy for this to work out."

"I'm ready to give it one hundred percent, which numerically is all an engineer can muster." When she popped his shoulder with the guide book, he rewarded her with a grin. "Got anything more on the park?"

"Here's something on programs. 'Every evening beginning in May, a floodlighting program is held in the Memorial Amphitheater at nine o'clock. Flags representing the forty-eight states line the avenue leading to a viewing platform for the sculptures. This highly photogenic setting is a favorite one for visitors. Otherwise, the carved heads are best viewed under morning light. Carvers Café provides food service by a park concessionaire during park hours.'"

He checked his speed. "That sounds ideal. I'm starting to catch your enthusiasm now, Miss Dawes."

"I hope enthusiasm is included in your one hundred percent participation, Mason. I think the flag-lined lane sounds like a top-notch photo opportunity."

"Which is why Midge has us dressed like two additional flags. I hear the Alaska territory might be on the cusp of statehood. It's just a matter of paperwork and land inventories."

"Please, don't give Midge any grief. She's taking her role seriously. She even made me buy new sneakers." She flexed a foot past the center drive train and offered her evidence.

"I'll comply with the wardrobe coordinator—just to prove I'm easy to work with. The rest of the crew gets my wait-and-see attitude."

"Oh, is that so? Well at least Midge gets a break. That should keep her happy."

"That's my plan…to keep my girls happy." His view slid from the rearview mirror to glimpse his scenic passenger. To maintain integrity, he kept both hands planted on the steering wheel. "Did we need a reservation at the floodlight program?"

"No, I asked specifically. It's included in the price of park admission. We'll be getting a two-day pass, which means that the Rinehart Filming crew had better show up on time."

He nodded. "We should have the better part of two hours to get the tents set up at the lake prior to embarking to the park for that night photo shoot. It might be a good idea to take a few pictures while we set up, but I doubt we'll have time to cook tonight."

"I agree. Edgar mentioned grabbing something to eat midafternoon when we stop for gas. The filmed cooking sequence isn't until we get to Devils Tower. The steaks are frozen solid, but we should plan to grill them by our third day on the road."

"There's something I can put my stamp of approval on. Oh, look. There's one of those new Datsun imports." He pointed out the oncoming car.

"Wow, that's small. We're not going to be overrun by these toy-sized imports, are we?"

"Time will tell. I don't know how safe they are, but they're supposed to be fuel efficient." Glancing in his side view mirror after it passed, the car looked like a toy.

"I watched 'Candid Camera' on TV last night. I don't know why that quirky show catches my attention, but I find it downright irresistible." She flashed a guilty smile before closing the park guide.

"You're not going to be the campground prankster, are you?"

"Not hardly. I'm as straight-laced as they come. Still, a good laugh is tough to beat."

"I'll remember that innocence claim if I get short-sheeted in my tent."

"That would be hard to do with a sleeping bag." She opened a case and brought out a bag of corn chips. "Want a snack?"

"You bet." He dipped a hand in and ate them readily.

"You should have said something if you were getting hungry."

"Sometimes, snacking has nothing to do with hunger."

"What? I'm boring you, aren't I?" She hesitated eating a corn chip, resting it on her lip.

"On the contrary, Glori. You're an indelible part of the trip."

She shook her head. "Possibly…right after the bacon and the steaks."

Elevated by her tease, he jutted his elbow in her direction. "But above the Vienna sausage. There, now you have a ranking platform from which to advance."

She grabbed his arm, leaned closer, and fed him a few more corn chips. "I'm not above baiting my way to the top of your list." She arched a shapely brow to heighten the admission.

Flush with the feminine attention, he rode the crest of a magnetic wave for several seconds before realizing she hadn't released his arm. For a plain plastics engineer, she made a fairly fancy attachment. As with the cooler's new lid, fit was everything—and hers proved pretty solid. "Thank you for picking me as your camping partner, Glori. I'll try not to let you down."

She lifted her chin to reveal two sparkling blue eyes. "I know you won't. Let's make the most of it, shall we? After all, the background scenery cannot get much better."

"Amen, and God bless America." He glanced at the clock on the dashboard, its luminous hands pointing out the lateness of the morning. He wondered how far they could overshoot high noon before someone would need to stop. They had but one direction—northwest—so he let the Belvedere climb through the plains of Nebraska, enjoying his immediate company more than he'd be willing to confess out loud.

~

Edgar balled the wrapper in his fist as he swallowed down the last greasy bite of his hamburger. Purchased after his gas fill-up in Nowhereville, Nebraska, he reached for his soda to clear his throat. Once Glori reappeared from the ladies room, he'd make his pitch. They had a little over five more hours of travel in his estimation. Their ambitious agenda would not allow for laggards, and he felt compelled to crack the whip to guard it.

Mason approached and tossed his cup in the trashcan. "I won't need another fueling stop for the Belvedere. That should leave us plenty of time at the campground before heading to the park. What do you think?"

"We should protect time whenever possible. They equipped my Ford Fairlane with an equally generous gas tank. As standard operating procedure, hold onto all your receipts for potential reimbursement after the trip. The sooner we get to the campground, the more comfortable I'll be about the photo shoot tonight in the park."

"How about snapping a few pictures of Glori and me erecting the family tent? You might be able to use those in a collage for advertising. Every clear day is an invitation to take pictures, because you never know when hovering clouds or pending rain will detract from your success."

He flinched at the amateur suggestion. "I'm the head of Marketing, so I think I know how to be opportunistic, Mr. Porter. Whenever I have the camera in my hands, it makes for more work for the others, especially Andy."

The engineer nodded sideways, as if to shirk off his authority. "How's my fishing partner doing in your backseat?"

"Riding silently like an emissary from heaven. It's Midge that's berating my sanity with her nonstop commentary. What do I care that the Hope Diamond is being donated to the Smithsonian Institute by year's end? She's a rambling trove of trivial rubbish. At least she's reading the road atlas to me, so I can better track our steady progress."

"Glori has a national parks guide we'll loan you for your enlightened entertainment. Maybe Midge will get absorbed in its pages."

"Leave the book in your car. I plan to swap out Glori for Midge for the second leg of our journey. I'm sure you don't mind."

The man sharpened his gaze. "That decision is entirely up to Glori. She seems to be enjoying the trip right where she is."

Challenged by the unexpected standoff, he wouldn't relent. "You pulled a quick one on me by insisting to drive, which forced a split in the group. Let's not play favorites and create ill favor at the outset, shall we?"

Diverting his gaze to a rack of candies, Mason selected a tube of peppermint Lifesavers. "As I said before, it's up to Glori." He turned his back and headed for the sales counter.

Steamed at the snub, Edgar stepped closer to the restroom entrance, pretending interest in salty potato chips. Before he could make a selection, the women joined him.

"Oh, that's a great idea," Midge said. "I should have packed a few snacks."

"I'm good in that department," Glori said, slipping past her.

Edgar jumped on the chance to make the shift. "Hold up, Glori. I wanted to request that you and Midge trade places for this second leg of the trip. That would give us plenty of time to catch up. We've both been terribly busy as of late." He smiled and dangled a bag of chips with a wise owl on it, to make the offer more attractive.

Glori looked past him as Mason shoved the gas station door open and exited. When she refocused on him, her expression turned quizzical. "Catch up? There's nothing to catch up on."

"Maybe if we went over the travel itinerary, we could iron out some possible wrinkles. Perhaps our schedule is too demanding at this pace. Let's take another look at it together."

Glori took a step toward the door. "We can do that at the breakfast table in the park's café tomorrow morning. Something tells me we'll have to wait for Rinehart Filming to arrive, so that's a better use of our time. As for the ride up, I'm quite comfortable where I am, thank you."

Before he could argue the point, she scooted out of the station. Stunned at the turn-down, he froze in place until Midge nudged his arm.

"Here, let me get these chips. I want some gum, too. Do you like Juicy Fruit?"

"Fine with me," he muttered as he handed over the chips. "I'll be outside."

"Wait—you might need to summon Andy out of the men's room." She nodded her head toward the alcove, swiped a pack of gum off the rack, and headed for the register.

Bile rose in his throat at this latest demotion. Maybe he should have pressed to trade Andy out instead. His assistant could have ducked Mason's wardrobe pole and rode cloaked from the afternoon sun. Not that it would affect the young man's keen ability to nap. Clenching his teeth, he gave the door a requisite knock.

"Be right out," the occupant called.

Edgar retreated to the Fairlane and decided to clean the

windshield while he waited. A sleek blue Plymouth pulled back onto the highway, a car that carried his fiancée—the star of his campaign. He spotted her laughing with the driver, which incensed him to no end. He took his anger out on the squeegee, and soon all the bug splats had been wiped from his windshield. Somehow, the cleared perspective made him feel better. When Midge exited with Andy, the highway beckoned to him like an unscratched itch. *Time to head up the road.*

~

Though the tent's twin peaks attempted to block her view, Glori made every effort to face the gorgeous lake to watch the setting sun reflect off its surface. Only a thatch of willow saplings stood between her campsite and Horse Thief Lake. Andy worked well under Mason's lead, and between the three of them, the tent stood tight and tall in no time. A subtle sense of ownership in this open space began to lend her comfort.

Mason came around front. "Andy, go unload some of the Coleman gear there by the picnic table. Then ask Edgar to bring the camera for some photos before the lighting gets too dim." He knelt and shoved a tent stake further into the ground.

She watched his muscles flex in the endeavor. "Wow, that's what I forgot to pack—brute strength. Guess I'll have to stay clever and provide the brains for our partnership."

He stood with a laugh, wiping his palms. "How do you like this set-up?"

"It's perfect in every way." She fiddled with the tent flaps for a distraction.

"I hope you're still saying that after the mosquitoes come out." He smiled before stepping over to help Andy unload his armful of gear. Their iconic Coleman lantern soon graced the picnic table. "Take the cook stove out of the box, Andy. Let's get set up for picture-taking."

Glori glanced at the unzipped tent entrance. "If bugs might be bad later, maybe I'll bring in my bedding now. We can leave the mesh zipped up and try to guard against invasion."

Midge walked up looking suddenly sober. "I'm all for that. Nothing makes the ground harder than a mosquito buzzing your ear all the live-long night. Let me get my sleeping bag."

Mason approached Glori. "I guess it's time for my first surprise then. I brought a gift to help make your tent more comfortable."

"I'm all for that. Meet you back here in a minute after I find my sleeping bag in Edgar's trunk." Excited for the surprise, she hastened to the car.

"This is a lot better than I imagined." Midge tugged out her sleeping roll from behind the heavy coolers.

"Yes, our spot is idyllic. Mason brought a surprise to make our tent more comfortable. Want to come see what it is?"

"Do I ever," she replied with a waggle of her brow. "You two seem to be getting along well. Is that practice mood-setting for your skits tomorrow?"

"No, we're just enjoying each other's company. How was the drive up with Edgar?"

"I don't think his lunch agreed with him. Maybe he shouldn't have ordered that spicy sauce on top. Anyway, I tried to distract him by keeping the conversation fresh. He came around after awhile."

Glori dug her fingers into the webbed belt that kept her sleeping bag in a roll. "Let's go see our first surprise." She returned to the tent with her best friend in tow.

Mason appeared with two rolled mats tucked under his arms. "These polyurethane foam pads came courtesy of a supplier who'd like me to diversify my plastics orders. I held onto them thinking they might be handy for camping. Can I ask you ladies to give them a trial run and tell me what you think?"

"Come to momma," Midge replied with an outstretched hand. "I sleep on my side which can be ruinous on hard ground."

Andy knelt by the opening in the mesh and soon leapt inside. His boots dangled from the tent's entrance. Once he flipped over, he sat upright and displayed the target of his hunt. "Andy found a missing prop."

Glori looked, and there was her missing shoe from the day of the platform collapse. "Goodness, my sneaker from the campaign launch. I wish I had brought its partner along."

Mason untied a twine string. "Save it for a spare. If we get muddy, you may need it." He handed Andy the foamy pad. "Here, buddy, roll this out for me."

Glori surveyed the set-up around her campsite, spotting the heap of canvas soon to be Mason's tent. "Please put mine on the left side, Andy. Midge can have the right side."

After making quick work of the installation, Andy reached for Midge's roll.

"Thank you for thinking of our comfort ahead of time, Mason. It reflects your thoughtfulness." Her eyelashes fluttered, though she hadn't intended to flirt.

"Well, if they make an improved difference, we can expand Coleman's line of camping gear with mats for our sleeping bags. These straight planks would be a cinch to generate. We could even emboss the company name in the corner."

After handing Andy her sleeping bag, Midge rested her fists on her hips. "Let me get back to you tomorrow morning. Depending on my level of soreness, I might endorse your new product idea." A June bug flew by, headed toward the willow thicket.

Before Glori could add her tease, Edgar joined the group. "Is anyone ready for a snapshot around the old campsite?"

"Start with Glori by the picnic table opening the cook stove," Mason replied. "I'll hold the lantern in the background and pretend to be checking inside the tent."

"I'd like a picture or two down by the lake afterwards," Glori added, a thrill shooting down her spine. "We can take the green cooler and a picnic jug down with us, so it looks like we've lingered awhile."

"Good suggestions." Edgar lifted the camera to his eye after motioning Midge away from the scene.

Glori glanced across the campsite to where Mason would be sleeping close by. That birthed a wistful smile as she lifted the top of the latest model Coleman cook stove. In the quietness of the moment, a camera's lens clicked shut and captured her contentment. She looked at Mason over her shoulder, and he paid her back with a tiny wink. The lantern in his hand swayed the tiniest bit, like a beacon marking the way home. When he pulled the tent flap back, she joined him by the entrance and placed her hand over his to guide the lantern at her whim.

Mason relinquished the lantern and slid an arm around her waist. He faced her toward the camera and several more shutter clicks commenced.

Glori muted her personal reaction, though his solid chest pressed her back. Reminding herself it was all pretend had no countering effect in the moment. Trying to break the spell, she pulled away. "I want the lake scene next—before the light wanes."

"It's more like before the clock wanes," Edgar replied. "You have ten minutes to get this shot in. Then, we have to leave for the park."

"Andy can help carry the cooler down," Midge added. "I'm running to the ladies privy."

"Let me help tote the cooler," Mason insisted. "Is it full?"

"To the top, I'm afraid," Glori replied. "I'll bring down the picnic jug."

"Let me go on over to the shore and find the right spot," Edgar said. With the camera strapped around his neck, he left as empty-handed as he could be.

Glori shook her head. "Don't expect him to be any help."

Mason walked beside her toward the trunk. "I don't expect him to be any hindrance."

She snickered as his comment hit the bulls-eye. "Something about this place is alluring. I already wish we could stay here longer." She caught his wink, though it came like the flicker of a bug's wing. Even the jug's weight couldn't bog down her happiness. The lake was hers to enjoy.

Chapter 16

Never given to hyperbole, even Mason had to admit the colossal sculptures detailing the cliff face were nothing short of stunning. Each face more familiar than the next, he studied the oversized artwork with an exacting eye. The tailings pile beneath the carving task spoke to the enormity of the project. By immediate contrast, the rock rubble lent the carved surface extra grandeur. Made dramatic in the floodlights' cast, the scene took on postcard perfection.

"Mount Rushmore at last," Midge said in a wispy tone.

"This is overwhelmingly unbelievable," Glori admitted. "We're going to look like ants posing with these giants."

Mason chuckled. "It depends on the camera placement, for sure. I agree that this is unbelievable as a construct of human endeavor."

Glori stepped closer, her gaze fixed on Mount Rushmore's faces. "If the designers truly planned this for the best roadside attraction in America, they may have overshot their goal."

"Yes, Criminy," Midge concurred. "Wonder if we should add a more modern president to this jumbo collection."

"Well, a certain Kansas war hero who currently holds the office comes to mind," Glori replied.

"We like Ike," he teased, poking a finger in her back.

She smiled and shifted her gaze down the illuminated lane of flags anchored by towering arches. "The little girl inside me wants to run down the center of that Avenue of the Presidents until she cannot get any closer."

"We'll do the entire Presidential Loop tomorrow, I promise."

He took her hand in his and began to walk toward the state flags fluttering on the first granite arch. "Come on, Midge. Grab Andy off the railing, and let's stick together."

"Sure thing. Wait for us." She dashed off to retrieve their helper.

"Let me improve the scenery for a moment." He turned Glori facing the café and framed her face in his fingers, catching the presidents in the background. "This is the shot I wanted."

"So take a picture up here," she teased, pointing to her temple. "The minds-eye always makes the best capture…and it doesn't require any film."

He inched closer, taking in the gem-like sparkle of her eyes. "I don't see how this setting could be a near miss. It's a real thrill to be here with you, Glori. Let me get that said before a hoard of people divide our evening." When she pressed her lips together, she created a first-class distraction from the monument.

"Cheer, cheer—the gang's all here," Midge quipped from behind. "Edgar must have gotten the new roll of film loaded. He's coming up the walkway like a stampeding bull. Let me check your outfits for a final touch-up." She stepped closer to Glori and tugged at the shirttail of her fitted blouse. "Remember to keep your chin up, so your profile matches the carvings."

When Midge turned to evaluate him, Mason held her off with extended arms. "Look, but don't touch."

"Finicky engineer," Midge muttered. "At least run your fingers through your hair. It looks like you've been driving with your head poked out of the car window."

Andy laughed like a donkey braying when he followed her suggestion.

Edgar walked up, huffing for breath. The essence of cigarette smoke soon followed. "We'd better get a few shots under our belt, in case the lighting changes. It's absolutely stunning right now from further away."

"How about we lean over the railing past the first arch there?" Mason posed. "I can put Glori in front, so her profile looks out beyond the four faces."

Edgar flipped his wrist, gesturing to make them move. "Hurry up then. We'll start with that location, and I'll move you around from there. We may have to back up some."

"Backing up means including the crowd," Midge replied. "I don't think we want that—not in these still photos anyway."

"You may be right, Midgey, but let the camera dictate our next move. The panorama may be more than I can fit inside the viewfinder." Edgar led the way to the closest railing.

Mason stalled a bit to relay a message to Glori. The bright lights accentuated her fair features, causing her to look even more appealing. "I may have to add a measure of pretend here, but I wanted you to know that I won't take undo advantage of you. I mean every pose out of the utmost respect."

She seemed momentarily perplexed. "But there's no script for tonight. We're taking still pictures."

"Yes, where I'll be holding you as a man holds his dear wife. Please, allow me the momentary liberty." He tilted his head in sincerity.

She wiped a knuckle across her bottom lip. "Fine. It's gentleman's honor then. I'm yours to hold for the moment." She swept away and soon joined Edgar at the railing.

Watching as they enjoyed the colossal edifice together, he garnered his courage and stepped into the world of make-believe, a fantasy world where Glori belonged in his arms. After Edgar posed her in his preferred spot, Mason tucked behind her and braced an arm between them. In a progression of shots taken from the rail nearby, he held a woman close and stared out into a far-away horizon.

"Chin up, Glori," Midge coached from the sidelines.

The camera lens clicked a couple of additional times. "Okay, your final enamored embrace," Edgar said from behind the camera.

Mason folded his arm across Glori's chest and drew her against him, his chin pressing her hair. The clean scent of honeysuckle disarmed his senses as his enchantment grew beyond the iconic scenery. Her tiny gasp played on his ear like an unrehearsed song. In a cataclysmic crush of time, he nuzzled against her bare neck. "My moment," he whispered, sure of little else.

Glori pushed from his arms and tore off in a full run. The camera clicked countless times as the woman-girl took flight down the avenue of her fancy. Even under the floodlight's validation, it looked like a migration of the inexplicable sort.

"What just happened to Glori?" Midge asked, her eyes as wide as saucers.

Edgar stepped from the rail and allowed the camera to dangle from its strap. He looked at Mason with a leer. "What a moron."

Midge wrung her hands. "Should I try to bring her back?"

"No, let's stroll down to the end," Edgar replied. "We can try to capture a few tear-filled shots from there. Talk about filling up the viewfinder, though. This may not turn out well." He grabbed Andy's shoulder and led the team down the central avenue draped by flowing flags.

Midge took a tentative stepped toward him. "Tear-filled? What in the world?"

Mason threw his hands in the air. "Quite possibly, it could be her adverse reaction to me." He blew all the residual breath from his lungs, wishing for once he was dead wrong.

~

From her perch on the picnic table, Glori watched the moon play across the seamless lake, moved to be part of their nightly ritual. High-pitched peeps echoed from the water's edge, signaling the veracity of spring. Enough of a breeze blew to rustle the willows' branches, which stirred her ragged thoughts into the gentle night—if only they would carry downwind.

Other members of the campaign had turned in earlier. From where she sat, she could hear Midge's routine inhalations through the tent's mesh door. Mason hadn't spoken a word to her since her exodus from the rail. She alternated between not caring what he thought, to feeling somewhat apologetic for the meltdown. Even with his hinted warning, the play-pretend turned tactile and oh-so real in a crush of masculine attention for which she was most unprepared.

A solitary hoot echoed across the lake. In a hushed interlude, a pair of sturdy wings caught the moonlight and shadowed the lake, all at the same time. The give-and-take of it affected her soul. *Lord, please be mindful of my precarious plight.* The ache of unfinished business ran down her length low and slow. Handicapped from its persistent grip, she slid from the table and unzipped the tent, hoping to hide beneath the anonymous shelter of sleep.

~

He stole from his tent under the cloak of night. No matter that the photo session had gone awry to mar their first shoot, he had an agenda that must play out. Tiny skirmishes never won the war, after all. His bare heels rubbed against his shoes as he approached the women's tent. In search of the corner off the back, he noted for the first time that they'd failed to erect the rain fly. No matter—he could cut another nonessential spot. After flicking his knife from its sheath, he sliced through a corner loop. In the moonlight, the tent began to sag. Content for now, he stole back to his private accommodations to wait for the morning light.

~

Mason strode up the Avenue of the Presidents in the glaring sunlight, a stark contrast to the focused spotlights that pinpointed the carved faces last night. Though the horizon had expanded, his task remained the same. Perhaps today, he could rely on the safety of scripted interaction and not push his co-star to the brink. That remained to be seen.

"I hope Edgar was able to reserve our table in the cafe," Midge said. "I'm plenty hungry this morning. Hey, that mat you gave me really helped cushion the ground. Thanks a million."

"You're welcome a hundred thousand and change," he replied.

Their young assistant moved into the huddle. "Andy is hungry like a bear."

Glori moved past him in a regal red sweep. She patted Andy on the shoulder. "Even though all the park signs say not to feed the bears, I think we'd better make an exception this time. How about we get Andy some breakfast?"

The young man's face animated. "Andy likes pancakes."

"Stack 'em high," Midge teased as she stepped over to open the door.

Unable to fight the shifting tide that forfeited sightseeing for subsistence, Mason gave the distant carved mountainside a fond glimpse over his shoulder and walked toward the café's rear entrance. "We like Ike…and maple syrup," he muttered to Glori as he passed to assume door duty. An elderly couple exited with a nod, and the Coleman team took Carvers' Café by storm. The aroma of cooking sausage soon moderated his tourist's regret to a more tolerable level.

"There's Edgar at the corner table," Midge said. She turned Andy on a dime and escorted him down a narrow aisle.

Glori glanced at him before falling in line behind them. "The film crew likely won't be here for a couple of hours. We should enjoy this leisure breakfast and its abundance."

He nodded, moving closer without touching her. "Still, we have to be aware of the advancing sun, since the photography is better in the morning. That doesn't mean I won't order the breakfast combo and take my sweet time clearing my plate."

She glanced over her shoulder while still a distance from the table. "This won't be anything like the breakfast we'll cook together tomorrow morning at Devils Tower."

The tiny coo riding her voice caused him to hear it like a dove's promise, one that extended an olive branch of peace. "Thank you for giving me yet another scene to look forward to, Miss Dawes. Until then, I'll loan you back to your friends…and the film crew."

"Don't forget our scripted scene later, on the Avenue of the Presidents."

"Forget? No, I don't think I could." Running out of private space, he winked and followed her like a good sport. Maybe he could pose a pancake eating contest with Andy and try to out-consume a self-proclaimed bear. He definitely needed a rigorous distraction. Plus, the company would be covering the tab.

After pulling out a seat for Glori to occupy, he slid into a sleek molded chair of his own, wondering from which type of plastic it had been cast. For once, he wasn't analytically-minded enough to pursue figuring it out. A platter of pancakes soon made its way over his shoulder while an empty plate landed on his placemat. Before he could ask, Glori passed the syrup dispenser, so he took a stab at the stack and made a sizable claim against the bear cub off his right shoulder. The eating contest was on with a growl—a stomach growl.

~

"That has to be the film crew," Edgar said, standing to go greet them. "Please, let me do most of the coordinating. First and foremost, this is a business proposition—and I'm the acting director." He walked toward the two men with a stiff wave.

"Hey, man. How you folks doing?" the taller man asked. He slid his sunglasses into the neckline of a ratty UCLA T-shirt. "I'm Larry, and my partner here is Cal. Sorry is we're late. Our departure didn't go too smoothly."

Edgar spotted Mason checking his wristwatch. He already knew it was well past ten o'clock, their agreed-to meeting time. He nodded in response and smacked the script across his open palm. "No matter. Do you have the filming equipment ready? As the sun advances, the faces fall into the shadows past noon. I'd rather avoid that if humanly possible."

"Yeah," Larry replied. "Our equipment's waiting right outside the door. Let's pick a spot and get this segment rolling."

Detecting a California-style casualness about the crew, they at least appeared ready for action. "I have scouted out a few spots, but don't know how far back the camera needs to be. We took some still photographs last night, but this is a whole different ballgame."

Larry gestured to the door. "Lead on, Mr. Sterns. We'll let you know if that angle works for us or not. The camera is a man's eye on the world. It never tells a lie."

Mason pushed past, rolling his eyes. When Glori followed, they became a color blur of feigned cooperation. Only Midge stood by him. "Fine, then follow me. We have an hour and a half to get some usable footage."

"You'll have more than you can use," Larry replied with a smile.

"You don't know my cast of amateur actors—but you're about to meet them, clumsy script and all."

"We've likely seen worse," Cal added, winking. He held out a callused palm and gestured for Edgar to lead.

"Come on, Midgey. Help me keep those two presentable." He headed for the door with her right behind him. He found Andy already outside with Glori and Mason. The urge to smoke hit him full force, but he didn't have a spare moment. The campaign swung into full forward gear, now that all the characters were in place, and he was literally paying for it by the production hour. A matter of pride, no one would dare gear down the wheels of progress with him at the helm. As soon as he shoved the door open, he shouted to the amateur cast. "Let's hit it." He held his head high and marched to his first spot, confident and in full control.

~

Glori repositioned at the film crew's recommendation. This third location had more privacy, which she saw as beneficial. A hedge of green shrubs blocked the foot of the slope, which left only the top of the tailings pile with the four majestic faces peering out from the crest of the mountain. As she waited for the cue, she noticed a detached look on Mason's face. "Hey, we almost have this one licked. Stay sharp with me for a few minutes, and then we get to ad lib our way into tomorrow."

He looked at her with a stiff turn of his neck, like he was trying not to get out of position. "This has grown a little too stifling for me. It's like Alfred Hitchcock goes off the far edge. Our director is so dictatorial, I'm afraid I'm losing heart for this entire project."

"Salvage the good out of their direction, and we can incorporate it for an improved tomorrow. We'll stop at the lemonade vendor before heading back to the campground."

He gave her a look from the depths of deprivation. "Do you promise?"

She melted a bit at his sincerity. "Yes, I promise."

"Okay, that audio is good," Larry called. "Let's run through the entire scene, start to finish. Everybody hold your places...and rolling."

As Glori expected, the camera Cal manned began to slide down a sled run. When he stopped on a dime, she delivered the opening line. She shifted her gaze from Mason up to the towering faces, remembering to smile.

Mason delivered his line to perfection. He even seemed comfortable in the process. Cal's camera pivoted to film from front to back, highlighting her affable campaign husband.

She stood and walked to him in a leisurely pace. Once she delivered the last line and stooped to draw his attention, she knew they'd aced the delivery. To finish it off, she gave him the affectionate look the revised script demanded.

"Cut," Larry shouted. "That's a wrap from Mount Rushmore. We'd better get moving."

Imbalanced, Glori teetered into Mason's lap. She squeezed her eyes closed and tried to become a real person in the process. A friendly hand began to rub her shoulder blade.

"Genuine emotion is so much better," Mason said in a low voice. "You think the camera lens would crack if we tried a heaping dose of that?"

"Maybe being real matches the escapism of camping better anyway," she replied. When his hands encircled her waist, she tried to stand on her own two feet.

Mason stood, his expression warming. "Do you still want to stroll along the Presidential Loop, Miss Dawes?"

"Don't I ever," she replied without hesitation.

Mason turned to Edgar and waited for a chance to address him without interruption. "Hey, I wanted you to know that Glori and I will need another hour or so at the park. We might not get back this way for awhile, and she wants to walk the loop."

Edgar diverted his gaze to her, his disgust evident. "Play like children if you must, but we'll roll out from the campground at three-thirty, whether you're there or not."

Like an interpreter ready to set the negotiation between two foreign dignitaries, Glori stepped between the two men. "We all deserve a break. It's been a long two days. Maybe you could have the film crew shoot some footage of the campsite while we're gone."

Midge stepped into the conversation. "Sure, Andy and I can pose the camping gear. It might be nice to have some scenery edited in without any people cluttering things up. It's a sales promo, for pity's sake."

Edgar looked at her and yielded. "Why do you always make such good sense, dear friend? As for the rest of you, get out of my sight." He flung a hand up and swiped the rolled script across the sky.

Glori laughed, hooked Mason's arm in hers, and pulled him into a run.

"Where are we going? The loop starts in the opposite direction."

"But the lemonade starts out here. I made a promise, and I plan to keep it."

His headshake produced a smile, one that cast off the dictatorial cares of the day. "I still like the idea of old Ike being carved into that monument."

She clutched him to her side, mindful of what a precious person he was. "I bet you could mold that image into plastic in no time flat."

"You D-double dare know I could." The gleam returned to his eyes, that genius gleam that told the world he could do anything he set his mind to accomplishing.

Treasuring his response, she sank deeper into the bottomless pit that mutual admiration had first dug. Now—without movie cameras rolling or work records endlessly unfolding—she was free to fall in love. Not that she could help it, but she finally mustered enough courage to allow it. Under the fixed gray eyes of the nation's forefathers, they would stroll around the loop in unforgettable togetherness. Love tasted lemonade-sweet, at least for the day.

Chapter 17

A column of rock jutted its prominence vertically against the sky while Mason eased the Belvedere up to the park's front gate. As national monuments went, Devils Tower pitched its eligibility case with unabashed grandeur. Only a short distance from Rushmore, they had arrived well before the dinner hour. The entrance line shortened, so he moved up a length behind Edgar's Ford. "If I had known how short the drive over was, I would have spent half an hour repacking the trunk to my liking."

Glori glanced up from the travel guide to regard him. "I know you need order, but we had to meet Edgar's deadline. I'll help you neaten up once we unpack."

"Andy has many commendable traits, but being a neat nick isn't one of them. Still, if he can focus on keeping the props in top form, then I can excuse some of the rest."

"I'm truly sorry there's no lake here at the campground. He seemed to enjoy your casting lesson last night."

He drummed his thumbs on the steering wheel. "Andy will get the hang of fishing yet. We have a week at Yellowstone, and I plan to fish in every river, lake, and stream I find."

"I'll cook what you catch—but you have to clean the fish. I can't stand that part." She shivered as if to accent her claim.

"Speaking of cooking, we need to move those steaks to the top of the cooler, so they can begin to thaw."

"Yes, thank you for reminding me. I told Edgar that we didn't need that second bag of ice, but he wants the cooler shots to look sparkling."

"He should snap that picture early then, because the sun looks like it means business today. I wonder if there's any way to juxtapose the tower against the sunset. Maybe I'll suggest something to the film crew."

"Or mention it to Edgar and let him formulate the plan. He likes to feel important."

He looked at her to gauge exactly what she meant. "I didn't sign on to give Edgar Sterns his strokes."

Her demeanor calm, she tilted her head. "Still, harmony between cast members is like oil dripping down Aaron's beard—a sweet fragrance to God."

He checked his knee-jerk reaction as the traffic moved forward. Edgar paid the entry fee just ahead, buying their privilege to take pictures in the park. "Fine. Today already holds one ace-in-the-hole, when we ad lib the script. I'll suggest the sunset shot to Edga, and let him run with it." After the park map made its way into the Fairlane, he prepared to approach the entry gate. He pulled up and reached for his wallet.

The ranger leaned closer. "Your admission was paid by the car ahead of you. Here's a park map, so you don't miss the campground turn-off."

Mason accepted the brochure with the familiar national park badge on the front. "Thank you, and enjoy your day."

The ranger nodded. "Watch your campfire for me."

"Will do," he replied with a mock salute. Once he pulled ahead, Edgar's car merged from the shoulder to lead again. "So, Miss Cook, what are you planning for our dinner tonight?"

"I opted for something easy, because I didn't know if the film crew would join us. I have hamburgers with baked beans and chips. How does that sound?"

"Perfect." The vista opened to a grassy meadow up ahead, and the paved road made an arc around its perimeter. Pleasing to the eye, Mason began to relax. Ever dominant, the columnar tower pointed skyward beyond the meadow's reach. "How's this for a glimpse of tranquility?"

Instead of responding, Glori gripped his shoulder. A tiny gasp escaped her throat.

He slowed the car to better study the surroundings. There, atop mounds scattered throughout the meadow, stood hundreds of prairie dogs, watching the cars pass by. Seeing a gravel shoulder on the far side, he checked for opposing traffic and shot across when the coast was clear. He nosed the Belvedere's grill into the post-and-cable barricade and turned off the ignition. "Ease out my door," he said, reaching for her arm.

Glori slid behind the wheel and followed him out in a crouch. "Oh, look. There's a mother and baby. So darling."

Mason leaned a hip on the front quarter panel and brought her up close beside him. Two larger animals stood on their hind legs to get a better view.

Glori's shoulder pressed his. "I think they're called sentinels—the ones that keep watch. They seem to call a different signal than the other family members."

"Look there—the baby is eating flowers." He pointed to the mound in slow motion.

"This scene gives me hope for the day. How simply wonderful they get to live here unthreatened in the park."

"Well, I'm sure they still have natural predators, but at least the space is set aside, and there's plenty of meadow grass to eat."

"And tiny flowers, too. Can we stay and watch awhile?"

When her blue eyes begged, he had no resolve whatsoever. He glanced up the road and spotted the film crew out on the shoulder setting up to video the colony with the tower looming in the background. "As long as the crew is out, we can stay. I never knew you were such an animal lover, but it's quite evident to me now."

Her fingertips brushed down the front placard of his sports shirt. "All of God's creation is precious to me, but I like the furbearing huggable forms better than the creepy-crawly ones. I would like to learn how to bird watch, because I'm terrible at separating out the different kinds. Some people want to know the names of the stars, but I'll never reach out close enough to touch a star." She broke off her study of the prairie dogs to lend him some direct attention. Soon, a fingertip touched his sideburn. "There's my favorite mole—a constellation all its own."

Drawn by her contact, he slipped an arm around her waist and pulled her against his hip. He stood there in a tight hug, allowing her to watch the colony's antics unfold on a mild spring afternoon. Minutes passed in harmony, feeling her breaths rise and fall against his chest. Finally, out of the corner of his eye, he spotted the crew's exodus across the access road. "The others are ready to get going. Should we join them?"

She smiled up at him. "For now, I suppose. But we can always come back, once we have the film segment done."

"As I'm about to suggest in my ad lib line, I want to spend some time along the perimeter trail. I hope to shoulder into that giant tower and make it lean while I walk by."

Glori broke away with a giggle. She pulled the door open and looked through the window opening at him. "Now, you're talking like one of those colossal heads back at Rushmore."

To match her imagery, he lumbered back stiff-legged, his arms up like a monster. Once he dropped into the car, he stared at her. "You've never looked more radiant than you do today."

"Oh, sure. Practice your lines on me to cheapen the experience." She brushed him away and neatened her hair.

"No practice, Glori. Your face was that of an angel while you watched those prairie dogs. I won't forget that vista for a long while." He winked and started the car, hoping not to fall behind. "Maybe you could open the map and navigate me to the campground entrance."

"Fine. Angels can be useful, too." She pressed her lips together and dimples popped up.

Content to remain behind, he kept his speed down, partly out of respect for the colony's well-being, and partly out of disrespect for their leader in the car ahead. A little independence never hurt anyone, which the next filming session would surely prove.

"The campground is four-tenths of a mile ahead to the left." She closed the brochure and leaned forward to peer at the tower. "I sure hope this scenery speaks to America."

"The land doesn't need our words. It's really about the gear anyway. We'll try the passive sell approach and see how it comes across." When she nodded her consent, he knew they were on the right path. This particular trail circumnavigated an ancient monolith, another precious treasure belonging to America's remarkable landscapes.

~

Glori found the campground only half as scenic as the previous one at the lake, but it came with welcomed shade. Large oaks towered over the campsite, lending a sense of protection. She almost had the hamburgers done in the iron skillet, and there would be plenty for all. The film crew disappeared hours ago and had not returned from their tour of the tower. She glanced up to see Mason putting the last touches on his tent supports.

Midge wandered over with paper plates in her hand. "I have the beans ready in the saucepan. Say the word when I can fit them on the cook stove. Andy's been pilfering chips so fast, I'm sorry I opened the bag."

"Offer him a sweet pickle chip and see if you can get him to switch over." She fiddled with a patty and checked its underside with the spatula. "These need three more minutes, and then we can heat up the beans. Did you find the buns and condiments?"

"Yes, the table's all set, too. Let me give the men a five-minute warning. I think we're closing in on a hearty dinner." She set the plates on the table and wandered down toward Edgar's tent first.

Happier than she'd been in a long while, Glori took a moment to thank God for such provision. She could be trapped at the HR office today, moving piles of paper around. Instead, she had the privilege of camping in the shadow of a world wonder. Through a break in the tree canopy, she spotted the tower and let it elevate her mood.

Mason squatted at her side. "Would you have some cheese to melt on those hamburgers, Miss Dawes?"

"Oh mercy. I've forgotten the cheese. There's a brick of cheddar in the cooler. Can you find it for me?"

"Will do." He winked and darted off to the cooler behind the picnic table. After closing the lid, he detoured to his tent. When he returned, a long fillet knife slit through the packaging at his expert guidance. "How many slices would you like?"

"Let's do at least half, so make it four."

"Correction—let's do five. Lunch was light, so I'm game for eating two. I prefer cheeseburgers."

"But, I'm trying to leave some for the film crew," she protested.

Mason offered the first slice directly off the blade of his knife. "No need. Cal's a vegetarian, anyway. That came up in our conversation of how California differs from Kansas."

"Oh, goodness. I hadn't given that a thought." She took the cheese and leveled it onto one of the larger burgers. Soon, three more slices came her way. "You might save some cheese for your scrambled eggs tomorrow."

His eyebrows shot up. "Right, let's guard our limited resources."

Midge laughed as she approached the table accompanied by Edgar, who seemed highly amused by her girlish antics. She stepped to the table and absconded with the chip bag, putting Andy's pilfering to an immediate halt. "Remember, everything has to be shared."

The young man dropped his chin. "Andy forgot to share."

"That's okay, Andy," Glori replied. "Dinner is almost ready. Edgar, do you care for cheese on your hamburger?"

"No, thank you. But I do prefer my beans warmed up instead of straight from the can."

"Coming up next," she replied. "Okay, Midge. Get your pot ready. I can get the cheese to melt by putting a lid on the skillet. You take the burner."

"Here, Glori." Mason beckoned to her. "Put the skillet on this tree stump. Let's not melt the plastic tablecloth."

She lifted the skillet with both hands and shifted off the stove. Once she placed it on the stump, she retrieved the lid and put it on the pan. "There, I guess that means that your fantastic plastic is not impervious to damage—even at the campsite."

Mason shrugged his shoulders. "Well, sheets of plastic are less durable, but even hardier castings may melt under direct contact with a heated metal pan."

"You mean, like your cooler lid?"

He worked his lips together. "Yes, let's say it makes a better stool or cutting surface than a trivet for hot pans. That lends selective uses that differ from our metal coolers."

Edgar dusted off his palms. "What's the advantage of shifting to plastic then? I don't see what the big brouhaha is all about."

Mason gave Glori a quick wink. "That's because you're having Handy Andy carry all the gear. Try hauling that steel-belted cooler around fully packed with iced-down provisions, and you'll get an inkling of where our improvement is headed."

"I'm all for it," Midge added. "Let's get those burgers in the buns over at the table. By the time we finish, the beans will be plenty hot."

"Coming right up." Glori picked up the skillet and followed her friend to the table where half a jar of pickle chips remained. When Andy gave her an impish grin, she smiled in return. "I made two burgers for you guys, thinking you might be hungry."

"I like the way you think," Mason replied, slipping onto the picnic bench. He moved down a space and took a plate with two cheeseburgers on it.

Glori took the pan back to the stump, while Midge brought the beans over. After helping ladle them out, she checked to make sure the stove was properly turned off. Without a word, she rejoined the group, took the seat beside Mason, and bowed to pray. "Lord, we thank you for this humble campsite. Bless our time together, as we acknowledge that your hand fashioned Devils Tower, though your lesser adversary got its naming rights. Forgive us when we err, and bless the food we're about to receive, amen."

She glanced up to locate the catsup and saw Edgar's mustache stretch to encompass a mouthful of hamburger. Grimacing at her tactical mistake, she should have sat with Edgar and looked across at Mason throughout the meal. A tiny pinch on her hip made her glance below the tabletop. Mason winked while he reached for his burger, causing her regret to instantly vanish. She scooped up a forkful of beans, forever grateful for the campout.

~

His secret pleasure led him to this—stalking around in the night. Camping offered the perfect foil, a less-restrictive community with canvas for walls. Better yet, the mesh panels keeping the night tolerable for sleepers made for opportunistic viewing under the naked moonlight. Born to be nocturnal, he crept to his neighbor's abode and studied its outline to place the night's harm. A small gesture, it still signified his ability to inflict damage on a whim. The rush it left stroked something else, a nameless alley of unmet want held deep inside.

He chose the back corner and made his way around the tent's perimeter, all the while catching glimpses of the sleeping female occupants. His blood warmed at the sight, another charming perk of his hobby. As he unsheathed the knife, he looked for the exact spot to monogram. Nothing could be rushed, least of all his signature puncture mark.

~

In and out of sleep, Mason rolled onto his side to place his back toward Andy. The addition of a folded towel earlier had remarkably reduced his partner's incessant snoring. Though he'd eaten a large supper, the leisure hike back to the prairie dog colony with Glori helped settle the meal. He repositioned his head on the small pillow and tried to fall asleep.

Minutes later, the unmistakable crackle of a plastic wrapper shot him back to full awareness. He sat up and listened for sounds of a marauding animal outside. Glori had been careful not to leave food out, taking pains to clean the pans and throw away the trash down by the bathhouse facility. Still, something could be on the prowl.

Again the plastic crunched. Perhaps a foot had eased off the wrapper, as the sound came muted though distinct. His senses heightened, he slid to the tent's door and began to force the zipper up the seam. Once he had it open far enough, he slipped on his sneakers and grabbed his fillet knife. The flashlight tempted him, but its beam would only give away his position.

He scanned the picnic table area in a crouch. Nothing moved. The cook stove sat closed on one bench, right where Glori had left it. Smoke from a smoldering campfire crossed with the light breeze. He waited, his eyes straining to see.

A slight movement off one corner of the women's tent caught his attention. Staying low, he crept toward the general location. He regulated his breathing and braced the knife's shank up his thumb for leverage. Unthinkably, the shadowy figure stooped to touch the tent. A reactive alarm fired off inside his head.

In three quick steps, he rushed the trespasser. His free hand latched a chokehold on the intruder. The knife blade came to rest broadside against the guy's jawbone. He added pressure so the blade's edge could be felt. "Real slow now, we're going to back away from this tent," he directed in a whisper. To prevent a backlash, he dragged the culprit before he could stand erect. They made it to the Belvedere, where he pressed his catch against the passenger door, belly-first.

"Stop it, Mason, you imbecile," Edgar said in a forceful hush.

"Tell me what you were doing over behind the women's tent at this hour."

"Resetting the loose tent stake I found on my way back from the restroom."

"Liar." He pressed the knife tip toward the man's Adam's apple. "You were up to no good over there, and I caught you red-handed."

"Prove it. Right now, it's your word against mine." He tilted his head back as if to avoid the blade. "Besides, if I told the ranger I was exercising my visitation rights as Glori's fiancé, you wouldn't have a credible leg to stand on."

"No, the shepherd goes through the gate—that's his legitimate access point. You weren't going in the front flap, you perverted stalker, so here's how it's going to be. When we set up at Yellowstone, you take a campsite away from the rest. Excuse yourself to needing more privacy—or whatever the lie. I want you away from the women. Do I make myself clear?"

"I'm not about to concede one fraction of an inch of my authority to you, golden boy. I still call the shots around here for the Coleman campaign. Don't make things miserable for the rest, because of your *misinterpretation* of what you tripped over tonight."

Mason tightened his grip until he could feel the cad swallow. Not satisfied the prowler had expressed due penance for his misconduct, he had to force the issue. "Fake engagement notwithstanding, the women are off-limits to you, Mr. Sterns. Do we have an understanding?"

Seconds ticked by. "All right," he replied, "for now. Have it your way."

He removed his chokehold, but used the freed hand to shove the deviant fop against the Plymouth. Something seemed left undone, as though he needed a guarantee of cooperation. Only intimidation could do that. He had to add some. "Guess there's just one more thing—the compelling need for your next lie. So sorry to hear you cut yourself shaving." With that, he inverted the knife blade and ran the tip across the man's jawline for a fraction of an inch. A shove sent the prowler backpedaling toward his pathetic pup tent.

Burning up from the inside out, Mason dropped onto the picnic bench and relaxed his grip on the knife. His next breaths came labored as he tried to sort out the avalanche of conflicting relations the encounter could possibly taint. The stream seemed endless. Whether to tell Glori became the loudest objector to downplaying the encounter. He wrestled with it for some time before resting his head on his arm and relenting to exhaustion right where he sat.

~

Glori rubbed Mason's arm, thinking he'd had a rough night if the picnic table was his idea of comfortable. "Someone doesn't look like himself this morning." She kept her tone melodic, to better encourage his awakening. When she saw his eyelids flutter, she crouched closer along the bench. "Don't tell me I'm hard to look at in the morning. That might burst my delusional bubble."

He moaned and rolled his head onto her shoulder. "Woe is me."

"Did Devils Tower come crashing down on your tent last night?" She nestled her cheek against the crown of his head. "Poor baby."

"Who's the baby?" Midge asked through the tent's mesh, fighting to pull out her last roller that set her bangs.

"Mason is. It looks like he didn't get his beauty sleep last night. That might not bode well for our filming session today." She ran a fingertip across his forehead. "Tell me if you're not able to cook breakfast with me. We can plan something else. In the meantime, I'll make you some strong coffee. How does that sound?" She'd tipped her head down far enough that her lips scraped his beard stubble.

He stirred under the close-up attention. "Yes, please—coffee. Your face is…most pleasant…for morning."

When he craned his neck to look at her, she saw something unguarded in his soft brown eyes that landed like a caress. No matter how much play-acting came their way today, it would pale by comparison. For a magical moment, the picnic table became a boat buoyed by a current not unlike the wind—unseen but certainly felt.

Midge stood in front of the tent in her rumpled bedclothes. She blinked in wide-eyed disbelief. "Get with it, you two. The filming session is scheduled for eight-thirty this morning. The show must go on. After all, that's why we're all here. If that ain't the folly of Miss Molly's good golly." She shook her head and departed toward the bathhouse.

Glori cupped his chin in her hand and tried to lift him off her shoulder. "You can let me be the strong player today in the skit, if that helps your…deficiency any."

He grunted and sat erect on his own power. "I'll manage somehow, but you can bridge the gap with some clever filler if I'm not following close enough behind your lead." He shook his head and turned to peer inside his tent. "Looks like Andy is sleeping in, too."

Glori couldn't squelch her grin. "Did you two have a break-up last night?"

"No, we're getting along fine, especially since I got him to stop snoring with an extra towel under his pillow. I thought I heard a wild animal rummaging around camp. Guess my vigil ended at the picnic table."

"You might regret that when you stand up to walk."

"I already have tons of regret." He stood and looked down at her for a long interval. "You look more radiant today than I've seen you in a long time, darling."

She chuckled at the familiar line. "Save it until you smell the bacon frying. Remember Larry—the tall guy? When he says 'roll'—that's not a place to spread your butter."

"I'll try to keep that in mind. Let me go get rid of these whiskers, or that wardrobe lady will be all over me. She's serious about her job." He departed toward the Plymouth's trunk.

Mindful of a task left unaccomplished, Glori headed for the green cooler, lifted the lid, and moved the wrapped package to the top. Semi-firm in her grip, the thawing process was well underway. This steak feast would crown their long day after the cast park-hopped to its final destination—Yellowstone. As Mason ambled to the bathhouse, she wondered what geysers might add to the landscape, or would improvisation and timed eruptions prove too odd to mix?

Chapter 18

Within an hour of arriving at Bridge Bay Campground in Yellowstone National Park, a rain cloud scraped across a mountain ridge and the bottom fell out. Glori sat in the big tent, wishing they could have spent time on Yellowstone Lake after arriving through the east park entrance. She didn't count the brief stop at Fishing Bridge general store as an attraction.

She overheard Mason being strict with Andy about not touching the tent's canvas walls to prevent leaks. It lent her comfort that they had chosen a spot close by. Edgar, ever the elusive brooder, took a site much further away and pitched his tent on it in solitude. The celebratory steak dinner would have to be placed on hold if this downpour kept up.

Midge shifted her sleeping mat to adjoin hers. Sitting with her legs crisscross, she animated her expression as a thunderous roar rolled down a nearby mountain. "I'm not feeling too protected despite the trees. I hope this site drains well, or we'll soon be sitting in a puddle."

"That should really remind you of our old days at Triple Star Ranch."

"No, I'd do anything for one of those sturdy cabins right now." She looked up through the rain fly as a distant thunder rolled.

Glori brushed a hand across her arms and tried to stay warm. "For some reason, I'm feeling kind of cozy here." A hearty masculine laugh emanated from the neighboring tent.

Midge leaned forward, her eyebrows arched. "Maybe that has something to do with your co-star. I noticed you two looking pretty chummy. Want to talk about it?"

"What you're seeing is the genuine interaction we promised each other, which is a far cry more authentic than Edgar's marketing script. Mason and I considered the non-pretentious approach a better match for the camping life anyway."

"So when he bends down and looks like he's about to kiss the daylights out of you, that's just for the camera? Is that what you want me to believe?" Her whisper held a sharp edge, turning the question into more of an accusation.

Glori rubbed an imaginary itch on her anklebone. "Mason is definitely special, if that's what you want me to admit. A girl could get used to that kind of attention."

Midge made a noise of disapproval in her throat. Pelting drops rattled off the rain fly as the young trees swayed in the wind. "You've got over two more months to let this engagement thing play out. Are you going to make it? Tell me now—because if you aren't—I might as well head south for cover. There are bound to be some ugly repercussions." Her tone sounded less sure than her words. She refused to make eye contact.

With the intermittent echo of Mason's voice from close by, Glori could scarcely dismiss his influence. Should preferences be told out loud, she'd much rather be trapped in a cozy spot with him than her present company. Just the idea birthed a magnetic attraction of what could be.

To thwart the rising feeling, she hooked her pinkie through Midge's finger and clenched the hold. "I'm trying to make it, mud sister. However, the fake engagement does bother Mason. He's an upright Christian man. In fact, he thinks my oath is an area of unaddressed sin. No doubt, from the outside, it has that glaring appearance."

Midge's eyes grew watery. "Try extra hard, Glori. Only a best friend would understand the sordid ramifications if this whole thing should collapse. I'll try to run interference for you and keep Edgar happy. He and Mason seem to have developed a knack for finding fault with each other. Whew, boy. How much more combustible can it get?"

"Plenty, I'm sure, so maybe the rain is a good thing. Still, consider my position as a play-acting wife and a pretend fiancée. Rest assured there are some real emotions making that rub increasingly uncomfortable. For the camera's sake, I'm trying to hold it together."

Midge wiggled her finger out of the hold and buried her hands in her lap. "We both have to do what's best for the group. That's the only way the campaign will come off a success."

Glori looked at her old friend and then gazed up through the sheeting of the rain fly, hoping God could clearly see their predicament. Only Midge would be well-served by her continued engagement. The oath became a dangling noose, not a ring of promise. *Forgive me, Lord.* She hung her head and let contrition run its course, right through her tear ducts.

About ten minutes later, a familiar pair of sneakers could be seen through the mesh of the tent's front flap. After several trips back and forth, Mason ducked down and jiggled the zipper pull. "Come out, ladies. I think the storm is over for now. Let's think about getting that steak dinner started. Thank goodness we don't have to depend on wet wood to get a cooking fire going. That would make a nice pitch for our Coleman cook stove, wouldn't it?"

"Right you are," Glori replied with a backhand wipe across her cheek.

Midge unzipped the tent and slipped out. "In fact, I'll go track down Edgar and suggest he snap some pictures of us cooking while wearing our rain ponchos—after I stop by the bathhouse, that is."

"Don't rush back, Midge," Glori called behind her. Standing, she examined the treed campsite and the cozy feeling overtook her again. She glanced at Mason and gave a coy smile.

"Let me rig our lovely cook a rain shelter over the picnic table with the tarp I brought. That way, if it rains again, I can still eat my steak dinner in her esteemed company."

Her fingertips played in a tiny puddle on the table. "Look who's being quite the capable camper again. I never should have questioned your contribution to the team." To make the compliment more tactile, she traced her wet fingers through his unkempt hair.

Mason held his gaze a few seconds longer, and then he took a step back. "I'll get that tarp from the trunk now. Are the steaks in the green cooler?"

"Yes, that's right. It probably needs to have the ice melt

drained. I'll dry off the table and wait for you." She sighed as she hunted for the oversized towel she'd taken inside the tent. At long last, the time for the much-heralded steak dinner had arrived, but the cause for celebrating remained unclear.

Like a reprieve, she remembered the new potatoes hiding in a flour sack. She'd have to boil and mash them under this scenario, as the wet ground held no affection for a long-simmering pit-fire for roasting. "I'll save my aluminum foil for another day," she muttered, dragging the towel into service across the rain-soaked tabletop.

~

Mason glimpsed into the dim mirror as he brushed his teeth in preparation for lights-out. The five o'clock shadow darkening his chin and cheeks would have to be shaved off in the morning for the day's filming episodes along sulfur vents and mud pots. Larry and Cal had seemed excited at the prospect. If the steak dinner could propel him into a state of extended sleep, he'd be ready for a piece of that action.

His tent mate banged out of a nearby stall and approached the sink. "Andy ate too much, but steak and mashed potatoes are his favorite."

Mason laughed and spit in the sink to play the tease. "I know the cook, so I'll ask for your least favorite tomorrow night." He pointed his toothbrush at the young man, hoping to get a rise out of him.

"No liver for Andy. He won't eat it." He shook his head hard as if to throw the idea out.

"Ha, no liver then. We'll have to see what the cook plans for us. In two days, we'll be at the lake catching fish. Go ahead and brush your teeth, so we can walk back together. I brought the flashlight in case we need it." He rinsed and tapped his toothbrush across his finger to dry it.

A woman's tittering laugh rippled through the open eaves of the bathhouse. Before long, a catchy sing-song ditty accompanied it. The woman's voice grew more pronounced.

By the time Mason shoved out of the spring-set door, the song had almost reached its crescendo. He hid around the corner to let the duet finish. When Andy prodded him in the back, he had no choice but to make an appearance.

"Hum-dum-de-dum-dum—summer camp," Midge shouted with gusto.

Something about Edgar's immediate flush made Mason hold back his comment. Their dishwashing escapade had obviously struck on a familiar note. Andy pulled the flashlight from his back pocket and shined it onto the footpath. "Do you two need a light?"

"Nope, we're about to finish up this chore," Midge replied.

Edgar stood and brushed off his dungarees. "I've invited Midge over to help me with the script for tomorrow. I didn't know I would need so many intermediate scenes prior to the grand finale at Old Faithful."

Mason nodded, working his lips to one side. "You have a lantern then?"

"Yes." Edgar jutted his thumb over his shoulder, indicating the Fairlane parked by his campsite.

"Please be the gentleman and walk Miss Kerr back to her tent when you're done. We wouldn't want anything to happen to our favorite wardrobe coordinator." He caught Midge's attention with the title and gave her a wink. "I'll take the dishes back and let Glori set them out to dry."

"Good idea," she replied with a wipe of her hands. "That was a great steak dinner."

"Andy's favorite," his companion added.

Edgar snickered, which made his penciled-in mustache dance. "We're finally at Yellowstone, so it feels like everything is bound to work out."

Mason assumed the dishpan from Midge with a clatter. He gave Edgar a protracted stare and glanced at Midge. "I sure hope you're right. Tomorrow, we'll let the sulfur vents decide."

"Larry claims it will look highly dramatic to the camera." Edgar smoothed his upper lip and tried not to smile.

"I hope the script is equally as dramatic then. Good luck you two." He nodded and took off down the path behind Andy. Play-acting to promote camping gear may have counted as the last thing he wanted to think about. He stubbed his toe on a tree root and the dishes rattled in the tub. "Slow down, Andy. I'm having a hard time seeing where I'm going."

The hulking figure took a smaller step. "Sorry about that. Andy's ready to call it a night."

"We'll get the sleeping bags out next, then." Once on the road, they walked together in wordless cooperation. The campsite gave the appearance of being abandoned, until he heard the soft feminine humming coming from inside the big tent. "Oh, it looks like Miss Glori has the same idea. I think she's unrolling her sleeping bag." He shifted the drying towel in place and began to unload the dishes on it.

His tent partner leaned closer. "Andy will laugh if she finds another shoe."

The running tease struck a funny bone so Mason chuckled. "You're pretty okay, do you know that?"

He shook his head and then got a serious look on his face. "Andy wants to work on the new cooler assembly. Plastics are where it's at."

"Yes," Glori agreed with a soothing tone as she joined them. "Plastics are definitely where it's at. I think if you talk to Mr. Coleman, he might allow you to transfer, Andy, but you have to pledge to work at it with all you've got."

Andy nodded and stepped toward his tent.

Mason halted him with a hand on his shoulder. "You're good at repetitive tasks, Andy, the things that need doing over and over. You could be a big help, especially when the plastic is still in slabs and needs to be fed into the lines for molding."

Glori stepped closer. "I can go with you to speak to Mr. Coleman, if that makes you feel better about it."

Andy shot a glance over his shoulder at him, a hint of vulnerability on his face.

The situation needed salvaging. "No, let me go along," Mason insisted. "Andy has already been a big help to me, unpacking an ungainly crate shipped from England. I'll suggest a work station along the assembly line and later train him to make sure he knows what to do."

Andy patted his hand. "I watch and you do, then I do and you watch."

This time, the smile came easily. "I appreciate your can-do spirit, Andy. Keep that in mind when we go fishing, okay?"

He walked to the car with a nod, pulled his sleeping roll out, and maneuvered it through the tent's flap. Before he could be reminded, Andy pulled down the zipper to keep the bugs out of their sleeping quarters. Close by, a click of tin cups reminded him of his unfinished chore.

Glori looked at him while she turned the dishes upside-down. "Did you lose Midge at the bathhouse?"

"Edgar invited her over to his campsite to help write the script for tomorrow. He didn't have anything prepared for the paint pot admiration scene. Larry might be taking us out on a limb with this one, but he thinks the sulfur vents are dramatic."

"Maybe they should have been named 'stink pots' then," she quipped. Her lashes made long shadows in the flashlight's beam as she continued her work. "If you're not too tired, I'm available for company this evening."

"Too bad there's no prairie dog colony to distract you. Believe me, I'm not too tired to keep the camp cook company. In truth, nothing would please me more."

"I wish we could sit around a fire. It always sets the proper mood."

"We have the second lantern. Let's set it on the fire pit's grill and pretend we're all dry and toasty." He rubbed his palms together and waggled his brow at her as he stepped into the dark. In short order, he had retrieved the lantern from the trunk. With the strike of a match, the mantles lit. He sat the lantern on the tabletop and adjusted the setting to a warm glow. After the last dish found a place to dry, he captured her hand and led her to the campfire site. A heavy iron grate soon served as the lantern's pedestal.

Her eyes invited his attention. "Tell me something about yourself, Mason. Besides your plastics work and education, I hardly know much about you."

"Fair enough." He crouched over a flat stone and settled onto it. "Here's something that I should reveal, if we're going to know one another better. I'm a self-taught numismatist." He opened his palms to show he had nothing to hide with the disclaimer.

Her brow furrowed. "I've not heard of that before. Is it a status or a club?"

He shook his head, enjoying her direct attention. "No, by every measure, it's a hobby. It simply means that I'm a coin collector."

She drew back, her lips forming a circle. "I saw you at Park Villa that day with Linda. You paid for the skeet ball and then were delayed at the counter. I thought you lacked the correct change, but you were on the hunt for rare coins, weren't you?"

"Indeed I was. I made the vendor an offer he couldn't refuse."

She covered her mouth and then slowly let her guard down. "You didn't place a wager on the outcome of our game, did you?"

"Oh, no. Everything remained above board, I assure you. I simply told him I was looking for wheat pennies and would offer him a two-to-one replacement if he had any."

"I know he humored you, because Linda and I had to wait. Did you collect any wheat pennies to make it worthwhile?" She slipped her sneakers off as if getting more comfortable.

He grinned as the latent truth became revealed. "I received two wheat pennies that day. But I'll tell you the secret of the search-within-the-search. While the merchant fingers through his coin collection, I train my eye to catch anything out of the ordinary—an off-center strike, a clipped planchet from a misfeed, or even a missing clad layer that makes a nickel carry a coppery sheen. He could be holding a treasure trove of imperfection in his stash and never realize it."

"That sounds fascinating. How did you get started?"

"When I turned twelve, my grandfather gave me a mercury dime, saying it wouldn't be around much longer. They replaced that coin with Roosevelt dimes in forty-six, so I kept collecting until I had over two hundred mercury dimes. I added wheat pennies along the way and even have a few 'steelies' that were only produced in forty-three."

"How fun that must be for you. I can see the enjoyment radiate in your eyes."

"It has been, yes. The mintage or rarity of the type drives the value, as does condition."

She made a humming sound in her throat. "Tell me what those condition ranges are, so I know how to be a good penny when I want to be of value to you."

"That kind of favoritism would start out at 'very good' and climb through 'fine,' 'very fine,' 'extremely fine,' and 'uncirculated.' But the ultimate realm of superior condition is 'brilliant uncirculated' which bears a perfect, bright, and consistent luster."

She crossed her ankles and rubbed her hands down her pedal-pushers. Seeming contemplative, she tilted her head and looked at him, her eyes reflecting the lantern's glow. "If you've developed such discernment, would you recognize a brilliant uncirculated specimen upon discovery—even under low lighting, like one might experience in a manufacturing plant?"

The nuance of her question floated out of the realm of hobby into something much more personal. Perhaps a lesser woman would have been fishing for a compliment, having voiced such a suggestive detour. But the earnestness of her tone spoke of another matter, perhaps a tentative measure of the heart. He'd have to find middle ground to play it safe. "Luster can occasionally seem like an internal quality, such as a radiance coming from within. It requires an expert eye and a keen discernment to value the ultimate state of condition."

"Would a man with a pocket full of ordinary pennies recognize the value of ultimate?"

He sent a wizened look across the lantern's low beam. "The closer one gets to the object of ultimate value, the more apparent its desirability becomes." He dropped his chin, but didn't break his gaze. "I know what I like. What about you, Glori? Do you collect anything?"

Her expression warmed. "When Linda turned one, I bought her the first of a set of fashionable dolls. She receives a new one each year. While searching for the right selection, I stumbled upon a line of miniature dolls whose eyes blink and tiny arms move. I purchase one each year from the birthday money my parents give me, with the thought of handing them down to my own daughter one day. I'm sure that sounds silly—a grown woman collecting tiny dolls."

"No, not at all. It sounds like there may be an extremely fortunate little girl someday, one with reddish blonde hair like her mother who might be the apple of her father's eye." When she folded an arm across her midsection, he worried that the night had grown too chilly. "It's cool out, because of the rain earlier. Let me move beside you and bring the lantern closer. That should chase off the chill." He made quick work of the move and enjoyed the improved proximity right away. "There, that's much better."

Glori stared at the lantern. "Would you like to ask the next question?"

Since one had been digging at him for awhile, he might as well get to the bottom of it. "I know you and Midge go way back. I heard you singing that camp song the night we coordinated wardrobes. Tonight when I left the bathhouse, I heard Midge and Edgar singing the same peppy song, so my question is, did Edgar attend the same camp, too?"

Glori gnawed her bottom lip before responding. "He did, as the sailing instructor at Triple Star Ranch. He's three years our senior, so we thought it pretty special to be noticed by such a big-man-on-campus during our lessons." She laughed, but it fell flat.

Though the information made him feel like the odd man out, he had to get at the crux of the matter. "If they're old chums, then I suppose I don't have to worry about Midge being over there alone with Edgar at his campsite."

Glori flitted her wrist as though to fling off the heedless innuendo. "No need to worry."

Her hasty dismissal dug his heightened discretion. "Is that because Edgar's engaged to you? Is that the safety net of proper behavior?"

"No, I trust Midge, that's why." She blinked and stared at him.

She had spoken with such matter-of-fact surety, Mason knew to drop it for now. He grew momentarily uneasy, certain that no relationship could be impervious to such a dagger-in-the-back as betrayal built on unfounded assumptions. For the first time, he sensed a gullibility about Glori that might leave a microscopic fissure open in her armor for hurt to permeate. Hoping to high heaven he might be wrong, he peered into the upper realms and found only occluded skies.

Glori picked up a stick and drew in the dirt. "A group of ranchers in western Colorado once spotted a light hovering above the evening horizon and thought they had discovered a new star. As it turned out, the light came from a Coleman lantern in a fire lookout tower some forty miles away. Tales like that lent our lantern the nickname, 'Sunshine of the Night.'"

"Those are the kind of tall tales the Coleman historian should be telling, not just sitting in some back room compiling Proof Books that will only yellow with time."

She stopped drawing and looked sideways at him, her eyes like dark sapphires set in alabaster. "We're now taking all interested bidders for the role of company historian. If you have a suggestion,

I'm listening."

Her radiant profile in the lantern light proved too much to resist. A traitor, his hand lifted and the knuckle of his index finger stroked her exquisite cheek. "There's much to be admired here. I hope the new script allows me to portray it fairly." His tone turned husky with the admission.

"I hope the backdrop of stink pots won't diminish your message then, Mr. Porter." She smiled and ducked into his touch, so much that her cheek soon lay in his open palm.

He leaned to deliver his message into her hair. "An engineer is not easily distracted."

She rubbed her arms and gave a tiny hum in response. When her head came to rest on his shoulder, it seemed the highest commentary of all.

Awash in the tactile aura of their connection, Mason rubbed his chin against the crown of her head and tried to think of a response to the historian dilemma. Someone still moving forward, but capable of looking back would embody the truest keeper of the company's record. Drawn from the assembly floor, talents like that were rare indeed. Since Andy wanted into manufacturing, perhaps someone wanted out. That juxtaposition played against the tender elements of the night until his arm found Glori's trim waist, and all logical thought vanished.

Chapter 19

A wooden catwalk wrapped the most primitive landscape Glori had ever observed. Seething and steam-filled, the earth's crust seemed to be at odds with the immediate atmosphere above it. Accumulations of sulfur encrusted every inch of surface, forbidding plants to grow.

She strode past two blue-eyed sink holes banded in orange and yellow. The film crew hoped to shoot across this color-rich dotted landscape from a distance to zoom in on the percolating field of mud pots, where the morning's promotional scene would be filmed. Dressed in maroon red, she certainly contrasted with the setting, so strike one up to Midge's intuition.

The molasses muffin purchased at the general store had made quick business of breakfast, another victim of a tight filming schedule. Once the culminating geyser scene was captured tomorrow afternoon at Old Faithful, Larry and Cal would head back to California, allowing their schedule to relax for the remaining three-day return to Kansas. She passed a strong sulfur-ridden area. When her nose began to burn, she broke into a trot to gain distance from its source. Without a breeze, the steam vapors pulled up from the earth like hastily-drawn curtains to ward off the unknown, a mystical spectacle.

Midge waved from a straight section of boardwalk. "You have to see these crazy bubbling pots," she called through cupped hands.

Glori threw her arms in the air and increased her pace to exhibit her cooperation. Where Mason knelt along the railing, the color had drained from the landscape. The unstable ground appeared a monotone tan-gray. No wonder the film crew had wanted to throw the vivid-colored sink holes into the foreground of this washed-out geographic error. At closer glance, she questioned whether they should relocate the scene.

Midge headed toward her in a clipped pace. "I need to get off the set before someone mistakes me for Lana Turner." She pressed her perm into place behind her ears. "That happens all the time, you know. I do feel sympathy for Lana." She smirked while passing, adding a wink.

"See if Andy and Edgar can help move Larry and Cal after the zoomed sequence," she called over her shoulder. She fixed her gaze on Mason, looking muscular and svelte in his burgundy sport shirt. With a force surpassing the sulfur fumes, the magnetism of attraction drew her toward him. She hesitated along the railing, steps away from his position. In deference to the camera, she knelt to match his lowered profile.

"Good morning, Miss Dawes. I hope you slept well after our welcoming rainstorm yesterday evening."

"Yes, too bad it didn't clear up this rancid sulfur vent curdling the morning air. If this is as fresh as it gets, I don't think this area will be my favorite." A low bubble of air escaped the earth's surface with a percolating sound, causing the mud around it to spatter. "Oh, my goodness. What just happened?"

Mason chuckled as he stood and leaned against the railing. "These are mud pots. The volcanic gasses rise slower here, so the mud coats the surface and burps now and then."

A pot further out gave a pop, which was soon followed by a symphony of slow motion activity. Mesmerized by the synchrony, Glori allowed the underplayed scene to reset her lowly opinion of the mud pot geologic feature.

"As to our conversation last night, I have a recommendation to make." He leaned on his elbows and turned to regard her.

"You're not going to suggest that I start collecting off-centered wheat pennies, are you?" Her brow hitched into her bangs to echo the absurdity of the suggestion.

A wry smile etched into his clean-shaven cheeks. With the mud pots firing off in the background, that combination composed quite an impressionistic painting. "No, coin collecting isn't for everyone. I meant regarding the vacant position of company historian."

That reference held enough open-ended interest that her pulse elevated a bit. A mud pot percolated nearby. "Do make your suggestion, Mason. I'd enjoy entertaining that thought."

"What about Lenard Sanders for the position? He can't go back to the lantern inspector's position. Given that he can still read, he might find that historian role stimulating." He held out a hand toward her, as if to lend the concept wings.

So taken with the possibility, she clapped her hands to her cheeks. "Oh, yes, good Lord above. That could be a match made in heaven, all right." The sputtering mud pots soon inspired a little hopping session when joy from the potential solution bubbled up in her chest and set her feet in merry motion. She laughed and extended her arms toward him to instigate a hug.

Instead, Mason stepped toward her, swept her into his arms, and twirled her around in a majestic circle. "Look who's lighting up the landscape now."

She laid back in his arms, kicking her feet up in merriment. "What an unbelievable way to celebrate the morning."

He nuzzled into her neck. "You're sweeping me away, Glori."

"Who knew mud pots could be so romantic?" When she stroked his chin, he turned close enough their lips almost brushed, launching a desire that they might collide on purpose. Across the railing, the mud pots' percolating puckers only heightened the sensation. Her throat grew dry, so she wiggled to get down, hoping to quell the internal fire being fanned by their connection.

Mason drew her against the railing at his side and seemed content to stand wordless, watching the semi-liquid landscape gurgle.

In scant minutes, Midge came running down the catwalk. She stopped with a grin and wrapped her in a huge hug. "Glori, that last action turned out downright marvelous. I don't know how you two came up with that twirling scene, but with the color pools in the foreground, it turned out to be something else. Wait until you view the footage, you're going to love it."

Bolstered by the outcome, Glori took heart. Maybe things would work out for a successful campaign. She hooked a crooked pinkie in the air and her friend joined hers with the same. "Mud pot sisters are the best."

Midge laughed. "Absolutely. Golly, Pete. Larry thinks you two have great chemistry for the video camera. In fact, he'd like to have it culminate in a kiss during the eruption of Old Faithful tomorrow for the final scene."

Glori clapped her hand over her mouth while her deepest-held desire somehow rose to the surface amid the mud pots. When she turned to gauge Mason's reaction, she read all-out apprehension on his face. She tried to swallow and tasted sulfur on her lips instead.

"Here's a warning," Midge said in a low tone. "Edgar stamped his foot in protest over the suggestion of an improvised kiss. You'd better get this worked out before tomorrow's session. The way it looks right now, having two husbands is more a curse than a blessing. Whew, boy." She shook her head in empathy.

"I'll see what I can do," she replied, attempting to look cooperative. Too bad only the mud pots had permission granted to pucker up any time they wanted. When she saw that Mason's expression had frozen to stone, she couldn't find an ounce of freedom anywhere in the vicinity. The film crew approached up the boardwalk to capture the next scripted scene, trailed by Edgar and Andy lugging gear. Cardboard characters or not, the filming sequence had to happen. She'd have to coax her engineer-friend back out of his shell like a good mud pot turtle, if such a wary creature even existed.

~

"Might I have a word with you, Glori?" Mason asked with mild expression.

Midge winged her with an elbow while collecting the tin dinner plates. "You go ahead, sweetie. I'll get these washed before taking a look at the final script with Edgar."

Glori wiped her hands on the towel and gave him a wistful smile. "I guess I'm done with duty, then. Sure. Would you like to take a walk?"

He gestured to the campground entrance road and waited for her to join him. Still seated at the picnic table, Andy tucked the flashlight into his back pocket when they passed. "Thanks, buddy. Watch over Midge for me until we get back."

She glanced up from her work with her brow knit. "Unless I'm with Edgar, of course. Andy, I'll let you know when I get back from his campsite."

Mason walked away from camp and established a leisure pace up the wooded lane. Soon, the trees thinned to allow a view of

Yellowstone Lake. Not trusting conversational banter, he'd wait until they found the right spot to have this loaded discussion. He needed isolation almost as much as he needed her cooperation. Things might get volatile—and then where would he be left standing?

After crossing the loop road, he stepped up onto a raised boardwalk that flanked the west bank of the expansive lake. With the vista opening up, perhaps he could derive some clarity as they worked through the present difficulty. They strolled twenty yards down the weathered planking until he spied an unoccupied bench with a perfect lake view. "How about here?" he posed, gesturing to the bench.

"Fine, that's nice." She pulled in her blousy shirttail and settled into the seat. "Thank you for breaking my pattern of nightly chores. I think I've traded up, most definitely."

He sat and slid back to rest against the wood. On the verge of being too late, he silently sent up another prayer that his course of action might be justified. At least he'd be out with the truth and maybe get some sleep tonight. When she folded her hands in her lap, it seemed like the proper time had arrived. "I wanted to talk to you about tomorrow."

"Yes, that's our Old Faithful scene. I believe it's scheduled for the ten forty-five eruption. Larry wants the sun overhead. If the wind blows just right, we might get a rainbow to halo the entire scene. That would make our grand finale perfect in my estimation."

He shook his head in disagreement. "No, not perfect—because of my involvement. I need to apologize to you up front, especially since you selected me for your campaign husband."

She turned halfway toward him. "What in the world? Honestly, you've been an excellent co-star, if you don't mind the celluloid term. I can't imagine having anyone else in the scenes with me, cross my heart on it."

He gave her a tired smile. "That places a soothing balm on my embattled heart, but I'm afraid further wounding is unavoidable at this juncture. You see, I simply cannot do the Old Faithful scene and give Larry the culmination he requested. I'm going to state the problem succinctly for your awareness, as I wouldn't want you to think it stems from any shortcoming on your part."

Glori turned and tucked one calf under her other leg, so she could better face him. "Speak your truth then, as it's important to me, more than you could know." She blinked and locked gazes with him, seeming ready.

He threaded his fingers together to keep from touching her, which would only exacerbate matters. "Every day that we spend time together, I feel like we're growing closer. I thrill at holding your hand, and then I hold your waist and soar even higher. I pick you up in my arms and suddenly I'm the grandest man on earth. However, I cannot trespass on another man's territory with a wandering kiss—I cannot, and I will not."

"I told you, Mason. This engagement is phony. This diamond ring leverages Edgar's inheritance coffer open prematurely. It means nothing more to me." She shook her head with an incredulous look on her face.

"Yet, you forget what it looks like to the rest of the world, Glori. It stands for a promise of furthered endearment. Were that *my* plight, to be so dearly held, but I'm the odd man out in this arrangement, while Edgar still sits cozy. So here's my proposition for you this evening. Please have the grace to hear me out."

She stood, wringing her hands. "I'm not so sure that I can. If you want out of the geyser scene, then find a way to sit out. Go fishing or something. I will commit to the filming schedule and see the campaign sequence through, husband or no husband."

"Please, come sit back down with me." He reached for her arm and helped guide her back beside him. "Thank you for humoring me. I want to be upfront about the kissing scene. It's not really about that one orchestrated kiss, it's about the one that happens afterwards—or quite possibly—the one that doesn't happen afterwards. Though I assure you my attraction is genuine, the whole situation had become too convoluted, like a knotted net of entrapment. For the life of me, I cannot swim into that kind of ordeal—not for you or for Coleman Company."

Her sapphire eyes fired with intensity in the day's dimming light. "What exactly do you want, Mason?"

"I want you to break off the engagement, that's what I came to request. You can have only one object of your utmost affection. I need to know if it's me—or Edgar. Simply put, the engagement must be off for the final scene at Old Faithful to hold my kiss. We cannot subsist on play-pretend, you and I. There's something more to be redeemed, and I want it honorably."

"If I break the engagement, I do more than rid myself of Edgar's dull company." She hung her head, neglecting the lake view. When she looked back up, her eyes had misted with emotion. "Once upon many summers ago, a hapless young woman attended camp with her head full of notions of growing up as a dearly-beloved wife. However, she came home as a tossed-aside love interest and became a mother-to-be for nine months instead. The baby was placed up for adoption, and the entire matter squelched, so that scars could heal and lives might go on."

Unexpected, the story numbed him as the sordid details emerged. "Dear Lord, Glori. You're not saying that young girl was *you*?"

She tilted her head, her eyes now clear. "Part of the oath I swore is to not speak the truth about the parties involved. The unadvised engagement was fashioned to fix all wrongs." Her laugh sounded more like a gasp.

"Do you mean that Edgar somehow found out about it and threatened to reveal the truth?" His stomach quivered at the lurid thought.

"I assure you that Edgar does not know the full truth. He eavesdropped on a vital conversation, but misconstrued the characters. If the engagement is broken before he inherits his grandfather's money, then his silence will be lifted—a leverage point he has made quite clear. Beyond my reputation, it might cost me my job at Coleman and my officer position with the Soroptimist Club. I've also had nightmares that the elders of my church will throw me to the curb. So you see that outcome is disconcerting at best, and catastrophic at worst."

He leaned forward, bracing his elbows on his knees. The rancor seeped deeper than he'd even imagined. No wonder Glori had lasted this long on the arm of that worthless fop. She had determination to keep the lid on a past mistake—albeit not her own personal error. That left a question he had to ask. "Would you confide the identity of the unwed mother to me, that I might better understand the implications of this tangled mess?"

She looked up, her gaze almost a caress. A tear found her cheek and her lips trembled at the corners. "I made an oath, so I cannot. Today, that oath still stands."

"And what of tomorrow, Glori? Will the oath still stand?"

"Who can see tomorrow from the edge of a lake?" Her shoulders shook before she stood.

He rose and took her elbow. "Let me have the honor of walking you home tonight, in the event my tomorrow never comes."

She only made in half a dozen steps before turning to collapse in his arms right there on the boardwalk. Together they stood as the breeze blew around them, united in an unbreakable hardship, contrived in deceit. On occasion, her chest heaved while she cried over the ultimatum, her arms entwined around his neck. Inside his collar, hot tears trickled down his chest to an unyielding heart. He would have her daily or not have her at all—with the latter seeming more likely, despite the moment's embrace. Only the nimble fingers of God could untie the knots separating them. For once, Mason doubted whether the Keeper of Justice would even want to.

~

At the first light of dawn, Glori awoke from a fitful sleep and began her morning meditations to remain mindful of God. If she could concentrate on his sovereignty, perhaps she could ignore this barrel she teetered over. Sick to her stomach at having to forfeit Mason and all the hopes he represented, she fought to gain her future while remaining protective of her past. *Could the two somehow coexist?* That had been the crux of her night-long prayer—to no avail.

The first sounds of the morning filtered through the mesh tent flap. The whir of a zipper pulling up meant that Mason had stirred to begin his day. What might he think of her reticence to make a decision in his favor? God forbid that he would accept any blame. No, the fault landed squarely on her shoulders, though she continued what she deemed necessary to restrain an unkempt hell from breaking loose.

"No, baby, no," Midge murmured from her bedroll. Her trunk twitched, and she released a low moan.

Glori reached for her and shook her closest shoulder. "Wake up, Midge. I think you're having a nightmare."

"Oh, what? Yes, it was frightful," she admitted in a weak

voice. "What day is this?"

"Thursday, our last day of filming, and then it's a leisurely drive back home. Come on, let's hit the bathhouse together." She rummaged through the bedding and found her clothes, which she shucked on without ceremony. The wrinkles matched her disposition perfectly. She unzipped the tent and rose to face the day. The bathhouse became her immediate destiny.

After washing her face and applying some cold cream, Glori began to experience a void of purpose. Without Mason's full attention and cooperation, the script would regress to lame perfunctory at best. She sighed and brushed through her hair until Midge joined her at the sink. "What am I supposed to wear today, mud sister? I've all but forgotten what comes next."

Midge turned back to her to unzip her cosmetic case. "I think you're in blue today—that medium blue cotton blouse with the sweet gathers at the neckline."

Glori caught an eyeful of something, but it sure wasn't blue. A smudge of Midge's red lipstick smeared the back of her collar. It's origin certain, how it got to such an odd spot was the question. "What were you doing with Edgar last night?" She glanced at her old friend in the mirror as if she scarcely knew her.

"I told you, we went over the final script. He caved in and wrote Larry's requested kiss into the geyser eruption." Midge shrugged her shoulders and pulled her eyelash curler out.

"Well, I think something caved in all right." With her blood running hotter by the second, she hoisted the smeared collar to the mirror so that Midge could get a good look at it. Her friend's guilt-laden reaction said it all. "You two have something going on, don't you?"

"Edgar had a bottle of wine. He wanted me to celebrate with him, so I had a glass—or two." She switched eyes with the curling clamp, acting as though it meant nothing.

Glori's lungs almost collapsed from the pressure. "Midge, I'm standing on a precarious ledge trying to protect you. Is this how you repay me in return?" She smoothed a hand over her shirt, trying to tame the ridiculous wrinkles that made her appear inept. With Midge one mirror over primping for the day's benefit, the difference in their positions became acute.

"What are you squawking about, Glori? That ring on your

finger doesn't mean a thing. Edgar is available, and he invited me to join him. I did what any present-minded girl would do and had a nice evening with an attentive man. End of discussion." She tossed the curler back in and pulled out her cake of mascara to paint black onto her eyelashes.

The ground under Glori's feet erupted—and not from volcanic activity. "This ring?" She flashed her hand in the mirror. "Don't you ever mention this godforsaken ring to me again for as long as we both live." She turned and could not exit the bathhouse fast enough. Spotting the Fairlane, she made long strides until she arrived at Edgar's campsite. Through the mesh, she saw him positioned to make his exit. She held back her steam, but like the geyser ready to blow, it came with pent-up pressure.

"Oh, good morning, Glori. To what do I owe this pleasure?" He halted the blossoming smile when he read her angered expression. Instead, he tucked his shaving kit to his chest.

"What in the world do you mean making out with Midge over here last night? Did you think I might find that acceptable? Well, here's what I say—you can forget this whole stinking arrangement. In all honesty, I'm tired of being caught in the middle of this travesty. I hereby break this phony engagement and all your expectations that go with it. I've had it up to here." She gestured over her head and then worked the ring off with all the drama the moment deserved. "Hold out your hand and take it like a man." When he did, she slapped the ring into it with extra force. For the first time all morning, she found her balance.

"You're going to be abysmally sorry, you little hothead. Midge and I were just having a few laughs, but I'm afraid when I'm done shredding your reputation, you'll have forgotten how to laugh. And one more thing, you have an obligation to this company to finish out the campaign. If I so much as see one capitulation of duty, I'll go straight to Mr. Coleman with it."

She backed away, counting to five in her anger like her mother had taught her. Next, she drew a calming breath. "You'll have your final script acted out, Edgar, and no one will be the wiser. Furthermore, I suggest you never try to one-up me with Mr. Coleman, as he and I are pretty close." She fought the urge to spit in his eye, though Edgar truly deserved it.

"When I shine the light on your past dalliance, maybe you will no longer be regarded as everyone's little darling. Did you ever think of that?" His eyebrows flinched to drive it home.

Sick of his presence, she wheeled around and headed back to the campsite in an effort to redeem the day. The unremitting urge to wash her hands looped over and over in her mind. Opening the back door of the Plymouth, she located the blue shirt with the gathered neckline and tried to match it to a darker skirt. Selecting a light shade of brown, she could play the role of a lone tree stump against the sky, a role that matched her emotional wardrobe to a tee. The aroma of bacon frying crossed the campsite, but failed to evoke even the first pangs of hunger.

~

Breakfast came marred by a wet blanket that snuffed out the amicable conversations he'd grown used to around the table. Mason passed a lone plank of cold bacon to Andy. "Are you ready to go trout fishing, buddy?"

Andy glanced at Edgar before sheepishly taking the bacon. "Andy is ready."

Mason nodded, not looking for similar permission. In a day lopsided with unreasonable expectations, starting off knee-deep in a glacial lake was the only remedy he could fathom. Resolute, he stood and scanned the picture-perfect campsite. Perhaps he was the only component with careworn edges. "Good, then. I'll get my tackle box, and we'll be off."

Edgar squelched an objection in his throat. "You know the final filming centers around the ten forty-five eruption, right?"

Mason tossed a glaring look over his shoulder. "Yes, I remember." As he stepped toward the Plymouth for the fishing gear, he spotted Glori pouring coffee grinds into an empty can nearby. He found the tackle box and hoisted it from the trunk.

His partner approached with two poles in his grip. "Andy has your fishing pole."

When he nodded his approval, his gaze drifted in Glori's direction.

She waved with the percolator basket, her vacant expression unreadable.

At the last second, he remembered to grab the spare cooler. After slamming the trunk closed, he fell into step alongside Andy, and they made their way beyond the campground into the heart of the park. A herd of magnificent elk grazed an open meadow, languid in the morning sun. Countering the thrill of unexplored territory, the weighty vision of Glori standing all alone played back against his mind's eye. Not until they'd hike three-quarters of the way to the lake did he realize her slender fingers had been bare against the percolator's basket. The breath he blew out turned into a whistling reprieve, and somehow, he regained balance in the lopsided day.

~

Glori stretched her shoulder out, stiff from carrying the gear. "Okay, but if anything does go wrong, we can set up for another eruption in sixty-five minutes." She traced the gathering cluster of on-lookers for signs of Mason and Andy. The ranger's sign predicted the time of eruption at ten forty-six, which gave the missing men six minutes to materialize.

"I'd rather not wait," Larry replied. "We have a long drive ahead of us." He put up a cordon rope between two cones and helped Cal get the rail track down for the in-motion camera.

"We'll make the most of it no matter who shows up," Edgar said to no one in particular.

Midge swatted her with the rolled-up script, her eyebrows arched in expectation.

To kill time, Glori took the script and studied the exchange, a total of six lines. They'd filmed the sequel scene this morning at the campsite to better feature the gear, so now they had to get this end cap in place. Metaphorically, the story would conclude, but Glori sensed a lack of closure that would need further addressing. For one, she needed a ride back to Wichita, though currently alienated from both drivers. She'd eat humble pie, if served by the ultimate outcome.

"Okay, let's get into position to film without the male counterpart," Larry said. His face soon disappeared into the viewfinder of his camera.

"What do you want me to do about dialogue then?" Glori asked. "I can't talk to myself."

Larry pulled back and studied the crowd. "Maybe you could talk to America—and not someone in particular. Most of the dialogue is your impression of the geyser, so share your comments on Old Faithful. Inspire the nation to go camping one last time."

"Fair enough." When Midge outfitted her with the tiny lapel microphone, she managed a brief smile. The crowd began to build around them.

"Go knock 'em dead, Glori. Prove that you're the centerpiece of this whole campaign."

"That's a pretty tall order, given that my current co-star is the most iconic geyser on the continent." She took a deep breath and straightened her back. Her character would be ready for the camera, even though the flesh-and-blood woman beneath the veneer was not. How she wished she'd discussed the situation with Mason beforehand, but he'd left with Andy to go fishing right after breakfast.

"Better get in position now, Glori," Cal said. "Remember, break left to study the eruption, as that's the direction I can migrate with you to pan the shot."

Edgar stepped promptly into her path. "Don't forget. We have no way of knowing if the eruption will last a minute and a half or a full five minutes. Get the requisite lines said in the first forty-five seconds, and then you can ad lib the rest—as you've demonstrated such an amateur fondness for doing."

"You'll have your dialogue, Mr. Sterns. How's my audio, Larry?" She turned to catch his thumbs-up signal. "Excuse me, then. I've never met a geyser before, and it's high time I did." As she broke away from Edgar's glare, an unseen force lightened her steps. By the time she stood at the cordon rope, the exhilaration of the encounter swept her into a higher state of mind. *Thank you, Lord, for lending me the grace to do this.*

A forceful steam bank rammed against the rocky crevice that split the meadow roped off by the park rangers. Seconds later, the first frothy splash of water spewed from the ground. As though a switch had been thrown, the pent-up pressure yielded a full-blown geyser next, earning a collective gasp from the crowd. While the awe still registered in her fast-beating heart, Glori recited the opening line of the dialogue, addressing the American people. She added a personal reflection on the phenomenal sight, and then broke left to begin the scripted meander.

As she delivered the next penned reflection, she caught motion from the corner of her line of sight. Turning from the geyser, she spied Mason running up the roadside, the red plastic cooler swaying in his hand. Touched by the poignant sight, she made a dash to unite, hoping the geyser's spout-off would last. "God bless America," she managed to say as her throat choked with emotion. Shed of the script, she tasted freedom and fled toward it.

"Mason—over here," she directed, giving a windmill wave over several latecomers. Determined for the meet-up, she brushed a tear away and leapt up to see over a large group advancing toward Old Faithful.

"Glori—I'm coming," Mason shouted in a sprint. He hauled the cooler over a roadside cable and made a diagonal dash toward her.

The distance between them evaporated to nothing, and when he set the cooler at her feet, she plunged into his open arms with unabashed laughter. "You made it, darling. You made it in time to see the geyser." Her eyes swept his features, eager to take in every detail.

"What geyser?" he posed, lowering his face to align for the closing.

Tingling with expectation, Glori tiptoed up to fill the gap, and soon her lips were sealed with his in a kiss that even Old Faithful couldn't stop. The pleasure it brought spoke of pent-up pressure, so she allowed a few extra seconds to let him vent—a masterful collusion of touch.

As if latent with his awareness of an unfulfilled obligation, Mason broke away and hoisted her off her feet. He positioned her on his shoulder and stepped closer to watch the remainder of the eruption with the admiring crowd.

She cupped her hand around Mason's chin and watched the magnificent water show in awe. From the perimeter, she spotted Larry giving a thumbs-up which released her from any further obligation for the campaign. The geyser took no such orchestrated direction while it continued to spout off for the full five minutes. *How absolutely glorious.*

Chapter 20

Lost in a productive work session, Mason hurried to neaten the table when he looked up and saw Mr. Coleman at the lab door. "Good morning, sir. Could I assist you in any way?"

The president stepped inside the lab, focused on his latest project—the picnic jug. "I believe you've already been of great assistance, Mr. Porter. I've just come from Marketing, where I previewed three magazine layouts for the promotional campaign. I selected the breakfast scene for the Ladies Home Journal advertisement. Between you and Glori Dawes, I think you hit that assignment out of the ballpark."

The first real feedback he'd received, relief filtered his next thoughts. "Thank you, sir. We tried to be mindful of the gear when staging the scenes, and then we let our love for camping steer us from there."

"All of which is evident. Now, regarding the photo shoot at the geyser, I've chosen to delay that affectionate exchange until the December issue."

"Were there photographs? I thought we were only filming, but in truth, I rushed onto the scene at the last minute, for which I'll blame six cutthroat trout—all longer than my forearm." A sporting smile chased his disclaimer.

"That explains the need for the cooler. In deference to Old Faithful spouting off in the background, that cooler is the only piece of camping gear in the entire picture. But the chemistry captured is so compelling, and Yellowstone is so iconic, I committed to using the photo. You understand the obvious hitch in all of this, don't you Mr. Porter?"

"Well, sir. That plastic cooler isn't available to the purchasing public yet. I don't know what we could do about that."

He gave a nod as he traced a finger around the opening of the newly-cast jug. "Here's a start on making that cooler available. There's no room here downtown for a second cooler assembly room. Hence, I've decided to convert the plant out on Hydraulic Avenue to house the company's cooler assembly and all future plastic products. We'll ventilate the room for your injection molding process and get you everything you need to begin. The most important thing is to get the line up and running. Holiday spending is critical to our entire product line, and sets the fourth quarter earnings in solid red. That's my kind of Merry Christmas."

Stunned, Mason searched for the proper word of caution. "Sir, that prototype hasn't received thorough testing yet. I jumped on a side track to get this picnic jug designed."

Mr. Coleman sidled up to the table's edge. "May I?"

"By all means." He unclamped the jug and held it up for his immediate inspection.

Taking the first installment in hand, the astute businessman took his time, turning it a full revolution. "This doesn't weigh a sparrow's lean ounce. How stupendous—especially since liquids aren't getting any slimmer."

"That's the inherent beauty of plastics, Mr. Coleman. They're lightweight. We'll use that to our full advantage, most definitely."

He walked a complete circle, ever surmising the situation. "I want this in our catalog of camping gear come Christmastime, too. Let's call it the 'Snow Lite Picnic Jug.' Keep this top band white and match the main portion with your plastic cooler. We'll market the two products together from here on out, which should announce to the world that plastics are here at Coleman to make a lasting difference."

Mason ran a hand through his hair. "Sir, with all due respect, the final design on both products will take me two months to complete. That includes perfecting the final cast, so the precision molds are fully developed when the assembly process begins."

"Good, now we're getting down to brass tacks. You'll have your two months for final development. That gives me time to remodel the facility. What else? Can you order enough raw materials? I was told we're importing that fancy plastic."

"Yes, at first I had to import, but now I can order high-density polyethylene from Dow Chemicals. I'd have to place the order this month, as they're fighting to overcome a six-month lag due to such high demand."

The aging man's brow furrowed. "What in the world from?"

Mason couldn't restrain a boyish grin. "Hula hoops, sir. Of all things, industry is stifled by a hip-hugging hoop."

"What a way to bring a giant to his knees," he replied with a chuckle. "Can I start you with twin assembly lines for the cooler and a single line for the jug? Since the processes and the materials match, I'd like to run them side by side."

Swept into the updraft of progress, Mason felt lighter than the jug. "That's a modest start, sir, most definitely. We'd have to figure out the packaging for the jug, but I think we could stack and ship the coolers without boxing each one. They'll be plenty tough enough for the journey."

He set the jug on the table and locked gazes. "They'd better be, as I'm staking my reputation on this new plastic version. Our steel-belted model earned us the title 'The Cooler Company,' so now we'll graduate into our lightweight line." He pulled out a pocket watch and glanced down at it. "Get the math done on that order quantity for the polyethylene and run it through purchasing, so I can see how deep it might hit us at the bank. It wouldn't be the first loan I've taken out against future earnings."

The gravity of the business risk hit Mason full force. "Thank you for this opportunity, Mr. Coleman. I'll do everything in my power to make it a success. From every indication, plastics manufacturing is the wave of the future."

"Ride the cusp of it then, Mr. Porter. And keep the cooler red for now. Red is perfect for the Christmas season, and I'm partial to it, as well."

"I can thank Glori Dawes for steering me in that providential direction, sir, giving intuitive credit where it's due."

He smiled for the first time as he headed toward the door. "She'll charm the whole country in that Ladies Home Journal ad. By golly, they'll even smell the bacon on that cook stove. Good day, Mr. Porter, and thank you for taking time off to promote our summer product line." He nodded and disappeared into the interior of the plant.

Racing to make time for all that had to be accomplished, he picked up the phone and dialed the familiar extension. He needed support and knew right where to find it. On the third ring, the call was picked up.

"Human Resources, Glori speaking. How may I help you?"

"Can you grab two cold lunches and meet me in my office? Thanks to your insistence, the darling plastic cooler pictured at Old Faithful will be making its debut for the Christmas season, as per Mr. Coleman's personal request. Unfortunately, I have miles to go with its development before that can happen."

"I clearly remember that scene at Old Faithful, so I'll take partial credit for the rush it puts you in now. Consider it my corporate duty to deliver those sandwiches to your lab on my lunch break. I believe they're serving roast beef today."

"Plan to stay and eat with me," he said in a fonder tone. "Even a genius needs occasional inspiration—and yours is the best."

"Flattery won't get you everything, my dear, but it will get you fed today. What more can I do? Oh, how about I launch a local campaign to stop the ubiquitous spread of hula hoops?"

He laughed right down the phone line. "I'm in an all-out battle for raw materials, for sure. Plastics are destined to appear under the Christmas tree this year. Let's just hope and pray it's the camping gear kind."

"See you in forty-five minutes, Mason. That gives me something to anticipate."

"Maybe if I could clear off a dining spot, we could do this more often."

"There's your motivational thought. I'm charmed to be a part of it. Here comes Midge, so let me go. See you at lunchtime, Mr. Plastics." The phone clicked into silence.

He grabbed the picnic jug with both hands, determined to sand off the seams. Then he'd run it through the ultrasonic testing to determine if he could advance the Coleman mettle. From this point, it had a Snow Lite chance to become a worthwhile fixture.

~

Their meeting extended the work day by ten minutes, but Edgar couldn't wait to share the good news. No one carried much sympathy for a Thursday anyway. With the new business moving ahead rapidly, he had to make the most of his planning time.

Lloyd Cox wandered into his office and began studying the campaign pictures sitting on the table by the door. "Hey, these turned out pretty good. I mean, I could have done much better as a handsome husband, but you have to work with what you've been dealt, right?"

Steamed that the ensuing break-up with his fiancée had forced him right to the bank for adequate collateral, Edgar bit his lip and decided to change the subject. "Things are falling together for occupancy of the club in short order, so I thought we might need to meet."

"Good with me. Is that other partner coming?"

A tall figure came through the door and Edgar stood to greet him. "Ah, here we go, all three forces together at last. I believe you two know each other."

Lloyd shook the man's hand and plopped into the guest chair. "Let's get this meeting underway. I've got bowling league tonight."

"Right, here's item number one. We will receive occupancy on the bar portion of the building on June first. The upstairs may be the hitch-up, but I think we can open the club and then extend the services to include that accommodation. You know, we'll ease the clientele in the door with the free-flowing bar taps and go from there."

Lacking a chair, the tall man sat on the corner of the desk. "How much lag time, you reckon?"

Edgar squinted while trying to come up with an estimate. "Well, if the plumbing can get fixed, I'd say less than three weeks. I forced the current building owner to address that issue, so naturally he took the low-ball bid for the work. They start improvements next week, which means we're underway. That brings us to the next item—staff."

Lloyd sat forward with a grin on his face. "I have ten women under contract for a three-month period. That's a standard duration for probation, until we see if things work out."

"Excellent work, Lloyd. We'll pull their pay off the top of our revenue. Did you promise a weekly payout?"

"Yes, cash every Saturday night." Lloyd sat back, looking

smug. "Because of the tempting accumulation in our money drawer, I'm making plans to provide security, too."

Edgar retrieved his ledger and made the notation. Satisfied, he slapped the pen down. "Next item—the liquor supply. If we open June first, we have to fully stock the bar by then. I'm talking beer and hard liquor, enough for our grand opening on the seventh."

The tall man gestured with an open palm. "Well, boss man, I managed to get you a locally-bottled red wine for less per ounce than soda pop. It could be a real money-maker."

Lloyd snapped his fingers. "The women might like the wine. I think it's a good risk."

"What about the rest of the supplies?" Edgar pressed. "Do we have the first month's inventory covered?"

"Covered and soon to be delivered. I have the key you gave me for the back door, so I can help unload the shipment one evening next week. Do you have that blank check for me?"

Edgar reached for the bank book, daring to crack it open and get the dream underway. How fitting for liquor to be the inaugural expense. "Tell me how to write it out."

"Make it to Ins and Outs Food Distribution. I'll write in the dollar amount and let you know the total. Do you want a receipt?"

Edgar looked from one man to the other. "For the liquor, yes. For the women, nothing gets written down, as I cannot claim their expense on my taxes." The downright cleverness of it birthed a smile, which the other two men soon shared. He signed the blank check and tore it from the book, launching the endeavor on a wave of bulk-purchased whiskey.

~

Glori almost scraped her shin on the coffee table trying to reach the insistent phone. Doubtful it was Mason again, she wondered who might be calling at this hour. She grabbed the receiver and pressed it to her ear. "Hello?"

"Hello, Glori. It's Myla Durand calling. Please excuse the lateness of my call. I just heard from Lorna Rae, and she wants to surprise Duncan with a birthday party. She claims it's his last year in a good decade, so she wants it to be memorable. I'm masking the party as a couple's dinner at our house next Tuesday, the twenty-seventh. Do you think you could make it?"

She glanced at the wall calendar tacked behind the front door.

"Yes, that evening looks clear. Are you inviting Mason Porter also?"

A girlish snicker tripped across the line. "Yes, but Weston thought he might need some persuasion to accept. Mason has been working out at the YMCA on Tuesdays and Thursdays. Here's an incentive you can offer him as a trade. Weston plans to invite the men to check out his weight room as part of the party's entertainment. Hey, if it makes them happy and keeps them from talking business all night, then I'm all for it."

Flooded by the ease of offered friendship, Glori could hardly wait. "Thank you for including me. Could I bring something? Mason has been providing fresh vegetables out of his neighbor's garden, so I could steam some asparagus, or whatever is ripening next week."

"Oh, that does sound good. My asparagus is struggling this year. Yes, please bring a vegetable dish, if you really want to. That way Mason will also feel like he's contributing. By the way, Lorna Rae insists on no presents for Duncan."

"Fine. Mason received some big news regarding his plastic cooler, but I'll leave him the privilege of announcing it."

"Hmm, it sounds like you two are getting along well. Does that mean you're dating?"

She hesitated to share, possibly because she held it as precious. "Yes, we've been out once since returning from the camping outing. I think we made hard decisions for some real togetherness after posing as camping husband and happy wife for eleven days. Some of those private moments were rather tough to share with the camera and crew, as you might imagine."

Myla laughed. "You'll get used to people interfering. If God means for you to be together, there will come a time when you'll have him all to yourself. But don't plan for that to happen on your wedding day—I can tell you that from experience."

She laughed at the insightful advice. "Maybe while the men are lifting weights, we can look at your wedding pictures."

"Sure, I'll set my photo album out on the dining room buffet to remind me. Maybe Lorna Rae will bring her photographs, too. That might send the clock's hands moving backwards a bit."

"I look forward to seeing you all Tuesday night then. Be sure to give Mason your address, if he hasn't visited before."

"Count on it. I'm calling him next, so he's the odd man out if he says no."

"If you tell him I want to come, he'll agree to attend. Mention the weights if he drags his feet." She cupped the receiver in her hand, thinking what a lifeline it could be.

"We'll have a wonderful time, I'm sure. See you Tuesday about six-thirty. Goodbye until then."

She hung up the receiver, aglow with the feeling of establishing mutual friends. These women had so much they could teach her, and she had a lot to learn. She wandered into the kitchen to make sure all had been left in order before turning in for the evening. From the clock on the range, she had time to read her Bible before bedtime, a perfect combination.

~

Mason winced at having to shift the conversation, even though he'd already committed to attend. "We'll leave it as the great unknown—asparagus or Swiss chard—whichever is prime for picking next week. Hey, Myla, could I trouble you to speak to Weston for a short minute? I'm thinking he could help me narrow down my choices for some pending inspections at work."

"Absolutely. Let me go get him. I'll see you Tuesday." A hollow click followed as she surrendered the phone.

The lantern problem flared up in his mind, unsolvable up until now. Maybe knowing who to ask was as key as knowing what to do about it. The newspaper clippings had confirmed that more than a couple of faulty lanterns had rolled off the assembly floor. Every indication pointed to a design flaw in the fuel line, and he sorely needed to pinpoint the exact location.

"Hey, Mason. Do you need to pick my brain about something this late in the day?"

"I'll take your keen-eyed input whenever I can get it. Not that I've had any time to address it, but that lantern problem is simmering on the back burner of my mind. It seems like such a simple inspection issue on that rubber gasket, but maybe I've been going about it all wrong. That's why I asked to speak to you, since Myla already had me on the line."

"I always start with a surface inspection. It often hints at the need for further evaluation, but at least it gives you a starting place."

"Fine, I'll run a surface inspection. Should I test the rubber sheeting or test the gaskets once they're stamped out of the die press?"

"Hold up a second. Are you talking about that two-sided cutter that resembles a giant waffle iron?"

"Yes, that's right. We stood right in front of it on our tour of lantern assembly."

"Now we're getting somewhere. That's made of metal and easy to inspect. All you have to do is coat it with Magnaflux, a fluorescent penetrant, and then view the surface under black light for defects. I'll bring some home from work and have it for you Tuesday night."

"Wow, that technique sounds too straightforward. I'll be relieved to start somewhere, though. There are other whispers in the night I'd rather hear than a problematic lantern."

"Tell me about it. Hey, Myla mentioned you were dating Glori Dawes. That sounds more like the kind of whisper a sensible man might want to hear. Good job on that initial scan."

"She's fallen for my plastics allure, I feel certain," he replied with a chuckle. "Thanks for bailing me out on this inspection hitch. That gives me more than one reason to look forward to Tuesday night. I'll see you then. Goodnight."

He hung up the receiver and drifted out of the darkened hall toward the bedroom. Glori had never seemed like an inspection project to him. Maybe her injury at their first encounter had cancelled the defaulting need to inspect, but he'd certainly been a sucker for her beauty at first glance. Such a forfeiture of discernment would scarcely lead to detection of hidden flaws, hence the allegation that love was blind.

He sat down on the edge of the bed, wondering if he had fallen too far under its influence to judge properly. Challenged by the possibility, he vowed to become a more careful observer Tuesday night. If she couldn't share his friends, then she couldn't share his life. He emptied the contents of his pants pocket, rubbing his thumb over a wheat penny he'd picked up at the gas station after work. Every day had some small element of gain, and he had a fine new penny to showcase for this one.

Chapter 21

The last week of May began with a sense of order. Glori noted the diminished stack of clippings on Leslie's table which calibrated the advancement of time. Satisfied that they were making progress, she returned her attention to the staffing expansion for the new cooler assembly line Mr. Coleman had ordered for an August start-up.

Leslie stepped up to the edge of her desk. "Here's the summary article you wanted for the June newsletter, Miss Dawes. I hope it reflects the value of looking back at the company's history. At least, that was my objective."

She glanced up and tried to radiate her appreciation. "Thank you for being so prompt with that, Leslie. Please put it in my in basket, and I'll use it to inspire the next issue."

"I need to take a break and grab a soda. Can I bring you anything?"

"No, thank you. I'll wait until lunch." After the young woman left, she dropped into a critical assessment of the labor force in the staffing request. Three lines would have to run simultaneously, involving a multi-staged assembly. Mr. Coleman's manpower estimate seemed to be conservative, a trait she'd witnessed before, yet admired.

Midge cleared her throat. "Glori, if you can make a minute for me, I feel like there's something we need to talk about."

"If it's job related, then go ahead."

Midge's mouth twisted, contorting her trademark red lipstick. "It will be work-related, in the long run, but it starts out kind of personal."

Glori dropped the staffing paperwork, sensing her assistant required some attention. "Please go ahead and speak your piece then. We've always kept an open door policy here."

Midge wrung her hands and finally put them behind her hips. "You and I have enjoyed a long friendship, Glori. It's always meant a great deal to me. However, during the camping trip, I began to see a few things in a different light."

"If I didn't thank you enough for all the behind-the-scenes wardrobe support, let me do it now, Midge. You kept me looking my best for the camera's sake, even though I found it difficult to keep pace. So thank you for all you did for me—and the campaign."

She squeezed a smile in place that didn't last. "We might need some space between us. That's mostly what I wanted to say. Men are causing a rub in our close friendship, so maybe it's natural to take a step back at this point."

The accusatory admission knocked the wind out of her lungs. She struggled for the right thing to say. "Can we not have our friendship and romantic interests, too?"

Midge stepped back. "You're full of advice, Glori, whether you realize it or not. That taints the friendship and leaves me feeling like I'm asking your permission to have a life—which I'm not. I've got a good head on my shoulders and can make my own decisions."

Because of her vitriolic overtones, Glori felt like she'd fallen under personal attack. "Yet you say this has something to do with work. I'm at a loss—"

"You're going to be at a loss for an assistant, all right. I plan to apply for the position of administrative coordinator for the new facility out on Hydraulic Avenue. I'll run the satellite warehouse and take care of admin support. You'll need a new assistant in HR by August. That should give us adequate space to co-exist." She sucked in her cheeks and stormed out of the door like a bee-stung filly.

Glori flattened her palms on the desktop and tried to regain her equilibrium from the lashing. Slowly, her ability to reason returned. For a tenuous few seconds, she tried to track Midge's possible line of reasoning, wondering if Mason or Edgar had set the schism into action.

The broken engagement seemed to claim yet another casualty, an outcome she hadn't seen coming. Purposeful not to assign fault for the fractured relationship, she took a deep breath and plunged back into the staff expansion request. At the bottom of the list, she spotted the administrative coordinator position, lying snake-like at the bottom of a deep pit. *Don't let this disappointment hurt so much, Lord.* Her eyes watered, but she would not allow herself to cry at work. No, she possessed a trunk load of professional dignity, which would get her through the workday. She sniffed and began to tally the new positions.

~

Mason took another glance at the wedding photo, noting his host boasted less hair now than on his wedding day. Likely a penalty of being a quality control ace in the aviation industry, it seemed a small price to pay for five years of success. Subconsciously, he passed his fingers through his abundant allotment of hair and glanced sideways at his attractive date.

Glori touched the scooped neckline of her blouse. "What beautiful lace. Is it Venetian?"

Myla looked at her with fondness. "Yes. I so wish I could take out my wedding dress and look at it on occasion, but it's been dry-cleaned and boxed for reuse by an heir."

"If we should be so fortunate to have one," Weston quipped from the doorway. "Can I invite the men into the weight room now, to see my unique set-up?"

Myla stood, making only brief eye contact with her husband. "Sure, go ahead. Dinner will be ready in fifteen minutes, so keep that timeframe in mind."

Duncan rose to his full height, nodding at Mason. "Come on, young blood. Weston wants to see what damage you can do on his weight bench."

He laughed, enjoying the challenge. "The damage will be all mine, I assure you." He tweaked the cap of Glori's shoulder as he passed by her on the sofa. "Don't have too much fun in here, ladies." A cat with plush gray fur jumped up and ran out of the room ahead of his host.

"Man talk is always fun," Lorna Rae replied with a quick wink.

He followed Duncan, a bit reluctant to leave the living room, given the pending subject matter. The sheepish grin Glori flashed seemed to lend permission. He trailed the men partway down a narrow hall and found the secondary bedroom that had been converted to something more useful. The closet doors had been upgraded to paneled mirrors, which made the room appear infinitely larger. Graduated dumbbells sat in descending order on a rack along that shorter wall, while a universal weight machine with dual stations consumed the rest of the space.

"I upgraded to this all-in-one fitness station under the guise of our first anniversary present," Weston said. "We agreed to always purchase something we could both use."

"Great idea," Duncan replied. "We tend to get new furniture to celebrate our anniversary. Having started out with nearly nothing, it's been a long process. With eight years under our belts now, I can say that we have a great marriage and adequate seating in our living room. Bunk beds for the two youngest children are next this fall, to get little Johnny out of the crib."

Mason nodded, thinking he had a long way to go before understanding the priorities of fatherhood. A metal jangle made him shift his focus. He unbuttoned his cotton shirt to prepare for exertion. Finding a towel bar near the door, he slid the shirt onto it and turned to face the weight machine—his immediate nemesis.

Weston held up a wide leather belt that sported a brass buckle. "Okay, who goes first?"

Mason clapped and followed through with a bicep bulge. "Let me at this thing. I'll go first, but start the weight stack on the light side. We can build up from there."

Weston relinquished the belt with a gleam in his eyes. "Forty pounds on the stack then, for dignity. We'll do forty, fifty, and sixty before switching out. Duncan, you're next. Just because you're about to turn forty doesn't mean all the power has drained out of your massive physique yet."

To play the part, the safety manager raised both arms and cupped his fingers onto an invisible ledge. "Thirty-nine and holding, thank you. I have to admit that I've gone for more duration holding that weight bearing, because Lorna Rae makes me hold Timmy every time we go out. Little Johnny only has eyes for his mother right now, so I get the five-year-old."

Mason clamped the buckle in place and took a deep breath. "Where do you want me?"

Weston patted a rubberized seat. "Right here. Get situated, and I'll pass you the bar. Duncan, you get ready to increase the weight stack. See this pin? Pull it out and shove it under the next ten-pound plate." He demonstrated the adjustment and the taller man nodded.

Mason gave him a questioning look. "I should have asked you to demonstrate the pull. Now, I feel like a mule all set to cross the mud pit without a lick of sense how to accomplish it."

The host laughed and reached over his head. "I'll make it easy for you, Old Sal. To head down the Erie Canal, just grab this bar and pull it down in front to about chest height."

He snickered through the reference to the old folk song. "What exactly makes that rendition so easy?" He felt the cool metal bar and took hold, leveraging it down with a grunt.

"Because this way, your biceps do the work. The other version that goes behind your head is the triceps curl. I don't think you're ready for that one right out of the gate."

"Somebody count," he growled as he forced the bar down. The stack made a clanking noise behind him, connected by cable to the bar.

"I'll enumerate," Duncan offered, "because I'm so good at it. That's one."

"Go to eight, Mason," Weston directed. "We'll add the weight while you rest between reps. Get ready, Duncan."

"Okay, coach." Mason paused to make the second pull-down. "I sure could use this team approach at work."

"Two," Duncan said. "Not a chance of that kind of aid, Mr. Plastics. I have to stay where the risk is higher. Those coolers don't have to fly. Three curls."

"Hey, I've got risk aplenty," he replied.

"Four."

"Yeah, but most of your pressure comes from HR," Weston quipped. "Loveliness can distract a man's footing at the ledge of risk. Better keep your feet planted on solid ground."

"Five."

"This is a set-up," Mason said. "You've got me pinned in place to hear your advice."

"Six."

"All women come with warning labels," Weston replied.

"Seven. Come on, one more," Duncan coaxed.

Not much of a strain, Mason completed the last pull and felt Weston take the bar. He shook his arms to rid the lactic acid build-up as a metal clink reported the added weight. "Any other nuggets of wisdom you want to sling my way, before I get distracted by this next round?"

Weston laughed at his receptivity. "Pray a lot?"

Duncan stepped around the teaser and gave him a friendly slap on the chest. "I wasted too much time trying to figure out my feelings for Lorna Rae, so here's my advice. If the situation requires a break-away move, aim in Glori's direction. That way, if calamity threatens to strike, you've got a running start to protect her. When the pressure's on, you'll understand how you feel, no question."

Mason nodded, sensing the wisdom of the offered advice. "What about my dilemmas at work? Do I get any help there?"

Weston laughed while lowering the bar into his grip. "Here's your prescription from Dr. Defect Detection. Take a bottle of Magnaflux for instant relief and call me in the morning."

Mason tried to belly laugh, but the added weight demanded core support, a direct muscular conflict. He polished off four reps before remembering to breathe. The muscle showdown became a rhythm of exertion and momentary rest, resembling the rest of his existence. The man in the mirror moaned halfway through the second set. No doubt, the third sequence at sixty pounds would be telling. Still, he couldn't be shown up by a hulking safety inspector fifteen years his senior. *Could I?*

When he teetered midway through the sixty-pound reps, both Weston and Duncan grabbed the bar to steady it for him. In a watershed of realization, he knew that they had his weak spot should the going get rough. He completed the challenge with leaden arms while the renewed appreciation for friendship lifted his spirits.

~

Glori slapped the yearbook shut, embarrassed they had asked so many questions. Maybe the four-layered coconut cake had set her nerves on edge, though the frosting tasted amazing. "There, that's enough about the young lady with stars in her eyes and heady aspirations. A few wrinkles of reality have set in since then."

"Nonsense," Lorna Rae replied, caressing the emblem on the cover. "Being voted 'Most Likely to Succeed' is nothing to shrug off. You had it going for you then—and still do."

Myla folded her wedding album closed. "I would wager there aren't too many women in senior roles at Coleman Company."

Mason ran his arm around her back. "No, there aren't. Glori does an outstanding job."

When Duncan yawned from the overstuffed club chair, Weston launched a throw pillow at him. "Looks like the years are beginning to catch up with you, my aging friend."

"Just the backlash from an overdone work week," he replied, rising. "Lorna Rae, we probably should go relieve Vivian of our rascally pack, so Bert will still acknowledge me on the shop floor tomorrow. Thank you all for coming to celebrate my collision with another year."

"Yes, thank you for making this such a wonderful evening," Lorna Rae added. "I think we truly surprised Duncan, which takes some effort to accomplish."

"Never thought I'd be thankful for a scheming wife." He reached for her hand with a squint that may have turned into a wink, which caused Lorna Rae to kiss his cheek.

The demonstration of abiding love sent a warm flush up Glori's neck. Muddled by the cake's sugary lift and befuddled by her increasing affection for the man sitting at her side, she dared to wonder what pictures her wedding album might contain. Even if those snapshots faded, she hoped their love remained as genuine as that expressed over the dinner table tonight.

"Are you ready to leave, Glori?" Mason hooked her gaze and gave his head a little nod.

"Yes, I was just reflecting on the wedding photos shared tonight. Thank you, ladies, for such a lively jaunt down memory lane. It was just the kind of trip I needed." She rose and lifted the yearbook off the coffee table.

Myla took a flimsy paper bag in hand, her brow arching. "Who brought this?"

"I'm sorry." Mason took the package from her. "I found this on the news rack and thought it would be fun to share tonight. It completely slipped my mind. He removed a glossy magazine from the bag and held it up for their hostess to see.

Myla examined the cover. "Ladies Home Journal?"

A shot of apprehension pierced Glori's heart. "No, it can't be. It's not even June yet."

Mason grinned. "Advanced copy. Check out the illustrious couple on page twenty-three."

Lorna Rae hummed, taking control of the magazine. Once she landed on the right page, she held it out for the whole group to see.

Glori peeked with one eye open. Instead of the half-page black and white photo, she found a full-page color ad. She blinked to test if the image would change. The cooking characters were easy to recognize, causing her to blush.

"Outstanding rendition," Duncan said.

"You both look so happy," Lorna Rae added. "It must have been a wonderful trip."

"Yes, it was," Mason replied.

Weston extended a pint-sized metal flask and a dark light bulb. "Here you go, Mason. Paint the Magnaflux on, let it dry, and then take a close look at the cutter under this fluorescent lighting. Oh, is this the ad campaign? 'America Goes Camping.' I like that sales pitch. And those two models aren't half bad, either."

Myla punched him with her elbow while leaning in to take a closer look. "What park is that in the background?"

"Devils Tower National Monument," Glori replied. "Our campsite was right up the road from the most adorable prairie dog colony on the planet."

Mason rested his chin on her shoulder. "The babies ate wildflowers, those cute little cusses. I don't suppose flower petals offer much in the way of solid nutrition."

"I recommend coconut cake," Duncan teased. "Thanks for saving the best surprise for last. Now, I know two impressive magazine models."

"No autographs, please." Mason's pompous look vanished with a laugh.

Glori frowned at her self-promoting escort. "Could we leave this copy with our gracious hostess as our thanks for such a lovely evening?"

When Myla's expression reflected keen interest, Mason shifted the magazine from Lorna Rae's hands to hers. "Happy viewing."

Duncan stepped toward the door, catching Lorna Rae in his arm. "Blessings to you all, from the elder of the pack."

"Hoot-hoot," Weston called with a clap. "See you at Cessna tomorrow."

Myla shot to the door. "Don't forget your wedding album, Lorna Rae."

She glanced back over her shoulder, her green eyes shining. "I've got a-hold of my man, at least my head's screwed on. Hope to see you all again soon. Toodles." She curved a finger wave back at them, while Duncan pulled her onto the porch.

Myla soon returned from the dining room bearing her chafing dish. "Here, Glori. While you're remembering to walk out with your campaign partner on your arm, I'll tuck your dish in for good measure."

"Boy, that fresh asparagus was delicious," Weston said. "Please thank your neighbors for sending it."

Mason hoisted the stain can. "You've got it. Thanks for the Magnaflux fix. I'll run it first thing in the morning and see what I can find."

"Call me anytime," Weston replied. "You've got my lab number, so feel free."

Myla locked her elbow around her helpful husband. "Thanks for my magazine. I'll be sure to share it with the ladies down the block. Our friend Glori might be a local celebrity before it's all said and done."

A dull ache started in her temple at the mere suggestion. "No, I'd like to remain safely anonymous, thank you just the same."

"She's still the most likely to succeed," teased Mason, leading her toward the door. "She doesn't want to be overly flashy about it, though." He winked at Myla and gave Weston a nod.

Glori followed his lead into the inky night. A streetlight illuminated the base of the bridge. The dull ache eased as tranquility became their backdrop.

"I thought that went well, didn't you?"

She tucked the dish into the crook of her elbow and handed him the yearbook. "Yes, such delightful people, the evening practically evaporated. What a precious look on Duncan's face when he saw us standing in the dining room." She started up the bridge's incline before noticing Mason had slowed his pace.

"Weston and Myla have a nice home. Have you ever given any thought as to where you'd like to live for the long-term?"

She reflected back on the little cottage, which contrasted with her apartment's high ceilings and drafty oversized rooms. "Mrs. Brougham might regard me as a traitor, but I thought the cozy cottage felt like more of a home. A bit newer build might be nice, though. Lorna Rae enjoys her double ovens, but I'd rather have a dishwasher if kitchen space is to be valued. Westinghouse has an impressive under-the-sink model with a handy roll-out wash-well."

When they reached the bridge's summit, Mason paused at the rail. "They're making such leaps in technology right now. Plumbing pipes are being converted to PVC plastic as rapidly as possible, making the metals shortage a moot point. I think if I settled down in a place of my own, it would have to be a new construction. Does that concept intimidate you, Miss Dawes?"

She shifted the dish to the rail so they could stand closer. "No, I think it matches your temperament perfectly. Will you stay within driving distance, so that I can find you?"

"You'll find me," he replied in a willowy whisper. The distance between them closed in kiss that also made good use of the space provided, a most romantic room.

She started with a hand against his chest and let it roam around his neck to reflect her contentment. Only when the headlights of a car swept the bridge did she pull away.

Mason shifted off the rail to protect her from the passing vehicle. "My gardening neighbors are thinking to sell ten acres along the river. The first offer to buy it is mine, so I need to decide whether Valley Center is the right spot for me."

She touched his cheek. "If you want my opinion…invite me out there." With one raised brow, she moved closer to encourage his response.

"Sunday afternoon then. I'll pick you up after church." He led her back to the car without another word. After slipping inside, he placed the can and the dark light bulb on the dashboard.

Glori tucked the chafing dish and yearbook on the floor mat, then slipped closer to see if the fondness remained in Mason's eyes. In one strong-armed sweep, she found her answer and so much more as he stole a lingering second kiss—and transfixed her heart in the process. *Such a lovely night.*

Chapter 22

The fluorescent light transformed the lantern assembly line into a scene out of "Alice in Wonderland" where nothing seemed exactly right. Inverted, Mason overcame a crick in his neck as he continued down the die cutter's surface, cage light in hand, trying to scrutinize the metal for any defect. With two flanks inspected and zero results to report, he shifted abreast the longer edge and took a deep breath to recalibrate his analytical mind.

Crouching, he searched the undersurface of the cutting machine, ever hopeful to discover something out of the ordinary. From quadrant to quadrant, the pattern of circular die cuts remained consistent and uniform. Only one more panel remained. He forced his eyes open wider to stay alert and bent back under the machine to complete the surface inspection. At least he could report back to Weston that he'd given it the old college try.

A mere two rows from the hinged edge that held the lid of the machine to the cutting surface, he spotted an odd linear reflection amid a sea of circles. Curious, he moved the light closer and pulled the magnifying glass from his back pocket. Up close, the fluorescent stain made it all too clear that one small die bore a substantial slice across its circumference. When magnified, it wore the irregular hacked-out serration of a knife cut.

The implications seeped into his consciousness like a disease, insidious and without allegiance. Someone had altered the equipment with malicious, premeditated intent. Mason took one more protracted look at the defect and resigned to pursue it through full rectification. No one else need lose an eye to a faulty gas tank seal on a Coleman lantern. Assessing his next move, he desperately needed a camera.

"What in the blazes do you think you're doing, Mr. Porter?"

Mason straightened and slid the magnifying glass into his back pocket. There stood Mack Insley, the floor supervisor, a dour expression drawing his face. "Good morning, sir. I'm simply conducting a surface inspection on the die cutter for the lantern's gasket." A bluish glow reminded him to cut off the light, which he did with haste.

Insley's expression didn't thaw. "I don't know what kind of cockamamie gadget you're using there, but the assembly line shift starts in five minutes, so I suggest that you scram back to your pampered engineer existence in the little lab space you've been granted."

"No need to get riled up over a routine inspection, Mr. Insley. I'm done here anyway. I'll unplug my equipment and go now, thank you." He backpedaled and unplugged the extension cord, then wrapped its length around his elbow until he had it wound up. Knowing his actions now bore scrutiny, he found the Magnaflux container and tucked it into a pocket on the sly.

With a curt nod, he headed back to his lab. Nothing felt pampered about the familiar surroundings whatsoever. In a minute's time, he had Weston Durand on the phone. As succinct as possible, he described his technique and laid out his findings. In an attempt to conclude, he shared one final thought. "The territorial feud flared up out of nowhere. He's lax as a floor supervisor and never lifts a hand to work or even help anyone, as far as I have seen."

"Then he's your first suspect, Mason." Weston said. "Don't overanalyze it, and, by all means, don't dismiss it. His odd reaction doesn't add up. Here's what you do. Go get a camera, and when the line shuts down again, take pictures from a couple of angles. In one shot, stick a ruler in the frame so you can provide some reference for the size of the defect. Got it?"

"Okay. That sounds like lunch break to me. Glori uses a camera in HR to take employee photos for her permanent records. I'll have her bring it when she delivers my lunch today."

"Here's one last word to the wise." Weston spoke in almost a hush. "Don't get Glori involved in this. Like the lantern, it could blow up in your face. I've got to go. Good luck."

As Mason hung up, the warning echoed in his mind. His quality control expert had yet to steer him wrong. From here on out, he purposed to maintain the fine line between disclosure and inclusion. Thinking of how long Glori had held on to that infernal engagement oath, he might have an unwanted battle on his hands. For her own good, she would need to relinquish.

He departed the lab to request the camera in person. When he passed the dining area, the aroma of coffee and cinnamon rolls drew him in. He decided to load up on bribery, hoping she wouldn't hold it against him. He could be downright charming. It just took extra effort.

~

Edgar dropped the envelope into the outgoing mail, having no compunction about using company postage to mail in his newspaper ad for the bar's grand opening. He had requested Friday's sport's page for its placement and enclosed a check to cover the eight-inch box. His finest freehand work, a customized beer tap embellished the space beside the scrolling font that spelled out "The Hangar Gentlemen's Club."

Possibly the best ad he'd ever designed, he knew the two-for-one drink offer would be too much to pass up. Business would be brisk. For the grand opening, he'd even supply salted nuts at the bar. Living it up would soon arrive in high style. He would guarantee that.

He had barely made it back into the Marketing office when a tall figure crowded the doorway. "Yes, may I help you?"

The man gestured to come in, his face unflinching.

Edgar bit back a reprimand. Instead, he motioned the worker inside and closed the door casually behind him. "Okay, Mack. This had better be good."

He looked at him with skittish eyes. "I think we may have a problem."

Edgar's short-lived joy over the open house shattered like cheap stemware. He bore no fondness for problems, because they always led to additional costs or untimely delays. On the rare occasion, they led to both. He need not let on to this hapless pawn, so he tried to brace for the revelation with forbearance. Not his strong suit, he'd have to fake it.

~

Glori shifted a stack of papers on her desk to give her guest more room. With the first of June approaching, she knew this pending employee matter had to be addressed. "Are you plenty comfortable?"

The man hooked the handle of his cane over the edge of her desk. "Plenty, yes. Don't you worry about me."

Her closed-lip smile might betray her on that aspect, but she continued the re-entry interview. "Speaking for Coleman Company, we are privileged that you can return to work in June. You may have anticipated that your disability will preclude you from functioning in your previous inspector position."

He tilted his head, his gaze questioning. "Could you put that in layman's terms, Miss Dawes? I want to be sure I understand you a hundred percent." He touched the eye patch as if it had slipped.

Glori leaned forward, embarrassed by her delivery. "Let's try this. You worked your way up the lantern assembly line to the position of inspector, because you learned everything there was to know about that product. You should be commended for that advancement."

"Well, though, look what it got me." He flashed his dark palms up as if to draw attention to his tattered state of being.

Glori fought to counter the negative comment. "Your employee record is exemplary. There's not a mark against your name, and the long trail of commendations fills several pages. That's the kind of employee Coleman Company wants to retain, let me assure you."

"I'm almost ten years from my full retirement, Miss Dawes. I'd do almost anything to keep those benefits from slipping through my fingers. In my mind, I'm still useful to the company, but the mirror tries to tell a whole different story."

"This morning I plan to suggest a new line of work for you, but I want you to stay open to fully consider it. Your visual impairment will not allow you to serve as inspector, so you have to move off the lantern assembly line."

He hung his head. "I figured as much."

"However, I want to suggest a position with a broader reach, so please hear me out. Where you were an expert on one specific line before, I am offering you a position that will require a working knowledge of our entire operation. We are opening a new department called Public Relations, and we're asking you to consider becoming our first liaison for that department." She paused to let the job title sink in while she gauged his receptivity.

He leaned back in the chair. "Please go on, as you might have lost me already."

"No, I'm not going to lose you at all. The job as I have designed it will be two-fold at the start. First, you'll coordinate and lead any tour groups or media that request to see the facility."

"Mr. Coleman is going to allow tours? He's never thought much of that in the past."

She gave a tiny wink. "We had that discussion yesterday. He's willing to give it a try, though he wants the school children to be restricted to second shift, so plan on late afternoon tours for them. Once we publicize the feature, I know we'll get lots of Boy Scout troops."

"Scout troops? I always wanted to volunteer with Boy Scouts, but I've been too busy working to do much about it." He laughed a bit under his breath.

"I don't know if you remember Herb Ebert, but he took retirement while you were out. That means the company needs a new historian, someone with a vast knowledge of our products, who can keep track of newspaper clippings, our print advertisements, marketing campaigns, and so on." She paused to read his expression, but her listener's calm reflected the still surface of a windless pond. "The second part of your position, should you decide to accept it, would be to act as the company historian."

"Do you mean the keeper of the Proof Books?"

"Yes, sir. That's exactly what I mean."

He took his chin in his hand and shook his head. After making several grunts, he stared out of the window. The interview ground to a halt.

Not sure if she should sweeten the pot, Glori remembered another aspect of the position. "That keeper of the Proof Books role is typically appointed for life—or your duration with the company up until retirement, like Herb."

He cleared his throat while leaning forward. "Miss Dawes, please let Mr. Coleman know that I'm humbled through and through with this historian appointment. I never thought to be looked upon so favorably to carry off that important responsibility."

Heartened, she sensed another question might be in order. "Do you enjoy telling stories about the old days at Coleman Company, like our productivity during the war?"

"Yes, ma'am, I do. Those were remarkable times, for sure. Every American infantryman carried a Coleman pocket stove, which made the added work pace around here worthwhile."

"I hope this seems like something you'd like to be involved doing. It catalogues and celebrates our contribution to this community—and to the industry. With over fifty years under our collective belt, I think Coleman Company is here to stay."

"Amen—and sign me up," he exclaimed, gesturing with an imaginary pen. A hesitant smile followed, like it might be rusty from disuse.

She turned the job description around to face him and circled the bottom line for his signature, then angled the pen toward the long-time employee. "I sure was hoping you would say that. Welcome back to Coleman Company."

As he scratched the pen across the page to ink the agreement, the office door flew open.

In rushed Mason, his hands balancing a cafeteria tray. "Greetings to my favorite Human Resources staff member," he said with enthusiasm. In servant mode, he whisked the tray through the air and allowed it to settle on the corner of her desk.

Stricken to make the forced transition, Glori blinked and defaulted to what felt most natural. "Mason Porter, I'd like you to meet the new company historian, Lenard Sanders. Mr. Sanders, please meet our new plastics engineer."

For a fleeting moment, Mason almost looked guilty of something inexplicable. His jaw gaped open and his hands flew into his pockets as if he had something to hide. In a boardinghouse reach, he retrieved the guest chair from Midge's desk and sat off to one side. "Mr. Sanders, I can't tell you what an honor it is to meet you at last. I'd not been in residence two weeks before your accident happened on the lantern line. In fact, I'm conducting inspections over there still, tracking down the possibility of any defects in the system."

Sanders nodded his head. "I'm relieved to hear that. Let me know if you find anything."

"I pledge to do that," Mason replied. "You know Glori has been your number one advocate all along, lining up the pooled sick day resources, so you could have extended leave to get well. She must recognize a valued employee when she sees one."

The aging man shrugged his shoulders. "Wish I could have come back sooner, but the doctors wanted to do some clean-up work on my face." He drew a finger along a scar in front of his right ear.

Glori needed to recapture control of this runaway interview, despite the benefit of Mason's interruption. "Mr. Porter, thank you for delivering our morning refreshments. Was there something you wanted from HR? I have yet to go over the location of Mr. Sanders' new office and the reporting hierarchy within Public Relations."

Mason rose from the chair like a jack-in-the-box. "I, uh…only need your camera, if you can spare it for the morning."

Relieved, she pulled open her bottom drawer and removed the camera. "Fine, here you go. I'll pick it up after lunch. I'm afraid I'll be running late today." She blinked and smiled to send him a coded message that she would have to stand him up for their midday meal together.

"That's positively perfect," he replied. Moving like a cartoon robot, he grabbed the gadget and advanced to the door. Turning back, he gave her guest a mock salute. "Welcome back, Mr. Sanders. It's mighty good to count you among our ranks again."

"I may have to stop by, so you can teach me something about plastics," he replied with a tap of his cane.

Mason managed to crack a smile. "I hope you do that. Come by anytime." He disappeared into the hallway and the door pinched closed.

"Oh, look. It's a cinnamon roll," her guest said, his tone sincere with interest.

"Let's stop and toast your new position then. I never could pass up our company cook's cinnamon rolls." She lifted a coffee from the tray and grabbed a packet of sugar. "Now, the coffee over there is a whole different story."

Mr. Sanders leaned toward her, trying to cover his snickering reaction. "Isn't that the truth? Those percolators have been building up caffeine residue since nineteen thirty-nine."

Glori blew into her cup, thinking what a treasured individual they had the privilege of redeeming. "You might want to write that down, Mr. Sanders—along with your other recollections of the early days. After all, you're going to need something to talk about when those groups start showing up on our doorstep."

He pulled off the wax paper from the bottom of the cinnamon roll with a grin tugging at his lips. "I haven't ever been at a loss for words yet, but I promise to fancy up my material to give the company a good showing. I've got to mention the first nighttime football game played west of the Mississippi, courtesy of Coleman lanterns hanging from poles along the sidelines."

"Yes, that's a grand claim to fame." Satisfied with the fit of his re-directed career, Glori allowed the day to turn casual so she could enjoy her snack. She'd have to thank Mason for his thoughtfulness later. With one more stir of the coffee, she took a nibble of the roll and let the icing bring her pleasure.

"After we eat, can we take a look at those Proof Books you were talking about?" His forehead wrinkled to accentuate the question.

Glori sipped her coffee and winced at its bitter aftertaste. "You bet. We've had a temporary intern working to update those from where Herb fell behind. Her last day is Friday, so you're coming back right in the nick of time."

"History never stopped for anybody," he quipped, right before taking a bite of the yeast-puffed pastry.

Glori made a note to take a picture of Lenard Sanders when he reported for duty Monday morning, as June second marked the beginning of a new historian at the helm. She pulled off a layer of sweet roll and appreciated the cinnamon caked between its spirals. "You're going to like your new office, Mr. Sanders. Herb set up camp in Accounting, but we're moving you a stone's throw down the hall from Mr. Coleman."

His good eye widened at the news. "Guess I'd better be on my best behavior then."

When he pretended to straighten his bow tie, they both shared a good laugh. Her job interacting with personnel certainly had its moments, and this reunion had proven to be a golden one. A sip of her coffee brought the antiquated percolators back to mind as the bitter brew scorched the back of her throat like a good old-fashioned stimulant should. She recognized a long-lived truth. The more things changed, the more they stayed the same.

~

No inspection job is finished until the documentation work is done. Mason moved in spy-like stealth as he entered the lantern assembly area. Lunch break had left the area a ghost town. He approached the die cutter, glanced around the room, and lifted the lid, making the hinges squeak. Determined to get the measurement snapshot first, he jabbed the ruler into the right vicinity and held the fluorescent light immediately beneath it.

The linear defect glared in the light's intended detection. He twisted almost upside-down but got the shot facing the cut mark. Deciding for something more oblique, he shot the next exposure across the machine's surface, where all the circular die shapes seemed perfect—all but one that bore a scar which measured a damage-ridden one-eighth of an inch.

He lowered the die cutter's lid to rest the hinges and collected his extension cord to depart. Beyond the dusty wall partitions that separated the assembly area, the sound of two men deep in conversation announced the end of his privacy. He retreated to a partial wall in back and held his position, hidden from sight.

By his tall height, the lead figure was clearly Mack Insley. The second man trailed and couldn't be made out as readily. Mack proceeded to lift the cutter's lid and allowed the other man to step closer. Both of them reached beneath it to adjust something under the lid.

Instinctive to protect the inspection scene, Mason leveled the camera and took an exposure with the men actively tampering with the equipment. His thumb worked to crank the film forward, hushing the camera's mechanism against his ribs. By the time he could ready the camera to take another shot, the men had lowered the lid and turned away. Shocked through and through as the second man's identity became apparent, Mason managed one more incriminating picture before they both left the scene.

While he waited out the interval, he rested his head against the wall to stop the reeling sensation birthed by their clandestine association. Against a corrupt lot, he had no idea what to do with the evidence he now had in hand. When he blinked, somehow Duncan Reed and his perpetual chase of safety came to mind. Revived at that stalwart direction, he would call in an expert next and get the professional assistance he desperately needed.

The skin crept up the back of his neck as he approached the die cut machine. Slowly, he lifted the lid to re-inspect the surface. There, fitted over the damaged circle, a cork had been affixed to neutralize its cutting surface. He took a quick snapshot of the alteration, closed the lid, and headed for the seclusion of the office, where maybe this would all make sense.

Chapter 23

Glori tossed Sunday's newspaper on her desk, intending to clip out the Coleman ad from the sports section for their new historian. Maybe she could toss in a lesson on what to look for as she got Mr. Sanders busy with his new position. June had dawned with the passage of Memorial weekend, and now the Tuesday-that-felt-like-Monday would consume her every thought.

Midge reported to work, passing her with a high-pitched whistle that continued until well after she'd sat at her desk. She made a few attention-seeking gestures, but refused to look directly at Glori for some odd reason.

"I trust you had a lovely holiday weekend, Midge. You seem bright and cheery this morning."

"Yes, I did, in fact. I'm helping Edgar clean up an old apartment above his new business establishment. They have the grand opening coming up this Saturday night." She grabbed the employee record book and snapped its binder tabs open. "Ah, yet another month passes us by. Something tells me June is going to be a scorcher—in more ways than one."

"How so?"

She gave her a coy look. "I'll let you figure that one out. Did you see my completed application for the administrative coordinator position?"

A cool trickle of detachment ran down her spine. "Yes, it's duly recorded and ready for Mr. Coleman's inspection. I'll likely pass on the handful of applications for the new facility by the week's end."

"Great. I think I'm going to miss having Leslie around. You

know, she might make a good temporary fill-in for me when I transfer in August."

"Well, Leslie's going to college full-time this fall semester, so I don't know how many hours she could be available. I'll call the agency and see if she plans to continue part-time."

Midge hummed her response and became engrossed in the work log.

Glori blew out a breath and sat down to start her workday. She flipped the newspaper open to the sport's page, but the back page of the local lifestyles section distracted her. A wave of déjà vu struck when she recognized a photo printed beneath a gossip-riddled headline. "What in the world?" she posed under her breath. "'Coleman Darling Hides Checkered Past.'"

"Show me," Midge insisted, popping up out of her seat. She peered over her shoulder and began to read the article. "'Marketing representative Glori Dawes shines in the Coleman Company's summer campaign ads, heroically hiding her tarnished passage into adulthood. The executive-turned-actress now acclaimed across America for her 'let's go camping' pitch in televised commercials and magazine ads may not be as all-American wholesome as she appears.'" Midge stopped to exchange glances, her mouth agape.

"Dear Lord above, what manner of yellow journalism is this?"

"God only knows. It sounds more like the National Inquiry's trumped up news to me."

"Well that photo of me with my darling niece isn't trumped up. It's real and it hurts. I'd better call my sister and warn her."

Midge snatched the paper and held it closer. "Oh, dear me. It follows with an account of the unwed mother giving up her baby for adoption down in Oklahoma City."

The words pierced her like a knife. "This information had to be leaked by Edgar Sterns," Glori said with a hiss. "With the truth twisted that way, it has to be him."

Midge's hands began to shake. "What are you going to do? Will you publically discredit the accusations? You need to be careful that one thing doesn't lead to another here. You gave your oath to keep this thing hidden, and I'm holding you to it."

The sensation squeezing her middle would hardly allow a breath. She needed to think this through, though a public rebuttal was clearly in order. "I cannot allow this slanderous article to question my integrity. It could cost me everything."

Midge made a few clucking sounds in protest and then her mouth fell open like a fish.

"I need to go see Mr. Coleman before the repercussions grow any worse." Glori quelled the unease making her stomach quiver. "Should Mr. Sanders arrive, please escort him down the admin hall to the new PR office I showed you last week. I've already moved Leslie's work down there for his use."

"In the meantime, I'm going to gulp down a cup of coffee like there's no tomorrow and hope this thing can blow over unnoticed." Midge stumbled back to her desk and plopped down in the chair with a huff.

Glori steeled her tumultuous emotions and set her gaze on the door to exit. "I'll verify your numbers once you calculate them, Midge. Let's not hold payroll up due to inflammatory personal matters." As much as it felt like the world had screeched to a halt, an ever-tending Creator still had matters in hand. She clung to that throne-of-grace hope—and the newspaper—all the way up the hall to the senior-level offices.

~

Not yet three months vested with the company, Mason shared a protracted moment of empathetic support for his president. While Mr. Coleman studied the equipment photographs he'd displayed in sequential order, he managed a conspirator's glance at his technical support. Duncan Reed made a faint nod and held his peace where he sat.

After a brief study of the situation, Mr. Coleman growled. "This looks intentional, yet I'm not well-versed at the surfacing of sabotage in the work place. I've made every attempt at countering happenstance that threatens safety, but this is a horse of a different color."

"A shameful color," Mason replied. "I'm sorry as I can be to have to address the matter with you, sir. I brought it in as soon as I could get the film developed. Otherwise, it would simply be their word against mine."

Duncan opened a broad palm toward the photographs. "You have enough evidence to press charges, Mr. Coleman. Safety in the workplace is a serious matter. Those who act against it forfeit the well-being of the general worker. The inspection Mr. Porter ran is state-of-the-art and quite telling, in this case. The odds that someone could zero in on that exact defect directly hints of a collusive responsibility. The legal system could indict the guilty parties on the photos alone. Plus, you have a witness in this case—the man holding the camera that took the pictures."

Though Duncan had likely intended it as a clincher to such a logical case, the divulgence seemed like a noose around Mason's neck. He tried to swallow and his necktie worked against it.

Mr. Coleman wiped a hand across his forehead. "*Why* though? Does that seem apparent to everyone but me? Why put a tiny fluke in a single die cut on the assembly line of a million-dollar lantern? I just don't get it."

Related or not, Mason had to come forward with what else he knew. "Sir, I'm not saying I can look into a man's mind or heart and reveal the devious aspects of it. I have to confess that I caught Edgar Sterns at the women's tent one night during the campaign, crouching behind the corner in pursuit of some manner of clandestine mischief. With the persuasion of my fillet knife, I managed enough intimidation to keep the staff safe and excommunicate our filming director to the campground's edge. The next time we broke camp, I found a series of odd-placed cuts around the bottom of the canvas walls of that main tent. As a sentry, I may have been inept. Still, I surmised that something untoward had been transpiring all along, that I had finally stumbled upon that night. This equipment defacement could be much the same situation."

Duncan rubbed a knuckle against his chin. "That report disturbs me, as abnormal behavior is a psychology unto itself. I've had some education on it in my risk management training, but the main thing is recognize something out of the ordinary is transpiring. That applies equally to your campground encounter and this equipment tampering. We may not know *why* until much later."

Mr. Coleman looked from one man to the other. "Make your best recommendation to me, Mr. Reed. Your reputation in risk management is unsurpassed. I'm blindsided here, as one of the accused is among my trusted ranks."

The silence that followed filled Mason's thoughts with incredulous ramifications. Things would get messy from here on out, depending on the speed at which they responded to the present threat. How he longed to return unadulterated to his undemanding plastics lab, where only his next patent-worthy discovery lurked as an unknown.

Duncan stood as if to draw his visit to a close. "Sir, if you have legal support, I'd turn the evidence over to them today. I've found it critical to halt further threat at the workplace by dismissing the suspect from duty, until such time charges can be brought. I've advised Mr. Porter to write down his methodology for the surface inspection, and the results it generated. His testimony should also include the cover-up visit to the machinery by the perpetrators. When the legal action defaults to police enforcement, you don't want that scene to unfold at the plant."

Mr. Coleman stood bent-backed, his knees shaking. "Thank you for coming out, Mr. Reed. I'm all about protecting my workforce. To that end, I don't believe I have any choice."

Duncan offered his steady hand. "The Coleman name is sterling, sir. Due diligence will keep it that way."

As the president accepted his handshake, a figure rushed into the room unannounced. Mason quelled his reaction at seeing Glori worked into a fury. Tears reddened her eyes, though she appeared to fight them off. Her emotion-flushed neck could not be camouflaged, however.

In deference, Duncan Reed stepped into the hall and gestured for him to follow.

Torn between two forces, Mason started out the door, but held back a step or two.

"Straight-out slander has hit the Sunday paper, Mr. Coleman." Glori halted her report as a sob worked up her throat. "They're claiming that, as your unblemished company spokesperson, I'm hiding a checkered past, but nothing could be further from the truth. Edgar Sterns started this smear campaign to counter our success in the camping campaign."

At the mention of the source, Reed's head jerked up as if responding to a silent warning.

Mason locked gazes with the safety expert. When he shook his head, a shiver ran down his full height. Dead-set on a collision course with trouble, he anticipated a backlash. No one held a knife to his throat—yet.

His heart pained as Glori finished her rebuttal and collapsed onto Mr. Coleman's shoulder, sobbing uncontrollably. The door swept closed between them as the iconic leader quelled the uprising by sheltering his wounded HR director with the protection of privacy.

Reed walked down the hall, gesturing to him again. His mouth twitched as they passed the Marketing office where Edgar Sterns' name was emblazoned in permanent black lettering on the door's glass panel. At the end of the hall, Reed pushed the door open to let mild-mannered June reconfigure the situation. "You've got a real powder keg here, Mason. Let the legal boys handle it and watch your back. Also, you should escort Glori out to her car after work daily. You've got a rebellious deviant on the loose, so you have to operate with caution."

"Right you are. Thank you for coming out, Duncan. I think it carried more sway with Mr. Coleman, plus you've banked a favor if you ever need a speaker for our engineering group."

A smile twitched at the corner of his mouth. "I like to pay the favor ahead, that's for sure." He glanced across the street as if locating his vehicle. "About the scandalous article in the newspaper, that seems more like a personal vendetta, if you ask my opinion."

"Well, Sterns had Glori trapped in a fake engagement to gain his inheritance early. I forced the break-up because of my earnest romantic intentions. She mentioned there might be some kind of fallout, and I guess it's just now washed ashore."

He extended his hand for a final shake. "She's going to need your unquestioning support."

Mason clasped it, knowing his friend wanted a confirmation. "Sometimes I feel like the outsider looking in on all of this. I'm ever looking for the truth and constantly praying for wisdom." He pumped his hand twice as he spoke.

"I pray God lends you both then. Weston and I stand at the ready, if you should ever need any help." He tipped an imaginary hat and stepped down the curb as the day's heat cranked up toward the point of combustion.

Mason turned toward the building and read the iconic Coleman name above the factory's main entrance. The bricks appeared stalwart along the façade, yet on the admin hall, a cankerous breech of reputation festered. He directed his steps back to the lab, where an innocuous potbellied picnic jug called for his professional attention.

~

Edgar neatened up his desk, appreciating the midweek's advance which brought the club's grand opening one day closer. Over the course of the day, he'd managed to get the remaining campaign spreads in the mail to three more magazines and two newspapers. His efficiency often impressed the senior staff, which he used to his advantage whenever possible.

Off the record, he'd also penned an informative narrative on the untimely fall of a rising starlet, targeted to a sleazy New York fish wrapper that didn't waste time checking its sources. Sensationalism was alive and well in the big city, where everyone enjoyed a juicy tidbit of gossip, especially ones that smudged a touch of dirt on a well-scrubbed face. He chuckled when he thought about Glori's pending discomfort as the country became aware of her cheapened nature. "You should have stayed under the engagement's protection, dearie."

He stood to put a file in his portfolio, so he could go over the liquor expense again tonight after dinner. No one could fault him for being lax in his business practices. He remained acutely aware of every factor, which would eventually make him an unmitigated success. Drawing the portfolio to his side, he left the office.

Two uniformed police officers approached him in the hallway. The older man assumed the lead. "Excuse me, are you Edgar Sterns?"

"Yes, that's right. How may I help you gentlemen?"

"You're under arrest, Mr. Sterns. We'd appreciate it if you came along quietly."

His pulse quickened. "Why should I? What are the charges? This is my place of employment. I think you're making a mistake."

The second officer stepped up, a pair of handcuffs in his grip. "I'd keep my trap shut if I were you, Mr. Sterns. Maybe your lawyer should do the talking for you."

Edgar froze while the man made good on his threat and locked one of his wrists in the device. He read the man's name from his uniform—Connelly—and committed it to memory. Bile rose in the back of his throat at being herded off like a hapless animal.

"The charge is corporate sabotage involving equipment defacement," the older officer said, pointing to the far door.

Edgar complied for a few steps and then halted. "Does Mr. Coleman know about this? He'd never allow you—"

"Mr. Coleman initiated your arrest. You might look elsewhere for your back-up support." With that, the younger policeman guided his shoulder with a touch of coerced cooperation.

At a momentary loss, Edgar complied. On a defensive, he wondered if what he carried in the portfolio might incriminate him further. Only the bar file would be found, and he was legal in that department. Fortunately, the U.S. Postal Service had possession of the rest. They marched past HR, where Midge stood bug-eyed in the doorway, witnessing the procession.

"Call Alton Landis for me, Midgey," he said with a controlled wink. Knowing she'd do anything he asked, his legal counsel would be forthcoming in short order. It would only be a matter of time before he could light up and drive the Fairlane back to his apartment. Too bad he needed that cigarette right now. *Better make yourself scarce, Mack Insley.*

Incompetence was so hard to cover. He grew weary of subordinates who had been weighed in the balance and found wanting. After exiting the building, he soon sampled the unforgiving upholstery of the squad car's backseat. Not one aspect of the situation met with his approval. He hadn't seen the capture coming, which singed his pride ever so slightly. As they pulled away from the curb, the ride seemed to steer him a new direction. He exhaled, trying to rationalize if he should ask to smoke now or at the station.

~

Sunrays shot across a low-banked cloud and illuminated the sandbar in golden light. Glori wandered to the edge of the water with Mason at her side. She'd cried so much, she felt empty now. Only the tether of his hand lent any sensation of being alive.

At his insistence, they'd come here to inspect the lay of the land along the acreage in Valley Center being offered for sale. Scenic and safe, the vista gave her an unexpected boost. Mason's company proved yet another matter. He'd been mostly silent during the late afternoon outing, undemanding and gentle. Not once had he asked her to talk about the character defacement, or pressed for further details. Her hopes of keeping part of the oath buoyed under such unsolicited trust.

When the sandbar submerged into the ribbon of river, Mason turned and wrapped her in his arms. "Here stands the incomparable Glori Dawes. What in the world am I going to do with her?" One eyebrow rose in magnetic expectation.

With his heart beating next to hers, the unity of the moment ushered out any quarrelsome doubts and left only peace. "You could love her," she suggested, a hint of timidity in her voice.

He touched her cheek with a solitary finger. "Indeed, I do." A tender kiss followed, until he swept her up in his arms and carried her back to the meadow's expanse.

She watched the river flow past as he tugged her toward yet another unexplored area. Perhaps this was how the land recovered from accumulated hurt, by having the river caress its edge. Her thoughts wandered to the adage about too much water passing under the bridge to allow reparation. Regarding the secret she continued to safeguard, she wondered how much was too much. At some point, truth would have to be redeemed. *Bless Mason, Lord, for not forcing the issue.*

Chapter 24

After consulting with Billy Dean during an exhausting weightlifting workout Thursday evening, Mason understood the need for clarifying the facts. He agreed a hundred percent that the slanderous report had not seemed totally fabricated, but if Glori had not been the mother, then someone else must have been. Perhaps that was the twist she'd mentioned earlier. Every ounce of rationale still didn't make this task any easier. He mustered his resolve and skipped up the steps to The Wichita Hospital, hoping for a little cooperation on a Friday afternoon.

The lobby opened to a front help desk. His heels clicked across the waxed tile floor, lending sound to his purpose. When a gray-haired woman gestured to him, he angled toward her. "Hello, I hope you can help me. My name is Mason Porter. I'm an engineer at Coleman Company who is researching a family tree of sorts. I get to the same place each time, but there's a baby's birth that seems to be missing. Is there any way to check your records for the maternity ward, so that I could clear up this gap in the family tree?"

"You want the Records Department, young man. That office is down the hall to the left. Miss Brinkley can help you find what you're looking for. They keep meticulous records."

"Which could be my salvation. Thank you." He smiled and headed for the hall she'd indicated. After finding the sign, he rapped his knuckles on the door and then pushed it open.

A young woman with thick glasses sat behind the counter. "Oh, you startled me."

"Forgive me for my persistence. I'm Mason Porter. The helper at your front desk sent me back here. I'm looking for a specific birth certificate to complete a family genealogy. Alas, I don't know the names of the parents—only the year of birth."

She studied him for a few seconds. "Then you're in luck, Mr. Porter, as we file the birth certificates by the year the baby was born. Then, the entries are arranged alphabetically by the mother's maiden name. That matriarchal system was put in place by the hospital's founding nuns, so no one has enough nerve to attempt an improvement." A smile flickered on her plain face as she stood and opened a gate to allow him passage into the archives.

"I so appreciate this. There doesn't seem to be another means of resolving the matter." He followed so close, he almost plowed her over when she stopped midway down the shelves.

"I'll need that year, sir, so I can get you started on the right box."

He reflected on the dated cover of Glori's yearbook and added a year to allow for the nine-month maternity progression. "I'm giving you my best guess—nineteen fifty-two."

"Perfect, this is what you need. Let's set you up back there at the research table."

"Please, allow me to carry the box. I don't mean to make unnecessary work for you today." He took possession of the storage box and followed her to a heavy-set table nearby.

"Just let me know when you're done, and I'll make sure you file it back in the proper order. I've already had my lunch break, so there's no hurry."

"That means you are one up on me, as I'm using my lunch break for my research today."

"I hope your efforts prove productive then. Best of luck." After turning on a rotating fan atop a high shelf, she returned to the front with efficiency of motion.

Riddled by a moment of doubt, Mason opened the box and sought out the records several inches into the column. Locating the names starting with the letter D, he only found Davis, Donaldson, Downs, and Dwyer. Glori Dawes did not have a child at this hospital in nineteen fifty-two. *What a relief.* Able to relax and address the task more systematically, he started again at the first entry and proceeded to review each one.

Almost to the middle of the box, he read a name that struck

him as familiar. On the third day of March, a Margaret Ann Kerr had birthed a baby girl. He remembered seeing that name in Glori's yearbook, though she'd pointed out the fellow cheerleader as Midge. The information generated a stinging sensation as Mason groped with what to do about the new revelation. Without a doubt, Glori had covered for her best friend as Midge became an unwed mother. Her loyalty stroked a heartstring, though he remained resolute to make the full truth known.

Mason pulled out his new Instamatic camera and laid the birth record on the table to photograph it as evidence. The fan tried to flutter the document from its spot, so he held it down with his thumb and took the picture one-handed. He took a close-up so the print could easily be read. When it came into focus, the white-on-black typing on the negative caused his shoulders to quake. There, listed as father, was an all-too-familiar name.

A convoluted cavalcade of questions started pouring through his mind. He pocketed the camera and stared directly at the document to make sure he's read it correctly. In this new light, the newspaper's smearing rendition of events made even less sense. He replaced the birth certificate in its proper spot and sealed the lid. Numb from the discovery, he moved with rote steps up the walkway and hoisted the box into place. When he got to the access gate, he paused to be released.

"I hope you found what you were looking for, Mr. Porter." The clerk opened the gate and pulled it back.

"I did find the missing baby's entry, so that much is a clear success. I'm at a loss as to what to do with the rest, I must confess." He stepped through and turned to gesture his farewell.

"You could take a tip from the founding nuns and start with the mother then," she quipped with an innocent smile.

Working past the foggy numbness clouding his analytical brain, Mason grappled for a grip. "You may be right about that. Thank you ever so much for the assistance today." He retraced his steps to the entrance, and practically stumbled down the front steps. To make the proper kind of progress, he's starting with the irresponsible mother, all right.

A stop at Old Mill Tasty Shop for a burger might be a necessary digression, but he promised to have a direct encounter of the truth-exposing type before the workday ended. Miss Margaret

Ann Kerr would not see him heading in her direction, so the truth would not be obscured by any premeditated dodging. That smoke-and-mirrors act had gone on long enough. Disgusted at the oblique oath-taking and a pervasive failure to own up, he unlocked the Plymouth's door and headed toward a confrontation of matriarchal magnitude.

~

Freed on bail, Edgar micromanaged the organization of the bar area in preparation of tomorrow's grand opening. He sat jars of roasted peanuts and bags of salty pretzels at regular intervals along the raised bar. If he couldn't locate any bowls to hold the snacks, he's seen some broad-rimmed brandy sniffers in the overhead cabinet that would work.

His probation status at work crept into his thoughts. Tonight, he'd update his resume with the latest sales campaign and mail it out to several prospective companies in town. With this sideline venture so young and promising, he didn't want to leave Wichita in the immediate future. Once his lawyer cleared him of any fault for the Coleman equipment debacle by pinning Mack Insley with the blame, he could salvage his reputation in marketing and continue his creative siege on the ready-to-spend consumer.

Remembering that Lloyd Cox had promised to drop by at five o'clock, he tried to order the remaining tasks for his afternoon. Too bad he couldn't pull off a miracle and have the upstairs ready for the opening event. Even with the cleanup completed, the city insisted on conducting a final inspection, having been notified of occupancy by the plumbing contractor.

Such was his imperfect life at the moment, though the feminine entertainment would commence by next weekend. What a gem to add to Wichita's crown, a sultry shade of red like a facetted garnet. He turned in a full circle to regard his polished-brass setup as a sense of accomplishment assuaged his damaged ego. This bar would represent his cunning recovery, an escape route from the ordinary with a subtle hint of impropriety. He smiled into the middle plate glass mirror, freed to be his alter ego at last.

~

Glori placed the latest application for the new cooler assembly line onto the stack destined for Mr. Coleman's desk within the hour. She glanced at the clock at couldn't believe the time. As the long hand lumbered past one-thirty, the listless Friday dragged on. A proactive move, she picked up her pencil to sketch in two blocks on her calendar for interview appointments around the middle of June.

The door pushed open and in walked Mason with two tall cups balanced in his hands. "Good afternoon, ladies. Does anyone have time for a chocolate milkshake interruption?"

"Jeepers, yes," Midge replied, popping up out of her seat. "My progress had been snarled for the last thirty minutes. I sure could use a boost."

After divesting a cup in her assistant's direction, Mason turned to her. "Glori, I'd be honored if you joined Midge in having some refreshments."

"You won't have to twist my arm on that one." When she reached for the cup, he hesitated to release it.

"Funny you should mention a twist, because in my afternoon research, I've hit a doozy." He relented on the milkshake and glanced between the two women.

Wanting to take a sip in the worst way, she decided to bait him with a question. "What kind of research are you up to today?"

Midge made a hum as she sucked on the striped straw.

Mason stepped closer until he stood midway of the two desks. "Well, I thought to write a rebuttal letter to the editor for Sunday's newspaper and set the facts straight on their 'Coleman Darling Hides Checkered Past' article in an effort to clear your name. A problem surfaced in that I didn't know the correct parties to assume credit—or blame—however one might look at it. So, I undertook a research venture at the local hospital to find the documentation of ultimate truth."

A funny churning started just under her ribs, so she stopped drinking the milkshake. "What kind of documentation? I don't know what you're talking about."

Midge lowered the cup, her expression frozen.

"It's called a birth record and can widely be used to substantiate unknowns such as date of birth, gender of the offspring, and the mother's maiden name, to list a few items." He gestured with open palms. "On March third of nineteen hundred and fifty-two, infant Starr Lynn was born at The Wichita Hospital."

"Hush your mouth," Midge insisted. "No one speaks of little Starr."

"That must be the case," Mason replied. "You're the ever-protective mother, isn't that correct, Miss Margaret Ann Kerr?"

Flooded with a sense of guilt, Glori stood up behind her desk. "Listen, Mason. You don't have to write that rebuttal."

"What? Here's the chance to clear your name. Don't you see? The oath to hide the truth is a moot point, as I now know the whole truth and plan to expose it."

Pressure started a ringing in her ears. "No, Mason. Think of Midge a minute. When you clear me, it indicts her. There must be some other way."

"You have heard mention of the plumb line of truth, have you not? That's the straight-up truth, not some vague rendering of the situation. Midge, please tell Glori why you're so insistent on keeping the news from emerging. You aren't just protecting yourself or the baby, are you?"

Midge's expression morphed through several changes until it situated in the realm of incredulous. "What do you hope to gain from all this, Mason? I don't understand why we can't let sleeping dogs lie with this one."

"Our deepest truths will someday be made known, that's why. Also, this cover-up seems to place the entire burden on an innocent third party."

Glori wrung her hands. "I didn't mind—"

"No, back then, it must have seemed prudent to protect a close friend, but it's played out into a farce," Mason replied. "I cannot let it continue another minute, so I'm rescinding the oath for you, Glori. As for your part, Midge, you've known the full truth all along. I now give you the option of confessing the father's name to Glori, or I'll promptly do it for you."

A vise clamped her ribs and stole her next breath. The thought of being used by her best friend turned her act of kindness into one of subterfuge. The latest smear campaign colored the whole effort black, a dark cape employed by a magician to pull off the cleverest trick. She stepped toward Midge in a fragile gesture to meet her halfway. "Mud sister?"

Midge faced her and swallowed. "That summer after our senior year, we both took sailing lessons on the lake at Triple Star Ranch.

Your lessons fell right before lunch, but I had the last session of the day. Things turned romantic and we decided to explore the island in the center of the lake until sunset. That detour repeated each evening, until it was time to come home."

The wind sucked right out of her lungs at the implication. "You and Edgar Sterns?"

Midge straightened her back. "Yes, the baby's father is Edgar. I didn't think it would matter, so I withheld the information."

Mason stepped between them. "And yet, Edgar penned the smear campaign to ruin Glori's reputation in the community. Does anyone else see the utter irony in that?" He glanced at Glori, and then at Midge.

"Dear Lord above," Glori replied in a faint voice. When her knees began to quake, she sat on the edge of her desk. "It's all been a huge wasted effort on my part…the initial oath…the pressured engagement…even the three-sided friendship. Looking back, it all seems equally fake, and I'm the brunt of the joke in the end."

Midge rushed toward her. "Golly, Glori. It wasn't intended that way. I had a baby to think about. We had to send her away and cover this whole thing up."

"When you say 'we,' did that include Edgar in the plan?" Mason posed.

Midge snapped around in his direction. "No, don't you understand? Edgar doesn't even know about the baby. Our romance cooled, and he went back to college in Ottawa. I did the only thing I could fathom at the time, and put the baby up for adoption."

Mason folded his arms. "So the part of the story that includes Oklahoma City is true?"

Midge glanced back at Glori. "Yes, I drove her down to the expectant adoptive parents myself. I…I had to see if they were good people, so I could let go."

To forestall the feeling of plummeting off the top of the building, Glori planted her face in her palms and tried to recover. How fitting to have been played the pawn and then dashed against the craggy bottom. The air grew stuffy around her. Spellbound, the trance broke with a tug on her elbow.

"Come walk me out," Mason insisted, his gaze steady. "One of us needs to go back to work this afternoon. Alas, I still have that rebuttal to write for the newspaper.”

She sighed and shifted onto her feet, seeing the wisdom of moving forward. When Mason offered his arm, she accepted it with gratitude. They walked to the door together, until he paused.

Mason turned to look back at her office assistant. “Midge, I’ll give you until Sunday to tell Edgar yourself. That might be better than reading your personal business in the newspaper.”

“Thank you, that’s decent of you, given the circumstances.” She placed a hand on the phone as if to get the process started.

Glori stepped into the hall with a shake of her head. “I should have seen it. In fact, I probably did see it going on right before my eyes.”

Mason patted her arm. “But you didn’t want to believe it, even if you had. Best friends believe in each other. You operated out of that trust. Midge had to operate out of the shame she found herself dealing with, so her motivation was more pressing, but less pure by contrast.”

She glanced into his earnest brown eyes and saw unflustered admiration. “Can I call you when I’m ready to walk out to my car?”

“Most certainly. I’d be devastated if you didn’t, after all, it’s Friday night. I need to be with my best gal.” He gave her a wink and released her arm to depart.

As she watched him turn the corner down the hall, she felt an overwhelming sense of emergence, like she’d begun to crawl out of the damaged landing where the oath had dumped her. Its restrictions now null and void, she contemplated the hard lesson learned.

“Miss Dawes?” Mr. Coleman asked. “Do you have those applications for the cooler assembly line for my review?”

Glori held her chin high and looked the icon straight in the eyes. “Yes, sir. They’re waiting for you on the corner of my desk. I believe there are fifteen or so. That’s a good start.”

“Well, I certainly believe in good starts. Say now, you’re not going to miss our Mr. Porter if I relocate him to the Hydraulic Avenue site, are you?”

She gestured into her office and gave it some thought. “No, sir. If I know Mr. Porter, he won’t let that happen.”

He chuckled as he made his way inside. “There’s nothing that says my HR staff can't make a monthly visit over there to handle any employee matters that might pop up."

Midge jumped from her desk, turning her back to rummage through the file cabinet in search of something.

Too familiar with her habits, Glori noticed Midge's tears before she managed to hide them. "Here are the applications, Mr. Coleman. There's also an in-house transfer request for the administrative coordinator's position. I believe that particular applicant is a close fit."

He saluted her with the stack and made his way back out.

Midge glanced over her shoulder to make sure the coast was clear. "You didn't have to put in a good word for me, Glori, but thanks for doing it anyway." She pulled a tissue and wiped her wet cheeks.

"I think I recognize a worthy candidate when I see one," she replied. As she sat behind her desk, a small portion of the world seemed to fall in order. Only three more hours to go and the workweek would be over. *What a wonderment.*

~

Thanks to a tip from Weston, Mason knew he'd hit the hot spot for seven-oh-seven jet landings this evening. He tossed the quilt across the back deck of the Belvedere and guided Glori into place from the back bumper. A double string of lights illuminated the main runway that stretched beyond the car. Only the rotation of a radar disc caused movement in the night. He tossed the keys through the open window and climbed up the viewing platform to join his date.

"This is the most outlandish thing you've thought of so far." Glori leaned forward and let him bury his arm behind her head.

"That's me all right—outlandish in every way." He chuckled under his breath at the exaggeration. Cicadas brought their rubbed chant to court the night until the roar of their entertainment began to take over. "Well, when you live in the Air Capital of the World, some of it's bound to wear off on you." Though he spoke with increasing volume, the seven-oh-seven overhead finally won the sound battle. Four afterburners lit the night with descending flames.

Glori covered her ears with her hands and snuggled into his side.

He curled his arm around her and held her close. Eventually, the sound of rubber wheels contacting the ground added a chirp of its own. "Yet another successful jet flight lands. It's amazing, if you really think about it."

"I hope your plastic coolers take off like that…and land by the year's end."

"That's far longer than I'm willing to wait for my other ongoing venture." When she glanced up at him, he planted a kiss on her forehead.

"I'm guessing that this other venture has nothing to do with plastics. Am I right?"

This time when she tilted her head up, he met her with an impatient kiss. By the time it relented, the next seven-oh-seven arrived seeking terra firma. He broke off the embrace to watch the landing glide to a distant success.

Glori placed a hand on his chest and rested her head on his shoulder. "I hope this side activity you're alluding to happens to include me."

"Only if you consent to it—when the time is right, of course."

"Now, you sound like a man of mystery. I think I like that."

"Well, the plan only works if the planner receives the cooperation he needs."

"I'll be sure to keep that in mind. Will there be any warning time up front? You know, a lead-in, so to speak."

He stroked his fingers through her wavy hair. "I have an inexplicable aversion to engagements, all things considered."

"This doesn't mean someone can't carry affection close to her heart and treasure it."

"Inseparably close," he assured her. The embrace he launched met with quickened doom, as the roar of the next jet overtook them. They watched the landing cheek to cheek.

"So, you say this venture might happen prior to winter, yet after summer, which leaves us most of autumn to make it come true." She scratched her fingers along his shirt placard. "Am I close to being right?"

He freed his arms and rested them up against the warm back glass. "I didn't intend this to become a scheduling exercise, Glori."

She shifted onto her hip to look at him directly. "Well, what did you intend?"

He sat up and blew out a breath. "Between kisses and near misses, it's been a hard week. I kept telling myself that I was the outsider walking into this mess, but that's not how it ended up feeling. I recognize that God brought me here for a purpose, and I don't mean the one where the camping world gets a lightweight cooler."

She snickered and laced her arm through his.

He brushed a kiss onto her fingers and then slid off the trunk of the car. Glancing skyward, he had half a minute at the most before the next aerial acrobat lowered in their vicinity. "This week I saw you be strong in the face of great hurt. Even in your weakest moments, I wanted to stand beside you and love you through it. Try as I might, I cannot watch over you from afar, so think about this. I want to marry you, Glori Dawes. I want to sit across the dinner table from you and hold you in my arms every night. Most of all, when we say goodnight, I don't want to have to part our separate ways. So, I'm asking you to consider it—without any lead-in time or running start. Will you marry me?" He remembered to kneel at the last second, he felt so rushed.

The seven-oh-seven's roar coincided with Glori's arrival off the trunk. If she spoke anything aloud, he never heard it. Her kiss became a tactile afterburner as they merged into a no-wait situation of mutual agreement, one that promised a date on the calendar without having to call it by name and number. Satisfied with that particular ambiguity, he locked her in his arms and let his deepest-held dream take flight.

Chapter 25

Fearing a ransacking, Glori peered up from her Life magazine to find Midge charging into her apartment. Stunned, she watched her twirl across the room until she stumbled onto the divan. "Who's the nincompoop who forgot to knock?" she asked, only partially teasing.

"Oh, me oh, my." Midge plopped her palms against her cheeks. "Where in the world do I start?" Her eyes glazed over like she had fallen under a charlatan's trance.

"General topic then. This is about—"

"I had lunch with Edgar, using the hook that I had something big to tell him. You would have been proud of me, Glori. I looked him straight in the eyes and told him about the baby. It took me six years to work up that much nerve, but I did it."

She put the magazine down to offer her full attention. "And then?"

"Un-be-live-able," Midge replied in a sing-song range of musical notes. "Of all things, he broke down and cried. I mean real tears. I almost couldn't get him to stop. Really, it made quite a scene. Good thing we had the back booth."

"I'm speechless. Edgar never struck me as the doting family man." She knit her brow.

"Tell me about it. That's what I couldn't figure out. It's like he had a family, and then he lost it in an instant." She snapped her fingers, her eyes looking wild. "He kept saying, 'Oh, Midgey, if I'd only known. Why didn't you tell me?'"

"Did that make you feel worse?"

"No, not at all. He kept hanging on my arm, like he needed to borrow my strength. I can tell you this—it was not an act. That man was distraught at the lost opportunity for something intimate like a family of his own. I don't think his home life was all that good growing up."

Glori had seen her far-away look before. "You're going to date Edgar, aren't you?"

Midge's eyes grew wide. "That is exactly the next thing we talked about. He thinks we should be a serious item. I was just about floored. When I pulled away, he grabbed my hand and almost started begging. The tears returned, and he started kissing my hand. Somewhere in the mêlée, my heart just flat-out broke for him. Once I relented, his face simply beamed."

"This sounds like one of his shallow scene scripts, Midge. My caution antenna is gyrating at full throttle. I'm not kidding about this. You need to be careful."

"That's why I'm here." She blew out a breath and sat at the far end of the divan. "He wants me to come out to his grand opening tonight—just for a few minutes—as it's largely a male clientele. But he wants us to share what he called 'a once in a lifetime memory.' Now, you tell me. How could I say no to that?"

Her astonishment picked up a side car of dread. "No, Midge. You cannot be serious."

"Edgar promised to keep me by his side the whole time. He wants to tour me around and introduce me to patrons. I don't even know what to wear. Do you think navy blue is too drab?"

Glori held out her arms as if to apply brakes to the entire situation. "I'm acting on your best behalf by asking you not to go." She kept her tone firm, as she meant every single word.

Midge looked pained. "Don't you get it, Glori? Edgar and I are meant to be together. I may have blown it by clamming up about the baby, but we have history to protect. All the nights sharing dinner at his parents, winning as canasta partners, pulling off the camping campaign—all of it. That makes perfect sense to me, which is why I have to be there tonight for Edgar." She rose and walked around the coffee table as if to leave.

Embattled, Glori fought for something to redeem the sudden rift. Reflecting back to the excruciating nights at his parent's house, she seized upon a peacemaking nugget. "Go then, Midge, and hold your head high. Edgar always liked you in red, so wear the sleeveless red chiffon. You'll be stunning, and he won't be able to keep his eyes off of you."

She snapped her fingers, solidifying the choice. "I feel like I'm going to the prom again. Oh boy, I'd better get busy primping."

Glori crushed a toss pillow to her chest to keep her heart from hurting so much. Unlike her friend, her anticipation was not the buoyant kind. It had a leaden quality that made it impossible to shake. When Midge floated down the hall, she thought of a parting comment. "Hey—close the door so us nincompoops won't wander out and hurt ourselves."

Midge gave her Lucille Ball laugh that sounded more like a woodpecker. She doubled back and eased the door closed with a giant wink. Riding high on clownish sentiments, she left.

"No Midge, my friend," she whispered. "Keep both eyes open tonight. Both eyes wide open." A sense of dread made her default to prayer, a destination she should have landed upon on more frequent occasions. By the end of her petition, she gave thanks that Midge still held her as enough of a friend to drop by and let her know how the tell-all had gone. Believing the reaction was difficult, as she recognized the scriptwriter's style and continued to abhor it. Midge had less scrutiny in such matters, so maybe the gentlemen's club was the right place for her.

~

Mason rinsed the garden's dirt from his hands, dried them, and reached for the incessantly ringing telephone. "Hello?"

"Hey, Billy Dean here. I'm calling to let you know we checked out that tip on the bar's grand opening you gave us. We hooked up with the state permitting office too late yesterday afternoon and missed getting that confirmation. My sergeant says we can still have a couple of guys casually drop by."

He scratched his temple. "I'm not sure having officers in uniform wander in would be the best approach. They're going to stand out like a sore thumb. If anything illegal is going on in there, like gambling for instance, it will evaporate the moment those guys walk in."

"So? A little intimidation never hurt anyone. You gotta let us do our job, right?"

"Well, I'd go in under cover, if it were me."

"You mean don't make it so obvious?"

"That's right. No telling what you might learn."

"Guess I could offer to dress casual and make that scene. Libby and I don't have anything planned for tonight. Let me see how that suggestion goes over. I just wanted you to know that the WPD plans to make an appearance, uniformed or not."

"Thank you for being open to John Q. Public and his unwarranted suspicions, Billy Dean. I'll let you go first on the weights next week."

"I'm definitely taking you up on that one, Mr. Q. Public. Stay out of trouble until Tuesday, you hear me?"

"For me, it's church on Sunday, and maybe an afternoon drive with my best gal."

"Good enough. Let me work on my boss about tonight. See you around."

Mason lowered the receiver while the sensation that something had been left unaddressed made the hairs on his arm stand on end. Edgar had nothing to worry about as long as the bar was on the up and up. Of all businesses for a decent man to undertake, a bar seemed the least likely. He shrugged it off and headed for the shower, thinking he might want to surprise Glori with a drop-in visit later. As stirred-up trouble went, that kind tended to be pretty sweet.

~

Glori evaluated her appearance in the mirror, trying not to look the part of a harlot. Her chinchilla-colored silk sheath dress draped her hips in a flattering fit, but didn't speak of anything flirtatious. For the umpteenth time, she tried to talk herself out of going. Without question, Midge needed an escort—possibly even a bodyguard. If she drove, she could guarantee that her friend didn't overstay her welcome. One of them had keen discernment, and it wasn't the woman in the flowing red dress.

She grabbed her clutch purse and headed out the door. Once on the landing, she ran into her landlady holding cuttings from her flower garden. "Hello, Mrs. Brougham. I hope you have a nice evening."

She sniffed the mixed flowers. "Where are you headed off to, young lady?"

"A grand opening for a friend's business. I won't be too late." She smiled and stepped down to the walkway to get the escort business underway.

~

A trio of friends seated at the bar laughed, adding gaiety to the front of the club. Edgar wiped out some stemware to lend Lloyd a hand at the bar. The three partners had agreed to rotate in and out of bartending duties to keep things moving as business picked up. Maybe hiring a part-time bartender would need addressing in their immediate future. They easily had the club half full, and it had only been opened for an hour. Smug in his assessment of the newspaper advertisement's strong response, he actually found himself enjoying the work. The three friends laughed again, causing a smile to tug at his cheek. The Hangar Gentlemen's Club was officially in operation, a major lift that made him feel invincible.

~

In a casual hurry, Mason slammed the door on the Belvedere and made for Glori's front door. As he approached the landing, he discovered an elderly woman on her knees scratching at the weeds beneath a rose bush. "Well, hello there. You must be Glori's landlady. She's spoken fondly of you on several occasions."

"Yes, I'm Theta Brougham. And who are you?"

He knelt to make the introduction more direct. "Mason Porter. Glori has become dear to me. I hope to be seeing much more of her. Just so you know, my intentions are honorable."

"That may be the case, but I'm afraid you're out of luck tonight. She's gone to some kind of fancy grand opening for a friend's business. At least that's what she told me when she left out of here all gussied up."

His next breath hitched against his ribs. That grand opening would be the last place on earth he'd want her tonight. If the situation grew confrontational, she'd be right in the middle of the fray. With the risk factor pegging the high end of the scale, he needed to formulate a counter plan. A perfect back-up team came to mind. "Because I think she might be walking into trouble unknowingly, I need to call in a quick favor with some law-abiding friends of mine. Might I ask to use your phone, Mrs. Brougham?"

She studied him for a long moment. "Help me stand up out of these weeds, young man. Then I can show you to my telephone."

He offered his arm and took her elbow with the other hand. In steps, his formative plan took traction, painfully slow arthritic traction. Worry began to seep into his rational thoughts, but he focused on Glori's retrieval as if nothing else mattered.

~

The dim joint smelled of alcohol and cigarette smoke as Glori stepped inside the open house. To the right, a sweeping bar lined with stools flanked the mirrored wall. Every seat was taken. As she scanned the table area, it appeared packed to overflowing. Empty glasses collected in the middle of tables as the service fell behind, attesting to the glib behavior of the imbibed clientele. Lots of drinking had already transpired—a measure of success for Edgar, no doubt.

Midge rushed around her and headed for the bar. She made an exclamation over the din of lively conversation and Edgar raised both hands in the air to welcome her. At the end of the bar, the two met in a generous hug.

Watching in the mirror's reflection, it became apparent to Glori that whatever Midge and Edgar had going, she would not be able to quell the attraction. He brought her around to the first table, his arm locked behind Midge's back. It struck Glori that she was the outsider.

On gut instinct, she realized she should not have come. Shoved by the next entering patrons, she stepped toward the bar and took an empty spot off the street end. From there, she examined the liquor dispensing and watched with detached interest.

A round-faced man wearing suspenders over a starched white shirt finally made his way to her spot. "What will it be tonight? All drinks are two-for-one."

It took Glori several seconds to recognize him from Coleman. "Hello, Lloyd. I didn't realize your were tending bar for Edgar."

He gave her the once-over and let a lurid smile ease his expression. "No, I'm Edgar's full business partner. Hey, I heard your camping campaign has been a big seller. I thought I had a shot at the husband position. Guess I got outcompeted by some enterprising engineer."

She needed to quell any further personal interest. "That's all behind us now. I'll have some ice water with lemon, please."

He stepped back, though his gaze dropped to her fitted bodice.

"Right, two virgin waters with lemon, coming right up."

She exhaled and glanced at her watch. *Would Midge think half an hour enough time?* She searched the crowd and found the proud couple at the back of the room, entertaining the group of elderly men in loud banter. With the smoke ever collecting in the room, she soon found it easier to people-watch using the mirror. After Lloyd slid the two water glasses in place, she gave in to the distraction of a modern-day saloon and eyed the reflection with detachment.

A nudge on her elbow broke the protracted spell. Soon, a figure hovered off one shoulder. A man's hand offered the brandy sniffer full of nuts.

"Do you come here often?" he posed in a velvety-smooth voice.

She turned to find Mason standing a narrow shadow's distance behind her at the bar. Guilt and relief choked one another for ultimate expression. Taking a cue from his calm demeanor, she put on her acting hat and answered him. "No, this is my first time. Please, join me in a drink." She passed the second water glass to him with a coy smile.

Mason accepted the offering and took a sip, then nodded. He glanced around the room and held the bar area in a protracted inspection. A muscle flinched in his jaw.

Glori traced his gaze to the back end of the bar where a storage room opened. A tall man leaned on the door jam. Too far away to identify, she wondered if he could be another partner. If so, Mason may have recognized him from Coleman.

"You look radiant tonight—like a shiny copper penny," he whispered, almost touching her hair with his chin.

"Would you be in collection mode, Mr. Porter?" She raised one brow and let her eyelashes flutter closed.

"Always, Miss Dawes. Consider yourself collected. We'll enjoy this one drink, and then we need to get out of here." His hand slid around her waist and clamped over her hipbone in direct violation of the silk.

"What about Midge? I brought her here so she wouldn't stay too long."

"She's a big girl, but we'll let her know when we're leaving. I wouldn't offer her my car keys, if I were you."

Glori checked the mirror and spotted a swath of red chiffon in the middle of the room. While she watched, Midge raised a wine glass to her lips and took a long drink. Mason was right. She'd have to beg Midge to come with them instead. As she started to say something, two men crowded them at the bar. Upon recognition, she could not have been more shocked.

"What are you drinking there?" Duncan Reed asked.

"Ice water with lemon," Mason replied.

"We'll join you with two more of those," Weston Durand added.

An imposing figure, Duncan snapped his fingers and Lloyd Cox appeared on the double. "It's hot as blazes in here. We'll have two more of these lemon waters."

"Yes, sir. Coming right up," Lloyd replied, wiping his hands. In no time, he returned with the drinks.

Duncan lifted his glass and held it up for a toast. "Here's to a peaceful night."

"Here, here," Mason replied, clicking his glass into the grouping.

Glori joined the toast, but didn't miss the circumspect demeanor of the toast-giver. She knew Duncan had a knack for assessing risk. She glanced in the mirror above the gathering smoke and didn't know what to look for. The din of the room cast a mesmerizing spell as Mason made idle conversation with his friends. Ill at ease, she couldn't partake. *I should not have come.*

Chapter 26

Mason sat the empty glass on the bar and turned to leave. He made eye contact with Billy Dean who had camouflaged his official presence with a baseball jersey and knickers. When his friend gestured toward the door, he gave a single nod and threaded his fingers through Glori's. "Gentlemen, that's all for us. Stay and enjoy the grand opening if you want."

Duncan surrendered his glass. "No, we'll walk you out. This is about as much nightlife as I can stand."

"I'm probably going to be in hot water with Myla as it is," Weston said with a testy grin.

Before Mason could add a tease, a commotion started at the door. Six uniformed police officers shoved their way into the packed room. Uninterested in witnessing the confrontation, he regretted they hadn't left a minute earlier.

The lead policeman lifted a megaphone to his mouth. "All right. The night's over, folks. We have an obvious fire code violation here for exceeding occupancy limits. Please leave the bar single file. I need to see the owners up front pronto."

"Dear Lord," Glori murmured. "This can't be good."

"I didn't see their state liquor license posted anywhere for public display," Duncan said.

"That will be tacked onto the full list of violations," Weston replied.

"And force a shutdown." Mason turned toward Glori. "If you'll keep an eye out for Midge during the exodus, we'll offer her that ride home."

Duncan jerked his shoulders square to shield them. "Get down and take cover."

Mason peered past him in time to see a crazed bartender hop up on the bar, a handgun clutched in his grip. Shouts went up across the room and a woman screamed. A metallic click from the megaphone amplified across the chaos as the police responded to the threat. He leaned against Glori's cheek. "Stay low off the end of the bar. Whatever you do, keep your head down."

"Okay," she replied, a tremble in her voice. "Let the police do their job."

Mason tucked her under the bar's overhang and followed a crouching Duncan Reed. Weston trailed him as they tried to move behind the first table for cover.

When the police rushed the poised shooter, he opened fire with a madman's rage. The lead policeman went down, and the rest scattered among the exiting crowd. People swarmed in every direction, trying to avoid harm.

"Chaos of the worst magnitude," Duncan muttered, moving a chair between him and the bar. "No safety to be found."

"We have to stay put and ride it out," he replied. A hand clamped his shoulder and he turned to find Weston seeking asylum beside him, his eyes wide with shock. His gut tightened in anticipation of the fallout. They were too close to the shooter's location. A quick glance told him that Glori had obeyed, on her knees with her head ducked and hands covering her ears.

The bartender fanned out his range toward the street side of the bar, his shooting intermittent. A second man appeared out of the stock room, but didn't have a visible weapon. One policeman who had infiltrated to the room's center, raised his gun and fired, striking the second man. That set off the trigger-happy bartender, who focused on the shooter and brought him down. Screams echoed from the crowd.

In a vulnerable moment, the bartender hesitated. As he fanned back toward the front entrance, Mason spotted a fast-moving figure dressed in a sports uniform climb atop a far table. With steady aim, the man shot at the assailant, but missed. In brittle response, the mirror off their side of the bar shattered into a million pieces.

A woman's moan almost cloaked the second shot. This time, the crouched sports figure hit his mark.

The bartender grabbed his side. He dropped to his knees as the police shouted orders for him to cease and desist.

On heightened alert, another low moan caught Mason's attention. He glanced over to check Glori and found her prostrate, blood seeping through the silk of her dress. Surrounding her, chards of the shattered mirror lay everywhere, proving out the end of order. "Glori's hurt." Without thought to his own safety, he darted away from cover.

In his peripheral vision, he saw the shooter react to his movement. Laid open, all he could do was watch the madman's gun raise and aim in his direction. He reached toward Glori, desperate to help her no matter the risk. A hollow shot rang out.

Beyond explanation, a figure lunged in front of him as a human shield. A guttural sound arose from his throat when the bullet struck its target. He fell to the floor, clutching one shoulder.

On his knees, everything began to seem surreal. A body fell from the bar and hit the floor with a thud. Sounds of the police controlling the crowd echoed across the mayhem, trying to restore order. A siren's wail cut through the ebbing chaos as he gained Glori in his arms. Her gentle weeping sounded like music to his ears. "Darling, it's over now. The police have the upper hand. We'll get you some medical help, I promise."

She laid her cheek across his knee, her hair matted with blood. A trickle dripped down her chin as her blue eyes flickered beneath heavy eyelids. "No more copper penny to keep."

He drew her closer, his heart breaking. "Hush that senseless talk. Let the expert decide what to keep. As for me, I see a coin of rare value. Yes, a penny brilliant and uncirculated, to be treasured for a lifetime." He kissed her cheek and looked up to gain some assistance.

Weston shifted closer, his hands shellacked with blood. "I don't think I can stop the bleeding." His gaze held a plea. "Come help me?"

Mason cradled Glori in one arm and skid across the floor on his knees. When he looked at the victim, there lay Duncan Reed, eyes shut and white as a sheet. Blood began to pool on the floor. At the sight, urgency knifed through his chest. With a tug at his pocket, he produced a handkerchief and moved toward the wound. After Weston pulled his knuckle away, he jammed it into the bullet hole as far as he could manage and applied direct pressure.

"How many wounded here?" a man asked, crouching in front.

Mason looked up to find Billy Dean staring down at him, waiting for a response. "Two, and one critical. He's lost a lot of blood."

Billy Dean glanced toward the door. "Help me get him out to the street. We'll give him the first ambulance, because the shooter sure won't need it anymore."

Mason kissed the top of Glori's head. "Let me get Duncan tended to, and I'll come back for you."

She struggled to sit up. "No, let me help carry him out."

His admiration swelling, he pulled her to her feet by his side. "You keep the pressure applied to the wound then, while we lift and carry." Once she nodded, he took the injured man's shoulders and glanced across at Weston, who hoisted his midsection. Billy Dean got Duncan's feet and began tugging them all toward the exit.

The protracted trip to gain the door resembled a shuffled funeral procession. Mason fought exasperation for such lowly treatment of the risk management genius. Glori's slender fingers kneaded the blotter centrally over the wound as they made it out to the sidewalk. When the ambulance attendants had stretched Duncan onto the gurney, he noticed Weston's tear-streaked face. The whole scene etched into his memory, a leaden plaque commemorating a horrendous end to the ill-conceived grand opening.

"Looks like we'll take her, too," a uniformed man said. He gestured for Glori to step toward the ambulance.

Torn by the threat of separation, Mason clung to her for a second longer. "Go and be brave. I'll get there as soon as I can. Remember that I love you."

She sobbed and tried to wipe the blood off her hands, sullying the silk even more.

With a kiss to her temple, Mason relinquished possession to the attendant, who escorted her into the back of the ambulance. The siren blipped a warning as they pulled from the curb.

Weston shouldered into him, causing him to momentarily lose his balance. "Duncan drove over, but I didn't think to get his keys. Can I ride over to the hospital with you?"

A growl rose in his throat to protest the outcome, and he shook to choke it back. Someone jostled him from behind, so he stepped to the curb. When he looked up, Edgar and Midge stood side by side. By all accounts, it had been a rough night for all concerned.

Edgar broke the silence. "I'm quite sorry—for your friend and everything else. I had no idea Lloyd was armed. I promise you that." His shoulder jerked, so he turned sideways, and the police led him away locked in handcuffs.

Midge trailed them by several steps, her expression blank. After pausing, she doubled back and offered him a small purse. "Here, take this to Glori."

Seeing her shock, Mason had compassion in the moment. "There's room in my car, if you want to go to the hospital with us."

Her eyes drooped under the weight of the heavy consideration. "No, thanks. My place is with Edgar tonight. Tell Glori I'll drop by in a day or two."

Mason nodded and watched her walk away, a fading childhood allegiance that melted like a mud sister in a heavy downpour of circumstance. His thoughts immediately shifted to Glori. "Let's get to the hospital, my friend."

Weston walked along the street edge and rapped his knuckles across the hood of an aging Buick as they passed. "Hold on, old steed. Duncan is coming back for you, so help me God."

By the time they'd arrived at the Plymouth, Mason's throat was parched, an ironic state given they'd just left a bar. He swallowed and tried to think of something to comfort his hurting friend. "There's no time like the present to pray down an almighty miracle."

"That's when a burden becomes a privilege," he replied, lowering into the passenger seat.

Mason started the car and threw it into reverse. After they maneuvered down Douglas Street, he felt the urge to make a plan. "I need to stay by Glori's side, so I can drive her home when they release her later tonight."

Weston leaned his head back and closed his eyes. "I'll stay with Duncan, at least until Lorna Rae can get there. Boy, that's one phone call I hate to make."

As Duncan's precious family came to mind, the sting of pending loss pierced a little deeper. "Can you ask Myla to come out to comfort Lorna Rae?"

Weston exhaled and looked out the side window. "That's another call I hate to make."

Mason waited out a red light before turning north. The towering hospital soon loomed on the horizon, its windows lit with activity. For the first time all evening, hope buoyed his low spirits. "I have to say this, because you and Duncan are the best friends I've ever had. You know I would be there for you and Myla if circumstances ever demanded it. Duncan Reed would be the first to tell us that when the chaos of evil rears its head, the righteous have to make a stand. That's the kind of battle we faced tonight."

Weston stretched his frame and bent both arms, flexing his considerable biceps. "I may need to upgrade my weaponry before the next skirmish then."

Assessing the nature of such a personal reflection, Mason shook his head and snickered, breaking the sullen mood. "Better try the full armor of God—and possibly work on quickening your reflexes."

Weston turned to him. "What? You're insinuating that I'm getting slow?"

"Not exactly. I'm saying that we can learn a thing or two from Duncan, who always sits on the verge of *go* in response to a spiritual prod. I want to be like that, a man after God's own heart. That's the kind of husband Glori deserves."

Weston nodded and stared ahead. "Why is it that most major revelations come to us in the shadow of the hospital?"

Mason pulled into a parking spot and turned off the car. He reached over and took his friend by the shoulder. "Life in the crossroads is a precious consideration indeed." Through the windshield, the emergency room entrance beckoned under a solitary streetlamp's light. In traditional Coleman Company fashion, he squinted to purposefully mistake the lamp for a far-off star. On nights like this, it paid a man to default to the heavens. Ever mindful of his limited reach, he began the trek toward the tower of hope.

Epilogue

Glori clutched the camera to her chest, her spirit soaring high above the lake. Sulfur vents cloaked the conifers on the horizon with a curtain of ground-birthed steam, making Yellowstone's landscape turn surreal. Back in one of her favorite places on earth in time for Labor Day weekend, only the remarkable man standing knee-deep in the lake's crystal waters garnered her full attention.

Mason's shout accompanied a gesture that lured his best friend from the water's edge. "No need to be a bystander, Weston. The water's not that cold."

Myla climbed along the rocky shore to join Glori from a higher vantage point. The afternoon sunlight shimmered on the lake's quaking surface which rippled Myla's reflection. "I might not get involved in this horseplay session."

Glori laughed. "That's why I'm holding the camera. Before things get too crazy for me, let me say how honored I am that you and Weston could join us for our special occasion."

She glanced over her sunglasses, her eyes sparkling. "We wanted to come. It's good to get away from home and spend time together. Besides, a strong representation of America will be in attendance, thanks to Mr. Coleman's generosity with the park passes."

When the petite woman stumbled cresting a rock, Glori reached out a hand to steady her guest. "I suppose you brought a sturdy tent?"

"Yes, Weston can hardly wait to set it up. Really, the three men would have been like overgrown campfire kids—if only Duncan

Reed could have made it."

Glori tried to work the lump out of her throat at the mention of Duncan's name. A loud squawk from the center of the lake made her notice the men had waded in deeper. Weston had locked his hands behind his neck as if to minimize contact with the cold water. Mason pretended to struggle just to create a well-aimed splash. When they began to wrangle with locked arms pulling and lurching, she decided to snap a keepsake picture.

"Good one," Myla said. "We'll make a lot of memories on this trip. Will you two stay around after the ceremony, or is the honeymoon car off to some distant horizon?"

"I'd be surprised if Mason gives up our perfect camping spot here for something unknown, but he's not letting on. There's always Yosemite to explore."

"Mercy, that's a long drive to California. I think I'd court around mud pots and sulfur vents right here. We're planning to drive over to Yellowstone River on Sunday, after the early morning eruption of Old Faithful. Weston drew up a timed schedule. When you marry an engineer, you get used to it—even for your leisure outings."

The way she rolled her eyes made Glori laugh. Across the lake, a wood-paneled station wagon honked its horn, pulling into the campground. Two little arms waved nonstop from the backseat. She spotted a blonde driver with a kerchief on her head as the car rolled to a halt. "What in the world?" she asked in a whisper.

A tall man unfolded from the passenger seat and slammed the door. Like a miracle come to life, there stood Duncan Reed in plaid Bermuda shorts, a sight to behold even with his injured arm stuck through a black sling.

"Come on out here, slowpoke," Mason called with an insistent beckon.

Glori slapped a hand over her mouth to keep from gasping. Were it not for the bravery of that man, most certainly one of them would be lying in the mortuary right now. Though she trapped the gasp, her burning tears had a mind of their own.

A satiny-light touch, Myla's arm interlocked with hers. "They simply had to come. I'm sure Lorna Rae took the lead on their trip. She's quite fond of national parks, as it so happens."

A second car door slammed, followed by two more. Soon, the

entire Reed family stood on the shore, the kids antsy to get wet.

"Give the men a minute out here," Duncan said as he waded out for the rendezvous.

Glori waved Lorna Rae over and watched her red capris make quick work on the rocky climb. "Okay, the blushing bride is now the surprised-beyond-belief bride. Thank you so much for coming out, Lorna Rae. You two are making this even more unforgettable for us. I can't even express how much." She swiped a tear off her cheek and leaned over to hug their wedding guest.

Lorna Rae returned the hug and then pushed away. "Hey, Myla." She looked the woman over head to toe. "How've you been feeling?"

"A little plucky in the morning, but it's nothing I can't handle." Myla flashed a grin rimmed with secrecy.

"Are you?" Glori asked, looking alternately between the two women.

"Probably. Well, I can't say definitely yet, because I have to tell Weston first. Lorna Rae had to fish me out of a wretched scene last week, so she figured out my condition on the sly."

Lorna Rae squared to the water's edge. "Not too many things miss this set of eyes. When you're a mother to three active children, you have to stay on guard. Okay men, this is your ten-second warning. I'm releasing the children after that."

Duncan turned and faced her, "Because you get to, Rae—not because you have to."

She dismissed him with a flap of her hand, but her cheeks soon bore dimples at his personal message. "Timmy, put that rock down, and then take off your shoes and socks so you can join Daddy. Trudy, please help little Johnny get barefoot." Her directive launched a flurry of activity from the children on shore.

Glori watched the men lock arms around each other's shoulders and bow their heads. Strength and weakness all rolled into one scene, it stirred her heart and constricted her throat. The steam vents in the background gave the scene a surreal aura. The sky could not have been bluer, a canvas of perfection.

Mason spoke a loud "amen" and raised his arms heavenward.

Glori lifted the camera's viewfinder to her eye and took a snapshot.

"Okay, send in the children," Duncan called.

"All children now report to your father," Lorna Rae echoed with a clap.

Glori took another snapshot as Duncan tried to figure out how to hold two wiggly preschool boys in waist-deep water while wearing the sling. When he finally handed little Johnny off to Weston, she laughed right into the camera. Trudy disappeared under the surface and bobbed up like a seal.

Lorna Rae cleared her throat. "Myla, I think you should go in."

"What?" Myla's incredulous question sounded full of air.

Glori lowered the camera as the realization caused her skin to tingle. "All children now report to your father, right?"

"It would make Weston's day—and then some," Lorna Rae added, her gaze on the men.

"Okay, on one condition, though," Myla countered. "After ten seconds, I'm not the only woman standing in that chilly lake. Do we have a deal, ladies?"

When Lorna Rae locked one arm around the dark-haired beauty, Glori was privileged to do the same on the other side. They strolled along the rock-lined shore arm in arm until the pebbles gave way to a sandy beach.

Myla waded out in straight-line fashion right to Weston.

"All children now report to your father," Lorna Rae called between cupped hands.

Weston pressed a palm onto his forehead. "What? Myla?"

She dropped one hand to wrap her abdomen in wordless confirmation.

Weston whooped and handed little Johnny to Mason so fast, the tyke couldn't spout an objection. He swept his wife off her feet and buried her in a wet hug. When the kisses came next, middle school-aged Trudy had to place blinders up to screen her innocent eyes.

Glori nudged Lorna Rae with an elbow. "We should keep our word and go in now."

"Even if I know you're right, it doesn't make it any easier to get soaked to the bone by this ice-melt lake water." She bit her lips, but a smile soon worked its way up.

Glori strolled to the closest boulder where she secured the camera. The rest of the scene would have to play out in precious living color, without any play-acting or film involved. The idea emancipated her to live it up a little. She kicked off her sandals and raced out to hug Mason, including little Johnny in her embrace. The warm kiss she received in return was all her own.

Lorna Rae soon leaned in to remove her baby boy. "Here it is—our fabulous life."

Mason held Glori and beamed his affection to her in his loving gaze. "No question—a lake full of the best life imaginable."

Glori wrapped her arms around his neck and held him until his breathing rhythm matched her own. "Tomorrow, I become your bride, Mr. Porter. What might you say about that?" She let her lips tickle his wet neck as she posed the question.

"All I can say is—come on, sundown," he quipped, lifting her off her feet.

Glori stole a glimpse to see the other two women enjoying similar treatment, wrapped in the husband's affections. Her heart began to overflow with joy. She tucked her face into Mason's neck and kicked at the lake's surface with her feet.

"I hope that persnickety geyser can stay regular for one more day," he teased. "I don't want it messing up on my wedding day."

"Just be at the altar when I come down the aisle at the lodge. They didn't name it Old Faithful for some nebulous reason."

"Call that God's little injection molding project—one that recurs with more hydrologic regularity than the moon's phases." He turned to her with a coy smile.

Glori touched a finger on her favorite mole by his sideburn, stroking his face. "A plastics engineer likely holds a keen appreciation for that degree of order."

"You can bet he does." He took a step and turned toward the others. "Let's go make camp, gentlemen."

"Tonight—we grill," Duncan replied. "Our treat, we brought T-bone steaks to celebrate."

Glori reached for Lorna Rae's arm. Soon, the adults were all connected while the children frolicked ahead in the shallows. The moment held a precious rarity too tender for words.

"I hope it's a boy," Lorna Rae said to Myla. "I saved my infant boy clothes for you."

Glori signaled to get down and soon had slippery rocks under her feet. She locked arms with Lorna Rae who linked up with Myla, and they waded from the shallows under the escort of three amazing and brilliant friends. "You were right, Lorna Rae. This is our fabulous life."

"Let's go be next-door neighbors," Lorna Rae replied. "I hope your campsite can hold two more tents."

"Yes, I'm sure of it. Let's start our own village." Glori looked up in time to catch Mason's approving glance. Tomorrow, he'd look at her like that over an open Bible at the altar, permission granted to expand her tent stakes, right in time for a new decade of remarkable togetherness under the hand of God. For that particular oath, she would let her yay be yay—and there would be no need for nay.

The End

Keep reading for the first chapter of Oil Field Maven

Chapter 1

El Dorado, Kansas 1951

Hell must have ascended and nailed him right to the middle of it. Duncan Reed passed his palm down the back of his neck to wipe away the sweat. A full crew of men stood at the ready as a monstrous fan belt gyrated around the powerhouse's interior. On assignment for less than a week, his first trip into the company's power generator pulsated with raw force. A nervous quiver shook the fan belt and a flapping resonance filled the air like chattering teeth.

Sol Edmunds, the larger-than-life floor supervisor, motioned with a gritty forearm. "Get back, boys." The men along the western wall responded by easing back a step.

Duncan leaned on the door jamb and slid a notepad from his shirt pocket. Second nature, his assessment began with a tally of the eight men out of harm's way. The giant belt cogitated through another cycle, straining against the spindles at each end of the building. As it shimmied up the eastern cylinder, an attentive worker guided it back into position with a greased wooden paddle. He scrawled a note and returned his gaze to the unstable east side.

A second man brought his paddle up to skim along the upper edge of the bucking belt as if to tame it. The belt retaliated with a bulging slap that seemed to set the entire rig loose. Secondary vibration contorted the rubber into a quivering snake, slithering around and around the spindles. The chattering teeth noise escalated to a full bone rattle, which solicited looks of dread on several dirt-smudged faces.

"No more, fellas. Back off." Edmunds crisscrossed his arms, his fists pounding his shoulders for emphasis.

A split second later, Duncan glimpsed the failure as it happened. The upper edge of the belt tore, making an ungracious slapping sound. Then it began to shear apart.

"She's going—everybody out!" Edmunds heaved the closest man to safety through the doorway right in front of him. Chaos followed as men careened for the exit, while the oversized serpent choked the life out of the powerhouse, its flap licking the stagnant air like a tongue.

Plastered to the plank wall, Duncan focused on every detail. Each piece would need to fit into his follow-up accident report, so he had to remain sharp. The west side workers had all gained freedom, and now the east side workers attempted to cross behind the front spindle. Right when the two men with wooden paddles ran past, the belt tore in half top to bottom.

"Heaven help us," Edmund exclaimed from the doorway. Free from the generator at last, the belt lashed out, striking two workers with unmerciful force. The slighter of the two men went airborne, landing against the far wall with a sickening thud. The stout man dropped where he stood, the air knocked from his lungs in a horrendous huff. The murderous belt thrust past him and coiled into a rubber mound in the corner. Spared by mere inches, the last four men dropped to their knees.

Duncan straightened from his post and pointed his pen at Edmunds. "Send for the ambulance." The supervisor scurried away, and a mousey-faced man peered into the room. Nothing stirred inside the threshold, an ominous portend. The man closest to the thrown victim checked his vital signs, while another laborer tended the heavy man.

Duncan pointed his pen again and pinned the mouse-man with a task. "Can you find Mr. Coates and advise him of the situation? The belt's gone out again, taking two men down with it. He will need to arrange a back-up, if we are to get this generator running."

"Yes sir. I'm on my way, Mr. Reed." Pained, he pulled a scruffy hat off, crumpled it over his heart, and then scurried away.

Fighting the urge to add a few notations, Duncan stepped past the motionless heavy victim to check the man by the wall. The laborer backed away, his eyes skittish. From the angle of the body, the man's neck had clearly been broken on impact. Light from a nearby window played a streak across him, highlighting something that glimmered on his hand. There, a narrow wedding band claimed the victim's left ring finger.

He squatted beside the man to be certain, unable to stop his throat from constricting. As he knelt on the floorboards, reality hit him with the weight of an anvil. How he loathed the follow-up portion of his job requirement—the notification of next of kin. He shifted toward the heavy-set man, while the victim's attendant shook his head and dropped his chin.

Death and industry made for strange bedfellows, a union he had never gotten used to during his ten years of service. *What a way to make a God-given living, chasing safety.* He took the notepad out and dated the preliminary accident report, May 4, 1951. It seemed hot for early May, even for central Kansas, but what did he know?

~

Neatness has no price tag. As the bungalow sat bathed in quiet, Lorna Rae had to hurry to get supper on the stove. When little Trudy awoke, she would demand her full attention. Tendrils of hair coiled damp against her face as she chopped the borrowed onion that would flavor their soup. Already too hot, a worry needled through her thoughts that she would have to serve more substantial meals with summer's pressing demands on the oil field laborers. If only Harley hadn't decreased her grocery money again this month without any explanation.

She raked the diced onion into the pot with the knife blade and fought back a tear, her reaction to the pungent vegetable. She looked for her next ingredient, a fat carrot. The chicken broth bubbled from a ring of heat below and lent her a soothing feeling, its aroma wafting to fill the tiny kitchen. She smiled when the embroidered tea towel caught her eye by the window over the sink. A wedding present from her mother, it hung from safety pins to form a makeshift curtain to block the afternoon sun. Otherwise, the swelter would be unbearable.

Standard housing for the oil field workers came with no embellishments, just a rectangle to contain family life. They were fortunate, as only the three of them had to fit. Poor Vivian next door had four kids to shoe-horn into her cottage, but it never seemed to dampen the woman's spirits. No, she was lucky to have Viv for a neighbor. Plus, she tended Trudy now and then to free her up for an occasional outing.

She scraped the outer skin off the carrot and began to slice off wafer-thin pieces to make the soup seem fuller. If she got the carrots tender enough, she could feed them to Trudy. They'd blow the slice cool together, and all that attention somehow made it taste better.

Lorna Rae wiped the cutting board clean and cut the heat down on the gas stove. Ready to move onto the biscuits, she dried her hands and scouted the overhead shelf for her canister of flour. She frowned at seeing it emptier than she thought, lowering it with care. She had no more set it on the counter when a loud knock came at the front door.

"Golly gee, they will wake up Trudy yet. Lord, please do not let that unpleasantness come my way today." She stepped through the bedroom straight into the front parlor where a man stood on her front porch, waiting for her to answer the door. When he started to open his mouth, she shushed him with a finger to her lips to let him know she meant it. Not wanting to seem harsh, she allowed a smile to curl the edge of her lips. She shoved the screen door open to join him on the porch. "I have a toddler asleep in the back, which is just the way I prefer her right now, a wordless Kewpie doll. Now, sir, how may I help you?"

The man shifted his weight from one foot to the other, concentrating on her face. He stood dressed in a starched white shirt and dark slacks that looked like they had seen extra duty of some sort today. Maybe he had never seen a housewife before. Some men were all work and no play. This guy fit the bill. When he turned into the sun, she could see he was not as old as she'd first thought.

"First, allow me to introduce myself. I am Duncan Reed, and I work for Mr. Coates."

"Mr. Reed, here in El Dorado more than half the population works for Coates Oil Company. Oil Hill is his domain. I am Lorna Rae Holmes."

"So you would be the wife of Harley S. Holmes then? Is that correct?" He withdrew a notepad to double check the name and seemed satisfied with his pronouncement of it.

"Yes. I'm Mrs. Harley Holmes, but Harley does not typically come home for another hour, Mr. Reed. I'm afraid you are too early if you have business—"

"No, ma'am. I came here to speak with you." Again, he shifted his weight and gave his collar a tug while he swallowed in a gulp of air.

Unease crossed the porch as Lorna Rae sensed for the first time that something menacing might be hiding behind this nice man, something Harley could be trying to hide from her. After all, he had been siphoning off her grocery money for months. She folded her hands, found the apron tie with her fingers, and pressed the rickrack like she could somehow straighten things out.

"Mrs. Holmes, there was an accident today at the generator house." He paused, and his gaze softened.

A steam kettle seemed to go off inside her head as unbearable speculation tainted her reasoning. Harley had gotten himself hurt. How in the world would they afford that? "I…I see." Her thoughts got chopped up worse than the onion, and the almost-tear she had in the kitchen tried to come back.

"Mrs. Holmes, I'm afraid I have come here today with the news that Harley lost his life trying valiantly to correct a damaged belt at the generator house. He was struck and killed instantly, so I can assure you that no suffering was involved." He reached out to touch her but drew back almost as quick.

"Oh, I see." Her mind raced past the gulf of initial shock as the immediate truth of not having Harley to provide for the two of them poked a hole in her lungs. What would she and Trudy do? Try as she may to push past the question, no answer awaited. "Where will we live?"

"I am so sorry to bring you this kind of news, ma'am. Please accept Mr. Coates' condolences, as well as my own. The company will bury Harley and pay all those expenses, rest assured. You name the cemetery, and we will make the arrangements for the family."

"Rosalia. His people are from Rosalia. The family plot is there beside the church. Is he still here at the oil field?" She twisted the apron tie until it became limp in her fingers.

"No ma'am. The ambulance came and took both victims to the

hospital to officiate the death certificate. That is standard procedure. I came over as soon as I could. The other fellow didn't have any immediate family."

"Where will we go? Do I need to move right away? I certainly do not want anyone coming to clear out my things without me knowing." Somewhere a protective bristle stiffened her backbone, and she stood taller to defend her homestead, company housing though it was.

"No ma'am. Harley had this month's rent taken out of his paycheck like usual, so you have most of one month to make plans for where you will head. Unfortunately, there is a waiting list for housing here on the oil fields, one that I am on myself. But I hope something will open up for you and the little one, maybe something back home?"

"Not likely." Lorna Rae inched toward the door, unwilling to consider the possibility. "Daddy and I had it out over Harley, but I do not mean to make that any of your business, Mr. Reed. Do I need to sign anything for you, or do we leave it like this? You delivered your message and I received it, standing right here in front of God and everybody. Is there anything more?" Not intending to, she backed into the door and the frame slapped shut against the threshold, sending a loud crack echoing through the house.

A glance up at her visitor revealed his genuine concern. She had not anticipated compassion from a company man, and it proved to be her undoing. A cascade of unblocked emotion broke loose, and the tear she'd been working up all afternoon finally got emancipated.

A tiny hand pushed against her legs right through the screen. "I waked up, Mommy."

"Come here, baby girl. Mommy needs a hug right now." Though her knees trembled, her voice held steady as she brought the girl out and lifted her for the hug, rumpled clothes and all. "Trudy, this is Mr. Reed. He works with the oil company."

The toddler took a look at the visitor who had tried to soften his stance upon her appearance on the porch. "He's my new fwiend." Implausible, her declaration crossed the planks while she twisted several blond curls around her finger.

"I...I would like that." He eased off the porch and paused on the top step. "A day like this one is pretty tough…without having a new fwiend, I mean."

"She has trouble pronouncing her R's. Say goodbye to Mr. Reed, baby doll."

She flexed her hand to wave farewell. "Bye-bye, Mista Weed."

The man gave them a long look and finally lifted one finger to return the gesture. "I will see you at the funeral, then. Goodbye, Mrs. Holmes."

"Yes, we will see you at Harley's funeral. Rosalia Cemetery, please don't forget."

"No ma'am. I won't forget. You take care." He stepped away, headed for a car parked down the block.

Lorna Rae turned and came inside, her thoughts speeding by a mile a minute. Harley would not be coming home tonight. Not tonight, or any other night. It was over—the makeshift marriage her father had sworn her to had not lasted long enough to properly detest it. Yet she did, every blame minute of it. Her father would not be amused at this outcome, not in the least.

~

Duncan took a seat at his makeshift desk in the corner of the medical clinic as the company doctor flipped the Open sign to Closed. "No, Dr. Lucas, I don't suppose this particular incident had anything to do with the undercover maiming scheme. I saw the whole thing. It was an accident, pure and simple. Tragic, but an accident."

"Then we are nowhere closer to gaining the truth. Pity that, as your inauguration hasn't come off too easy, young man." Dr. Lucas patted his shoulder as he passed by.

"I would say it's been a rough spring so far. Guess I am still getting over General MacArthur being canned last month. What a perfect time to leave D.C. behind and relinquish the home fort to the Truman haters."

"You have to wonder what the Commander-in-chief might have been thinking in the heat of the moment. I suspect that General Ridgway may not have the same war-ravaged ilk that Doug MacArthur had. Change is difficult, especially with battles still raging."

"My kid brother is finishing a stint in the U.S. Navy. He wrote that morale has plummeted among the troops. Thank goodness his ship is headed back from Korea. I expect a visit next month." He brought out his notepad to begin transcribing details onto the company's standardized accident form.

"I would like to meet him and thank him for his service, if we can arrange it. Would that be during our company picnic? He could certainly attend as your guest."

"No, but thank you, sir. Sam is scheduled to arrive the week after, mid-June I think, depending on when the train can get him to Kansas from San Diego. I am hoping this place will be a true slice of American pie."

"Ah, R and R for the midshipman. Not to mention solid ground. Sounds like a healthy dose of Midwest normal." The doctor jiggled some glassware in the sink on the back counter. Soon water splashed to announce the end-of-day clean-up routine. "Say, if he's here for two weeks, maybe he could stay for the Independence Day celebration. Mr. Coates told me the citizens of El Dorado would be in for a treat this year."

"Fireworks are nothing but a distraction, sir, if you don't mind me saying so." Duncan rested his pen on the first blank and tried to recall the day's date. With pessimism as his newfound companion, the overtime work this evening would likely be quite protracted.

"Well, when the men striding terra firma cannot think of anything more lofty to pursue than maiming members of their own lot and wearing that disfigurement like some type of badge, maybe we need the distraction of looking heavenward, Mr. Reed. I wish you a focused report completion and a better day tomorrow. Mrs. Lucas promised to make my favorite meatloaf tonight, so I dare not be late. Remember to block out time for the funeral day after tomorrow. Mr. Coates requires his administration to attend in deference to the victim's family."

"Yes, sir, I will. You go enjoy that meatloaf. I have half a sandwich left that will hold me over. Here's to tomorrow and a better day." He lifted the soda bottle and tipped it to the doctor as he donned his hat to cross the threshold into a personal life, a realm Duncan didn't know. He inked in the words "Generator House Accident" across the top line and when the date came to him, he entered it next. With only two months until Independence Day, he had miles to travel to unveil the truth, a bloody path of sordid collusion. Why the image of a curly-haired little girl flashed to mind next he had no earthly idea, but he lacked any control whatsoever to stop it.

~

Rain blurred the vista beyond the hood of the hearse, which Lorna Rae accepted as God's protective provision. Still numb from the brief memorial service at the oil field chapel, she could not handle too many more details. Bless Vivian for playing the piano before the service. Otherwise, the whole affair would have been far too somber to bear. She had sat on the front row trying to keep Trudy from squirming as the men gave testimony to Harley's strong work ethic.

She had wanted to add an invective about his flawed family ethic, but her mother had taught her not to speak ill of the dead, so she sat quietly and held Trudy in her lap. Maybe red had been a poor choice for her daughter's dress, but all other options had grown too snug or too short. Time marched on, and now it had to leave their income provider behind.

Like trees in a forest, men that had busied themselves removing the simple casket now reappeared outside of the rain-streaked car window. In an instant, they would extract her for a graveside service interminable in length, given her present state. Trudy fidgeted against her on the seat, and she reached out to draw her closer.

"Listen to Mommy for a second. This is the funeral I told you about, where they put daddy's body in the ground. Remember, they are not hurting daddy. He is already in heaven."

"With Jesus?" The girl searched her face with innocent eyes.

"Yes, baby girl. He is with Jesus. Maybe they both wanted it to rain today, so God could water the flowers to tell us everything will be okay. You be good and stay close to Mommy, okay?" The car door opened in a flash, and a man's arm hooked inside. Mr. Coates bent down into the door frame like a humble patriarch and guided her hand onto the arm of his suit jacket. His expression bordered on kindness. The concern mixed in seemed genuine. He gave her hand a pat and stood to draw her out.

Lorna Rae slipped from the car shielded from the rain by a black umbrella. The steady drum of the downpour lent her entrance a mourner's cadence. Realizing she didn't have Trudy with her yet, she turned back to witness a second man dressed in black removing the brightly-clad girl from the back seat, carrying her on his hip to spare a muddy encounter. She sighed in relief and stepped toward the grave site.

The tent protecting the grave from the elements must have shrunk in all the dampness. Women from the oil field community sat beneath its shelter. A group of men huddled in the soaking rain along the tent's edge, some without hats or overcoats. Thank God above she had insisted on a brief graveside service.

Mr. Coates escorted her to the front row seat, while the preacher from First Methodist Church downtown took his position between two modest sprays of yellow daisies. She sat down and saw a red blur as Trudy slipped into the adjoining seat. When the attending gentleman straightened, Lorna recognized the man who had delivered the death news, Mr. Reed. His dark eyes fixed on hers for the briefest of moments, and then he stepped away into the crowd.

Across the belts hoisting the coffin above the rectangular grave, she spotted the Holmes clan, with Mama Reese wearing her navy blue Sunday dress. She nodded at the woman who immediately deflected her full attention to her oldest son. Lorna Rae reckoned this marked the last day of her being considered a Holmes, as the family members had only extended forbearance to placate Harley. No need existed to keep up that pretense any longer.

"We have come here today out of respect to this dearly-held man, Harley Holmes, a fallen co-worker, husband, and father." Clear-voiced, the preacher paused to acknowledge mourners on both sides of the grave with a nod. The rain intensified and a few more men crowded under the tent's edge for shelter.

"And beloved son." Mama Reese clutched her purse to her lap, while shooting the errant clergyman a caustic look for his inexcusable omission.

"Yes, ma'am, and such a beloved son." The preacher added the phrasing without breaking rhythm and proceeded to lay out the scripture-laden eulogy full of "thee" and "thou" swimming among other antiquated words that drew the finishing line on Harley's mortality. Hushed by the rain, the man of God soon closed his Bible and stepped toward her, whispering inaudible words of pity-padded relinquishment.

Lorna Rae fought the rain's comfort and sat rigid in the hard folding chair. With her gaze on the coffin, she recalled Harley on their marriage day, so attentive and eager to be wedded to her. How quickly things had degraded into something less than desirable when Trudy came onto the scene. As a wife, she had not been enough for him, and now the whole lousy situation fell beyond rectification. *What a mess.* Her attention trailed away and traced a rivulet of water running off the grave mound. An impulse shot through her to do the same.

Still beside her, the preacher mumbled the first words of a closing prayer, and she blinked before remembering to close her eyes. The funeral home attendants shifted into place as she lifted her chin upon the pronounced amen. When Trudy squirmed into her lap, she pressed the child against her chest, while the hoist squeaked and lowered the coffin into the grave. As it settled to the bottom, she yielded to an overpowering urge to stand, bringing Trudy with her.

She approached the vacuous hole that held her deceased husband and reached for the closest floral arrangement. Taking a fistful of daisies, she offered the child a flower and then tossed the rest onto the coffin. Trudy mimicked her actions without a word.

Thunder rumbled from a far horizon, and she gave in. Lorna Rae walked away from the gravesite, the mourners, and the truncated marriage to leave it all behind. With the hearse as her immediate target, she had almost made it on her own when a protective umbrella graced the sky over her bowed head.

The man pulled the rear door open and took Trudy, so she could manage the maneuver of sitting gracefully in a tailored skirt and high heels. The ground turned to mush under her feet, but she somehow got inside and reached up for her daughter.

"Trust God that tomorrow will be a better day." Humanity expressed itself in the eyes of the helper as he relinquished the child with a look that embraced the depths of compassion.

Well, well. Who'd have thought Mr. Reed would have such empathy in him? The door slammed closed to the pelting rain. Next the passing of attendees transpired, where humanity blurred once more into trees within a distant forest.

AUTHOR BIO

Cindy M. Amos lives and writes inspirational fiction from Wichita, Kansas. With her background in natural resources management and endangered species conservation, she typically writes about man living close to the land. "America's Fabulous Fifties" is her first historical regional romance sequel, allowing her to feature her transplanted homeland, the American Midwest, in its post-war pride. Married to an aviation engineer with two college-aged engineering sons, science rules the roost at the Amos home. On weekends, the author helps work on the family's fifth generation ranch in the Flint Hills of central Kansas near historic Council Grove. She enjoys nature, wildflowers, riding her bike along Rails to Trails, gardening, and home-canning. She can also throw a mean made-from-scratch cherry pie on the dinner table when the occasion suits her fancy. Her books are available on Amazon.

Member: American Christian Fiction Writers (South Central Kansas Chapter Secretary)

Review her full book-list on her website at:
http://cindymamos.wixsite.com/natureink

Also check her Amazon author page at:

https://www.amazon.com/Cindy-M.-Amos/e/B01JTDIPOQ/ref=dbs_p_ebk_rwt_abau

Find her on Facebook at:
https://www.facebook.com/natureinkbooks

OTHER BOOKS BY CINDY M. AMOS

Landscapes of Mercy Series
Redeeming River Rancher
Saving Bicycle Man
Justifying Sound Strider
Sanctifying Ace Aerialist

Lifting Lock Runner
Salvaging Doctor Junk

National Parks 100th Anniversary Romance Collection

Everglades Entanglement
Mesa Verde Meltdown

Christmas 3-in-1 Collection

Running Out of Christmastime

Taming the Cowboy's Heart Collection
Warming Stone Cold Lodge

50 States Collection
Secondhand Flower Stand (Kansas)
Red Cloud Retreat (Nebraska)
Tidewater Lowlands (North Carolina)
Canyon Country Courtship (Utah)

John Denver 20th Anniversary Collection
Calypso Reimagined

Loving the Town Hero Collection
Cascading Waterworks

Cowboy Brides Collection
Renegade Restoration

America's Fabulous Fifties Series
Oil Field Maven
Airfield Aptitude

Small Town Christmas Collection 2018
Gift Tag Tree